Lit

DEATH'S DOOR

DEATH'S DOOR

A Billy Boyle World War II Mystery

James R. Benn

Published by Soho Press, Inc.
853 Broadway
New York, NY 10003

Library of Congress Cataloging-in-Publication Data

Benn, James R.
Death's door / James R. Benn.
p. cm.
ISBN 978-1-61695-185-6
eISBN 978-1-61695-186-3
1. Boyle, Billy (Fictitious character)—Fiction.
2. Murder—Investigation—Fiction. 3. Italy—History—German occupation,
1943-1945—Fiction. 4. Vatican City—Fiction. I. Title.
PS3602.E6644D43 2012
813'.6—dc23
2012012676

Printed in the United States of America

10 9 8 7 6 5 4 3 2 1

For Debbie
First reader,
First in my heart

Satan arrives at Pandemonium, in full assembly relates with boasting his success against Man; instead of applause is entertained with a general hiss by all his audience, transform'd with himself also suddenly into Serpents, according to his doom giv'n in Paradise; then deluded with a shew of the forbidden Tree springing up before them, they greedily reaching to take of the Fruit, chew dust and bitter ashes.

—John Milton, *Paradise Lost*, Book Ten

DEATH'S DOOR

CHAPTER ONE

THEY MUST BE in love, I thought, watching the couple as they danced to a scratchy tune on the Victrola. It was late, and the place was empty but for us, the dancers, and a waiter at the front entrance, trolling for customers. He'd gotten bored refilling my wineglass, so I poured the last of the vino myself and listened to the song. Again, since it was the only record in the joint.

"Who's that singing, Kaz?"

"Carlo Buti. Very popular in Italy. Billy, are you listening to me?"

"Sure. Guy named Carlo Buti. What's the song about?" I could count on Kaz to know stuff like this. He was smart in seven languages, but he didn't know everything, like when to mind his own business. He'd been yammering at me for the past hour, and I'd been doing my best not to pay him any mind.

"He is singing to his lover," Kaz said, leaning back and listening. "Love is beautiful when he is near her. It makes him dream, it makes him tremble. The usual romanticisms."

Kaz had his reasons to play the cynic, so I let it pass. He was probably right about the song anyway. The couple on the tiny dance floor swayed to the music, ignoring us and the waiter at the door, who called to a group of British officers to come in and try the mussels with fava beans. The dancers ignored the war, too, in a way Kaz and I could not. They were together, their arms interwoven, their passion thick in the night air. They were young, maybe nineteen or twenty, tops. She rested her cheek on his shoulder as his hand caressed the small of her back.

"They must be in love," I said, out loud this time.

"Indeed," Kaz said, finishing the wine in his glass. "And moneyed, as well. She is wearing silk stockings, and he has a decent wristwatch. No visible scars or injuries on the young man either, so it is likely he is either very lucky—which comes with money—or he avoided military service with the Fascists. They are drinking a Brindisi Rosso Riserva, so he can afford more than a common table wine. He has been sneaking glances at his watch, so he must need to get her home soon. This is the only time he can be alone with her, and hold her, which is why they are dancing."

"Not bad," I said. "How do you know she's not a prostitute?"

"Her shoes. They are expensive, and new. Also, they are still here, long after the meal is done. The young man would not wish to dance all night if he could take the young lady to bed. Therefore, he cannot. It is only a guess, but her parents must trust him to let her go out unattended. But, it is wartime, and these things may not be so important anymore."

"You might have a career as a detective, Kaz."

"You've taught me to study a room and the people in it as soon as I enter. We have been at this table for so long, I've had ample time. What are we doing here, Billy?"

"Having dinner, enjoying the view." I gestured to the harbor, across the road from the *ristorante*. A Royal Navy destroyer was tied up at the dock, and the muted sounds of sailors moving about drifted across the wide street that separated the wharf from the city. A line of palm trees rustled in the breeze. February in Brindisi was not much like February in Boston.

"We finished eating hours ago. The wine was tolerable, more so than your company, I must say. Billy, face it. She is lost. By now, there is no hope. Why won't you listen to me?"

Love is beautiful when you are near the one you love. When you can't be, it is terrible. It makes you dream, but the dreams aren't happy ones. And I tremble, too, along with Carlo Buti.

"I do listen, Kaz. Is it true that the old Roman road ends here, in Brindisi?"

"The Appian Way? Yes. Just around the corner, as a matter of fact. A Roman column marks the end as it comes down to the water. Why?"

"So we could leave here, start walking, and end up in Rome?"

"Well, yes. But it is almost three hundred miles, and the German Army might have something to say about it."

"Yeah, that's a problem." I watched as a jeep full of American MPs drove slowly by, checking out the clientele. I rested my chin in the palm of my hand, tilting my head against my fingers to hide my face. The music had ended, and the young couple were gathering their things to leave. Almost midnight. The jeep stopped, and the MPs watched the lovebirds depart. There was a blackout in place, but the MPs were easy to spot with their white helmets shining in the moonlight. Light spilled out into the street, but the MPs didn't say anything, simply rolled on, probably admiring the young lady.

"Are you in trouble with the MPs, Billy?"

"Not that I know of," I said, my hand going to the table. It was true enough.

"Good, because this late, they may stop to question anyone out near the harbor."

"Yeah, especially pretty girls. I think we're safe." Safe. I trembled.

"Billy," Kaz said, laying his hand on my arm. I shook it off. "We heard a week ago. The message took two days to get here. You know what that means."

"*Due grappe,*" I said, signaling the waiter. Maybe another drink would shut Kaz up, but I doubted it.

"It means that by the time we learned she was taken, the Gestapo had let her sit alone in a cell for two days, listening to the screams of the tortured," Kaz said. "To soften her up. Standard Nazi practice."

"*Grazie,*" I said as the waiter set down the drinks. I raised my glass, but Kaz ignored me.

"The first day might not have been too bad," he continued. "They apologize for keeping you waiting, offering tea, coffee, cigarettes. A rational discussion, to size the prisoner up. Some might give up information then, in the hopes of staying alive and keeping their fingernails."

I drank half the glass down, the fiery liquor harsh in my throat. I didn't look at Kaz.

"But it is all a ruse," he said. "To raise the prisoner's hopes and then dash them. Later that day, the actual torture begins. That would have been six and a half days ago. And the Gestapo would have worked fast, knowing that once an agent is captured, the rest of their group will go into hiding as soon as they hear of it."

"When did you become an expert in Gestapo torture?"

"I was briefed by an SOE colonel." The Special Operations Executive, Great Britain's spy and sabotage outfit. Set up in a villa outside of Brindisi, they sent the young and the willing to do the dirty work of winning a war for the old who had too much to lose. They had their own Royal Air Force squadron at their beck and call, plus a small army of forgers, tailors, demolitions experts, commandos, and smugglers. "You don't want to know the rest. Suffice it to say, six days is more than any mortal can stand."

I finished the grappa.

"They call their torture chambers kitchens," Kaz said. "That should give you some idea of what they do. If prisoners don't talk, they will likely die from the interrogation. If they do talk, they are often shot once the information is verified. Or sent to a concentration camp. Either way, she is dead by now, or beyond all redemption."

"How does SOE know all this?"

"It is their job to know these things."

"But how can they, if all prisoners are killed or sent to concentration camps? There would be no way to learn those details."

"There have been some escapes. And a very few people have been let go. Even the Gestapo makes mistakes."

"Interesting," I said.

"No, it is terrible. And what is worse is that you should cling to any hope." Now it was Kaz's turn to drink. He took one gulp, and then finished the rest. His lips curled against his teeth as he swallowed, and the scar on the side of his face seemed to redden. Our eyes met, and I wondered which of us was the worse off. Kaz had been head over heels in love when I first met him. And Daphne Seaton had loved him too, but that all ended in an explosion that killed her and maimed him in body and soul. Daphne was never coming back, and that certainty haunted Kaz.

I was haunted by uncertainty. Was Diana, Daphne's sister, alive? Diana Seaton worked for the SOE, and had been reported taken by the Gestapo in Rome, where she was operating undercover as a nun. Was she dead? I couldn't believe it. But I couldn't do anything about it either, and it was tearing me up inside. Not that I would ever say it to Kaz, but I was jealous of him. He knew, straight out. I wondered, wept, and trembled again.

"Let's go," I said. I threw cash down on the table, probably enough for a dozen dinners. "Show me the Appian Way."

Kaz led the way, passing a bombed-out building, around a corner and up too damn many stone steps. At the top, a single Roman column stood, next to a pedestal where its twin had once been.

"It is more correct to say this is where the Via Appia ends," Kaz said. "There is no beginning here."

The wind whipped around us as I gazed out over the harbor, the moon reflected in the low, lapping waves. Warships of all sizes floated in the calm waters, their immense guns immobile. Why weren't they helping us get to Rome? Why did they sit, useless, in the Mediterranean night?

"How much longer are you here?" I asked.

Kaz—Lieutenant (and Baron) Piotr Augustus Kazimierz, of the Polish Army in Exile—had been detailed to liaison duties with the Polish II Corps, currently making its way to the Italian front from Egypt by way of Taranto, on the heel of Italy. Kaz and I both worked for General Eisenhower, and we often found ourselves loaned out when the General had no pressing matters at hand, investigating murders and other crimes that might impede the war effort.

"I have orders to return to London at the end of the week. Getting the Polish Corps supplied and coordinated with Eighth

Army is nearly complete," Kaz said. "I am sorry I haven't been around to help you. Too much paperwork and meetings. All terribly boring."

"Nothing you could have done," I said. I'd spent every day, every hour, trying to get information about Diana—from the SOE, MI6, even Allied Command at Caserta—but had come up empty all around.

"What about you, Billy? Have you heard from Colonel Harding?" Harding was our immediate boss in General Eisenhower's head-quarters.

"Yes, I have," I said, pulling a thick wad of documents from my jacket pocket. "Orders to return to London two days after we found out about Diana. Orders to proceed to the airfield at Brindisi for priority transportation to London. Inquiries demanding to know my location. And today, orders for me to return immediately or face court-martial for desertion."

"Billy, you have to leave. You can't ignore orders from Supreme Headquarters."

"Oh yeah?" I held the papers up over my head and let them go. The wind lifted them and carried them out over the harbor, where they fell like tears into the sea.

CHAPTER TWO

THEY FOUND ME the next morning. I'd hoped that I might have a day or two of grace, but Brindisi was full of Brits and not many Yanks, so I knew my chances were slim. There were no pretty girls to distract them this time, and I was in a part of town that wasn't known for officers' quarters.

I'd left the billet Kaz and I had been assigned a couple of days ago and gotten a cheap hotel room on the Via Cittadella, between a bordello and a bombed-out haberdashery. I'd met some of the officers from SOE when I was on official business, just before we got the news about Diana, and I simply kept showing up, carrying orders I had no intention of obeying, and asking everyone from the clerks on up if they had any further news of Diana. The orders had come from Colonel Harding in London, but no one at SOE in Brindisi knew what they were about, or that I was absent without leave. They were the left hand that didn't know what the right was doing.

But the snowdrops knew. They were waiting by my jeep, outside the hotel entrance. It was one of the few US Army vehicles in this part of town. One of the only vehicles, period. It probably was a dumb move to park it next to a whorehouse, but I had paid the concierge to keep his eyes peeled and to chase the *scugnizzi* away when they got too close. I could see some of them now, eyeing the military police from behind piles of rubble. Street kids, orphans most of them, a common sight in any Italian city that had been bombed or shelled. They were grimy, always hungry, and clothed in rags that had once been uniforms, impossible to tell from which side. One of the MPs glanced in their direction and they vanished into the rubble as if invisible.

"You got me dead to rights, boys," I said, flashing my friendliest grin. "What'd I do?"

"You Lieutenant Boyle?" the sergeant asked, his white gloves, helmet, and leggings sparkling in the morning sun.

"Call me Billy, Sarge, everyone does."

"Let's go for a ride, Lieutenant. Someone wants to see you." He hitched his thumb in the direction of the passenger's seat. No pat down, no handcuffs. A good sign.

"What about my jeep?" I asked.

"Be right behind us," he said, and snapped his fingers. One of the MPs took my jeep, and the sergeant climbed in behind me. He was a big guy, square-jawed with a deep, growling voice. He needed a shave, which probably meant he'd been up all night looking for me, or throwing drunks into the stockade. Whichever it was, it hadn't put him in a good mood.

"Where we going?" I asked, as I buttoned the collar of my trench coat and held onto my garrison cap.

"You should be going to the stockade, like all the other deserters, but you seem to have friends in high places."

"Hey, I didn't desert, Sarge. I'm only a little late heading back to London."

"Everybody's got an excuse, Lieutenant. I've heard 'em all."

"Don't bet on it. You going to tell me where we're headed?"

"Nope."

"Aren't you going to take my weapon? Put the cuffs on? Shackle me or something?"

"Only if you're planning on shooting all of us, and I don't think you have what it takes. No need to cuff you either; me and my billy club can take care of a dozen wiseass lieutenants any day of the week. I do have a dirty rag back here though, and I will gag you with it if you don't shut up."

I got the message. I sat back and enjoyed the view as we circled the harbor, heading north. It was the same route I'd taken to the SOE station, past the rusting hulk of a bombed-out freighter in the harbor, the barbed-wire fence surrounding the ammo bunkers, and the open pit where army dump trucks deposited mounds of Uncle Sam's garbage every day. Dozens of women and *scugnizzi* sorted through it, the luckiest of them wearing discarded combat boots— German jackboots, GI combat boots, British ammo boots—some of them reaching up to the knees of the smaller kids. They looked up warily as we passed, ready to scatter, but went back to their scavenging when the MPs paid them no mind.

"Those kids will steal anything," the sergeant said. I took this as an invitation to converse.

"Most are orphans," I said. "If either of their parents are alive, they were probably taken by the Germans as forced labor. It's a hard life for a kid, all alone, home destroyed, no one to look after them. Hard to blame them for snitching K rations when they can."

"Bunch of them tried to steal a truckload of liquor," he said. "The kid driving had blocks of wood strapped to his feet so he could reach the pedals. They're thieves, plain and simple."

"What did you do with him? Break his legs?"

"Shut up before I get that rag out, Lieutenant. We're almost there." He tapped the driver on the shoulder and pointed to the access road for the airfield. He showed his orders to the Royal Air Force guard at the gate and was waved through. We drove past Halifax four-engine bombers, painted flat black, with the RAF roundel on the fuselage and not much else in the way of markings. Same with the Lysanders, the rugged single-engine craft used for quick landings behind enemy lines. These were the aircraft of 148 Squadron, assigned to the SOE for the work of delivering arms, agents, and saboteurs behind the lines. It was all night work, which was why the aircraft were on the ground, under camouflage netting, waiting for the sky to become as dark as their airframes.

We passed the warehouse where SOE had a packing station for parachute containers, and drove on to the edge of the airfield, where a dirt road led to a villa, perched on a small hilltop overlooking an inlet. It was surrounded by cypress and palm trees, the breeze off the Adriatic Sea producing a calm rustling sound at odds with the grimness of the enterprise.

I was puzzled as to why we were here. I'd expected to be taken to the nearest provost marshal's office, or at least to a US Army facility. But a British outfit? The same SOE station I'd been haunting for the past week? It didn't add up. If there were news about Diana, they wouldn't send American MPs out to find me; they knew I was bound to show up sooner rather than later. Which of my friends in high places did the grumpy sergeant mean? For the first time, I felt uneasy. I figured I could talk my way out of the desertion charge; although that was perhaps technically correct, it was an overstatement. I was still in uniform, out in the open at the last place my orders had sent me. Not counting the orders to London, that is. But being delivered by American MPs to a British SOE unit got my hackles up. It meant somebody wanted me, and the last time the Brits wanted me, I got shot, along with a few other people. None of us enjoyed it.

"Wait here," the sergeant said as he got out and spoke to a guard at the door. British Army uniform, no markings.

"Do you have any idea what's going on?" I asked the driver. He was a young kid, a private, nineteen years old at most.

"Not a clue, Lieutenant. But I know one thing for sure. Sarge ain't as tough as he makes out. He gave that kid a spanking, then sent him on his way with Hershey's bars and Spam."

"That qualifies as both cruel and unusual punishment. So why bring me here? Don't you guys have your own hoosegow?"

"Yeah. We use an old *carabinieri* station. Kinda bombed out, but the cells still lock."

"How come we didn't go there?"

"Because Sarge said to go here. That's how things work in the army. You should stop talking now."

"Hey, I'm a fellow cop, don't sweat it. At least back home I was. Detective, Boston PD. You looking to get into police work after the war?"

"Maybe. Can you beat prisoners who won't shut up in Boston?"

I was beginning to irritate the kid, but I didn't have much time. Sarge was signing some paperwork with an officer who'd appeared in the doorway.

"Senseless. But we frown on turning our collars over to the feds, and we'd never give up one of ours to foreigners."

"These guys are our allies."

"You Irish by any chance?" I asked, going for the long shot.

"One quarter, on my grandpappy's side. The other three quarters are glad to get rid of you. Good luck, Lieutenant. I truly have no idea why we're here."

Sarge walked up and motioned me out of the jeep, his jaw clenched. My detective skills told me he was steamed, at me, at the Brits, at whoever ordered him to deliver a shavetail to a secret headquarters, no questions asked. They sped off, spitting gravel, before I had a chance to say, "Call me Billy. Everyone does."

CHAPTER THREE

"ANDREW CROFT," SAID a British captain, grinning and shaking my hand as if I were a welcome houseguest. "Follow me, Lieutenant Boyle," he said, pronouncing it *left-tenant* in the odd British way.

Croft was tall, with a strong, dimpled jaw, thick blond hair, and a weathered look to his face. A guy used to the hard life, not a paper-pusher. His uniform was bleached-out khaki, as nondescript as the guard's had been. But his had the look of being worn in the salt air and hot sun, and I wondered if I were being shanghaied for some against-all-odds mission. At the end of the hall, French doors opened to a balcony overlooking the Adriatic. It was impressive. Clear blue water to the horizon, waves throwing foam at the rocks below. Maybe it was going to be tea and crumpets, not death-defying odds.

"Not the worst digs possible," Croft said with a sly smile. "You know what the regular army chaps call SOE? 'Stately 'Omes of England,' since we seem to find the choicest estates to bed down in. Coffee is on its way. You do want coffee, don't you?"

"Sure I do. And that quip is hilarious. But what I really want is for you to tell me what the hell I'm doing here. Then we'll have some joe and swap jokes."

"Don't we all?" Croft said. "I haven't a clue myself. Orders came from the top to wait for you and a Yank courier from Naples. All will be made clear, one hopes. Ah, coffee."

A silver coffee service was set down between two chairs on the veranda by a corporal wearing a revolver and a long knife on his belt, and a scar across his forehead.

"What unit is this?" I asked. It felt more like a pirate's lair than a British Army headquarters.

"They call us Force 226," Croft said as he poured. A breeze came up off the water, blowing his thick blond hair back. "We do a bit of business everywhere, from Corsica to Crete and points in between."

"Just how high up did those orders come from?" I asked.

"The very top." Croft sipped his coffee and leaned back in the chair, letting the sun wash his face.

"As in Kim Philby?"

Croft raised one eyebrow at the mention of Philby. "Best not to name names, even among friends," he said. "There's no reason to let on you are that close to those in exalted circles. Could get you killed if some bloke repeats it."

"Almost has," I said. Kim Philby was with the British Secret Intelligence Service, head of MI6's Mediterranean Section. We'd worked together before, done each other a favor or two, and I thought we were even. Maybe I was wrong. "When is the courier due in?"

"He's here now, finishing breakfast in the kitchen. I thought it would be good for us to chat first, get to know each other."

"Why? Are we going on a trip together? Someplace exotic, with explosives?"

"I've no idea, Lieutenant Boyle. But if we are, I'd like to know the sort of man I'm traveling with."

"I'm an unhappy man, Captain Croft. I'd rather be somewhere else right now, with someone else. The sooner we get this over with, the sooner I can go back to being miserable." I drank my coffee and inhaled the sea air. I felt guilty, with Diana in a Gestapo cell while I sat in the sun, powerless to help her. Or too late.

"You do have the look of a man who needs to *do* something," Croft said, turning his blue eyes on me. "Anything but sit here far from the shooting war, I'd dare say. Restless. Haunted, perhaps. Why?"

"Everyone's got a story," I said. "Mine is too complicated to tell."

"Ah, a woman," Croft said, smiling.

I felt like taking a swing at him, but he couldn't know it wasn't a laughing matter. It wasn't that the course of true love never did run smoothly; it was more like its path was marked by torture, death, and finality. Croft was sharp, and likable, but I saw no percentage in giving anything more away. So I drank his coffee and let him think he had me figured out.

"Here's our man now," Croft said, as the sound of heavy footsteps echoed in the tiled hallway. "Not the highest-ranking confidential courier I've ever seen, but certainly the largest."

It couldn't be, I thought, as I put together the visit to the kitchen, the heavy footsteps, and the comment about rank and size. But damned if it wasn't Staff Sergeant Mike Miecznikowski himself. Or Big Mike, as everyone from privates to generals called him.

"Hey, Billy," Big Mike said, raising his hand in the least possible semblance of a salute.

"When did they let you out?" I asked, ignoring the salute and giving him a slap on the back. No mean feat when you took into account Big Mike's shoulders. He looked like a cross between a linebacker and a lumberjack, stuffed into the largest olive-drab getup Uncle Sam had in stock.

"Couple of days ago," Big Mike said, puffing out his cheeks as if he'd run up a dozen flights. He sat down heavily, beads of sweat on his forehead. The last time I'd seen him was more than a week ago, in a military hospital in Naples, his head swathed in bandages, coming out of a deep sleep after a nasty blow to the head.

"Do you need help, Sergeant?" Croft said, a look of confusion on his face.

"Naw, I'm fine, thanks." Big Mike had a way with officers. Most guys couldn't pull it off, but he had the knack. Unless he sized up one of the brass as a real twit, he treated him like one of the guys. He knew when an actual salute was called for, and he could toss off a nice one when he had to. Otherwise, it was like old pals chewing the fat. And who didn't mind a likable strongman as a pal?

"You don't look fine," I said. I wanted to find out what was going on, but I was more concerned at that moment about Big Mike. He was pale, and his face looked thin and drawn—and thin was a word I'd never applied to him before. "Are you sure you shouldn't still be in the hospital? Or on your way back home?"

"I'm okay, Billy, only a bit winded," Big Mike said. "I was in bed for a week, that was enough hospital for me."

"Were you wounded?" Croft asked, giving Big Mike the once-over, looking for telltale signs. Big Mike took off his garrison cap, revealing a crescent-shaped incision on his skull, above the right ear. His hair was shaved down to a crew cut, and the red, angry scar still showed where the stitches had recently been removed.

"Subdural hematoma?" Croft said, peering closely at the scar. Big Mike nodded, his eyes closing as he did, trying to shut out the pain. "Acute?"

"No," Big Mike said. "The doctors called it subacute, or something like that. Are you a medical man, Captain?"

"Not exactly, but everyone in Force 226 is trained in emergency medicine to one degree or another. It helps to assess the effectiveness of men in the field. I'd guess you should still be on bed rest at least. Discharged from the service at worst, although perhaps you wouldn't think of that as the worst outcome."

"No need to discharge me yet, I'm fine," Big Mike said. I watched him take a deep breath, like an old man in a rocking chair. Then I understood.

"Big Mike is a career policeman," I said to Croft. "I'll bet he talked his way out of a medical discharge because the Detroit Police wouldn't hire him back with a certified head injury. Am I right, Big Mike?"

"Can't say I'd mind going home," Big Mike admitted, shaking his head wistfully. "But I can't risk losing my spot on the Force, or my pension. So I told Sam to keep me in Naples as long as it took to rest up and get back in shape."

"Sam?" Croft said.

"Colonel Samuel Harding," I explained. "He works for General

Eisenhower, and we work for him in the Office of Special Investigations."

"Exalted circles, indeed," Croft said, raising an eyebrow. "The air you breathe is positively rarified. Sergeant, we are both restraining our curiosity about what comes next. If you are able, please get on with it."

"Sure, sure," Big Mike said, resting his hand on a manila envelope marked Confidential and sealed with red tape. "I've got a pile of paperwork here, orders, briefing information, memos from MI6 to SHAEF with copies to Captain Croft. But maybe you want the long story short?"

"Paperwork gives me a headache," Croft said. "Please, in your own words." I was beginning to think this guy was okay.

"There's been a murder," Big Mike said. So far, no surprise. Murders that get in the way of the war effort are our stock and trade. "A priest named Edward Corrigan took a shiv between the ribs. A monsignor, actually."

"Corrigan? Was he Irish?" I wondered if this were leading to another trip back to the old country.

"Nope. American. Now comes the tricky part. He was murdered in Rome. At the Vatican."

"Rome," I whispered. Diana. I felt my heart race, and hoped God would forgive me for how glad I was that someone knifed Monsignor Corrigan. In Rome.

"A pity, to be sure," Croft said. "But what does it have to do with SOE, or Lieutenant Boyle, for that matter? Vatican City is neutral territory. Surrounded by German-occupied Rome, another problem altogether."

"I'll answer the one about Billy first," Big Mike said. He spoke slowly, each word a struggle, and I worried about the toll this trip had taken on him. But I wanted to know more about Rome and getting closer to Diana, and I willed him to get on with it. "Monsignor Corrigan is, or was, an American. But he held Vatican citizenship, and had lived and worked there for years."

"Corrigan worked for the Pope," Croft said.

"For the Holy Office, to be precise," Big Mike said. "He was a lawyer, and drafted statements on church doctrine for the cardinals to review, that kind of thing."

"What does this have to do with me?" I asked, impatient for the other shoe to drop. The death of a priest in a city of priests was hardly earthshaking news.

"What it's got to do with you is that Monsignor Corrigan is a cousin of Bishop John Murphy Finch, of New York. Him and FDR are childhood buddies. From what I hear, when Bishop Finch got the news that cousin Edward was murdered, he gave FDR an earful. FDR passed it on to General Marshall, who passed it onto Ike, who handed it over to Sam. Sam got the news before he left Naples for London, and told me to bring the details to you once plans were in place. It helped keep me from getting sent home, since I was under orders from Ike himself."

"Forgive me, Sergeant," Croft said, "but in the British Army, noncommissioned officers are not usually privy to the thoughts of the general staff."

"I got a few pals at SHAEF," Big Mike said. Supreme Headquarters Allied Expeditionary Force in London was where we were based, and where Big Mike rubbed elbows with General Eisenhower, not to mention his chief of staff at SHAEF, General "Beetle" Smith, who knew everything about everybody. Nobody got along with Beetle on a regular basis, except Big Mike. "We stay in touch."

"So President Roosevelt wants me to find out who murdered Monsignor Edward Corrigan, so he can tell Bishop Finch justice has been served," I said, getting the conversation back on track, and trying to understand what was being said—and what wasn't.

"You got it. I hear the bishop and all the other Catholic voters in New York state will be very happy to receive the news," Big Mike said, giving Croft a sidelong glance and a shrug. "But then I'm just a noncom, what do I know?"

"Forgive me, Sergeant, I am obviously in the presence of a born politician. And let me guess, my role in all this is to find a way to bring Lieutenant Boyle into Vatican City."

"Exactly. Billy and Kaz, that is."

"Lieutenant Kazimierz will be dining with us tonight," Croft said. "Orders from on high, received last night. Now I see why."

"Sam wants you and Kaz here until you leave," Big Mike said, handing me the file. "Top secret on this one. Why don't you read through this stuff and we'll talk some more later."

"I'll organize a place for you to rest, Sergeant," Croft said.

"Thanks, Captain. Feel free to call me Big Mike."

Croft smiled, as if he'd been asked to join the most exclusive club in London.

"Whatever you say, Big Mike."

Croft left us alone on the veranda, the sun warming the tiles at our feet. I was enticed by the possibility of getting closer to Diana, but I had to calm down and focus. We sat in silence, and I let the wheels turn. I thought about all the deaths in Rome, in Italy, and all throughout Europe. I thought about what I knew of politics and the Roman Catholic Church, and revenge. The wheels turned some more and I didn't like where they ended up.

"Tell me why you're really here," I finally said.

"To give you a direct order from Sam," Big Mike said. "He didn't want to give you this assignment, but Ike insisted, I guess because he had no choice." I could tell he was stalling.

"What's the order?"

"Stay away from Diana Seaton," Big Mike said, sitting up and looking straight at me. "You are not to attempt to contact her or free her from prison. You are to take no action which would jeopardize the successful conclusion to this assignment, and make no contact with any other agents."

"Why?"

"Sam said that would be the first thing you'd say, so here goes." He cleared his throat, and closed his eyes, reciting from memory. "Any interference in the affairs of Vatican City, as a neutral state, would have a detrimental effect on our relations with the Italian government and the Papal State, and endanger the neutrality of the Vatican. Your assignment is to assist in the apprehension of a murderer within the Vatican, while avoiding any clandestine operations or situations that would imperil the neutral status of the Vatican." He opened his eyes. "Got it?"

"Got it," I said.

"No, Billy, I mean do you really get it? This isn't like all the other orders you've ignored, like not returning to London. Sam said he can't protect you if you disobey. There's a lot of pressure on this one, and it goes all the way back to Washington. That's one heavy load of bricks ready to come down on your head if you go off the reservation."

"What else is going on here?" I asked, my teeth on edge. "What's the real deal? There's got to be dozens of operations going on in Rome and Vatican City. SOE, OSS, or half a dozen other secret outfits."

"Exactly," Big Mike said. "That's why you're ordered to steer clear of anything except this murder investigation. You could get agents killed by charging into their operations. You know that."

"Maybe so," I said, grudgingly. "It still stinks. Diana gets thrown to the wolves, and I'm dancing like a puppet while someone in the Archdiocese of New York pulls the strings."

"Hey, Billy, you know as well as the next guy how things work in the army."

"I get it, Big Mike. It's political. General Eisenhower wants to keep General Marshall happy, who needs to keep the president happy. Corrigan's already dead, so he doesn't care about being happy. Diana's probably dead, or will be soon. And me? I'll know I did nothing while the woman I loved died. Hell, what's the difference? Two, three hundred miles or two miles away?" I stood up, kicking the chair away, angry at the world but taking it out on Big Mike because the rest of the world wasn't here. "I could be two hundred yards away and all she'll know is that I left her there to die."

"Billy," Big Mike said, getting up and resting his arms on my shoulders. "So far it's all been bad news. Here's a little good news. Sam said to tell you we know Diana is still alive. As of two days ago, anyway. In the Regina Coeli prison."

"How do you know? Are you sure?"

"Sam's sure," Big Mike said, his voice trailing off. I watched his face go pale and felt his arms slip from my shoulders. His eyes rolled up and he swayed like a tree about to be toppled, until he fell, right on me.

CHAPTER FOUR

I'D TAKEN THE weight of Big Mike's fall and gotten more banged up than he had. The hardest part was getting him back on his feet and half carrying him to a bed. Croft had summoned a doctor from the RAF hospital on base, who examined Big Mike and then asked who the devil had discharged him from medical care so soon after surgery. Big Mike was silent on the subject, but agreed to stay prone for the rest of the day. I took the file he'd brought and settled into an easy chair in the library. Croft was right, SOE knew how to live. Not to mention die.

It quickly became clear that Monsignor Edward Corrigan was connected, and not only to FDR via his cousin the bishop. He worked for the Supreme Sacred Congregation of the Holy Office, the outfit that until the start of the century had been called the Inquisition. I was pretty sure they weren't burning heretics at the stake anymore, but it made me wonder if there was any religious connection to the killing. I'd been an altar boy back in Boston, and I heard enough gossip about bishops and archbishops to know that church politics was a game of hardball.

But murder? Revenge, maybe. He'd been killed up close, face to face, with a knife thrust between the ribs, and that could mean it had been personal, the murderer wanting Corrigan to see who was ending his life. Or the killer simply knew how to use a knife.

An orderly brought me tea. I'd hoped for more coffee, and had been surprised when Croft had had it served this morning. This was an English outfit after all, and tea was in their blood, even though I noticed more Brits picking up the java habit whenever they could get ahold of American supplies. I read through the file, focusing on what little information there was, trying to read between the lines to tease out any thread of substance that would give me something to go on.

I spread out the documents on the floor, and soon was sitting cross-legged among them, as I'd seen my dad do dozens of times, when a case was going nowhere. A Boston PD homicide detective, he'd often come home with a leather briefcase stuffed with documents, and after dinner he'd be in his den, on his knees, staring at the papers all around him. It was a good long time before he'd let me look, the crime scene photos not being meant for kids in short pants.

So I played out that scene here, far from my home in Southie, leaning into the motions of my father, hoping by some mysterious means to fall into his routine and absorb his experience—moving files and papers around, tapping key phrases with my finger as if casting a spell and drawing out the truth from a mass of tangled details and the occasional well-placed lie. I found myself doing this more and more, copying the rhythms of my old man, fooling my mind into thinking I had half his smarts, until I failed all on my own—or something clicked and the movements became my own, the memory of then mingling with the here and now, and I saw what had been hidden in plain sight. But not today.

I was lost in thought when Kaz came in and flopped down in a chair opposite mine, hitching his trousers up as he crossed his legs.

"Well, this ought to be fun," he said.

"You heard?"

"Captain Croft gave me the news as soon as I got here. The driver stopped at that fleabag hotel of yours and packed up your gear. It's in the room next to Big Mike's. He was sleeping when I looked in on him."

"Easy for him," I said, getting up and closing the door, keeping my voice low. "He's not visiting Rome ahead of the Allied armies."

"Billy, we are on a secure base, in an SOE building. Do you think there are spies about?" Kaz gave a little laugh, to show he wasn't serious, but I saw in his eyes that he was, as worry briefly furrowed his brow.

"Of course there are spies here, Kaz. That's what these people do. Which means there could be double agents, too. Or SOE security checking on us." It sounded crazy, but the secret stuff was the craziest part of this war, and that was saying something.

"You have a point," Kaz said, in a tone that said it was one I'd taken too far. "As for Rome, it is where you wanted to go, you said so yourself last night. Now we have the SOE to get us there. It is a gift from heaven," he said, twirling his fingers upward.

"Well, God Himself does have something to say about it," I said. "Our orders come direct from the White House. General Eisenhower's only the messenger." I told Kaz about FDR and the bishop, and the warning to steer clear of Diana.

"That does complicate things," Kaz said, tapping his finger on his knee, already figuring the odds. "It seems as if we must fool not only the Germans, but our own people. It would not be the first time, Billy."

"True," I said. "I'd hoped you'd go along with it." It meant a lot that he would, but I expected nothing less. Kaz and I were bound together in this war. Each of us had risked his life for the other, and we both cared deeply about Diana. Kaz, because of his love for her sister Daphne, and all that she had meant to him. Me, because I loved her, and felt I had something to live up to, a responsibility to the dead to make the most of life. It was complicated.

"It *would* make things more interesting," he said.

Kaz liked things interesting. He didn't have a lot to look forward to, and when he got bored, he tended to dwell on that fact. Things weren't as bad as they once were, but I still worried about him. Yet I knew I could count on him whatever the odds. He was a thin, bookish-looking guy with horn-rimmed glasses, but he was tough, too. The real thing, the kind of toughness that didn't show until the odds were ten to one.

"I will see what I can find out about the prison, the Regina Coeli," Kaz continued. "Now tell me what else we know about the unfortunate Monsignor Edward Corrigan."

"Well, he was a smart guy. Went to Columbia Law School after he became a priest. I'm guessing his cousin the bishop helped grease the skids since he got sent to Rome right after that. He went to work for the Supreme Sacred Congregation of the Holy Office," I said, looking up to see if Kaz knew what that meant. Kaz knew something about everything.

"The Inquisition," he said. "Much tamer now than in previous centuries. Go on."

"He also worked for the Sacred Congregation for the Propagation of the Faith, which sounds like missionary work."

"Yes, it is called by its Latin name, *Propaganda Fide.*"

"Kaz, how do you know so much about the Vatican? Are you religious?" I knew that Kaz, like most Poles, was Catholic, but I'd never once asked him about what he believed. We'd talked about love, death, fear, and loss, but never about God. It felt strange asking now, after so long.

"No, not at all. I was an altar boy for a while, which made my mother happy. But I asked too many questions which the father could not answer, so he asked me to leave. That made *me* happy, since I preferred reading the newspaper on Sunday mornings. I never could take all those Bible stories seriously."

"I was an altar boy myself," I said. "I kind of liked it. The ceremony, being part of something larger than myself, separate from everything else." I shrugged, embarrassed to admit I liked getting dressed up in white lace.

"You will have plenty of pomp and ceremony where we are going," Kaz said. "I've been there, to visit an older cousin who became a priest. He worked at Propaganda Fide, teaching students from Africa."

"Is he still there?"

"No, they sent him on a mission to Bulgaria, to evangelize among the members of the Eastern Orthodox Church. He was never heard from again. He was quite happy with his life in Rome, and was distressed at being sent to the Balkans. He was not the evangelizing type."

"Quiet and studious, like you?"

"Yes. We were close. Our families would spend time each summer in the mountains, and we got along well. I was glad when he became a priest, not because I believed in all that nonsense, but because the life suited him. Until they sent him to Bulgaria. There is still resentment toward Catholic missionaries there among the Orthodox, and I am sure he was killed for his efforts."

"Dangerous work," I said. "But our man Corrigan never left Rome. Looks like he mainly did legal work for the Holy See."

"He was a *scrittore*," Kaz said, heaving a sigh and returning to the present, leafing through pages of the report. "It means 'writer,' but is used as a rank for lawyers within the Vatican."

"It looks like the typical career of a successful bureaucrat. Good schools, influential relatives, plum assignments, and leaving the tough jobs to others, like your cousin. Except for this," I said. I handed Kaz a file of letters. "They're all from British POWs who wrote home about visits from a delegation from the Vatican."

Kaz flipped through the letters, scanning them quickly. "They all mention Father Corrigan," he said. "How helpful he was."

"Right. Seems that with the war on, there wasn't much news on the missionary front, so the Vatican sent out a delegation to tour the prisoner-of-war camps in Italy. Corrigan was part of that delegation, and helped bring letters out to families, and supplied winter clothing to a lot of the POWs who'd been captured in the desert."

"Interesting," Kaz said. "It gives us somewhere to start. Perhaps he picked up some information that was too dangerous for him to possess. Or got mixed up in spy business. We can try to find the rest of the delegation. I wonder if the Germans allowed them to visit prisons in Rome, like the Regina Coeli?"

"Maybe we can arrange something," I said quietly. I still didn't trust everything about this setup.

"There are no photographs of the body," Kaz said. "Where was he found?"

"Outside one of the main doors to Saint Peter's Basilica," I said. "His body was found before dawn by one of the Swiss Guards."

"Which door?" Kaz asked.

I looked through the report. "The left, facing the exterior."

"Quite interesting," Kaz said. "The leftmost door to Saint Peter's is only used for funeral processions. It is called the Door of Death." He raised an eyebrow, and grinned. "It seems Monsignor Corrigan was indeed found at death's door."

"Odd place to leave a body," I said.

"Our killer has a sense of the macabre," Kaz said. "Or was it coincidence?"

"There are no coincidences," I said, remembering what my father drummed into my head. "Only reasons that we haven't uncovered yet." Did that hold true for Diana as well? Was there a hidden reason I'd been picked for this job? Was there some thread of a relationship between Corrigan's murder and Diana being picked up by the Gestapo? If there were, would it lead me to her? Or to the Gestapo? I shook off these useless musings. Dad would have said not to worry about what the future holds until you look it in the eye.

"Anything else of value in these papers?" Kaz said, pawing through the sheets on the floor.

"Not that I can find. They're all secondhand reports, no names mentioned. Except for references to 'Rudder,' which sounds like a code name."

"Ah," Kaz said, finding one. "Rudder reports that Commissario Filberto Soletto of the Vatican Gendarmerie Corps had been a regular informer to the OVRA, the Italian Fascist secret police, and now reports to the Gestapo."

"Which is why we can't expect much help from the Vatican police. Soletto has already decided that a Jewish asylum seeker killed Corrigan when he refused to help him. Most of the Gendarmerie are straight arrows, according to Rudder, but Soletto keeps a lid on things, and has powerful allies among the more conservative cardinals."

"We will have to find this Rudder as well," Kaz said. "He is obviously feeding information to the Allies. We could use his help."

"Something tells me we're not going to get much help with this one," I said. I didn't like how many powerful men had a stake in this investigation. FDR, Bishop Finch, a crooked Vatican cop, and the cardinals who protected him. That wasn't even counting the Germans who ringed Vatican City, watching those who entered and left.

"Hey, Kaz, maybe the Germans saw something. They have to watch the border day and night, right?"

"Yes. Most of the Vatican is walled, but Saint Peter's Square is wide open. The Germans painted a white line to mark the border, and I understand they patrol it constantly."

"But the locals can go in and out, right?"

"Certainly," Kaz said. "Anyone who did not raise suspicion could have walked right by a German guard and killed the monsignor."

"And walked out again," I said.

"Yes," Kaz said. "The doors to the basilica are behind large columns; it would be quite difficult to see from the square. But we need to know when he was killed, and nothing here states that. If it was in the evening, then many people would have been leaving the piazza. Late at night, or early morning, I think it's likely that the guards would have questioned anyone leaving."

"Well, it hardly matters. I doubt the Krauts will cooperate with our investigation."

"One never knows," Kaz said. "Perhaps we will find a way to speak with someone at the Regina Coeli. It is on the Tiber River, a quick stroll from the Vatican."

"As long as we can stroll out, and back in again," I said.

"Excuse me," a voice said from the doorway. It was an American, tall and lean, with thick blond hair and a weathered look around the eyes, like that of fishermen I had known back home. I hadn't heard the door open, and wondered how long he'd been standing there. "Either of you guys seen Andy around?"

"Captain Croft?" Kaz said. "He was in his office a short time ago."

"Sorry to interrupt," he said, and turned to leave. His voice was a deep, mellow baritone, and he seemed familiar.

"Have we met?" I said, standing. I was sure we had. I got a look at his insignia and saw he was a lieutenant. A US Marine lieutenant, a rare sight in Italy.

"No, Lieutenant Boyle," he said, his lower lip jutting out a bit as he looked down at me. "We haven't. See you later." With that, he was gone.

"Who was that?" Kaz asked.

"Don't know," I said. "But he looks so damn familiar. How else would he know my name?"

"Perhaps you are right, and the walls have ears," Kaz said.

"This is supposed to be a secret operation, using the British SOE to smuggle us into Rome," I said, throwing myself back into my chair. "So what's a US Marine lieutenant who knows me by sight doing here?"

"Another mystery," Kaz said. "I also wonder why they sent Big Mike here. Captain Croft said he should still be in hospital."

"Far as I can tell, it was to tell me in no uncertain terms not to try to spring Diana. They probably figured I'd take the personal approach more seriously. And you know Big Mike—he'd insist he was fine as soon as Sam asked him."

"It is a pity we cannot speak directly with Colonel Harding."

"We can do the next best thing," I said. "All we need to do is find a communications unit and send a radio teletype to SHAEF."

"Why not ask Captain Croft? He may have the right equipment here; there are radio masts on the villa roof."

"I'd rather not," I said. "Let's blow this joint."

It was a good idea. Too bad the guard at the door ordered us back into the villa. My jeep was nowhere in sight, and there was security at every exit. We were prisoners.

CHAPTER FIVE

WE SPENT THE afternoon being turned away from the SOE radio room, Croft's office, and every door that led out of the villa. Kaz and I went through all the reports again, and again. Nothing new. A directive from Colonel Harding stressed the importance of not violating Vatican neutrality, but what he really meant was not to get caught violating Vatican neutrality. The big worry was that the Germans would use any excuse to occupy Vatican City and take the Pope into protective custody. Meaning he'd be a hostage to the Third Reich.

I understood all that. It wasn't going to stop me if I saw a chance in hell of freeing Diana, but that was probably an accurate description of the odds, so I didn't worry about it. What I didn't understand was why we were being held incommunicado, and the sudden appearance of the Marine lieutenant. Or what the hell was going to happen next.

It turned out that dinner was next. Kaz, Big Mike, and I were led into a dining room where Croft, his Marine pal, and a couple of British officers were mixing themselves drinks.

"Welcome, gentlemen," Croft said, approaching us as if we were weekend guests at his country home. "Will you join us for a drink?"

"The hell with drinks," I said, steamed at the runaround and now the soft soap. "Why are we being held here and what's he got to do with it?" I pointed to the marine.

"Lieutenant Boyle, all will be explained. . . ."

"Don't try that polite crap with me, Croft. I don't care if you're a captain or a cardinal, I want the truth, and I want it now."

Croft raised his eyebrows, glanced at the marine, and asked the two other Brits to give us some privacy. He eyed me until they closed the door behind them.

"You'd do well to remember the rank, Boyle. A captain trumps a lieutenant, and SOE trumps every other branch, so mind your manners."

"This is war, not a goddamn tea party," I said, my temperature rising. "What the hell is going on, and what aren't you telling us?" I stepped closer to Croft, my fists clenched and arms pressed to my sides. It wasn't his fault, I knew. He was only following orders. Orders that might make sense or might not, but clearly came from over his head. Still, I wanted answers. I tried to hold my temper in check, but the thought of Diana in prison kept it white-hot. If I did have a chance to get near her, I didn't want any SOE funny business to interfere.

"War or tea party, we're all on the same side," the marine said. His deep voice sounded so familiar. "Let's have a drink and sit down, okay fellas?" He had an easy smile, and clapped his hand on Croft's shoulder, breaking the tension in the room. The two of them looked like cousins from across the Atlantic. Both tall and blond with well-weathered faces, they moved with a grace that comes from confidence borne of challenges met and mastered. I didn't like the idea of them arrayed against us, but if so, I wasn't going along with their schemes without a fight.

"Agreed," Croft said. "Let's begin again. Drink?"

"Yeah," I said. "Irish whiskey, straight. You know, like the truth."

"Irish whiskey I believe we have in ample supply," Croft said, with a barely suppressed grin. "Have you met Lieutenant Hamilton?"

"No, we haven't been introduced," I said, taking the glass Croft offered.

"Sorry, Lieutenant Boyle," the marine said. "John Hamilton, US Marine Corps."

"You sure we haven't met?" I asked.

"Yeah, I'm sure," he said, wearily, as if he heard that line often. "Big Mike, Baron, what'll you have?"

"Vodka," Kaz said. "Truth on the side, please."

"I'll have what you're drinking," Big Mike said. "I never drank with a movie star before."

"Aw, Christ," Hamilton said, pouring Kaz's vodka. "Don't ask a bunch of stupid questions about starlets. I hope you like tawny port. Love the stuff myself."

"What?" I said, trying to figure out what was going on.

"Tawny port," Hamilton said. "Great stuff, packs a wallop."

"No, I mean—"

"*Bahama Passage*," Big Mike said. "I saw him in it before I left the States. I don't remember the name, but it wasn't John Hamilton."

"Gentlemen," Croft said, chuckling at Hamilton's discomfort, "allow me to introduce Sterling Hayden, otherwise known as Lieutenant John Hamilton. He is our liaison with your American OSS."

"I must have seen that movie too," I said. "I was sure we'd met. Don't recall it, though."

"For good reason," Hayden answered. "It was only my second film, and might be my last. Silly way for a man to make a living. Come on, let's all take a load off and talk this thing through."

"What does the OSS have to do with this operation?" Kaz asked as he took a seat at the table. I saw Croft and Hayden exchange glances, Croft giving a subtle nod.

"Okay, we'll play it straight with you guys, since you sound like a no-nonsense bunch," Hayden said. "The orders that Big Mike here brought with him came via a slightly different route than he thought."

"I got those from Colonel Harding," Big Mike said, his mouth set in a grim line. "I wouldn't like to hear him called a liar."

"If he's a friend of yours, I'd hate to call him one," Hayden said. "And I won't have to. Or General Eisenhower either. There's just a missing link in the story. It wasn't the president that Bishop Finch called when he heard of the murder. It was another old pal, this one from Columbia Law School."

"Let me guess," I said. "William Donovan. Head of the Office of Strategic Services." The OSS was the American equivalent of the Special Operations Executive. We were newer at the game, but eager to make up for lost time. "Your boss."

"Right on both counts," Hayden said, slapping the table with glee. "Wild Bill—that's Donovan's nickname, one he doesn't mind a bit—Wild Bill didn't want OSS to be connected to this operation, for security reasons and out of the same concern for Vatican neutrality that Colonel Harding has. But Wild Bill wants to do his pal a favor and find out who killed Monsignor Corrigan, so the story was altered a bit in case anyone spoke out of school."

"As for your being detained," Croft said, "that is standard procedure before a mission. Nothing sinister about it."

"So other than keeping watch on us, Lieutenant Hamilton, or Hayden, what's your game?"

"Hey, call me Sterling if you want, but don't spread it around. I'd prefer to keep the movie business quiet. It's all a load of horseshit anyway. And hell, I'm not here to watch you boys. I'm here to drive the boat."

"Boat?" Kaz said.

"Sure, the boat. We're taking a little trip up the Adriatic," Hayden said, a wide grin spreading across his face.

"Lieutenant Hamilton is an experienced seaman," Croft said. "He makes regular runs to Yugoslavia to deliver arms and supplies to the partisans, and brings out downed Allied airmen."

"Billy and Kaz are going to Rome, not Yugoslavia," Big Mike pointed out.

"Yes," Croft said. "And we will get them there, via the Adriatic. We can't use the western coastline, since there is heavy activity around the Anzio beachhead. So Lieutenant Hamilton and his men will take you up the eastern coast, past the front lines and into Pescara."

"Why don't we fly out in one of those Lysanders you have parked outside? Isn't that what they're used for?"

"Quite," Croft said. "But we've had some losses recently from Luftwaffe interceptions. We think there may be agents nearby watching our flights take off. We're taking countermeasures, but we can't wait for them to take effect. So I asked Hamilton here for a favor."

"I didn't know the SOE and the OSS were so chummy," I said.

"We have to be," Hamilton said. I decided it was too confusing to call him by two names, and if he wanted to go incognito, that was fine by me. I liked him for it. "We spend as much time fighting the brass as we do the Nazis."

"The OSS is dependent upon the Royal Navy for shipping," Croft said. "And when it comes to sharing resources with Americans, who seem to have so much of everything, it brings out the worst in some officers."

"Same goes for American regular army types," Hamilton said. "They don't want to cooperate with the Brits and learn from them, even if they've been at this cloak-and-dagger stuff for years. Stupidity knows no boundaries. Guys like Croft and me just want to get things done, so we help each other out."

"If the Royal Navy isn't helping you out, what kind of boat are we talking about?" I asked.

"An Italian fifty-foot sailboat with a rebuilt diesel engine. Looks like an ancient wreck, but she's gotten me home safely every time. Crewed by a dozen Yugoslav Partisans, able seamen, all of them. Damn good fighters, too."

"Well, Billy," Big Mike said. "What do you think? They sound like our kinda fellas."

"I'm game," I said. "Kaz?"

"I do not like boats," Kaz said, and downed his vodka.

CHAPTER SIX

IT WAS FOUR in the morning. I stood at the window, watching the stars and the silvery water below. I couldn't sleep, while everyone else was dead to the world. I could hear Big Mike sawing logs in his room, and watched Kaz thrashing, dreaming of all that had been lost, or at least that was my guess.

I'd slept for a while, and dreamed of horses. Galloping horses with black manes, against green fields and blue skies. They were all around me, and I held out my hands to feel their flanks as they sped past, my fingertips grazing warm, silky hides. The horses slowed and circled me, shaking their heads, frosty plumes of breath pumped from heaving lungs. They came closer, nuzzled me, pushed me forward until I fell against a saddled horse and felt a booted heel in the stirrup. I looked up. It was Diana. Suddenly the sky turned dark as thunder crashed and lightning flashed hot white. The horses reared in terror, large brown eyes wide with fear. As one, the herd turned and galloped away, taking Diana with them, leaving me alone in the field, watching them disappear into the rain and darkness.

I'd awoken, gasping for breath, not knowing where I was, but thinking instantly of Diana and where she was. In prison, but alive. I knew it now. The first time I'd ever seen her, she was on horseback, bringing horses to the safety of her father's barn as a thunderstorm drew close. It was a message, I was certain. She wasn't dead. She was waiting, waiting for me to follow where the horses led, and carry her to shelter from the storm.

I felt a calm I hadn't known in days. I got up, dressed, and waited. Waited for the other dreamers to rise and bring me where I needed to go. I watched the sky until I saw the first faint trace of sunrise edging up from below the horizon. It was time.

One hour later, Kaz and I said our good-byes to Big Mike, and made him promise to take it easy for a while. Croft said he'd watch out for him, and Big Mike, still not quite trusting how things had turned out, said he'd watch Croft for us until we got back. I felt fine on both counts.

Kaz was relieved when he found out the first leg of our trip was not by boat. Croft drove us out to a Halifax from 148 Squadron, already warming up. We stood on the tarmac, prop wash whipping at our clothes as the engines roared. Croft went over the final details while crewmen loaded gear into the belly of the black bomber.

"You'll have an escort of two Spitfires north to Termoli," he said. "It will be a quick hop. Hamilton will look after you from here on out. You've got your clothing, identity papers, and everything you'll need for Rome in duffle bags, marked with your name. He'll take you by sea from Termoli to Pescara. Any questions?"

"Yeah," I said, shouting to be heard above the din. "You seem to have this well organized, but you've missed one thing."

"What's that?"

"How the hell do we get out of Rome? Or is that not part of your plan?"

"One step at a time, Lieutenant. Find that murderer first. Someone from SOE will contact you when the time comes to smuggle you out," Croft said. "Good luck."

The hatch closed behind me, the metal clang echoing inside the fuselage. The Halifax, converted from bombing to ferrying men and supplies, wasn't built for comfort. Kaz, Hamilton, and I sat crowded on a narrow bench, surrounded by wooden crates and canvas bags. The aircraft lurched forward and picked up speed, the four engines snarling as they carried the plane out over the water, climbing until

Brindisi was nothing but a smear on the horizon. As we headed north, I thought of Diana waiting for release in Rome. I trusted the truth of my dream more than I trusted what I'd been told by Croft and Hamilton. Not that I thought they were lying to me, only that the chances were good they'd been lied to. The OSS had already hidden their involvement from General Eisenhower himself; what else had been hidden from their own junior officers? If Colonel Harding didn't know the whole story, what had Captain Croft missed?

Diana was alive, I was certain of it. I couldn't say why—other than because of the dream—but I was. Clandestine organizations like SOE and OSS played fast and loose with the truth—of that I was dead certain. What was waiting for us at the Vatican? Of that I was less sure. A helluva lot less.

"After we land, I'll brief you on the route in," Hamilton said, his voice raised against the engine noise and the wind beating against the bomber. "We set sail as soon as it's dark."

"I do not like boats," Kaz said, as he peered out the small Perspex window. "Look, that must be our escort. Four—no, six fighters." He pointed to small dots in the distance, descending from high cloud cover.

"I thought Croft said two Spitfires," I said.

"Goddamn!" Hamilton said. "Those aren't Spitfires." Faster than I thought possible, the fighters were on us, machine guns chattering, tracers white-hot against the blue sky. The Halifax picked up speed, but outrunning Me-109s in a lumbering bomber wasn't in the cards. Rounds hit the wing and the top of the fuselage, shredding the metal and sounding like a thousand stones blasting a tin roof. The Halifax's machine guns answered, their fire trailing the German planes as they split into two groups. One probably going after the escort, the other coming in for the kill.

We didn't stand a chance. A single bomber, no matter how many machine guns it has, is no match for fighters. Bombers were meant to fly in defensive boxes, covering each other with their guns. Alone, the fighters would swoop down on us, like a cat batting at a cornered mouse.

"Hang on," Hamilton said, as the aircraft banked left and began a slow dive, the pilot using gravity to increase our speed. Not a bad idea, until the ground got in the way. I hung on, as Kaz kept his nose pressed to the window, watching the show. Hell, why not? It might be the last one we ever saw.

Two Me-109s came at us from the port side. Their noses were painted bright yellow, the rest of the sleek, deadly plane in dappled camouflage. They were overhead in a second, the noise of machine guns, cannons, and throaty engines incredibly loud. I thought they missed us until I saw one of our engines spew black smoke. In a flash, another fighter was coming in, but this one was a Spitfire, the distinctive spade-shaped wings instantly recognizable, and welcome. But he wasn't coming to the rescue. He twisted and turned, then dove, trying to shake off two Me-109s on his tail.

The Halifax was vibrating now, the damage we'd taken slowing it, making us even more vulnerable. All of the bomber's gunners opened up, meaning we were being hit from every direction. Tracer rounds stitched through the plane, leaving blackened and smoking holes of jagged metal. I looked at Kaz and Hamilton, all of us wide-eyed at not being hit.

The firing died down, but I knew it would only last a moment while the fighters gained altitude for another run at us. It might be the last.

"There!" Hamilton shouted. "He's going for that cloud bank."

Ahead of us, a wall of dark cloud rose in the distance. Safety. The Halifax strained in an even steeper dive, as fighters swarmed around us. I saw the two Spitfires, still aloft, circling higher in a tight weave, pulling the Me-109s away from us.

"Look!" Kaz said, pointing to a trail of black smoke heading for the sea. One Kraut fighter down.

"That got their blood up," Hamilton said. "They're going after the Spitfires."

The sound of firing faded as the bomber descended and the fighters drew away. We were almost to the cloud as the pilot feathered the stricken engine. The propeller stopped as part of the cowling flew off and a last burst of thick, black, oily smoke billowed from the engine, turning the wing black before the cloud swallowed us in protective, gray nothingness.

Compared to the noises of the fight, it was silent. Only the remaining three engines and the sound of hearts pounding against terrified chests competed with the hydraulic whirr of turrets as the gunners remained alert, knowing the clouds could disappear at any moment. We listened for the snarl of engines, straining to pick out the sound of approaching fighters. Minutes passed and the cloud cover held. I felt myself relax, and saw Hamilton puff out his cheeks, exhaling a breath of relief.

"I've decided I do not like airplanes either," Kaz said, crossing his legs as if he were in a London parlor. Hamilton and I looked at each other for a long second, then burst out laughing. Laughter that comes from cheating death, the relief of feeling life for another hour, appreciating the sensations of the body as the reaper retreats, vanquished. The giddiness of war.

CHAPTER SEVEN

"BOTH SPITFIRES WENT down," Hamilton said. "One pilot bailed out. The other didn't make it." He lit a cigarette and blew out a long plume of smoke, keeping his eyes fixed on the ceiling. "Damn shame."

We were in the RAF mess hall in Termoli, waiting for a truck to take us to the boat. Our pilot and crewmen sat at a table opposite us, nursing mugs of tea and pointedly ignoring us, as if we were to blame for running into a Luftwaffe fighter sweep. Maybe they had a point. At the next table, half a dozen Italian laborers sat smoking, their old army uniforms grimy and stained.

"If enemy agents were observing the Lysander flights," I said, "wouldn't they report a Halifax taking off as well?"

"They might," Hamilton said. "That's why we had an escort. We weren't even crossing the front line, so it seemed unlikely they'd find us before we got to Termoli."

"Who knew about the flight?" Kaz asked, glancing at the Italians.

"Me, Croft, the aircrew, and my first mate. Likely others at the Brindisi RAF base, not to mention OSS headquarters in Caserta," Hamilton said. "It wasn't out of the ordinary. We fly back and forth all the time."

"Getting jumped by six Me-109s is damn well out of the ordinary," I said. "That Spitfire pilot getting killed was out of the ordinary."

"No, it wasn't, Lieutenant Boyle. You know that. Yeah, maybe someone blabbed, or maybe the Luftwaffe wanted to show us they still can pack a punch. It's war. People die." I couldn't argue with that.

"He's right, Billy," Kaz said. "We can't change what happened. But we need to be sure that not too many people know about the rest of our route." He eyed Hamilton, then turned his attention to his tea.

"Okay, okay," Hamilton said. "We have to set sail tonight, and make our rendezvous in Pescara, there's no getting around that."

"Why?" I asked.

"Tides and minefields. The tides have to be just right to navigate around the minefields. I have two of my men ashore with a radio. They'll contact us if anything looks suspicious."

"Do you trust them?" Kaz asked.

"One of them has a sister," Hamilton said. "She's a Partisan too. The Ustashi captured her last year. Sent her back with her arms cut off. What do you think?"

"I think we don't have to worry about him," I said. "But who are the Ustashi?"

"Croatian fascists," Hamilton said. "The Nazis set them up as a puppet government in Croatia. They happily kill Jews, Serbs, Gypsies, anyone who isn't a Croatian Catholic. They're so damn bloodthirsty the Germans had to step in and disarm some of their militia units, since they were driving so many of their opponents to join the Partisans."

"More violent than the Nazis," Kaz said. "An uncommon occurrence."

"They are enthusiastic about killing in the name of religion," Hamilton said. "A Franciscan monk is the head guard at the Jasenovac concentration camp. Defrocked, but he still likes to wear his robes. So don't worry about a little trip through the Italian countryside with good papers and a decent cover story. You could be going to Zagreb, not Pescara."

"Okay," I said. "I get it. What about after Pescara?"

"The Germans have a garrison there, so we'll land you outside of town. The plan was to bring you inland to meet up with an OSS team. They were detailed to bring you overland, to a rail yard north of Rome, at Viterbo."

"Sounds like a lot of people must be in on that plan," I said.

"Yep," Hamilton admitted. "A dozen, at least. So we'll do something different. Hide you in plain sight."

"What does that mean?" I asked.

Hamilton leaned across the table, turning his face away from the others in the room. We did the same, foreheads almost touching. "It means we'll see how good your forged identity papers are. You're going to buy tickets at the train station in Pescara. You'll be on your own almost all the way. You speak Italian, right?" Hamilton said to Kaz.

"Yes, but not well enough to pass as a native."

"Doesn't matter. Your papers say you are a Romanian priest, Baron. And you, Boyle, an Irish man of the cloth. A neutral and a German ally, both on Vatican business, traveling back to Rome."

"So we just ride the train straight into Rome? Then call a cab to take us to see the Pope? This sounds risky as all hell," I said.

"The good news is that no one else knows this route, until you get to Viterbo. Your papers look good, and there are documents on actual letterhead from the Holy See. You're inspecting the refugee situation and reporting your findings. I'll give you the train schedule and the route you should take. Very plausible—they have priests traveling all over Italy now that they can't leave the country for missionary work."

"What happens at the Viterbo rail yard?" Kaz asked.

"We need a safe method to get you into Vatican City," Hamilton said. "The closer to Rome and the Vatican, the more checkpoints and roadblocks the Germans have. Once you're in the Vatican, it's fairly easy to move around, with the right papers and some luck. But the Nazis are watching the approaches. They're after Allied agents, Italian partisans, escaped POWs, deserters—you name it. Everybody wants to get to Rome, and everyone on the run wants to get to neutral ground. So we have a safe passage prepared for you."

"What is it?" I asked.

"The Vatican has its own railroad station. Railcars bring in food and supplies from the north, and they enter through a special gate."

"Yes," Kaz said. "A sliding iron gate that retracts into the wall. I've seen it, along the Viale Vaticano."

"That's your way in," Hamilton said. "We have a trusted agent, a railroad worker, who will seal you in with a load of produce at Viterbo. We only use him for priority missions, and it's worked every time. When the doors open, you'll be inside Vatican City."

"The Germans don't search it?"

"They oversee the loading and lock the doors, but they don't search it before it enters the Vatican," Hamilton said. "Wait on the platform at Viterbo for trains bound for Florence. There will be less scrutiny there. A worker in a blue coat will approach you and ask for two cigarettes."

"Why two?"

"Because anyone might ask for one. Say no, they are too expensive these days. He will place you in the produce car and seal you in. When you reach Stazione Vaticana, another contact will take you off the train."

"An OSS agent in the Vatican?" I said, wondering why we were making the trip.

"Let's just say someone who provides favors now and then. Not an actual agent."

"So all we need to do is evade the German guards and jump in with a load of rutabagas? I gotta say, you have a way of making the impossible sound downright simple. This isn't a Hollywood movie, this is the real thing, *Sterling*." I said his real name as loud as I could, knowing he wanted to keep it under wraps. His optimism was beginning to bug me.

"Hey, I'm giving you a choice, buddy," he said. "You can go either way, but you're going. You can take the planned route, which means you'll have to trust the people moving you along it. Or you can take the train and trust your papers. Me, I'd go on my own if I had a cover story as good as yours. Less complicated."

"It can't be *that* easy to move around in occupied Italy," I said.

"I never said it was easy. Sailing back and forth to Yugoslavia isn't easy either, but we do it all the time. Have some confidence, goddamn it!" He slammed his fist on the table, splattering lukewarm tea on the surface. People turned and stared, then moved away, leaving us to our subdued argument.

"All right, sorry about the Hollywood wisecrack," I said. "It seems so tenuous, that's all."

"Tenuous," Hamilton said, relaxing a bit. "That's a good word for life these days, and I can tell, you're not a guy who minds tenuous. I think you can handle tenuous. So why so jumpy about which way you go in?"

"I want to be sure we get there, that's all." Hamilton was sharp, I had to give him that. I looked away, not wanting my eyes to meet his.

"What brings you here, Boyle? There's something different about you, something you're holding back," he said as he leaned across the table and fixed me in his glare. "Most guys going behind the lines are nervous or busy working hard not to show it. You seem to be somewhere else, like you have your own private war going on. You're not nervous about the Germans; you're nervous about not getting into Rome. Who are you, Boyle, and what's your game?"

"I'm a man on a mission," I said. I was sure Hamilton and the rest of the OSS didn't know about Diana, and I wanted to keep it that way. The fewer people who knew, the fewer there were to stop me. I tried to stare him down, but Hamilton had his own tough-guy face, maybe from the movies, maybe for real.

"Can you keep a secret?" Kaz asked.

"Hell, secrets are my business," Hamilton said.

"Billy is General Eisenhower's nephew," Kaz said. What that had to do with anything, I had no idea, but it did move the conversation away from Hamilton's questions, and I guess that's what Kaz intended. "We both work for him."

"No shit?" Hamilton.

"It's the truth," I said. "I was a cop in Boston before the war, and Uncle Ike wanted a trained detective on his staff." The truth was more complicated than that. I was related to General Eisenhower, on my mother's side, sure enough. But when the war broke out, Uncle Ike was an unknown general laboring in the bowels of the new Pentagon building in Washington, D.C., not the head of Supreme Headquarters, Allied Expeditionary Force. We were a family of cops, Boston Irish, and proud of both. My dad and uncle were both on the force, and they'd lost their older brother Frank in the First World War. According to them, this was another damn war to protect the British Empire, and not worth another Boyle family sacrifice. Since I wasn't a fan of either the English oppressors of my ancestors or of dying, I tended to agree. So the family called in some political favors and got me a commission and an assignment to work for Uncle Ike in D.C. and sit out the shooting war as an officer and a gentleman. Worked like a charm, until Uncle Ike got sent to London and decided to take me with him.

"So that's why they picked you for this mission, being a detective," Hamilton said, rubbing his chin and giving me a fresh appraisal.

"Yeah, and Kaz because he knows a boatload of languages." I didn't mention that I owed my detective rank to the fact that my Uncle Dan sat on the promotions board.

"Well, if there's something else going on and you want to keep it to yourselves, that's fine with me. Glad to help out a fellow New Englander. I began sailing out of Gloucester, used to go drinking in Boston every now and then. Maybe you rousted me once or twice, eh?"

"Maybe. I've tossed a few drunken sailors in the clink. Guy your size though, I would've left him in the street."

"Good one, Boyle! Let's go." Hamilton pointed to the doorway, where a bearded figure stood, a head taller than anyone in the room. He wore a brown wool cap with a bright red star, along with a well-worn British uniform, a Sten gun slung over his shoulder, and a menacing look on his face. He noticed the Italians, and his eyes narrowed to hard, dark slits. A sneer crept into his mouth, and one hand moved to the revolver at his belt. The Italians froze, fear etched across their brows.

"Best not to keep Stjepan waiting," Hamilton said.

CHAPTER EIGHT

STJEPAN WAS AT the wheel by the time we got to the jeep. Hamilton took the passenger seat, and Kaz and I scrambled into the rear as the scowling driver took off.

"Everything set?" Hamilton asked, one hand holding his cap, the other clutching the windshield as the vehicle accelerated.

"Set, Hamil-tone," Stjepan said, speaking deliberately and enunciating each syllable as he turned to glance at us. "Priest clothes will fit. Good enough."

"Good man," Hamilton said, slapping the Partisan on the shoulder. "We'll cast off as soon as everything's loaded onboard."

"What else are we taking?" I asked.

"It's not for you," Hamilton said. "After we land you at Pescara, we head due east and make a delivery across the Adriatic."

"Guns for Partisans," Stjepan said, turning to look at us again, indifferent to the other traffic on the road. "Kill Germans and Ustashi. You make us wait."

"Sorry," I said. "I just found out about this trip myself."

"Waste of time," Stjepan said. "Partisans need guns now. You will die like others. Waste."

"What others?" I asked, suddenly more interested in the conversation.

"S-O-E," he said, pronouncing the letters slowly. "English talk too much. Like god-damn Italians."

"Don't worry these boys, Stjepan," Hamilton said. "They're in our hands now. Ah, there's the boat."

If I was worried about Stjepan's prediction, I now had something else to worry about.

"I do not like any boat," Kaz said. "Especially not that one." The jeep descended a curved road leading to a line of rotting docks, home to three rusted fishing trawlers and a sailboat that looked like it had been through one too many hurricanes.

"Good boat!" Stjepan roared, pounding his fist on the steering wheel. For the first time, he smiled. "Damn good boat, eh?"

"Aye," Hamilton said, nodding in appreciation. "She's a twin-masted fifty-foot schooner. Completely rebuilt diesel engine runs like a charm, right Stjepan?"

"Charm," Stjepan agreed as he braked enthusiastically, halting the jeep less than a foot from the dock.

"She's not much to look at," I said.

"Exactly. We prefer not to draw attention to ourselves," Hamilton said. Where there was paint, it was peeling, showing gray, weathered wood below. Instead of railings, there was a rough framework of boards filled in with smooth stones from the beach. Armor, of a sort. Yugoslavian Partisans were busy loading crates of weapons and supplies, lashing down what didn't fit below on the exposed deck. "She's seaworthy, don't worry about that. We keep her looking sloppy, which is more work than you'd think."

"Don't the Germans stop you?"

"They haven't yet. We make our moves by night, and hole up in some small inlet, under camouflage nets all day." Hamilton led us aboard as the Partisans eyed us suspiciously. They were clad in a variety of uniforms, the only commonality a red star on their caps and a pervasive odor suggesting bathing facilities were hard to come by in the mountains of Yugoslavia. They were also well armed, here on this dock on the Italian coast, far from the front lines. Pistols and knives at their belts, Sten guns and rifles near at hand. These were men—and a few women—who lived on the edge, in that place where sudden violence could erupt at

any moment, and you were either prepared for it or fell victim
to it.

"Hamil-tone," a voice boomed out from belowdecks, stretching
out his name the same why Stjepan had. "Have you brought me
those fucking excellent cigarettes?"

"Goddamn right I did, Randic," Hamilton shouted. "Come up
and meet our guests."

The door to the companionway slammed open and a short,
thickset man burst through. He embraced Hamilton and let loose
with a volley of what I guessed was Serbian. He had long brown hair,
sticking out at all angles from under his wool cap with the standard-
issue red star. His mustache was broad and nicotine-stained, but it
did little to hide his devilish grin.

"Hell with guests, where are my god-damn Lucky Strikes, you
American bugger?"

"Right here," Hamilton said, pulling two cartons from his pack.
"Randic, this is Lieutenant Piotr Kazimierz and Lieutenant Billy
Boyle."

"Our freight, yes? Come, below," Randic beckoned. We followed
him down the narrow steps as Randic tore open one of the cartons of
smokes. The main cabin was filled with stacked supplies: blankets,
crates of ammo and Spam, brown greatcoats and medical supplies.
Randic slid in on a bench and gestured for us to take a seat around a
wooden table marked by cigarette burns and carved initials as he lit up.

"Randic is the commander of this detachment," Hamilton said
as he grabbed a bottle of wine and four glasses that could have used
a scrubbing. He poured, and I figured the grimy glassware was all
part of the boat's disguise.

"God-damn all, Hamil-tone, I am," Randic said. "But it is your
boat and your supplies, so we must take these men north for you.
Ziveli."

"*Ziveli*," Hamilton said, answering the toast. "Let us live long."

"Funny, eh?" Randic said after he'd drained his glass. "How many
dead men have made that toast?"

"*Faol saol agat, gob fliuch, agus bás in Éirinn*," I said, raising my glass.

"What bloody god-damn language is that, my friend?" Randic said.

"Gaelic. It means 'Long life to you, a wet mouth, and death in Ireland.'"

"I like it, you god-damn bugger. Life, wet mouth, death in your homeland. What else is there to drink to? You Irish from America?"

"Yes."

"And you," Randic said, pointing at Kaz. "Are you a son-of-a-bitch Romanian?"

"No, I am a son-of-a-bitch Pole, but I speak the language. Why?"

"Good," Randic said, pushing his glass toward the wine bottle. Hamilton poured. "Your papers are excellent, but this one—Boyle—he looks too well fed, even for a god-damn priest. You, Pole, you are good. Skinny. Not much food in Rome, even for the Pope."

"Did you get the clothes?" Hamilton asked, finishing off his second glass. He and Randic were puffing on Luckies and downing red wine as if they were in a drunkards' race.

"Yes, yes, cassocks, shoes, everything you asked for, even underwear, all Italian."

"Fellas, we need you to strip down and leave everything behind," Hamilton said. "You'll be outfitted as two priests traveling on church business would be. No weapons, nothing out of the ordinary. We have two small suitcases and some food for you to take along. Boyle, we didn't change your name, to make it easier for you. Lieutenant Kazimierz, your Romanian name is Petru Dalakis."

"Everything real," Randic said. "God-damn Italian priests are freezing asses off now, eh?"

"You didn't rob a couple of priests, did you?" I asked.

"Why? You holy boy? Kiss the Pope's ass?"

"If two priests report their clothes were stolen, the Germans might be on the lookout for imposters. But what's your beef with priests? And Italians for that matter? They're on our side now, if you haven't heard."

"Beef?" Randic gave Hamilton a quizzical glance.

"He means what is your problem," Hamilton said.

"Ah. Beef. God-damn funny language you have. First thing, no priests will make report," Randic said, raising an eyebrow in Hamilton's direction. Maybe he was kidding, maybe not. "Second thing, there is no now, where Italians are friends. There is only what has happened. It will always be that way. For you, perhaps, there is *now*. For us, never." He rapped his fingers on the tabletop, grimy nails tapping out an insistent rhythm.

"Why?" I asked.

"Hamil-tone, do these boys know nothing?" Randic struck a match and lit an oil lamp, the wick catching, inky black smoke floating to the ceiling until the flame held. The sun hadn't set, but the cabin was dark with shadows, smoke, and surliness.

"We know about the camps," I said. "Concentration camps for Jews, Gypsies, and anyone else the Nazis want to kill."

"I did not lose my family in god-damn camp," Randic said. "Wife and two little boys were walking down the street in Valjevo, going to market. They pass hotel where Italian garrison lives. Italian soldier is on balcony, reading newspaper. Nice day to be outside. He sees my wife and children, puts down newspaper. Picks up machine gun. Shoots them in street. Puts down machine gun and goes back to newspaper. Do you think that man is my friend *now?*"

"No," I said, in a soft, weak voice. "Never."

"God-damn right. Same thing with priests from Rome. You know the Ustashi?"

"Only that they're Croatians, right?"

"Fuck, you know nothing. Marshal Tito is a Croat, and I would die for him. Ustashi are Croats, yes, but. . . ." He waved his hand in the air, searching for the right words.

"Fanatics," Hamilton said. "Right-wing, Roman Catholic fascist fanatics."

"All that," Randic said. "We are Serbian Orthodox Church. Ustashi want to kill or convert us. Prefer killing. Kill Jews, Muslims, Serbs, everyone. And your Pope, he loves them, that bugger Pius."

"Listen, we're not involved in your politics," I said, wanting to change the subject. Not that I was a holy roller, but I was Catholic, an altar boy from South Boston, and I didn't take to bad-mouthing His Holiness. But our lives were in this guy's hands, so I didn't want to fight over religion with him.

"Politics! Listen, Hamil-tone, he calls it politics when Ustashi bastards murder us. Is that how politics goes in America, Mr. Boyle? Knife to throat? Women raped? Sons shot and thrown in pit? Ah, you are a fool. But I hope Nazis no kill you anyway."

"Thanks," I said. "I feel the same way. I didn't know it was that bad in Yugoslavia."

"The world should know," Hamilton said. "Tito has raised an army; they're much more than a guerilla force. He's fought the Italians, the Germans, the Royalists, Chetniks, and Ustashi, and held them all off."

"Josip Broz Tito is a great man," Randic said. "He fights." We drank to Tito as the diesel engine growled to life and the boat began to move.

"Tell me about the Pope and the Ustashi," I said. "What does he have to do with them?"

"You tell, Hamil-tone," Randic said, emptying the bottle into his glass. "I drink."

"The Vatican doesn't have diplomatic ties with the Ustashi puppet state," Hamilton began. "But the Pope granted the prime minister, Ante Pavelić, an audience when Mussolini and Hitler put him in power after the fall of Yugoslavia. The archbishop in Sarajevo, Ivan Šarić, is a pure fascist. Plus, there are many priests active among the Ustashi, from Pavelić's bodyguards to those running his concentration camps."

"Ivan Šarić," Kaz said. "He's the bishop who writes horrible poetry, isn't he?"

"He butchers both words and people," Randic said.

"Yeah, he runs the Catholic newspapers in Sarajevo, so he can print whatever he wants. Poems about the magnificence of Hitler, about money-grubbing Jews, the joy of forced conversions of Serbians—all terrible stuff," Hamilton said.

"And your Pope, Mr. Boyle, he does nothing about it. The

Ustashi murder thousands, the archbishop sings their praises, and the Pope lets Pavelić kiss his ring. But they send you to Rome because one priest is murdered. Ha! What can a man do but drink?"

"*Zeveli*," I said as the vessel picked up speed and began a gentle, rhythmic roll.

"I do not like boats," Kaz said, staggering from the room.

CHAPTER NINE

KAZ DIDN'T LIKE boats all the way to Pescara. The wind kicked up about an hour out, as darkness settled in and clouds covered the stars. Kaz spent most of the night above deck, leaning over the side, moaning when he wasn't cursing in Polish. As we neared the German-occupied shore near Pescara, the crew helped him change out of his soaked uniform and into his priestly garments. By then he felt well enough to give his Webley revolver to Randic, telling him he hoped he killed a good number of "god-damn" Ustashi with it. This gesture endeared him to the Partisans, who laughed, clapped him on the shoulder, and gave many Serbian well wishes for our safety. Even green at the gills, Kaz showed his knack for getting along with all sorts of people.

With the first glimmer of false dawn lighting the horizon to the east, a small boat rowed us ashore, Hamilton at the bow, Thompson submachine gun at the ready. The crew paddled into a small bay and brought the boat up onto a shingle beach, each wave rolling stones and pebbles, creating a cascade of sound that muffled the splashing of the oars and whispered commands. They beached the boat and Hamilton motioned us to stay put as they jumped out and pulled it onto dry land.

"Don't get your feet wet," he whispered as we got out, holding our long cassocks up like ladies at a garden party. "The Krauts at the train station might take notice."

"Okay," I said. "Where are the men we're meeting?"

"Right there," Hamilton said, pointing down the beach, about ten yards away. Two men, dressed in nondescript uniforms with rifles pointed in our general direction, had appeared from nowhere. "Good luck."

"Same to you in Yugoslavia," I said. We shook hands, and in seconds he was gone as the boat slid back into the water. Our new guides motioned for us to follow. We did, our shoes crunching on smooth, round stones worn down by the sea.

A hundred yards from the beach, we came to a rough track where a mule cart was waiting. An old woman dressed in typical peasant black from head to foot sat with the reins in her hands. She did not look at the two men, or at Kaz and me. They gestured for us to get in the back, and by the time we were seated, they were gone. The woman snapped the reins and the mule plodded forward.

"*Buongiorno, signora,*" Kaz said. She ignored us as we sat facing each other, our cheap suitcases on our laps, phony papers in our coat pockets, and a pallor to Kaz's cheeks. The cart trundled along, the early morning sun warming our faces. It was eerie, this sensation of falseness, everything about our identities a lie, every lie necessary to keep us alive. Armed only with disguise, from the clothing labels in our overcoats to the two-day-old newspaper from Rimini in the north, we had placed our lives in the hands of a silent old woman in a mule cart. At least our shoes were dry.

An hour later, we reached the outskirts of Pescara, which by wartime standards was unlucky enough to have a harbor, a main coastal road, and a railroad intersecting near the town center. It had evidently been recently hit by air raids. Rubble lined the roads, and some gutted buildings stood open, with floors of masonry, furniture, and the debris of families and businesses spilling into the street. Civilians, mostly women, were working at the bombed-out structures, stacking bricks with that *click-clack* sound I'd heard so many times before, the sound of life attempting to assert itself in the face of destruction. Around the corner, a church presented a gaping wound, the roof and side caved in, the altar exposed to the elements.

The front wall was still intact, but the main doors had been blown off. Above the shards of wood, carved into a limestone lintel, it read *Chiesa del Rosario.* Church of the Rosary.

As we neared the railroad station, I saw where all the male civilians had gone. German troops guarded work gangs of Italian men and boys repairing damage to the rail line. Some were in coveralls, others labored in suits and white shirts caked with dirt and sweat. The Germans must have picked them right off the street and brought them here to fill in craters and get the rail bed back in shape. The air was filled with thick, gritty dust. Men looked up for a moment as we passed, and then bent back to their shovels and pick-axes, casting wary eyes at their overseers.

The mule cart stopped as we neared the station. We got off and Kaz thanked the woman, who, true to form, said nothing and urged her mule on. Probably best not to get involved with the passengers in her business.

Trees had once lined the road where it passed the train station. Now there were ruined limbs, blasted trunks, and a bomb crater filled with mud. The windows of the station were shattered, but other than that it was still standing. Good news, if you didn't count the German guards at the door and along the platform. We had nowhere to go but forward. I clutched my suitcase, put one foot in front of the other, and prayed.

"*Dokumente,*" the first guard said. We handed them over. He looked at Kaz's first, checked a list on a clipboard, and handed them back with a curt nod. As soon as he looked at mine, he called for his *Leutnant.*

"*Irischer Bürger,*" he said, handing the papers over to the officer. I figured it wasn't every day an Irishman got on a train in Pescara, so I wasn't worried. Not much, anyway. He studied the identity papers and the travel documents from the Holy See.

"You are on Vatican business?" the officer said in clipped, precise English.

"Aye, that I am," I said, laying on the accent. "Seeing to the refugees up north, not to mention those right here. Was it the damn

English who did this? They destroyed the Church of the Rosary, did you see, man?"

"Yes, it must have been the Englanders. Only the British bomb at night."

"Cowards that they are," I said.

"You are on your way back to Rome?"

"Yes, Father Dalakis and I are returning from an inspection of the refugee centers in the north. As you can see," I said with a smile, pointing to the letters, which were written out in German and Italian.

"What was it like?" he asked.

"Up north? As you'd expect. Many families separated, not enough food, churches packed with refugees. And the bombings, by all the saints, it's terrible," I said, crossing myself at the invocation.

"*Suchen Sie ihr Gepäck,*" he said to the guard, who took our suitcases and opened them. "My apologies, Fathers, but we have captured a number of saboteurs in clever disguises. There are also many prisoners of war on the loose, since the Italians surrendered, all trying to make their way to Rome. This is simply routine."

It was. Underwear, socks, a clean shirt, a Bible, and that two-day-old newspaper from Rimini. The officer looked at the newspaper and nodded to the guard, who stepped back.

"All is in order," he said. "You may take your bags."

I felt a flood of relief and hoped it didn't show. A priest in my position would be used to this by now. Exasperated, maybe, but not relieved. We closed up the suitcases, ready to buy our tickets.

"One more question, please," the officer said as we began to walk away. I remembered what Kaz had said about the Gestapo. They'd treat you nicely as first, to soften you up, then hit you hard. I felt my hand shake and put it in my pocket, another nonchalant traveler with a suitcase and a train to catch.

"Certainly, *Leutnant*," Kaz said. I tried to look bored.

"You came from Rimini by train?"

"Aye," I said. "And points north."

"Then please explain how you got through. Ancona was heavily bombed for the last two nights. There have been no trains."

My mind went numb. Was this what Diana had felt? Cornered, outsmarted, with nowhere to hide? I stood, unable to speak, hoping the pounding in my chest couldn't be heard as thoughts of Gestapo kitchens ran through my mind.

"You are misinformed, *Leutnant*," Kaz said with certainty. I broke out in a sweat, and worked to keep from looking around for a place to run to. For a second, I couldn't catch my breath until I realized I was holding it. "We visited the Duomo there. Do you know that cathedral is almost a thousand years old? It is magnificent." Kaz chattered on about the architecture until the officer waved us along, bored with the recitation.

"Kaz," I whispered as we entered the station. "How were you so sure about the railroad?"

"It was obviously a trick," he said. "And if it wasn't, we were dead men anyway, so why not?"

"It wasn't obvious to me."

"Father Boyle," Kaz said in a low voice. "If the rail line had been cut between here and Rimini, how did Hamilton get the newspaper in your suitcase?"

"Bless you, Father Dalakis, that was quick thinking," I said, giving Kaz his due.

It should have been obvious to me. Not only the newspaper, but the interrogation technique. It didn't matter that we'd come in on the train as we'd said. The *Leutnant* was looking for a reaction, that flicker of guilt that gives a liar away when he's been found out. And I almost gave it to him. I should have picked up on it, but my mind had gone right to Diana and what she must've gone through. I needed to get my wits about me and focus on getting to Rome, not to mention avoiding the Gestapo kitchens.

I listened to Kaz get our tickets and heard the cities named along the way. From Pescara to L'Aquila, then Terni, then Viterbo. He paid with a wad of lira, and we sat on hard wooden benches, waiting for our train. I practiced not thinking about Diana. It didn't go well.

CHAPTER TEN

WE DIDN'T TALK much. Speaking in English was bound to attract attention, and whispering in English was likely to draw fire. The train was packed with a mix of civilians, Kraut soldiers, and Italians in the uniform of the Republican National Guard, the militia that stayed loyal to Mussolini after he was deposed and rescued by the Germans. Those were just the passengers. German military police walked through the cars at every stop, but they were more interested in their own troops, probably on the lookout for deserters. Our white collars seemed to make us invisible, two meek priests amidst uniforms and weapons of war. I tried to sleep, but the train rattled and rolled so much it was impossible. The locomotive chugged along, slowly, up steep mountain passes and through long tunnels carved out of rock.

I figured any good priest might read the Bible, so I took the one out of my suitcase. I had my own back home, of course, but I'd never actually read it. I skipped all the begats and tried to find the stories, the kind I remembered from Sunday school, anything to pass the time and look the part. It was in Acts that I stumbled across the tale of the Apostle Paul, who came to Rome to preach the new religion.

And when we came to Rome, the centurion delivered the prisoners to the captain of the guard ... after three days Paul called the chief of the Jews together: and when they were come together, he said unto them, Men and brethren, though I have committed nothing against the people, or customs of our fathers, yet was I delivered prisoner from Jerusalem into the hands of the Romans.

"Kaz," I said in a low voice. "Do you know what happened to Paul the Apostle?" He drew a finger across his throat. I shut the book and closed my eyes.

As night fell, blackout curtains were drawn and the lights dimmed. We ate the bread and cheese that had been packed for us, and shared a bottle of wine with no label. The air in the car was thick with tobacco smoke, the smell of stale food, and unwashed bodies. I prayed for sleep, and awoke hours later with a stiff neck and Kaz asleep on my shoulder. The conductor walked through, unleashing a string of Italian in a bored monotone.

"We are almost to Terni, Father Boyle," Kaz said. "The train will stop for one hour."

"Shall we stretch our legs then, Father Dalakis?" I said, putting on the brogue. By this time, the two odd priests were old hat to the other travelers, and as we stood, one departing German soldier gave us an "*Auf Wiedersehen.*"

In the station we found a bar serving coffee, and ordered "*Due espressi, per favore.*" As we sipped the bitter drink—no sugar to be had—two trucks pulled up outside and German soldiers piled out. For a moment I thought we were in trouble, but then I saw the medics, with their white helmets and big red crosses. They were unloading wounded, a few walking, most on stretchers. Kaz raised an eyebrow to let me know he was relieved as well. Some of the bandages were soaked with fresh blood; something had happened to these men not too far from here, and I hoped it wouldn't stir up security. As we finished our espressos and left the bar, a German officer ran up to us. From the look on his face, it wasn't to ask for our papers. His uniform was dark with soot, one arm bloodstained, and the blood didn't seem to be his. He was wild-eyed, as if he might be in shock.

"Bitte, Vater, werden Sie einem sterbenden Soldaten letzte Riten geben? Er ist katholisch."

"Letzte Riten? Ja, sicher," Kaz said. "Father Boyle, one of his men requires last rites. Would you like to perform the sacrament? *Er ist Irischer,"* he added, for the benefit of the officer, a captain.

I understood from the look in Kaz's eyes that he had no idea what to do. But I did, having seen police chaplains give emergency last rites to cops a couple of times, not that I was taking notes.

"Yes, of course, Father Dalakis. Take me to the poor boy." The captain looked confused for a moment, but recovered quickly. He nodded and we followed him to the sidewalk where the wounded were laid out. The dying soldier was obvious. A kid set apart from the others, a medic at his side, holding a bloody compress to his chest. The captain knelt by him.

"Hans, Hans," he said, squeezing the boy's hand. Hans opened his eyes, his straw-colored hair splashed across his forehead. His eyes were crystal blue, and seemed to be looking at something far, far away. I didn't want to do this, but I couldn't say no. It didn't seem right, since only a priest could perform the sacrament. But Hans was dying, and he'd never know the difference.

"I have no holy oil," I said to Kaz. I heard Kaz whispering to the captain, hopefully a story that would hold up. I was glad he didn't let Hans hear. I got down on my knees, took Hans's hand from the captain, and laid both of my hands on them, just as I'd seen Father Kearny do back in Boston.

"Vater?" Hans gasped. The captain said something reassuring, and Hans focused on me. With each breath, a thin, pink bubble formed on his lips, then burst. His eyes widened, waiting for me to perform the blessing. He gasped in pain as he fumbled at his neck and held up a small medal. Saint George, the patron saint of soldiers, the slayer of dragons. He kissed it, and I struggled to remember the words I needed to say, hoping they'd give comfort, and not betray my falseness.

"Through this holy unction may the Lord pardon thee, whatever sins or faults thou hast committed. Thus do I commend thee into the arms of our Lord." The benediction flowed without thought, from that place where I kept all things holy, memories of what I had been taught about goodness before I learned evil. I laid Hans's hands, still clutching the medal, high on his chest, above the bandage. His breath was ragged and his eyes desperate. He knew he was about to die. I touched both his hands with two fingers, then his forehead, just as Father Kearny would have anointed him with oil. He took hold of my hand, both of his hands bloody from his wound, as tears fell across his cheeks. He was a boy, but old enough to kill and be killed in turn. I leaned in close to his ear, and whispered a fragment of a prayer that had always stayed with me. "May He, the true shepherd, recognize you as one of his own. Amen."

Hans squeezed my hand, and with a rattle of breath from his lungs, let go. I leaned back, aware of a circle of soldiers around me, their heads bowed. I was in the presence of mine enemies, as the old psalm said, walking through the valley of the shadow of death. I unclenched Hans's hand from mine and stood. The captain took my hands and poured water from a canteen over them, washing away the sticky blood, perhaps my falseness too, but certainly not my sins. "*Danke sehr,*" he said.

"I am sorry," I said, and could not look him in the eye. I had probably committed a sin against the clergy and church, if not God himself. Maybe Hans would put in a good word for me.

Kaz took me by the arm and turned me toward the train. No reason to linger, he was right. We hadn't gone ten steps when the captain called out to us, "*Moment!*" He pointed to us, and two soldiers led by a sergeant trotted our way, rifles at the ready. Kaz and I looked at each other, wondering how we'd given ourselves away and what to do. If we ran, they'd cut us down in seconds.

"*Komm,*" the sergeant said, motioning us to follow him to the train. We trailed him, the two others on either side of us. The platform was full, lines of soldiers and civilians waiting to board the train. The sergeant pushed his way through with a ruthlessness that spared no one. Angry shouts went up, but no one in the crowd objected to the small formation. At the door to our railcar, we saw the holdup. Several SS men in gray dress uniforms were questioning everyone boarding the train, checking identity papers and consulting clipboards with long lists of names.

Our sergeant spoke to the SS men and in no time an argument erupted. I glanced at Kaz, but this was no time to ask for a translation. Behind us, more shouts broke out, and I saw the wounded from the trucks being led toward the train. The lead SS guy was yelling something at the sergeant, his hand on the pistol in his holster. That was a mistake, since the sergeant held a Schmeisser MP-40 submachine at the ready and had a squad of men on the way. He and the other soldiers pushed the security detail aside and waved the wounded and their medics on board. There was a lot of indignant shouting, but the SS knew they were outnumbered, and by actual combat soldiers at that. They retreated to a corner of the platform and glared at everyone who looked their way, lighting cigarettes and shaking their heads.

The sergeant gave us a smile and a wave as the train pulled out, crammed with travelers, the wounded, and perhaps a few other fugitives. I couldn't help waving back. I even smiled. It was one crazy war.

CHAPTER ELEVEN

"ITALIAN PARTISANS," KAZ whispered. "They mined the road, then machine-gunned the convoy. The captain said he headed here to put the wounded on the train for Viterbo, since it was the fastest route to a military hospital."

"That's why the SS was checking papers: looking for partisans," I said. "We're lucky he took a liking to us." The groans of the wounded increased as the train took a curve. Stretcher cases were laid over the seat backs, and the less seriously wounded lay beneath them, or sat up if they could.

"I don't know if we need to worry, Billy," Kaz said, in a very low whisper. "I think our papers are real. Have you studied them? The letters have Vatican watermarks."

"Even so, my guess is those SS bastards are going to want to get back at these boys for being pushed around. When we get into Viterbo, I'd bet on a heavily armed reception committee. Watermarks or no, I don't want to get caught up in that."

"But we have someone to meet at the station," Kaz said. "Trust in the Lord, Father Boyle," he said in a louder voice as the conductor passed us by. The train moved slowly on switchbacks around a mountain, and then sped up on the downside. Kaz and I finished what food we had left, and watched the countryside slip by. We were running along a riverbed now, in a narrow valley with a parallel roadway. I watched the wounded, and was glad they were all well enough to move and speak, even if in moans. I didn't want to go through last rites again. It was one thing to kill an enemy soldier in combat—bad enough, but necessary. But Hans's death came after the adrenaline of the fight, one more fatal aftermath, a passing that lingered for the living to witness longer than anyone wanted. I wished for death at a distance, if I had to deal in it at all. Not as close as Hans, with his wide blue eyes and wet tears, fooled in his last moments by another soldier in disguise.

"*Jabos!*" one of the Germans yelled, his head out of the window, craned at the sky. I knew that much German. *Jagdebomber* was the word for fighter-bomber, the curse of anything moving, and this train was moving straight and slow. I looked out of my window and caught a glimpse of two single-engine aircraft banking away, probably getting set up for a run. They looked like P-47 Thunderbolts, and that was bad news. They carried rockets and bombs, along with eight .50-caliber machine guns, which could turn these cars into toothpicks within seconds. Voices rose into frantic screams as the word spread, a cacophony of German and Italian that didn't need translation. The train seemed to pick up speed, the engineer probably pouring everything on, opening up the throttle and hoping to outrun the deadly planes. But where was there to go?

We rounded a curve and I could see what he was heading for. A bridge spanned the river we'd been following, and then the tracks entered a tunnel in the next hill. Plumes of white steam flowed from the locomotive; the *chug-chug* sound sped up, as the pistons drove the wheels faster. The engineer opened the steam whistle in one long, mournful note, for no reason I could see, except that I knew I'd do the same.

The snarl of the two P-47s grew louder, turning into a steady drone as they dove and then leveled off, setting up for a strafing run. "Get down," I said to Kaz, throwing him to the floor between the seats and covering him with my body. I felt the train take the curve leading to the bridge, too fast maybe, but not too fast with death descending upon us. We slid against the wall as the car entered the turn, and heard the first bursts, the rapid chatter of the .50-caliber rounds getting closer until the first ones hit home—shattering glass, splintering wood, flinging bodies into ripped and bloody pieces. It only lasted a second until a new sound assaulted my ears, a harsh metallic pinging as we reached the bridge and bullets pelted the steel girders, some hitting the train, others ricocheting away.

As fast as it began, the strafing stopped as the aircraft pulled away, their quarry out of reach. Darkness blanketed the chaos as the train took to the tunnel and the engineer hit the brakes, the squeal of metal on metal harsh and insistent as he struggled to stop before exiting cover and giving the *Jabos* another chance. Men fell, tumbling over each other in the dark. Cries came from the wounded, mixed in with the tinkling of glass as it fell from shattered windows. I helped Kaz up, and as lights came on, we did what we could to sort the living from the dead.

We carried the dead into the last car, and the medics treated the newly wounded—soldiers and civilians alike—as best they could. They seemed to be short on even the basics, and I didn't see any sign of sulfa powder. I should have been glad, since it meant that some of the Krauts would undoubtedly die of infection, but it was hard to wish any more suffering on the poor devils riding this train. No one questioned my English, and I didn't worry about our papers. Kaz translated for the Germans and Italians, as we checked the patch of sky ahead for *Jabos*. Funny how shared suffering and near-death turns *them* into *us* pretty damn quick.

The locomotive pulled out of the tunnel, slowly at first, as if sensing a trick. It was late afternoon, and I hoped that all the P-47s in Italy were back at their bases, pilots safe in the officers' clubs, drinking and telling tales of blowing up trains. It seemed they were, and as we picked up speed, the mood lightened, survivors glad to be alive, the dead stored away in the back car like a memory stuffed in the far corner of the mind. We stopped in a village as the sun was setting, a small castle tower at the top of the hill watching over the countryside. I hoped the Germans didn't have troops up there; it would be a shame to destroy such an ancient and lovely thing, not to mention the village clustered below it. But it would make a perfect observation post to call in artillery strikes on anyone within miles. Maybe I should make a mental note for the report I'd write up when this was over. Or maybe I'd pray the Germans took off when we finally broke out of Anzio and took Rome. Not very military of me, I know, but I was wearing the Roman collar, and I couldn't help hoping for mercy and peace.

We stretched our legs and kept an eye out for the Gestapo, who harbored no such good wishes. The train whistle bellowed, and as the night sky lit up with stars, we pulled away from the village station for the final run to Viterbo and our rendezvous with an OSS operative and a load of produce bound for the Vatican. It was a simple plan, really, and stood a good chance of working, given that the agent was in place and could be trusted. The only problem was that no one had clued in the Royal Air Force.

We saw the glow in the sky, a distant smudge of light at first, every time the train took a curve and gave us a view to the south. Probably the pathfinders, dropping incendiaries. Then the searchlights came on, stabbing at the black sky, hoping to pin a bomber for the antiaircraft batteries. It looked like Viterbo was getting hit, and hit hard. As in most Italian towns, the rail line and the main roads likely went through the center, which is where the bombers would aim, going for the transportation hub surrounded by churches and homes, where generations lived close together, away from the threat of the open countryside. Little could they have known.

The train slowed, then stopped, the engine releasing great gusts of steam as if sighing at the destruction ahead. We felt the ground shake with explosions as the bombs fell, and covered our ears against the thunder of antiaircraft batteries until the noise receded, the fury of both sides spent, the silence stunning in its fullness. The train nudged itself forward, moving slowly and carefully in case of damage to the tracks. Smoke drifted through the broken windows, along with the acrid smell of burning fuel and rubber, the air punctuated by secondary explosions, the sign of another convoy caught in the conflagration. We neared the city center, bathed in the yellow light of flames rising from ruined buildings, licking the night sky. Firemen worked a hand pump, sending a pitiful stream of water against a wall of fire and smoke. Trucks and armored vehicles lay in the road that ran alongside the tracks, broken and cast aside as if they were play-things. Soldiers stumbled around them, bleeding, burned, and in shock. We rolled on.

The train halted short of the station, which lay in ruins. No one said a word as they gathered their belongings, helped the wounded, and got off next to a piazza that somehow had not been badly dam-aged. The dead were left to fend for themselves.

"We need to search the station," Kaz said, without much enthu-siasm.

I was too tired to come up with anything else, so we held our suitcases over our heads, protection against the hot embers floating down from the burning city. We followed the tracks, working our way around a smoking crater, looking for the northbound platform. The smoke made it hard to see, and I tripped on a sign that had fallen from its post. In red letters, the word *Nord* stood out. North.

"We're here," I said, kicking at the sign, a laugh escaping my throat as I looked around at the collapsed walls and burning timbers.

"Look," Kaz said, pointing to a figure stumbling through the wreckage in our direction. He wore a worker's rough boots and a blue coat. His eyes were wide, darting everywhere, stunned and frightened. His hair was singed, his face black with soot. He held a hand up to shield his eyes from the bright light of the sparking flames, and stared at us, studying our faces, trying to fathom what had happened to his world and what we were doing in it. He blinked, a glimmer of awareness returning.

"*Per l'amore di Dio, ha due sigarette? Per l'amore di Dio!*" Two cigarettes, for the love of God.

"*No*," Kaz said. "*Sono troppo cari. Spiacente.*" Kaz gave the response Hamilton had fed us, and added his apologies. We each took an arm and let him lead us, hoping he knew where he was going, and that our train was still in one piece. With shuffling, stumbling steps, he took us down a siding, where three freight cars stood undamaged. A storehouse a few yards off was burning, and next to it a flatbed truck lay on its side, oily black smoke roiling from the tires. He pointed to the middle car and fumbled with a set of keys. The smoke made it hard to see, and we all coughed as it got into our eyes and throats.

Finally, he got the right key and unlocked the padlock that secured the latch on the sliding door. He pulled it back, the metal screeching in protest. As the door opened, we all turned as another sound came from behind us. Footsteps.

A figure slowly emerged out of the inky smoke, his face blackened and bloody. One arm hung limp at his side, wisps of smoke curling up from the torn fabric.

"*La santa madre di Dio*," our guide said, imploring the holy mother of God.

"*Aiutame*," the man croaked, asking for help. Kaz stepped toward him, supporting him by his good arm, reassuring him in Italian as he brushed the dirt and dust from the man's uniform, which was almost unrecognizable. Almost, until we saw the dark-gray uniform jacket and black collar tabs. One of Mussolini's RSI officers, part of the Fascist army that had rallied around the deposed dictator.

"*Fascista*," the railway man said with venom, the appearance of the RSI officer snapping him out of his shock. The officer gave him a quizzical look, as if he couldn't understand the man's insolence, his defiance of authority. His eyes flickered and squinted, trying to focus and take in the scene before him: the open railcar door, two priests, the keys, the curse. I watched his eyes as he assembled the pieces of the puzzle, working through the fog of pain, smoke, and surprise. Maybe he was a security officer on duty, or maybe he was passing through and got caught in the air raid. But it didn't matter. He was on to us, all of us, and he wasn't on our side.

His hand went to the leather holster at his belt, but Kaz still had a grip on his good arm. He twisted it behind his back with a savage thrust, and the officer gasped as Kaz threw him to the ground, then fell on him, trying to keep his hand from getting to the pistol. The officer slammed his injured arm at Kaz, loosening his grip. In a second, the Beretta was in his hand, his face contorted in pain from using his bloodied arm. I gave that arm a kick, and he screamed, his mouth round and his eyes wide with animal fear and pain. The pistol was still in his hand, and I dropped on it, pinning his good arm to the ground. Kaz was next to me, and his hands grasped the officer's neck, choking him, desperate to silence the threat. The guy was strong and his legs thrashed, shiny black leather boots pinwheeling behind us. His neck bulged as he gasped for air, and I wondered if Kaz was strong enough to do the job.

I wrenched the pistol from the guy's hand and hit him with the butt. Hard, twice. His legs stopped moving and he went limp, his face still showing the rage he'd fought us with. It was the last emotion he'd ever show. Kaz rose from the body, clenching and unclenching his hands.

"There couldn't be a witness," I said, tossing the pistol on the ground.

"No," Kaz said, shaking his head as he brushed himself off. "He would have gotten us all killed."

Our guide felt no need to justify what had been done. He spat on the body and dragged it by the heels to the burning truck, leaving the RSI officer crumpled on the ground, an obvious victim of the bombs. He trotted back, full of energy now, motioning for us to climb in, impatient to get away. The car was packed with supplies, crates of food, barrels of wine—a month of feasts. He led us down a narrow passage to the back of the car and pushed against the rear wall. There was a click, and the wooden slates moved, enough for them to slide sideways and allow Kaz and me to squeeze inside. The door closed and we were in total darkness. We heard the railcar door shut and the latch lock in place. Then nothing.

I lit a match and we surveyed the space. A couple of blankets. Space enough for the two of us to sit on the floor facing each other. Not much else to see.

"I wonder if this compartment opens from inside," Kaz said.

"Let's hope we don't have to find out," I said. Engine sounds drew closer, and I could feel the vibration coming up from the tracks.

A thump announced that a locomotive had hooked up with the cars, and seconds later we lurched forward.

"Rome, next stop," Kaz said, trying a bit hard to be the life of the party.

"We had to do it," I said.

"Yes. There was no alternative."

I should have felt bad. I'd helped kill a wounded man. I'd been shot at, bombed, and I'd sent a poor soul on his way with ersatz last rites. But the only thing I really felt was tired. Bone tired from too little sleep. Tired of disguises, lies, and the kind of war where bashing an injured man in the head was the only logical thing to do. I fell asleep against the rough wood planks, but not before a tiny voice in my head, a dream perhaps, told me that my body might rest, but my soul would be grievously tired for a long, long time.

CHAPTER TWELVE

THE TRAIN FINALLY came to rest hours later, the brakes taking so long that I thought we had stopped until that final little jolt pushed me forward against the rough wood wall. I must have slept, because bits of light were filtering in between the slats, barely enough to let me make out Kaz slumped opposite me.

"Tell the porter to bring coffee," Kaz said, grunting as he tried to sit up.

"I will, as long as he isn't wearing a German uniform," I said. Muffled voices sounded outside as the door to the railcar slid open. Footsteps thumped closer, followed by a sharp rap on the false wall. It opened, and a workman in a blue coverall held his finger to his lips. I followed him out, clutching my suitcase and blinking my eyes against the morning light. Waiting outside the boxcar was a well-dressed gent in a black topcoat and shined shoes. He was at odds with the workers who stood at a distance, ready to unload the train, but they seemed to wait patiently for him. He touched his snap-brim fedora and inclined his head as we jumped down, giving us a little salute.

"Fathers Boyle and Dalakis, I take it," he said, his English accent sounding polished, but with a hint of Cockney underneath. "Welcome to the Vatican. My name is John May."

"I'm Boyle," I said, shaking his hand. He had lively eyes that watched us and everything else at the same time. His bushy eyebrows stood above high cheekbones, and he reminded me of some smart hoodlums I'd known back in Boston, the confident way he oversaw this smuggling operation. "We're in Vatican City? Neutral ground?"

"Indeed. Since you came through that wall." He pointed to the iron door that was shut tight in the wall behind us. We were between the train and the railway station, and as I looked up, the dome of Saint Peter's loomed high beyond the station. "You're both a bit worse for wear, aren't you?"

We were. Soot and dried blood covered our black cassocks, probably not the usual attire within these walls. May had a hurried conversation with the workmen as he took off his topcoat. He gave it to me, and another coat, considerably more worn, appeared for Kaz.

"Put these on and leave the suitcases. They will be delivered later. Follow me, but at a distance, about twelve paces. Try to look contemplative."

"Why the secrecy?" I asked. "Aren't we safe here?"

"Safety is relative," May said. "We have to pass by the Gendarmerie headquarters, and I don't want to attract attention. Trust me, we'll be safe and sound in no time."

"I thought we were," Kaz said. May ignored him and walked off. We followed, leaving our suitcases behind, trailing our mysterious guide.

Contemplative was tough. We were in Rome, behind enemy lines, smuggled inside a neutral enclave. Saint Peter's dominated the skyline, and even though it was winter, the gardens and pathways were green and well tended, cypresses and cedars forming a backdrop that softened the hard reality of the wall and encircled this tiny domain. I tried not to gawk like a country bumpkin, and stayed behind May, glancing around for anyone taking notice of us.

May turned his head and looked at a building on our right. It was five stories of soft, beige limestone, with the yellow-and-white Vatican flag flying over the main door. Men in blue uniforms came and went, Vatican gendarmes. I didn't know if we had to worry about all of them or just their boss, Soletto, but May seemed to be steering clear of the whole crowd. So I bowed my head and folded my hands, sending up a quick prayer to Saint Michael, patron saint of policemen, asking him to keep the local cops occupied while we got on with things.

We made our way through a formal garden and ended up in front of a long, narrow building, much fancier than the police headquarters. Marble steps led up to the main entrance, with two wings extending on either side. But May didn't head for the front door, which was flanked by two gendarmes standing at attention. He took a garden path that led to the back of the building, and headed for a side door, which he unlocked after consulting a heavy ring of keys.

"Where are we going?" I asked when we were alone in a staircase with May.

"To see Robert Brackett, of the American delegation to the Vatican. This building is the Governatorato, where most of the major delegations are housed. Mr. Brackett has been waiting for you."

"Do you work for him?" Kaz asked.

"Goodness, no. I am employed by the British ambassador, Sir D'Arcy. Here we are," he said, stopping at a door and giving a discreet knock before opening it. "I will be back to collect you shortly."

"Where are you—?" But the door shut before I could finish, and we were left alone in a well-furnished sitting room. It was small, but its tall windows overlooked the graceful gardens below. The rug was plush and soft underfoot. I felt out of place in my filthy clothes.

An inner door opened and a maid entered carrying a silver tray, the aroma of coffee dispelling any worries about my attire. She set the tray down and asked in very good English if she could take our coats. It took her only a second to hide the look of surprise as she saw the condition of our clothes, and then act as if disheveled, blood-stained priests came to visit every morning.

"Ah, there you are. Robert Brackett, at your service." Brackett was graying at the temples, tall, and a bit stooped over, as if his height had begun to work against him in middle age. He needed a haircut, and his three-piece suit was worn, shiny at the knees and with threads sticking out at the seams. We introduced ourselves, and he nodded absently, as if names were bothersome.

"Are you the American ambassador?" Kaz asked as Brackett poured coffee.

"There is no American ambassador to the Vatican," Brackett said, motioning us to sit. "FDR had to settle for a personal envoy to the Pope when Congress got into a snit about an official representative. They said it was about the separation of church and state, but it was really anti-Catholic bias. So the president sent a personal envoy, who didn't stick around when war was declared and the rest of the staff was sentenced to the duration in this gilded cage."

"You don't sound too happy about that," I said, savoring the hot coffee.

"That's a beautiful view out the window," Brackett said. "But try looking at it for over eight hundred days." He frowned, gazing at the view despite himself.

"There are worse places to spend a war," I said.

"Absolutely. But that doesn't change things; it only makes one feel vaguely guilty for the resentment. Tell me, how was your trip?"

"Eventful, long, and uncomfortable," I said. "So, are you in charge here?"

"*Father* Boyle," Brackett said, stressing the title sarcastically, "you are going to have to learn the ways of the Vatican. Lots of formal small talk. It's a long journey to the truth here, whether you're asking the time of day or for an opinion on a point of diplomacy."

"Point taken. I'm usually big on chatter, but for right now let's get to the point. Who are you, and do you know why we're here?"

"I know why you're here, although you probably don't know the whole story. As for me, I'm only the deputy *chargé d'affaires*. My job is to keep an eye on you and ensure you don't do anything to endanger Vatican neutrality and American interests."

"See, you can skip the small talk just fine," I said. "What part of the story don't we know?"

"Why do you think you're here?"

"We've been told that Monsignor Corrigan was a cousin of

Bishop Finch of New York, who is pals with President Roosevelt. The bishop called in some favors to find out who knifed his kin, and that was enough horsepower to get us where we are."

"That's a fine story," Brackett said, pulling out his pipe and fussing with it, the way pipe smokers do. "Parts might even be true. What's missing is one key fact." He tamped down the tobacco and lit a match, puffing his cheeks like a pair of bellows.

"Yes?" Kaz said, as Brackett finally tossed the match in an ashtray.

"It was Donovan who sent you here. William Donovan, head of the Office of Strategic Services himself. I don't know about Corrigan and Finch, but I do know that Donovan and Corrigan attended Columbia Law School together. They were fast friends, then and now."

"Are you certain of this?" Kaz asked.

"Damn certain. I was one year ahead of them. The monsignor and I talked about old times quite often."

"Did he talk about Donovan?" I said. Brackett's news made sense, given what Hamilton had told us about Wild Bill's involvement.

"Never," Brackett said, frowning at the pipe, which had gone dead. "His silence told me that he was still in contact with him, one way or the other. So forget about FDR and the good bishop. You're here because Wild Bill Donovan wanted you here. And that can be quite dangerous."

"Dangerous for whom?" Kaz asked.

"The Pope, directly, and the war effort, indirectly. The last thing we need is the OSS running loose in the Vatican. If the Nazis catch on, they'd have the perfect excuse to invade, which would take about two minutes. They'd claim they were protecting the Pope, or were forced into it by the presence of enemy agents."

"We are not the OSS," I said.

"Tell that to the Nazis when they march in here. You're doing Donovan's bidding. So keep a low profile, a damned low profile."

"What does your boss say about all this? Does he feel the same way?"

"He's instructed me to keep both of you at arm's length from him. He doesn't want to meet you or have anything to do with you, in case he needs to deny your presence here."

"Wonderful. Who exactly sent for us anyway?"

"No idea," Brackett said, pulling at a thread on the sleeve of his coat. "But I'd wager half of Vatican City knows you're here."

"Why do you say that?"

"The Vatican is like a small town, filled with people attuned to nuance. They notice everything. Plus, you've got scores of diplomats and their families crammed in these hundred damn acres. All the countries that declared war on Italy and Germany, from France to the smallest South American tin-pot dictatorship. Secretaries, wives, children, servants. People who were used to Roman cafés and fine restaurants, the opera, the wine country. All cooped up in a city not exactly known for its nightlife. What do you think they do? They walk in the gardens, watch each other, and gossip."

"Does anyone ever leave?"

"The Germans guard the border along the entrance to Saint Paul's. There's a white line that they patrol. Worshippers can come and go, and sometimes people blend in with the crowd. But if they're found out, it means internment, in surroundings less pleasant."

"What about over the wall?" Kaz asked.

"It's been done, I'm sure, but I think most have turned inward. We get decent food, and money can buy good liquor on the black market. As time passes, the allure of the outside world, the risk of it all, lessens. And with the food shortages, café society is not what it used to be. People have adapted. Changed." Brackett went silent, his gaze wandering to the gardens, and I wondered what changes he'd endured.

"Who do you think killed Father Corrigan?" I asked, to bring him out of his daydream.

"It's Monsignor Corrigan," he said, sitting up straight, his face flushed red. What sort of thoughts had conjured up embarrassment? "You don't call a monsignor the same thing you'd call a common priest."

"You and the monsignor were friends?" Kaz asked.

"Of course we were. There aren't that many Americans among

the Roman Curia, and we both enjoyed a change of pace from our respective vocations."

"I was an altar boy, Mr. Brackett, but my knowledge of church structure ends there. What exactly is the Curia?"

"The administrative apparatus of the Church in Rome," Kaz said, "it includes foreign relations and all the congregations, yes?"

"Correct," Brackett said, sounding more comfortable talking to Kaz. Most people did, which is why we're such a good team. "The Holy See—that's basically the same thing as the Vatican—has its own secretary of state, who governs for the Pope. There is a separate structure for the Vatican City State. Police and military functions, that sort of thing."

"Did Monsignor Corrigan have any run-ins with Filberto Soletto, head of the police?" I asked.

"Soletto? No, why would he?"

"Don't know," I said. "It's why I asked. How about you? Do you know Soletto?"

"This place is one hundred and eight acres. It takes up less than one-fifth of a square mile. His office is a stone's throw away. Of course I know Soletto. How could I not?" Brackett crossed his legs, fidgeting with the crease of his trousers. The sole of his shoe was worn down, and I could see where his socks had been darned. It was evidently a life of genteel deprivation.

"How is his investigation going?"

"He's decided that a Jew on the run killed Corrigan. Don't ask me why, but he's stuck on that idea."

"Maybe because someone powerful told him to be?"

"That would have to be a cardinal, at least. I doubt it."

"Oh yeah, those guys got where they are by being sweet and gentle, I forgot."

"Listen, Boyle, that kind of talk won't go well here, no matter how true," Brackett said, sucking at his pipe. The tobacco smelled bad, harsh with the faint odor of burning leaves.

"Back in Boston, you know what Archbishop O'Connell's nickname is?" I asked.

"As a matter of fact, I do. Politicians call him Number One, last I heard. You're right, politics here can be bare-knuckle, but everything is done quietly, covered up with flowery language and lace robes. Don't suggest involvement in murder without proof, and think it through even if you have proof. You'll stay out of trouble that way." The voice of experience?

"Did Soletto have a specific suspect, or was it any Jew on the run?" I asked.

"Oh, he caught the fellow," Brackett said. "Found him hiding somewhere in the Bernini colonnades. Had blood on his coat, I think."

"Where is he now?"

"Handed over to the Italian police. Likely dead by now."

"I had no idea the Vatican was a dangerous place," Kaz said, encouraging Brackett to say more.

"It was for Monsignor Corrigan," Brackett said. "He wasn't the type to shy away from things."

The maid came in with a tray of bread, butter, marmalade, and cheeses, setting it down next to the coffee. As she arranged the dishes, Brackett stared silently out his window, relighting his pipe. Not a man of danger himself. He gestured for us to help ourselves, and I didn't hesitate.

"What sort of things?" I asked, grabbing a plate.

"Some priests do their job, others have a calling. Corrigan had a calling. I guess you could say he didn't let common sense get in the way of helping people, even if it wasn't his business. I always thought he would be more at home working in a soup kitchen, rubbing elbows with tramps."

"He was a lawyer in the Holy Office," Kaz said. "How did he get into trouble helping people?"

"You've had experience with lawyers, no doubt," Brackett said, permitting himself the slightest of smiles. "He volunteered for a mission to prisoner-of-war camps last year. Italian and German camps, up north. Mostly British prisoners. They collected letters for relatives, worked with the Red Cross, delivered blankets, that sort of thing."

"Seems like he did what he was supposed to do," I said.

"Perhaps, but he and another priest were recalled. Apparently they were working too hard at it. The bishop in charge of the visits liked to stay in fine hotels, maybe visit one camp a day, then have a nice meal with a good local wine. Corrigan went to two or three camps a day, then came back to Rome to read out the names of POWs on the Vatican Radio."

"Was he sending out messages?"

"No, only names, so families would know where their loved ones were. Maybe he made the bishop look bad, or maybe the Nazis didn't like news bulletins about prisoners. Someone put the pressure on, Corrigan got his hand slapped and went back to his legal work."

"Who could tell us more about that?"

"Another monsignor, name of Renato Bruzzone, also in the Holy Office. He and Corrigan worked together and got in the same hot water. Might have been something to it, since after Italy surrendered, and the POW camps were left unguarded, a lot of British prisoners came here, making a beeline for neutral territory," Brackett said, frowning as if he disapproved. More mouths to feed. "Also Monsignor O'Flaherty in the Holy Office. A loose cannon, that one. I'd stay away from him if I were you."

I resisted the urge to tell him I was damn glad he *wasn't* me. "The escaped prisoners were given sanctuary?"

"Yes, but very quickly the Swiss Guard was given orders to bar their entry. Again, a question of not antagonizing the Germans. Now they turn them away quietly." He made it sound as if they were granting a favor to his allies and countrymen seeking refuge. Beggars on the street to him.

"How many made it in?"

"Dozens, perhaps. It's one of those well-known secrets no one talks about."

"For fear of offending our enemy," Kaz said.

"You would do well to remember our enemy is not the enemy of our host. Antagonize Vatican officials and you could find your-selves tossed out on the streets of Rome."

"Yes," Kaz said, with a glance out the window, and back to Brackett, who blew a plume of smoke toward the ceiling. "A terrible fate, indeed."

"Have the Germans arrested any priests recently?" I asked. "Or nuns?"

"Not on Vatican territory, no. In Rome they arrest whomever they please. Or shoot them. Hardly the thing we can keep track of from within these walls."

"No rumors? Gossip about priests or nuns gone missing?"

He frowned. "Missing? As in murdered?"

"No, as in taken by the Gestapo."

"You'd have to inquire at the Regina Coeli," Brackett said. "For your sake, I hope the opportunity does not arise."

"Thanks for the concern," I said. "Can you get a message out in the diplomatic pouch for us?"

"No. While we are permitted to use the Vatican courier to Switzerland, we cannot send any coded messages, and nothing on military matters. The Germans would be certain to invade if they knew the diplomatic courier was used for Allied espionage."

"Well, somebody had to send out a message about Corrigan, otherwise we wouldn't be here."

"Quite," Brackett said wistfully. "But the death of an American citizen, even if he also held a Vatican passport, was a legitimate item for comment. Who acted upon that information is another matter. In any case, your association with the OSS makes it all the more important that you not violate the neutrality of our hosts."

"Is there any way we can talk with Soletto?"

"It may not be wise, or useful, but I can ask. He's not entirely sympathetic to the Allied cause, but that may change, the closer our tanks get. Won't be too soon for me."

We talked some more, Brackett telling us again not to ruffle feathers. He said he had a meeting to attend, and I wondered what they would discuss. The war? Or the difficulties of getting decent tobacco? He made his apologies, and left us to wait for John May to return. We ate the rest of Brackett's food, in the hope it might give him the feeling of contributing to the war effort.

"That was an interesting conversation," I said, licking the last of the jam from my fingers. "Did you notice that he never answered my question when I asked who he thought killed Corrigan?"

"Perhaps he considered it undiplomatic," Kaz said.

"Eight hundred days within one hundred acres," I said, as I stood to look at the view.

"Some have been in POW camps longer," Kaz said. "And they don't have pretty maids serving them coffee."

"There was another interesting comment," I said. "He said he felt guilty."

"Vaguely guilty," Kaz corrected me.

"Even more interesting," I said. "He couldn't even fully admit it to himself. I have a feeling it wouldn't take much to push our Mr. Brackett over the edge."

"I think he is as worn and frayed as his suit," Kaz said. "It would be interesting to pull some threads and see what lies underneath."

CHAPTER THIRTEEN

"GENTLEMEN, FOLLOW ME please," John May said. He'd returned with two new plain, black overcoats. They weren't as nice as his, but he didn't strike me as the vow-of-poverty type. He led us out of the Governatorato and into the gardens. Even in winter, the grounds were stunning. Thick green grass, evergreens, broad-leaved plants and palms created a sense of warmth and peace. The dome of Saint Peter's drifted above the landscape, like the moon on a summer night. We passed a plain two-story house, set within the lawns like a small jewel, so odd in its everyday simplicity. A wiry, gray-haired man with a thick mustache leaned on his rake and nodded a greeting to May.

"*Buongiorno, Pietro,*" May said in response. "The Vatican gardener. Excuse me, I must have a word with him."

Kaz and I admired the gardens as May talked with Pietro. The smell of fresh manure drifted up from the flowerbeds. Palm trees rustled their fronds in the light breeze. Eight hundred days is a long time, but this beat any slammer I'd ever had to cool my heels in.

"Pietro is a lucky man," Kaz said. "He lives in beauty that he tends with his own hands, and may leave when he wishes."

"And he has a beautiful wife," I said, watching as the curtains parted on the top floor, just below the orange-tiled roof. Lace gave way to a cascade of dark hair, large brown eyes, and translucent skin. She saw us looking, and hastily snapped the curtains shut.

"Or daughter," Kaz said, smiling. "I may return to ask him how he keeps the bougainvillea in bloom."

"Beware the farmer's daughter," I said, and noticed the quizzical look on Kaz's face. I'd have to explain that one to him later.

Pietro reached into a wheelbarrow and gave May a burlap sack. May glanced around before slipping his hand in his pocket and then shaking hands with Pietro as he took his leave.

"Fine fellow, Pietro. He has a cousin with a farm in Cerqueto, brings in the manure for the gardens," May said.

"That's not what you have in the bag, is it?" I said, sniffing the air.

"Hardly," May said. "There's a false bottom in the manure cart. The Germans don't bother an old farmer with a cart full of ripe cow droppings, so it's an excellent way to bring food in. A fine cut of lamb today, with potatoes, carrots, and a pecorino cheese."

"Why all the bother?" I asked. "The train we came in on was full of food."

"Three boxcars of supplies won't last a week here. There are thousands dependent on the Holy See to feed them. Everything has to be brought in—water, electricity, food, and fuel. The only natural resource here is prayer, and that does little to fill the belly. The food brought in by train is basic stuff, and Sir D'Arcy requires a level of dining to befit his status here."

"So you deal in the black market," Kaz said.

"Please, such a horrid term. I prefer to think of it as cutting out the middleman. It's much more efficient to purchase food directly from the farmer who cultivates it, don't you think?"

"That sounds reasonable," Kaz said. "Pietro and his wife must enjoy the fresh food from his cousin, no doubt."

"His wife died last year. He keeps to himself these days. He has some laborers who work in the gardens, but they don't live here. He's a nice chap, but shy, likes to be left alone. His cousin provides for us quite nicely. I hope you won't be disappointed."

"What do you mean?" I asked as Kaz and I exchanged raised eyebrows, both of us thinking that Pietro had good reason to value his privacy.

"You will be dining with Sir D'Arcy tonight," May said, as we left the gardens behind and approached a long, narrow building, three stories high, taking up a full city block. "Stay close to me, we're going inside. Don't worry about the Germans."

Before I could tell him I always worried about the Germans, May was chatting with one of the Vatican police guarding a side entrance. They shook hands, and I noticed the gendarme stuffing a pack of cigarettes into his pocket before opening the door and ushering us through.

"What exactly is it that you do for the British ambassador?" Kaz asked, clearly impressed.

"I am Sir D'Arcy's butler," May said, as if it should be obvious.

"Of course," Kaz said, his continental background kicking in. He was a baron, after all. "That explains everything except why it was you who met the train."

"All things in good time, gentlemen," May said, opening the door to a wide passageway. "No English for a while, if you please."

We stepped into the corridor, the vaulted ceilings glittering with gold leaf and brightly painted decorations. Closer to the ground, the colors were more gray-green, as German soldiers strolled past us, studying the frescoes that lined the walls. Maps. They were all maps of the Mediterranean. Italy, Sicily, North Africa. Medieval maps, but they showed the same lands and seaways we were fighting over. Not for the first time, I saw.

I brushed past two Germans pointing at a map of Sicily, surrounded by cobalt-blue waters and ships of the line in full sail. Their fingers traced lines in the air, and I understood they were talking about their days in Sicily, charting their withdrawal across the Strait of Messina. Had we shot at each other? Had I killed some of their pals, or they mine? For the moment they were tourists, unarmed, off duty. I had a strange desire to join them, to move my finger along the coast, into the interior, and see if our lines intersected.

"*Padre, bitte?*" One of them said, holding up a camera in that universal request to have a photograph taken. I nodded, trying for serene. The two of them posed in front of the Sicily fresco, arms around each other's shoulders. I took the picture, hoping one of them might show his grandchildren this snapshot one day.

May shot me a look and I caught up with him. I didn't see any reason to worry within these walls, especially not from a couple of privates gawking at the artwork. We left the museum building and walked along a roadway, passing a round tower that looked like it belonged on a castle. May took us under an arch in a narrow wall, and then we were there.

Saint Peter's Square. Magnificent colonnades circled the piazza, with a view of the Tiber River one way and the façade of Saint Peter's Basilica the other. Between them, a white line was painted on the stones, marking the border between the neutral Vatican and occupied Rome. German paratroopers guarded the line, their eyes searching those who approached. These guys were not off duty. Helmeted and heavily armed, they stopped and questioned several people approaching the square, eventually letting them all through. I noticed that people strolled out easily; it was those who wanted to enter who came under scrutiny.

"I thought you might want to see the scene of the crime," May said. "As well as be cautioned not to get too close to the line. I wouldn't put it past the Jerries to snatch a fellow if he came within arm's reach."

"All right, take us to Death's Door," I said, feeling a bit melo-dramatic as I said it.

The portico was gleaming white marble, the floor inlaid with the crests of Popes who had the clout to get the top billing. The central three doors were bronze, flanked by two plain oak doors, the Door of Death on the far left side.

"He was found here," May said. "On the top step at the base of the door. The Swiss Guard who came across him at first thought he was an escaped POW or refugee sleeping under the cover of the por-tico. When he got close enough, he saw the cassock. And the blood."

"Was the weapon found?"

"No. Soletto had the trash cans searched, but nothing was discov-ered. He was certain he had his man, so the search was halfhearted."

"We were told that Corrigan had been stabbed between the ribs," Kaz said. "It that the case?"

"Well, yes, in a manner of speaking," May said. "He was stabbed a number of times. The killer finally thrust one into the heart."

"How do you know all this?" I asked.

"I have friends among the Swiss Guard. I do them favors from time to time, and they repay the kindness. Sir D'Arcy likes to be well informed."

"The duty of any good butler," Kaz said.

"One aims to please," May said, his mischievousness showing for a brief second.

"We need to come back tonight, to get a sense of the scene when he was stabbed," I said.

"Pitch black," May said. "The Vatican is blacked out at night, like the rest of Rome."

"If Corrigan willingly came here," Kaz said, standing on the marble steps leading up to the door, "it was to meet someone in secret, in the farthest, darkest corner of the square."

"I'll bring you here after dark, but let's move on now. There's nothing to see and it will only attract attention." He took us through the colonnade to the left of the portico and held up his hand. "We are going to that building, through the Piazza del Sant'Uffizio. We have to cross a bit of open ground."

He pointed to the white line, which went from along the base of the colonnade and crossed a road leading into the piazza. A group of monks crossed toward us, and two nuns in the other direction. Two German paratroopers watched them with bored expressions.

"It looks safe," I said, working at convincing myself.

"It is," May said. "We took the long way around so I could show you the door, and avoid Soletto as well. It would have been a short walk from the Governatorato. But as you can see, people cross here as a matter of routine. They are not stopped if they are clearly crossing from the square. Look as if you belong."

I held my hands together in contemplative prayer and followed. The paratroopers lit cigarettes and ignored us.

"Here's where you'll be staying," May said a minute later. "The German College, but don't be worried by the name. The nuns who run the place are German but quite loyal to the Pope. It was used to house German priests and seminarians who traveled to the Holy See, but that traffic has dropped off a bit, as you can imagine. One moment, please." With that, he approached the Vatican gendarme who stood at the main door. They shook hands, chatted for a moment, and then the door was opened for us, the gendarme bowing like the doorman at the Copley Plaza.

"Why a guard at the door?" I asked as we stepped inside.

"This area is actually in Italian territory. The college was built up against the old wall marking the boundary of the Holy See. This is a public street, but the college has extraterritorial status and inside is considered sovereign Vatican territory. The guard is there to keep the public out, not to spy on you."

"Tricky jurisdiction," I said. "Let's hope no bodies are found here."

"Indeed," May said with a lift of his bushy eyebrows, as if it were a real concern. He showed us to a small room, clean but Spartan. A bed against each side wall, a table and chairs in between. A wash-stand with a pitcher of water completed the scene.

"Your bags, gentlemen," May said, indicating the suitcase on each bed. Next to them was a clean set of clothes, cassocks, the whole nine yards. "The clothing is complete with tailor's labels from Rome, to be on the safe side."

"You're amazing, May," I said. "Thank you."

"It is nothing. I am sorry that hot water and heat are in short supply. There is a bathroom down the hall, with a good supply of warm water at best. His Holiness has decreed that all Vatican build-ings are to go without heat this winter, since fuel is so scarce in Rome. He doesn't wish the people to think we live a life of luxury in here."

"It's February, for crying out loud. Do you mean that the Vatican has no fuel at all?"

"No, there is a large supply of coal in bunkers hidden within the gardens. But it is not to be touched until the people of Rome have fuel restored. Now rest, and someone will bring you to Sir D'Arcy's residence at eight o'clock."

"The gendarme outside is okay, even if he works for Soletto?"

"He's one of the best. That's why he's guarding your door. Have a rest and don't worry. I imagine your journey must have been difficult."

"Interesting," Kaz said after May had left. "Two men, Brackett and May, in the same circumstances. One retreats inward, not daring to take any chances. The other seems to thrive, rising above the situation he finds himself in."

"You never know about a guy," I said. "Before the war, Brackett was probably a big shot, and May a servant. War, even if it isn't a shooting war, puts pressure on everyone. Some can take it, others can't. There's no predicting." I looked at Kaz, who'd been a skinny student before the war. He probably never thought he'd go near a gun or harm anyone. Now he was a scar-faced killer—wiry, wary, and strong.

"No," Kaz agreed. "Life is strange, Billy. It is why I have come to appreciate it."

CHAPTER FOURTEEN

WE WASHED UP, changed, and waited. Our window looked out upon a small, well-tended cemetery, bordered by a brick wall and decorated with cypresses and palm trees. This was the German College, so I figured it was filled with dead Germans, as was a lot of Italy.

"We made it, Kaz," I said, thinking about how close we'd come to the wrong side of the grass. "There were times I wasn't sure we would."

"You're a priest now, Billy, you must have faith," Kaz said, adjusting his new cassock. Kaz managed to wear anything well, including these ankle-length priestly garments.

"Faith was easier back in Boston."

"When you were a choirboy?"

"Yeah. And when there wasn't a war chewing up half the world. Back then, everything had its proper place, you know? Church on Sunday, carrying in the candles, every week like clockwork. Seemed it would stay that way forever. Safe, predictable."

"I think the church wants you to have faith in more than ritual," Kaz said. "Although they certainly do love that."

"I know," I said, sitting on my bed and swinging my legs up. "It's all the death, destruction, and fear that makes it tough. Hard to imagine this is all part of God's plan." Fear was the big one for me. Fear of dying, fear of mutilation, fear for Diana. It was hard to shake.

Shattered buildings could be restored, better than new, but not the heart and soul after fear had gnawed at them.

"That's why they came up with the idea of faith," Kaz said. "It answers all questions without giving anything away. Clever."

"You're not big on faith yourself, are you?" I asked.

"No," Kaz said, gazing out the window. "Dust to dust, I think it is no more than that."

"I see now why you had a short career as an altar boy."

"Yes." Kaz laughed. "My thoughts on theology were not welcome. Nor was my suggestion that the church should give all its riches away for the poor. Now here we are, at the Vatican itself, surrounded by immense wealth and an ample supply of coal. Yet, we are chilled to the bone. As I said, in life one encounters many strange things."

"Like giving the last rites to a dying soldier. He had the ceremony, but not the absolution. We have fuel, but no warmth."

"He is dead, Billy. You gave him comfort in his last moments. That is all that matters. Priest or no priest, it makes no difference."

"I wish I were that sure, Kaz." I laid my head down on the pillow, closing my eyes as if that would stop the doubts and questions.

I tried to think through what I knew about this murder. That didn't take long, and a heavy blanket of weariness weighed on me as confused images swam through my mind. Dreams of burning cities, dead soldiers, priests in their billowing, black cassocks, and a sharp, pounding noise that wouldn't go away.

"Billy," Kaz said, shaking me awake. I threw off the blanket—Kaz must have put that on me—and stood, realizing the noise was someone knocking at the door. I blinked myself awake, and noticed Kaz stashing something in his suitcase before going for the door.

"Welcome, Fathers," a voice boomed out as soon as Kaz swung the door open. The accent was Italian, the pronunciation precise, as if he worried about getting every word right. "I am Monsignor Renato Bruzzone." Bruzzone tossed off a cape, under which he wore a black cassock with red trim and a purple sash, showing off his rank of monsignor.

"Monsignor," I said, unsure of how exactly to address one. "I am Father Boyle, and this is Father Dalakis."

"Yes, yes, but I know these are not your real names. No matter, I am glad you are here."

Monsignor Bruzzone had a full head of thick, black hair, and a good start on a five o'clock shadow. He was taller than me, with broad shoulders and dark, steady eyes that studied us, watching the confusion on our faces.

"Real names?" Kaz said, a look of practiced befuddlement worrying his brow.

"Come now, gentlemen, I am here to help. Sit, please." He gestured to the table as if we had come to visit him. Rank has its privileges everywhere. "Your arrival has been noted by many. The Vatican is a small place, with many big ears and eyes. As well as tongues!" He chuckled at his little joke, lifting an eyebrow, inviting us to join in the laughter.

"How did you note our arrival, Monsignor?" Kaz asked.

"Some of those eyes and tongues work for me. It is helpful to watch the comings and goings here, especially in this building."

"Why this building?" I asked.

"Surely you know?" Our blank stares answered his question. "This is one of the two buildings where escaped Allied prisoners of war live. The other is the barracks of the Swiss Guard. Amusing, isn't it?"

"Monsignor, you certainly know more than we do," I said. "But I do know you were a colleague of Monsignor Edward Corrigan's. Have you come here to tell us what you know about his death?"

"Sadly, no," he said, his lips pursed. He fished in his pocket for a pack of cigarettes and lit one up, his silver lighter polished and gleaming. He offered the pack to both of us, and we declined. They were Junos, a German brand. "These are terrible, but in times like these any tobacco will do. No, I cannot tell you much about Edward, except that he was a fine man. It is a shame for him to end that way."

"Dead?"

"Well, yes, but to be attacked by someone he was trying to help, that was terrible."

"How do you know he was trying to help the man who stabbed him?" Kaz asked.

"It stands to reason. He was a Jew with no place to hide. He must have escaped the roundup of Roman Jews last October and been at his wit's end. You'd be surprised at how many refugees we have hidden here. Not just POWs, but Jews, antifascist Italians, and even German deserters. Somehow, this poor fellow must have heard about Edward and made contact. Perhaps he panicked, perhaps he had gone mad. Who knows? It could as well been myself, or Monsignor O'Flaherty."

"Who does know?" I asked. "Where is this alleged murderer?"

"The Italian authorities took him. As part of the treaty between the Holy See and the Italian government, Saint Peter's Square, while it is Vatican territory, is under the legal jurisdiction of Rome because of all the visitors who come here."

"And what are the chances of a Jew turned over to the Fascist authorities still being alive?" Kaz asked.

"Next to none, I am sorry to say. The Nazis shipped all the Jews in Rome to those camps months ago. If he was not killed outright, he was sent north. To them, the greater crime is the religion of his birth. They are fiends, but you know that."

"There was no thought of that at the time?" I asked.

"Truly, there could not be. Commissioner Soletto is pro-fascist, to be sure. You must have been warned about him. But even someone with the opposite viewpoint would have had to do the same. The Lateran Treaty, which outlines these territorial responsibilities, is quite precise. It even delineates exactly where the Italian authority ends: at the bottom of the steps leading into Saint Peter's Basilica. We struggle constantly to maintain our rights within the treaty, which means the Holy See abides by the exact letter of that document. To do otherwise would be to open up the possibility of abrogation."

"Which would mean the Germans take over," Kaz said.

"Yes. Can you imagine? His Holiness taken to the Third Reich for his own protection, or some such nonsense? No, that must be avoided at all costs."

"Yet you hide escapees and refugees here, on neutral ground," Kaz said.

"Yes, we do. To do otherwise would be a sin. It is simply a matter of not getting caught! So far, we have not."

"Does the Pope know about all this?" I asked.

"His Holiness has not told us not to proceed in this manner, and we know he has opened his summer residence at Castel Gandolfo to refugees without regard to religion. The estate is territory of the Vatican State, and many Jewish refugees have found sanctuary there."

"So you have no direct orders from the Pope, but you think he approves?" Kaz said.

"Yes. He is a good friend to Monsignor Hugh O'Flaherty, the most visible of us. I have witnessed His Holiness looking down on the square from his palace windows, watching Hugh meet escaped POWs and direct them to safety. So, until Pius tells us to stop, we continue. You Americans have a saying, that something is done between a nod and a wink, yes?"

"It's with a wink and a nod," I said. "But I understand."

"A wink and a nod. Yes, that is how we do things. Good."

"You and Monsignors Corrigan and O'Flaherty worked together visiting POW camps?" I said.

"We did, until we were recalled. Our activities were too enthusiastic for some."

"I heard you made a bishop look bad?"

"In part, but the real reason was we became involved in rescue efforts with Jewish refugees from France. You see, Italy occupied part of southern France, and the Italian anti-Jewish laws were not as harsh, or as strongly enforced, as the Vichy French laws. When Mussolini fell and the Italian Army withdrew from southern France, many Jews followed into Italy, hoping to avoid deportation. But they had no identity papers and little money. The archbishop of Genoa set up a network to provide funds, shelter, and papers. His Holiness sent money to the bishop to help."

"Let me guess," I said. "Your POW camp-inspection trip was a cover for that."

"Yes, very good. It was, but the visits to the camps were important too. Many of the POWs who escaped after the fall of Mussolini remembered our names and came here seeking sanctuary."

"What happened in Genoa?" Kaz asked.

"We became too visible. The Gestapo began questioning people we came into contact with. Our Vatican passports protected us, but not the other clergy in Genoa. So we turned over our funds to the Delegation for the Assistance of Jewish Emigrants, an underground group doing good work, especially with children."

"Did the Gestapo know about Corrigan?" I asked, wondering if this had been a revenge hit.

"Yes, they questioned all of us. Politely, of course, given our diplomatic status. They said they were concerned about our safety, given the Jewish and Communist bandits who were running loose. The usual lies, but we understood the meaning."

"What about here in Rome?" I asked, fishing for information about Diana. "Has the Gestapo been arresting clergy?"

"Father Boyle, there are many priests and nuns at the mercy of the Nazis. Little is ever heard of those taken." Bruzzone lit another cigarette, flicking the lighter shut with a click, blowing smoke to the ceiling.

"If a member of the clergy is taken into custody, you are not informed? The Vatican, I mean."

"If the person holds a Vatican passport, yes. But of the thousands of priests, nuns, and monks in Rome, very few do. Unless it was brought to the attention of Cardinal Maglione—he is the secretary of state for the Holy See—nothing could be done. Even then. . . ." He ended with an eloquent lift of the shoulders. Who is to know?

"Is there anything else you can tell us about Father Corrigan?" Kaz asked.

"Nothing other than stories of his goodness. But in the morning,

I will show you to his room. Perhaps you will find something there to help."

"Didn't Soletto have it searched?" I asked.

"No, he thought it not necessary. I had it locked and kept the key. No one has been in since the murder. I will show you tomorrow, but now I will escort you to dinner with Sir D'Arcy. To be sure you do not take a wrong turn and end up in the hands of the Nazis."

"You are well informed as to our plans," Kaz said.

"It is important to be well informed. It could save your life." Bruzzone crushed out his cigarette and stood, donning his cloak.

"We need to speak to Soletto, or at least the officer in charge of the investigation," I said. "Even if he's an informer."

"One thing you would do well to remember: Trust no one until you know which side they are on, and then keep your own counsel if they are not friendly. The Vatican City State may be neutral, but the great majority who live here are Italians. Many welcomed Mussolini and his Fascist Party and were glad to see them in power instead of the Communists. Some wish he would return, and hope for a German victory. Be very careful."

"Would any of them kill for their cause?" I asked.

"We of the clergy have more experience as martyrs than murderers. But both welcome death, do they not? Follow me."

With that cheery thought, we followed the monsignor out into the cold evening air.

CHAPTER FIFTEEN

"SIR D'ARCY OSBORNE, Envoy Extraordinary and Minister Plenipotentiary to the Holy See," May intoned. Gone was the playful smile. Dressed in a dark suit and wearing white gloves, he bowed slightly as he introduced us.

"Sir D'Arcy," Kaz said, more comfortable with the ways of the upper class than I was. "Thank you for inviting us."

"Ah, Father Dalakis, I assume, from the accent. And Father Boyle. Welcome." We shook hands all around. May disappeared to do some butlering as D'Arcy led us into the dining room. Bruzzone had delivered us to the Hospice Santa Marta, a short walk from our rooms, but a world away. It was like stepping into an elegant London flat. The furniture was heavy and plush, the curtains thick, and the candelabras gleaming. There was a framed portrait of the king, but I think it was Sir D'Arcy himself who made it feel like a bit of old England. His receding hair was fine and light, his cheekbones high, and his posture perfect. Unlike Brackett's, D'Arcy's three-piece suit looked new and well tailored. His shoes were shined and I'd bet there were no holes in his socks.

"Forgive me if I do not ask about your journey," D'Arcy said as we sat at a table set for four. "I'm sure it was terrible, and that you can tell me little for security reasons."

"Right on both counts," I said. "Speaking of security, how many people do you think know we're here?"

"Quite a few, but let's discuss all that after dinner. Our other guest should be here soon."

May entered and poured wine for us. D'Arcy sniffed it and held it up to the light, as if he knew what he was doing. He tasted it, and nodded his approval to May. I took a slug and realized this wasn't the sort of vino I'd been drinking in Italy. They must have been hiding all the good stuff in Rome.

"Brunello di Montalcino," Kaz said, his eyebrows raised in admiration. "Excellent."

"And increasingly rare," D'Arcy said. "The Germans are taking all the best wines from Tuscany. May works wonders at keeping our cellar stocked."

"He has a clever delivery system," I said, then took a smaller sip of the wine.

"I don't know how he does it, and I don't wish to," D'Arcy said. "The position of Allied diplomats within the Vatican is precarious. We must not do anything overt to threaten the neutrality of the Holy See. That includes the black market, smuggling food, and hiding those on the run from the Nazis. So, I drink this fine wine in happy ignorance."

"Leviticus tells us that if a man sins through ignorance, then he shall pay for his trespass a ram without blemish from his flock," a voice boomed from the hallway. "But I shall settle for some of that lamb being prepared in your kitchen, Sir D'Arcy."

"Monsignor O'Flaherty," D'Arcy said, introducing us.

O'Flaherty was dressed in the full monsignor getup, but it didn't disguise his liveliness. He was tall, broad-shouldered, with a thick head of hair that curled down over his forehead. His grin was pleasant, and he shook our hands warmly. His wasn't what you'd call a handsome face, with a good-sized nose, thin lips, and round glasses giving him an owlish look.

"Father Dalakis," O'Flaherty said as he took his seat. "I've been around this part of the world long enough to have an ear for accents. You're certainly not Romanian. Polish-born, I'd guess. And you, Father Boyle, a Yank if I ever heard one. But I'd guess your granddad was from the old sod. You've got a trace of the brogue right at the edge of your tongue, boy."

"My grandfather came from County Roscommon," I said. "Last of his family to survive the Potato Blight."

"Awful times," O'Flaherty said, slowly shaking his head, and then flashing a ready smile at D'Arcy. "But out of respect for our English host, we'll talk of other things. Politics and good food do not mix. My own home is in County Cork, where I'm glad my family is safe from this war."

The food was brought in, and it smelled a whole lot better than army chow. For the next hour, we feasted on grilled lamb, thick strands of pasta seasoned with cheese and black pepper, green beans and tomatoes, and more of D'Arcy's wine. O'Flaherty told stories of his assignments for the Vatican in Egypt and Czechoslovakia before the war. He and D'Arcy talked golf, the Irishman being quite the player.

"The monsignor is also a pugilist," D'Arcy said. "Perhaps you'd like to give him the opportunity to fight a new opponent, Father Boyle. He's worn out most comers by now."

"I don't think I could hit a priest, much less a monsignor," I said.

"What makes you think you could lay a glove on me, boy? Anyway, in the ring it's just one man against another. No white collar, no rank. A bit like life, eh? Sometimes you have to leave certainty behind and come out swinging." He and D'Arcy exchanged looks, and the Englishman stood.

"Gentlemen, I must take your leave. I thought it best if you and Monsignor O'Flaherty met and talked, so as to avoid any confusion in your investigation. He has a rather active organization, and you are bound to cross paths. You may trust him in all things. May will join you shortly."

"The ambassador keeps things at arm's length, it seems," Kaz said after D'Arcy had left.

"Don't be fooled," O'Flaherty said. "When I first came to ask for his help, I thought the same thing. He said he didn't want to know any details, and then called for his butler. I was about to storm out, but I stayed long enough to meet John May. The most artful scrounger you'll ever come across. Sir D'Arcy also supplies us with large amounts of cash to buy food and pay those who shelter our people. In public, he can truthfully say he knows nothing of our operation."

"Just who are your people?" I said. "Escaped POWs?"

"There are many of those, mostly British, but a fair number of Americans now, and a scattering of others from the Commonwealth countries. Even a few French colonial troops. This is why we had this little dinner party tonight, so I could brief you about a number of odd things you might stumble across."

"Such as?"

"We've placed many escapees in Rome with families or in vacant buildings. But hundreds are within the Vatican. The Pope has a militia, the Palatine Guard, normally drawn from citizens of Rome. Their ranks are swelled by about three hundred Jews who escaped the roundup in October. They're housed in the Swiss Guard barracks. We have Italian antifascists who escaped the Nazis and the Fascist secret police after Mussolini fell. Italian officers who fought the Germans before the king fled, and who now have a price on their heads. Jewish converts who thought they were safe, until the roundups began. Aristocrats and deserters, we have them all."

"How do you feed them?" Kaz asked. "The food situation seems desperate."

"We are dependent on money from many sources—the church as well as a number of wealthy supporters. We buy on the black market, where John works his magic. Tell me, do you have any idea when the Allies will reach Rome? Liberation is what we really need."

"No," I said. "The line around Monte Cassino is still holding, and the troops at Anzio are boxed in. Months, I'd guess."

"Ah, that's bad news. Well, nothing we can do about that. Now, how can I help you?"

"Do you have any idea why Monsignor Corrigan was killed?" I asked.

"If it had happened in Rome, outside these walls, I might suspect it had something to do with his other activities."

"What other activities?" I asked.

"You don't know? He was in contact with the OSS. His code name was Rudder."

"Jesus," I said, taking this in.

"Watch it, boy. That better have been a prayer to heaven. I don't like to hear the Lord's name spoken in vain."

"Sorry. I've read reports from Rudder, but had no idea who it was."

"It makes sense," Kaz said. "It is a more logical explanation for why we were sent here."

"Do you know who his contacts were? Did he have a radio?" I asked.

There was a discreet knock and two servants came in to clear away the dishes. One returned with coffee, but O'Flaherty waved him away and poured it himself.

"I only know that there is a radio team somewhere in the city," he said. The coffee cups were delicate bone china. The coffee was the real thing, hot and bracing. "He'd be gone for a day whenever he had a message to send. They could be anywhere, close by or outside Rome."

"But he confided in you," I said. "Did he tell you anything else?"

"No. Two months ago he said he needed to limit his activities with the escapees. He said his other work made it too dangerous, and if the Gestapo got onto him, it could compromise us all. He told me about the code name in case he ever needed to get a message to me, but he never used it."

"So for the past two months, he hasn't been active with your organization?"

"No," O'Flaherty said. "But we'd see each other almost every day, in the normal course of our work. We were friends. I miss his company terribly."

"Monsignor Bruzzone as well? Is he part of your group?" Kaz asked.

"Yes, has been from the beginning. The three of us were on the first inspection tour of POW camps in the north, mostly around Genoa. We helped the bishop there with Jewish refugees flowing in from Vichy France. Bruzzone and Corrigan worked mainly with them, while I focused on the POWs."

"That was when you were recalled," I said.

"Yes," O'Flaherty said with a grin. "I know I can be too enthusiastic at times. One of my many failings. I made the bishop who was in charge look bad. But that didn't last long. Monsignor Montini sent us back to Genoa with money and false papers for the refugees."

"Who is Montini?"

"The Minister of Ordinary Affairs in the Vatican State Secretariat. Ordinary meaning he has jurisdiction over affairs within the Vatican City State itself. But he is a favorite of His Holiness, and often acts in areas beyond his brief."

"Where did the false papers come from?" I asked. "The OSS?"

"Strictly speaking, they were not false," O'Flaherty said. "Vatican passports, baptismal certificates, all printed on official paper courtesy of the Vatican print shop."

"So Corrigan had access to ready money and identity papers," I said. "Vatican and OSS cash for refugees, plus the papers. A tempting target."

"Walking around with thick stacks of lira is commonplace," O'Flaherty said. "We dispense funds all over Rome. The papers, yes, they are valuable. The right identity papers are life itself. But it would be a simple matter to rob us on any back street. Why do so in Saint Peter's Square?"

"Food is the currency of the day in any case," John May said as he entered the room, a thick file folder under his arm. He sat at the table in the seat D'Arcy had vacated and poured himself coffee. I didn't think butlers normally sat in their boss's chair. Despite the veneer of English respectability, this was a place where the rules of polite society did not apply. "It'd be worth your life to carry bread in some Roman neighborhoods."

"What do you think was worth Corrigan's life?" I asked.

"I wish I knew," May said. "But I have some information for you. This is the Gendarmerie file on Corrigan's investigation. I have to return it within the hour, so look quickly. Do you read Italian?"

"I do," Kaz said. He took the folder and handed me the photographs. They showed Corrigan's body from several angles. There were knife wounds in his torso and slashes on his arms. It looked like it had been a sudden, ferocious attack, but an unskilled one. The murderer had stabbed Corrigan repeatedly until a thrust to the heart finished him.

"The killer is strong," I said. "And determined, but not experienced."

"What makes you say that?" O'Flaherty asked, looking at the pictures of his friend and shaking his head sadly.

"Multiple wounds," I said. "He probably had never stabbed a man before, and struggled to find the right spot. Corrigan fought back, but the first thrust had already weakened him. It takes strength to keep stabbing a man. Killing a guy with a knife is hard work if you don't know what you're doing. Harder than you'd think." I studied the pictures. There was a large, dark pool at the base of the steps. Not surprising, since the heart, or the major arteries leading to it, can pump out a lot of blood before the body gives up the ghost.

"Yes," Kaz said, "the report states that there were numerous wounds, some superficial, others not very deep. The killer finally found his mark with a single penetrating wound between the ribs into the heart."

"Even so, it appears Edward did not die immediately," O'Flaherty said, pointing to a trail of blood on the steps.

"Right. It looks like he dragged himself up the steps to lie against the door."

"Perhaps he was trying to get into the basilica," May said.

"No," O'Flaherty said. "That is the Door of Death. It is kept locked except for funerals. Edward knew that."

"People do odd things in their last moments," I said.

"Odd to those of us still full of life," O'Flaherty said. "But I'd wager a man who knows he is in his last moments would not waste them on oddities."

I had to admit he was right. I'd seen some strange last moments, at least the ones that weren't sudden or the stuff of nightmares. Lots of guys reached for a picture, or a letter, or a religious medal, some memento they carried to remind themselves of a life beyond the battleground. But I never saw anyone who dragged his dying body up three stone steps.

"Who found the body?" I asked.

"One of the Swiss Guard, on his rounds at first light."

"What about the supposed killer?" I asked Kaz, as he flipped through the typewritten report.

"One Severino Rossi. He carried a French passport, marked with a red J for *Juif*. Jew." He passed a photograph around. A gaunt, unshaven face gazed dully at the camera. His hair was long, curling over his forehead. His eyes were dark, his mouth gaped open in surprise, or fear. The steps of the basilica were visible in the background.

"One of the many who fled Vichy France," O'Flaherty said. "He may well have been in the wrong place at the wrong time and been a convenient scapegoat."

"He was found behind one of the Bernini colonnades," Kaz said, scanning the report. "Covered in a bloodstained overcoat, asleep. Apparently that was enough evidence for Soletto."

"What it lacks in plausibility it makes up for in convenience," I said. "This guy Rossi knifes Corrigan, for no discernable reason, then takes a catnap a few yards away? It doesn't add up."

"It might," May said. "Perhaps he was meeting Corrigan to ask for his help. If Corrigan refused, he may have lost control and attacked him in a blind fury. Then, where could he go? The Swiss Guard had all the entrances covered, and the Germans were at the border. They would certainly question anyone leaving at that hour. His best bet might have been to wait and leave with a crowd."

"Could be," I said. "But he still sounds like a patsy to me. Anything else about him in that file, Kaz?"

"Born the first of June, 1921. Brown hair, brown eyes. It lists his height, weight, occupation, the usual from his passport. From Toulon, and lived in Genoa after he escaped Vichy France, until the German roundups began. Then he went into hiding. Nothing else."

"Thanks for the file, May," I said. "Any chance we could talk to Soletto about this? And not have him turn us over to the Nazis?"

"I think so. He is a Fascist sympathizer, and we know he has informed in the past, but he values his position here, and he can see which way the war is going. He may not be very cooperative, but I don't think it would be a risk. Monsignor?"

"No, especially if we arrange an instruction from on high," O'Flaherty said. "Monsignor Montini, I think."

"Monsignor Bruzzone advised against it," I said. "He thought it would be dangerous."

"I think it's worth the chance. Soletto may appreciate the opportunity to ingratiate himself with the Allies," O'Flaherty said. "I'll contact you tomorrow once things are set up."

"And I must return this file," May said, "if you're done with it."

"Sure," I said. "Thanks, not that there was much of value in it. What did it cost you?"

"A piece of cheese, no larger than my hand. Sad, really."

"Well, lads, what's next?" O'Flaherty said, after May was gone.

"Monsignor Bruzzone is going to show us Corrigan's room in the morning. Then we'll wait to hear from you," I said.

"Anything else I can do for you boys?"

"Tell me, Monsignor," I said, trying to keep my voice steady, "what is it like on the streets of Rome? Are there German patrols? Have any of your people been arrested?"

"There are Germans everywhere, but you've got to be careful not to show fear. For the most part, they go about their business, and if you do the same, you'll blend into the background. But when they set up security checkpoints, that's when it gets dangerous. They might block off a street and search everyone. Or stop a tram. Why, are you planning on seeing the sights?"

"Just curious, Monsignor. We might get lucky and find that Severino Rossi is still in custody."

"Well, if he is, he's in the Regina Coeli. Going in isn't the problem. Getting out is."

"Are they holding any priests or nuns there? It might give us an excuse to visit and look for him."

O'Flaherty looked at me, studying my face. He seemed to be weighing the risk of sharing information with me. Which meant he had information. "Leave that to me, will you?" O'Flaherty said, holding my eye with a steady gaze. "It's a soup I don't want too many cooks stirring."

"Excuse me," came an urgent whisper from the doorway. "Monsignor, I must speak with you." A woman stood in the shadowed darkness of the hallway, where all I could see was her face. It was enough. Wide, dark pupils beneath elegantly arched eyebrows. High cheekbones setting off lips as red as a cardinal's robe. She stepped forward hesitantly. We all stood, but Kaz positively snapped to attention as if a four-star general had walked into the room.

"Gentlemen, this is Princess Nini Pallavicini," O'Flaherty said, introducing us after she'd whispered an urgent report to him.

"I heard you had arrived," she said with the slightest Italian accent. "Welcome to our little cabal." She wore a beret and a raincoat, with water beaded on her slim shoulders. She held out her hand, and I shook it, unsure of the protocol. Kaz wasn't.

"Baron Piotr Augustus Kazimierz," he said, taking her hand in his and giving a little bow, his heels snapping, his lips brushing the air above her small, delicate hand. "Currently serving as a lieutenant with the Polish Army in Exile. Charmed, Princess."

"What sort of secret agent are you, Baron, to give me your real name?" She let go of Kaz's hand after a few seconds of graceful hesitation.

"Forgive me," he said. "Father Dalakis will return in a moment. But I could not bring myself to lie to a princess."

"What interesting visitors you have, Monsignor," she said, her eyes lingering on Kaz. "But I must take you away from them. We have a problem. Is John about? I need some supplies."

"Yes," O'Flaherty said. "Go find him and I'll be with you in a minute."

"A princess in the Vatican?" I asked as she left the room.

"Princess Nini Pallavicini comes from one of Rome's oldest aristocratic families," O'Flaherty said. "Her husband was a fighter pilot, killed over Sicily. She was involved in the antifascist uprising after Mussolini was deposed. When the Germans took Rome, the Gestapo came to arrest her, and she escaped by jumping out a second-story window and making her way here. I gave her sanctuary, and she has been a great help to our cause." O'Flaherty rose and donned his cape. "But I must leave you now. An emergency. Please find me tomorrow morning and we'll sort out your visit to Soletto."

"One question, Monsignor," Kaz said. "Does the princess harbor any ill will toward the Allies for her husband's death?"

"No. She reserves that for the Nazis and the Fascists."

"Good," Kaz said.

CHAPTER SIXTEEN

"DO YOU THINK we will see the princess today, Billy?"

"I don't know, Kaz," I said. "If I spot her, you'll be the first to know."

It was the third time that morning he'd asked the same question. Most guys, head over heels for a dame, walk around with their heads in the clouds and spout the goofiest stuff. I've done it myself, but at least I knew I sounded like an idiot. Kaz didn't have a clue.

"I wish I were not pretending to be a priest," he said, running his finger around the white collar as if he wanted to rip it off.

"I'd settle for you pretending to be a detective," I muttered as we walked up a gently sloping path in the gardens behind Saint Peter's. If Kaz heard me, he was too distracted to pay me any mind. I couldn't begrudge him a romance, anyway. Not after what he'd been through. Horror, loss, sorrow. A little joy would do him good. I wouldn't mind some myself.

After last night's conversation, I was sure Father O'Flaherty knew more than he wanted to tell me about priests and nuns held by the Gestapo. I was also sure he was the careful sort, and wouldn't spill unless he had a good reason to. A cautious type like Brackett might think him a loose cannon, but to me he seemed a decent guy. If all else failed, I could always try the truth. Might even work.

"I wonder what the trouble was last night?" Kaz said. "When the princess came in, I mean." As if there was another topic of conversation.

"Let's ask when we're done searching Corrigan's room," I said. "I need to get more out of him."

"About Diana?"

"Yes." Was she still in a Gestapo cell, dead, or on her way to a concentration camp? I didn't like any of the choices, but at least I'd have a shot if she were still alive and in Rome.

We walked in silence, passing an ancient church, tiny in the looming shadow of Saint Peter's, sandstone wall the color of rust. Skirting the *Governatorato*, we passed the gardener's house. The fellow with the ample mustache wasn't in sight, but the woman who had peeked from behind the curtains yesterday was. She stood outside with two small children. A cloth sack hung from one shoulder, her arm supporting the weight of it. The kids, a boy and a girl, maybe five and six years old, played on the lawn while the woman kept watch, glancing in every direction, averting her eyes after she spotted us. As she turned away, the sack slipped from her shoulder and the contents spilled to the ground. Tins of food. Cheese and a small salami. She scooped them into the bag and called her children into the house.

"She looks wary," I said. "Even here."

"That is probably how she stayed alive," Kaz said. "And kept her children with her." There was a chill in the air, but the sun was bright and the grass still green and lush. The boy and the girl looked like children the world over, playing without a care, satisfied with the moment at hand. Their mother stood hawk-like, ready to defend her young with her last ounce of energy.

We circled around the basilica, crossed a small square, and came to the Medieval Palace, where Monsignor Bruzzone was due to meet us. He'd told us exactly where to wait, which was good since the buildings all ran into one another here. The Sistine Chapel, the Pope's living quarters in the Apostolic Palace, and the Medieval Palace were all connected by passageways and corridors. They didn't look like palaces, but more like government architecture from the last century jammed together at all the wrong angles.

"Here, Fathers," Bruzzone called from an archway leading into one of the buildings. We crossed a small piazza as he spoke to a Swiss Guard at the entrance. The guard stood aside to let us pass. "*Buongiorno,*" Bruzzone said as he patted the shoulder of the guard in his gray field uniform. For the duration of the war, the Swiss Guard had traded in their colorful striped outfits for a more modern look.

"You and Monsignor O'Flaherty both seem on good terms with the Swiss Guard," I said.

"Yes, with all our activities, it pays to know them by name," Bruzzone said, pushing back his thick black hair from his forehead. "I also minister to them spiritually. Tell me, did you have an enjoyable dinner last night?"

"Quite," Kaz said. I wondered if he was going to describe the virtues of Princess Nini Pallavicini for the monsignor, but he held back. "You have an interesting circle of friends, Monsignor."

"To say the least, Father. Here, this way." Bruzzone led us down a narrow, arched corridor. Marble columns lined the passageway, lit by ornate brass chandeliers, giving the stone a soft, warm glow at odds with the sudden chill that settled upon us once we were out of the sun. "The next building is the Apostolic Palace, which you may have heard of. It is where His Holiness lives."

"And what exactly is this building?" Kaz asked, going along with the tour-guide routine.

"The Medieval Palace is where the secretary of state has his office, and other officials as well. One floor is living quarters, small apartments for those who live here permanently. Come, this way."

We went up a marble staircase, the walls decorated with artwork, mostly paintings of high-level Holy Joes from the distant past. Cardinals, they looked like. Maybe this was the reward the also-rans got when they didn't come out on top in a papal election. Not a bad spot for your portrait to spend the centuries. The ceiling gleamed with gold-leaf trim, a contrast to the jade-black marble at our feet. Back in Boston, I'd been impressed with the lobby at the Copley Plaza. Compared to this, it was a cheap flophouse. Bruzzone led us to a hallway on an upper floor. This section wasn't as fancy, the floor tiled and walls empty of paintings. A slot by each door held an elegantly lettered name tag. We stopped at Corrigan.

"Here," Bruzzone said, drawing an old brass key from his pocket and opening the door. "I have not been inside since the day of Edward's death. No one else has, either."

"I am surprised that Soletto did not have it searched," Kaz said. "Even if he was sure of his suspect."

"Monsignor Corrigan was a man of great faith and good works," Bruzzone said, clearly offended. "Whatever the faults of Commissario Soletto, he knows that much. What do you expect to find? Evidence otherwise?"

"Not at all, Monsignor," I said. "It is simply procedure." *For any decent cop*, I wanted to add, but saw no percentage. I stood in the doorway, taking in the room. To the left was a narrow bed. One dresser against the wall. Straight ahead, a small table placed by the single window with a view of an interior courtyard. A sink and washstand in the corner. One bookshelf, crammed with books, magazines, and loose papers. A worn carpet covered most of the wood floor. A single easy chair was placed at an angle to take advantage of what view there was. An end table held more books and magazines. On top of the pile was a biography of Sir Thomas More, the bookmark at the very beginning. Beneath that was a Rex Stout novel, *The League of Frightened Men*. That bookmark was near the end. Had Corrigan been reading this the night he was killed? I tried to imagine him in the room, rising from his chair, perhaps covering the mystery with the weightier biography, a bit embarrassed by his nonreligious reading material, thinking he'd finish when he returned. Murder makes fools of us all.

"Okay," I said. "Kaz, you check the bed, I'll work from the other end. Monsignor, thank you for your help."

"It was nothing. I will stay, if you don't mind. To lock up afterward."

"Sure," I said. "Don't touch anything." Bruzzone hung back in the doorway, shaking his head, perhaps thinking it had been a bad idea to bring us here.

Kaz had already started methodically pulling the bedding apart. I began in the corner, going through the washstand, and worked my way out. I could sense Bruzzone's disapproval, and I knew it wasn't pleasant to watch us go through his pal's stuff. It was a long shot, but we might find something that would tip us off to why Corrigan was killed, or maybe who he was meeting in the middle of the night at Death's Door. If it wasn't Severino Rossi.

There was a good chance it was, I had to admit. The war pushes people right to the edge. Some, like the mother with her two children, hang on right at the precipice, fingers dug into the slippery clay of life. Others, seeing only the certainty of death, lash out like a drowning man climbing on the back of his rescuer, desperate to grab a few seconds of breath and life. Was Severino Rossi drowning when he met Corrigan? From what I'd learned from Diana, there was no drowning man like a Jew on the run in Nazi-occupied Europe.

I replaced Corrigan's toiletries, feeling Bruzzone's eyes on my every move. I checked the bookshelf, fanning pages, looking for anything interesting. Nothing but scraps of paper floated to the floor, bookmarks and notes, hastily scrawled comments about the text. The detritus of a scholarly mind.

"Find anything, Kaz?" I asked, more out of boredom than anything. Searching a room is dreary business. The pieces of someone's life after he's died take on a weighted, lonely feel. As if a matchbox or a pencil were suddenly more important since it may have been the last thing the dead guy used, the warmth of his touch still fresh, clinging to the wood or paper. It ought to be the other way around. They're junk now, ready to be swept away. Useless, and sadder than they should be.

"Nothing, Billy. The usual." He was going through Corrigan's clothes, checking pockets, socks, and the normal contents of a man's dresser.

"How long do you expect to be?" Monsignor Bruzzone asked, leaning in the doorway.

"Not much longer, I'd say. We might have better luck at his office."

"That may not be," Bruzzone said. "His work was transferred to another monsignor. He went through all of Edward's papers and cleaned out his desk. Feel free to look, but I doubt anything is left. We did not think there would be anything of importance regarding his murder." He gave an apologetic shrug.

We kept at it, finding nothing. Corrigan did have a well-used street map of Rome, but there were no marks, no cryptic references to Rudder, the OSS, or a radio. Nothing but creases and folds, which showed that he must have carried it with him a lot. I stuck it in my pocket. You never know.

"I will return shortly, gentlemen," Bruzzone said. "My own rooms are down the hall and I cannot watch this any longer. I know you must, but forgive me, seeing you handling Edward's things is too much." He shut the door, and we heard him walking down the corridor.

"Emotional fellow," I said.

"Southern Europeans are more emotional," Kaz said. "Or I should say, they show their emotions. The farther north, the more contained we are. For me, I should be glad to have you search my effects if I am murdered."

"Good to know, Kaz. But try and leave a clue or two, will you? Corrigan wasn't much help in that department." I put the cushions back, coming up with one five-lira coin and a ticket stub from the Teatro Reale dell'Opera. "Let's go and put the monsignor out of his misery."

As I went to open the door, I noticed a coat hanging from one of two hooks. I'd missed it when the door was open. When I checked, I felt something small and hard in the inside pocket. I knew right away that this was something which didn't belong in the Spartan room of a priest.

"Kaz, do you remember what was listed as Severino Rossi's occupation on his passport?"

"Yes, he was a jeweler. Why?"

"This is why," I said, holding what to my eye looked like a flawless two-carat diamond. I'd seen a few diamonds in my time on the force, and I knew quality because thieves knew quality. No self-respecting thief went for the cheap stuff.

"What is it worth?" Kaz asked.

"Maybe a thousand smackers or so. If Rossi was a jeweler, he may have had more. The question is, why did Corrigan have this one?"

"Are you done?" Bruzzone asked from the hallway. I slipped the diamond in my pocket and signaled Kaz to keep mum. No need to spread the word around.

"Yes, all done," I said as we left the room, thinking that Bruzzone had left just in time to avoid disappointment. "You can lock up now."

"You found nothing?"

"No, Monsignor. Thank you for helping, though. I know it was difficult."

"Life is difficult, when we are tested. And these days, the Lord tests us constantly." He inserted the key, the old lock resisted, grinding metal on metal until it gave way and the bolt fell into place.

CHAPTER SEVENTEEN

"KAZ, SNOOP AROUND and find out who's in charge of keys around here. There's got to be somebody who hands them out and keeps track of them."

"Do you think someone planted the diamond?"

The wind whipped our cassocks against our legs and sent the spray from a nearby fountain across our path as we made our way back to the German College.

"Could be," I said. "But first I'd like to know if there are other keys floating around out there. If there are, then the field is wide open. If not, it's more likely Corrigan had the diamond, which would establish a relationship between him and Severino Rossi."

"But the diamond could be for anything," Kaz said. "A gift, or to buy food for other refugees. It does not mean Monsignor Corrigan was corrupt."

"You're right. Gems make for great portable currency. Easily hidden, always valuable. Nothing wrong in Corrigan having them, but it does link him to Rossi, which is something we didn't have before."

"Right. I will go back to the palace and see if there is a porter who may know about the keys. Where will you be?"

"Wherever Monsignor O'Flaherty is," I said.

I found him right where the nuns at the German College said he'd be—at the top step leading up to Saint Peter's Basilica, not far from Death's Door. He wasn't hard to spot, with his red-and-black monsignor's outfit and wide-brimmed hat, not to mention his tall, athletic frame. He held an open Bible in his hands, his head bowed, but as I approached I could see his eyes traveling across the square, scanning the thin crowd.

"Good morning, Father Boyle," O'Flaherty said. "What can I do for you?" His eyes flickered in my direction, then shifted to the people wandering through the square, glancing occasionally at the German paratroopers patrolling the white demarcation line.

"Waiting for someone, Monsignor?" I asked, avoiding his question for now.

"In a manner of speaking, yes. I wait here for two hours every day, in case some weary traveler needs my help. The time and place are known to those in Rome who help us, and they send the poor souls my way."

"How many have come your way?"

"Hundreds. More, most likely, if I gave in to the sin of pride and kept count."

"Are they all hidden within the Vatican?" I asked, as a cold breeze snapped at our cassocks.

"Oh no, they'd be hanging out the windows, Father Boyle. We bring them in, feed and clothe them, and then take them to safe houses in the city. As safe as can be, at least."

"How do you feed them all? It must be tough."

"That it is. We have couriers who bring money to the families who are hiding prisoners and to the religious houses that have taken in refugees and escapees. It's a dangerous business, to be sure."

"Monsignor, I have to ask you something, and I can't explain much about it." I hoped O'Flaherty wouldn't ask too many questions. I trusted him, but it was dangerous for too many people to be in on this secret.

"Go ahead, son. No reason you shouldn't add to the mysteries of the world."

"Is there a Sister Justina among those who help you?" That was the name Diana used, taken from a nun she'd met from Brindisi who had taught her the local dialect.

"Ah, so that is why you are so curious about any nuns who have been arrested, is it?"

"Yes, Monsignor." I didn't know what else to say. I needed O'Flaherty's help, but I couldn't explain why. It wouldn't make sense anyway, and he might think it too dangerous to take a chance on a phony priest he'd just met.

"You are a spy, Billy." He said it softly and simply. Not an accusation, merely a statement.

"I am not who I say I am, yes. But within these walls, I don't think of myself as a spy."

"Outside, the Germans would. And they would shoot you for it."

"Yes, I know."

"Of course. Any spy would be aware of the consequences." He let the words hang there, his gaze fixed on mine. He knew. Maybe not the details, but he knew. Which I didn't mind, since there was no pity in his eyes, which meant Diana was not dead. Yet.

"I love her," I said, whispering as if in the confessional. "Tell me how I can help her."

"Do you now, lad? Really love her? In this time of killing and desecration, you hold love in your heart? Or is it guilt, or lust, or any of those other terrible sins that drive men?"

"Monsignor, I was brought up to respect the Church and those who serve her," I said, barely containing the fury building within me. "But even given your faith and your good works, who are you to question me like that?"

"A poor sinner who wonders at his own motivations, late at night, when sleep won't come, when I wonder if my actions have caused others to suffer and die." O'Flaherty rubbed his eyes, as he must have done in those small hours of the morning, awake with his thoughts. "Do you ever have such thoughts, Billy?"

"No," I said. "What keeps me awake is the thought that I might not do enough, or worse yet, nothing at all. Maybe it is guilt."

"Not at all, lad. Guilt is for what you've done in the past. Fear is what you suffer from now. Fear of what may come, regardless of your efforts."

"What I fear most may have already happened."

"No, it hasn't," O'Flaherty said in a low voice that the wind nearly carried off. "Look there, do you see that fellow in the brown coat and cap?"

I was dumbstruck, wanting to ask more, but his voice held an urgency that I couldn't resist. I followed his gaze and spotted the man amidst a crowd of older women.

"Yes," I said. "Are you sure, about Sister Justina?"

"Later," he said.

We watched as the man in the brown coat detached himself from the group and wandered close to one of the Swiss Guard at his post near the bronze doors. The guard looked up toward Monsignor O'Flaherty, and the man headed our way.

"Another guest," O'Flaherty said. "The Swiss Guard are under orders to turn away anyone seeking asylum. Which they do, following their orders to the letter. They also mention that they may wish to return during the times I stand here, to gather them in."

"You know how to walk a fine line, Monsignor."

"It's all about having friends in high places who can adjust the line when needed." He raised his eyes and looked at the Papal Palace, rising above the north side of the colonnade. I caught a glance of a figure in white, standing at an open window. Then he was gone.

"Was that the Pope?" I asked.

"His Holiness himself," O'Flaherty said. "He watches me most days. We both act the part of the careful shepherd. You need a haircut. Come to my room tonight. Rino will give you a trim."

"What? Wait—"

O'Flaherty flashed a grin as he descended the steps to greet the guy in the brown coat, steering him through the Arch of the Bells to a safe haven. I wondered if I could bring Diana to safety as well, get her to neutral territory. Anywhere but in the Regina Coeli. It seemed possible, now that O'Flaherty confirmed she was alive, and I was so close. I needed to find the right way in. As for the haircut, I had no idea what O'Flaherty's game was. But I'd play it, that I knew for sure.

Thoughts of Diana preyed on my mind as I stood looking out over the square and down the long avenue that led to the Tiber River. All I had to do was head that way, take a right, and in a few minutes I could knock on the prison door. Or walk under the windows, calling for Sister Justina. Foolish thoughts, but they were all I had.

A prayer wouldn't hurt, I thought, as I walked into Saint Peter's Basilica. Saint Jude, the patron saint of lost causes and long shots, might give a listen if I sent up a prayer from here. Inside, it was another world. Hushed. Magnificent. Huge. Marble floors that reflected like glass, statues and paintings adorned with gold. I walked along the nave, watching two German officers, cameras around their necks, consulting a guidebook and speaking in whispers as they stood at the Chapel of the Pieta. The sculpture of Mary, with the body of Jesus draped across her lap, silenced even the conquerors. I had to pull myself away from that terrible beauty of a woman mourning her son and move on, not liking to be so close to my enemies, even here, in the safest of sanctuaries. Or was it death that drew my eye?

I came closer to the tomb of Saint Peter, if I remembered my Sunday school lessons right. It was in front of the massive Papal Altar, with four black-and-gold curved columns reaching to the ceiling under the great dome. At that moment, sunlight streamed in from the windows at the base of the dome, lighting the people standing underneath, bathing them in luminous brilliance. I spotted Kaz, shoulder to shoulder with Princess Nini, their necks craned as they studied the altar.

I wasn't as close as I'd thought. The scale of the basilica threw me off as the vastness and grandeur of the building overwhelmed my senses. Kaz and the princess were tiny, as if they were miles away, or was it a trick of the light? I looked up to the ceiling and the room swirled around me, the colors thick and heavy, the weight of centuries pressing on me. I covered my eyes and looked again, and Kaz was still distant, mingling and disappearing into a crowd as clouds killed the sunlight, turning the interior into a cold, gray murkiness.

I left the holy place as if it spit me out.

I sat on the cold steps, my head in my hands. Something terrible had happened to Diana, I was sure of it. It wasn't the Pieta, or the Germans, or the dazzling light. It was a scream in my brain, and I was certain where it was coming from.

The Regina Coeli.

CHAPTER EIGHTEEN

I WANDERED THROUGH the gardens, making my way back
to the German College. My brain was in high gear trying to figure
some angle that would get Diana out of that damned prison. But
this wasn't my town and I had less pull here than a hooker in a
monastery.

"Father Boyle," said a voice from behind. I nearly jumped out of
my skin. It was Robert Brackett, the American deputy chargé
d'affaires. I didn't like being surprised, especially by a heavy-footed
civilian. Stay focused, I told myself. Diana worried me, a lot. But I
needed to worry about a murder as well. Not to mention the murderer.

"Out for a walk, Mr. Brackett?"

"I was looking for you, actually. You asked about seeing Soletto."

"Right," I said. I'd forgotten we'd asked Brackett to arrange that,
since he seemed less than enthusiastic about our investigation. "You
have any news?"

"Yes, he's agreed. I had to go through the Pontifical Commission
for the Vatican City State," Brackett said, knocking ashes from his
pipe and tucking it into a pocket of his rumpled suit.

"That's a mouthful," I said, pleasantly surprised at Brackett's
sudden interest.

"It did take some talking. The commission is the executive
branch of the Vatican government, and they take any hint of a

violation to their sovereignty very seriously. But given the severity of the crime, they approved it, with one restriction."

"What's that?"

"A representative of the commission must be present at all times, to insure that the rights and privileges of the Vatican City State are respected. That's an exact quote, by the way."

"So who's my minder?"

"Bishop Krunoslav Zlatko. I'm not sure if they did us any favors with that one," Brackett said.

"Why?"

We sat on a bench near a grove of small pines as the wind swayed the branches, creating a sound like waves on the shore. But Brackett didn't look like he was having a day at the beach.

"Zlatko is here as the representative of Archbishop Ivan Šarić in Sarajevo, Yugoslavia," he said, as if that explained everything. "Or, as he'd insist, in Croatia. Zlatko is one of the Ustashi. You know what they are?"

"Yeah," I said, remembering what Sterling Hayden and his Partisans had told me. "Killers."

"There are a lot of killers these days," Brackett said. "The Ustashi are a fanatical Croatian militia. They hate Serbs, Jews, and the Eastern Orthodox Church with equal passion. They've killed thousands, tens of thousands, maybe more. As you can imagine, precise information is hard to come by."

"My guide to justice within the Vatican is one of them? Is that someone's idea of a joke?"

"It may well be," Brackett said. "There are factions within factions among the cardinals. Some support the Croatian state and the Ustashi as a bulwark against Communism. They hate Tito and Stalin, and the feeling is mutual. If a strong Catholic state gets created out of the ruins of Yugoslavia, then they figure the godless Marxists can be held at bay."

"So thousands of bodies are a small price to pay?"

"Yes. Especially when the bodies don't contain Catholic souls. The Croatian government has a policy of dealing in thirds. One third of the Serbs to be driven out, one third to be forcibly converted to the Roman Catholic Church, and one third to be killed. There are cardinals within the Holy See who consider it a bargain."

"Let me guess. Those are the same cardinals who would not care for the work Corrigan was doing with Bruzzone and O'Flaherty," I said.

"Now you're getting the hang of how things work around here. But Bruzzone has eased up a bit on the cloak-and-dagger stuff. He hasn't left the Holy See for months."

"Are the police on the lookout for him?"

"That's what I figure. Word must have gotten around. O'Flaherty himself takes to a disguise now and then, so he won't be recognized visiting his safe houses."

"These guys deserve a medal," I said.

Brackett shrugged, as if their work was nothing remarkable. "Now don't expect Zlatko to be a big help. Of course, the official line is that he speaks good English and Italian, and since he doesn't know the people involved, he can be fair to all sides—your need to investigate, the Vatican's desire for secrecy. Say, you happen to have any cigarettes?"

"No, I don't smoke. Does this have the Pope's approval?"

"All this goes on within the Pontifical Commission and the Secretariat of State. Pius is above it all, or so he lets the world think. Different factions vie for dominance, and meanwhile people die while we sit in this pleasant garden."

"That's the way of the world," I said, not wanting to get drawn into Vatican politics. It wasn't a fight I could win, and I didn't want to end up like Brackett, bemoaning my fate to whoever would listen and bumming smokes. "Right now I'm only interested in one dead person, and that's Monsignor Corrigan. If it takes an Ustashi bishop to get me to Soletto, then so be it."

"Only trying to give you the lay of the land, Boyle. You wanted to see Soletto, go see him. You'll find Zlatko in the Governatorato building. I've done my bit, now you do the rest. Jeez, what I wouldn't give for a Lucky Strike."

I left Brackett on the bench, content he'd done his duty, dreaming of American cigarettes. I made my way beneath the shadow of Saint Peter's and went in the front entrance of the Governatorato this time. A gendarme at the door directed me to Zlatko's office and I walked between large pillars, across the marble emblem of the Vatican on the floor, the crossed keys of Saint Peter gleaming up at me. Yesterday we'd been snuck in the side door, and today I was on my way to see a bishop. Funny how quickly I'd become accustomed to the place, confident in my false identity, at home with the solemnity. Everything about the Vatican was majestic, constructed to an enormous scale, one measured by centuries and souls. It felt natural to bow my head as I walked, to give deference to the art, beauty, and order all around me. Maybe it was being brought up as an altar boy. More likely it was my desire for a place of peace and calm amidst the world at war. Either way, it wasn't the right move. If there was a killer prowling the holy grounds, I needed my eyes up and wide open. I needed to be afraid, not awed.

As I arrived at Zlatko's door, I tried to shake the cobwebs from my mind. Diana wasn't far away, I reminded myself, and she was hardly calm and at peace. Corrigan was very far away, maybe at peace, who really knew? Here, something corrupt lurked beneath the surface. I had to protect myself from being lulled by sanctity and Renaissance architecture. I took a deep breath, and knocked.

Opening the door, I braced myself to see a stern-faced monster, a fanatic Croatian fresh from the crusades. That wasn't what the petite guy behind the desk looked like at all.

"Ah, you must be the American," Zlatko said, in a delicate, airy voice, as if he might break into song at any moment. He set his pen down and invited me to sit. The room was plain—a wooden desk, a couple of chairs, a picture of Pius XII on one wall, a crucifix on the other.

"The passport is Irish, Bishop Zlatko," I said. "I'm sure you understand."

"Of course, and I will play the charade with you, Father Boyle, and help you any way I can." Zlatko folded his hands on the desk and took a breath. He was small. Thin, with delicate hands. His close-cropped hair was flecked with gray, but his face was smooth, the skin pink and healthy. The kind of complexion some priests get, the ones who don't drink too much. I always figured it was from a life of being taken care of. No manual labor, not much wind and sun on your face, nuns keeping house, cooking your meals and washing your clothes. It was like looking at a boy in a middle-aged body. But the eyes were deep and aware, no childish twinkle at home there.

"I understand you will be my escort when I speak to Commissario Soletto," I said.

"Yes, that is a good way to put it," he said, the only trace of an accent being a hardness in the consonants. "The *commissario* speaks only a little English, so I can assist with translation as well. Have you had any success in your investigation?"

"Nothing yet," I said. "Which is why I need to find out what the Vatican police know."

"Do you think it is true, what they say about the Jew?"

"I only know what Soletto's opinion is, and that's secondhand. What do you think, Bishop?"

"Who can understand the nonbeliever? The Jew, the Serb, the Protestant—none are of the true Church, and I have pity for them. Perhaps in his twisted mind, this young man struck out at the hand which helped him, not understanding Christian charity."

"If he didn't do it, there is a murderer walking free, within these walls."

"Then I pray for his heart to be healed. I am more concerned with your presence here. Have your brought your conflict with you? Shall you divide us, or bring ruin down upon this house?"

"That's not my plan. Justice is all I want."

"Justice often requires sacrifice. What will you ask of us? Will you push the Holy See closer to taking sides in the war?"

"I have no such grand plans, Bishop. If justice sounds too threatening, then I'll settle for the truth." *Even though I know it is a long shot*, I wanted to add.

"Ha! That is even worse. Your truth, Serbian truth, Italian truth, English truth, my truth—which shall it be?"

"Good point, Bishop. From what I hear, your truth is pretty rough on a lot of people back in Croatia."

"We are a new nation, and sometimes nations in their youth go too far. Perhaps we have. Still, Croatia stands for civilization amidst chaos. The chaos of Communism, Zionism, the false Eastern Church. After all, it was His Holiness himself who called Croatia the outpost of Christianity. We live in the wilderness, my American friend. Our backs to the Adriatic, Serbs in our midst, godless Russians to the east. Do not judge us for defending our lives and faith."

"There's a lot I don't know," I admitted. It was true enough, and the last thing I needed was to pick a fight with my ticket to Soletto, so I backed off.

"And I as well," Zlatko said. "You have become acquainted with Monsignor O'Flaherty, haven't you? What is he like?"

"He seems to have a good heart," I said. "As every priest should."

"Ah, yes. I understand he brings escaped prisoners and criminals into the Vatican. Sanctuary for all."

"I wouldn't call them criminals," I said. O'Flaherty's activities were an open secret, so it was useless to deny it.

"The civil authority in Rome has ordered all Jews to be transported north. Those who do not comply are in breach of the law. Therefore, criminals."

"Do you know what that means, Bishop? Transport north?"

"That is not the point. The Germans run Rome and make the laws. The warmhearted monsignor is risking the Holy See itself with his actions. He is violating their laws and the neutrality of the Vatican State. As are you, Father Boyle." Zlatko smiled apologetically.

"I'm here to solve a murder, not settle a question of diplomacy, Bishop. There is a logic to what you say. But there is also logic to what O'Flaherty is doing."

"And what logic is that?"

"Isn't there something in the Bible along the lines of 'I was a stranger, and ye took me in'?"

"Yes, the logic of Matthew," Zlatko said, closing his eyes and reciting. "And the King shall answer and say unto them, verily I say unto you, inasmuch as ye have done unto one of the least of these my brethren, ye have done unto me."

"The least of our brethren are everywhere these days, I'd say."

"*My* brethren are not the heathen Jews or godless Communists. Certainly not the heretical Protestants or Eastern Orthodox Serbs. My brethren are my fellow Catholics. You, Father Boyle, or whatever your real name is, you are among my brethren." Zlatko leaned forward, his eyes locking on mine in what he must have thought was brotherly love.

"Wasn't it Saint Peter himself who told us to practice fervent charity, to cover the multitude of sins? To give hospitality without grudging? Isn't that was Monsignor O'Flaherty is doing?" The good saint's words were always part of the talk Sister Mary Margaret gave in school about giving to the poor and to the church, although not necessarily in that order.

"You know your Bible, Father Boyle. As does the devil."

"Only bits and pieces from Sunday school, Bishop. I was an altar boy, but Father McGonigle did call me the devil's own once or twice."

"Of that I have no doubt," Zlatko said with a sly grin. "You have a pleasant way about you, Father Boyle, I must say, in spite of your misguided belief in the monsignor. Although I doubt he would be so successful without the help of the English ambassador and his disappearing butler."

"Disappearing? Do you mean John May? Where is he?"

"Oh, he is always somewhere. In Rome, or visiting the hiding places within the Holy See. I wonder how he has time to take care of the ambassador, don't you?"

"He seems quite capable, although I don't know much about butlers. I have a cousin who was a housemaid, though."

"You Irish are lighthearted, indeed. It must be from living on an island with a cold sea between you and your enemies. We Croats are too wary of knives at our throats to joke so much."

"Shouldn't we go find Soletto now?" I had to get out of there before I gave him a history lesson that might involve a right hook.

"Certainly, if now is convenient for you," Zlatko said. He stood, smoothing down his black cassock and adjusting the scarlet sash. Then he spoke, standing with his hands clasped behind his back. "One thing you should remember about Saint Peter. He was first called Simon, and only later became known as Peter. When Jesus said to him, 'on this rock I will build my church,' he may have been making a joke at his disciple's expense."

"What kind of joke?"

"Peter—*Petros*—means rock in Greek. It may have been a commentary on Simon Peter's mental prowess more than his steadfastness. Remember, he was the one who denied Jesus three times after he was arrested."

"I don't follow your meaning, Bishop."

"As a matter of doctrine, the Pope is infallible. But we should also remember that the Church of Rome was founded by a mortal, one who needed help and assistance, as does the Holy Father today."

He smiled and bobbed his head, letting me know he was ready to leave. A gentleman. He'd never raised his voice, never shown a glimpse of anger. But as we left, I knew that hatred simmered beneath that smooth skin and that soft voice, and a line had been drawn. I also had the feeling that I'd been interrogated, and that Zlatko had gotten a lot more out of the conversation than I had.

CHAPTER NINETEEN

THE TRIBUNAL PALACE that housed the Gendarmerie Corps was a squat, five-story structure that would have been at home in any city stateside—plain and unassuming, with a main entrance like any other police headquarters. A flag flapping in the breeze, guards at the door, and a handful of officers off to the side, smoking cigarettes and talking. They glanced at us, with that sideways look cops give when assessing a newcomer or a potential threat. Their eyes didn't linger. Bishops were commonplace, and another harmless priest didn't rate a second look.

If it weren't for their fancy-pants uniforms, the Vatican gendarmes could have been cops anywhere. But they still wore a getup from the last century, with white pants and a black short coat, complete with gold epaulets and silver buttons. Napoleon would have felt right at home under one of their red-plumed hats. As a guard opened the door for Bishop Zlatko, I noted their sidearms were strictly twentieth century, .32-caliber Berettas in shiny, black leather holsters.

Soletto's office was on the third floor. The walls along the corridor were hung with the portraits of generations of Vatican cops, mostly dressed in the same getup. The floor was marble, inlaid with the crossed-keys crest of the Holy See. A guard at the double doors to Soletto's office opened them for Zlatko, with me in tow. Were we expected, or was the bishop a regular visitor? With Soletto supposedly pro-fascist, and Zlatko friendly with the pro-Axis Croatian government, it made sense. The door shut behind us with a decisive, quiet sound, the kind that comes from centuries of craftsmanship, not the low-bid, thin sound of a Boston city government office.

Soletto had himself a big piece of real estate at the corner of the building, and I almost had to squint to make him out across the expanse of carpet. His desk was right in front of a window with a magnificent view of Saint Peter's. The light shining in made it hard to focus on his features, and I could tell he knew it.

"*Benvenuto, Vescovo,*" Soletto said as he rose to greet the bishop. They exchanged rapid-fire Italian as we walked to the chairs set in front of the massive desk. Polished walnut with a deep, dark color, it was probably an antique when the Boyles were still in Ireland. It held one telephone, an ornate model with gleaming brass, a blotter, a fountain pen, and one folder, which took up about a tenth of the space. The rest Soletto probably used to check his reflection. He was a stocky fellow, with wiry, graying hair. He had the look of a politician about him, that attention to grooming that marks a guy who wants the world to notice him. Since there wasn't much ordinary criminal activity within the Holy See—no prostitutes, drinking, or gambling must do a lot to keep the crime rate down—I figured his job was mostly political, which maybe meant crooked too.

"My English, not good," Soletto said.

"*Il mio italiano non è perfetto,*" I said, trying to say the same thing back to him about my Italian. It was a practiced phrase, and got a laugh. Soletto opened a drawer, offered cigarettes, and he and Zlatko lit up. They were Echt Orients, a common German brand. Not a good start.

"Please thank the *commissario* for seeing me," I said. "Any help he can provide will be greatly appreciated."

Zlatko translated, and Soletto blew smoke in my face as he answered in staccato Italian.

"Commissario Soletto says he is seeing you as instructed by the Pontifical Commission," Zlatko said. "He considers the investigation closed and the guilty party has been turned over to the proper authorities. As you would be," Zlatko added with a hint of apology in his voice, "if he had the authority to do so."

"I understand," I said. "I was a police officer myself before the war, and I would not stand for any hint of interference either." I waited for that to get through, hoping for some brotherly solidarity.

"The *commissario* says you are still a spy now, and should be handed over to the Germans for violating the neutrality of the Holy See. He says that as a fellow officer of the law, you should understand his position."

The Boyle charm was obviously failing. Zlatko gave a little shrug, as if to say, *What did you expect?*

"Ask him what specific evidence he has against Severino Rossi, and if I may see it," I said. I'd dropped the word "please." That would show him.

As Zlatko spoke, Soletto turned to look out the window, admiring his view. From here, I could almost see where Rossi had been found among the colonnades.

"*È Ebreo,*" Soletto said. "*Con il sangue sulle sue mani.*"

"He is a Jew," Zlatko said. "With blood on his hands."

"Really? On his hands? I thought it was only on his clothes? Or are we talking metaphorically?"

"Do you really want me to ask him that question?"

"For laughs, yes."

Zlatko did so, and Soletto answered angrily. "He says it makes no difference," Zlatko said. "Rossi was covered in blood, Monsignor Corrigan was dead. It was enough for him. He suggests you take matters up with the Gestapo if you wish to learn more."

"Does he know if Rossi is still alive?" As I spoke, I thought I saw a reaction on Soletto's face. Did he understand English better than he let on? If so, what was it about the question that caused that quick blink, the look away, as if he had something to hide? Or something he didn't want to face.

"He does not know," Zlatko said when the translation was complete. "The Gestapo does not keep the Holy See informed on such matters."

"One last question, then. Ask him why he thinks Monsignor Corrigan dragged himself up to the top step at Death's Door." Zlatko ran that by Soletto, but I'd seen his eye widen as soon as I said it. His English was maybe not as poor as he claimed.

"Where did you hear that?" Soletto growled, waving off Zlatko.

"Is it the truth?"

"There was a struggle. Monsignor Corrigan, he bled everywhere. *Molto sangue.*" He shrugged at the sadness of it all.

"I saw a distinct trail of blood in the photographs. The ones your gendarmes took."

"All you had to do was ask," Soletto said, stretching out his arms. "We would have provided them to you. You cannot rely on someone who takes bribes."

"I agree. Your English is very good, Commissario."

"There are so many Englishmen here these days, one has the opportunity to practice," Soletto said. "I would prefer to keep to Italian, but the *Inglesi* do not bother to learn it. You said that was your last question, yes?"

"You didn't really answer it. Are you certain Monsignor Corrigan did not move from where he was left?"

"He could not have. His injuries were too severe."

"Thank you for your time," I said, rising from my chair. There was something Soletto was hiding, something that made him nervous. There was no reason he should be, nothing that I could pin on him. Rossi was dead or in the Regina Coeli. Case closed.

Or was it? I felt for the diamond that was in my pocket. It was a long shot, but if Soletto was in cahoots with the killer, then a wedge between them might do the trick.

"By the way, have you found any more diamonds?"

"*Diamanti?*"

"Yeah, like this one." I held the sparkling gem up between my thumb and forefinger, letting it catch the light.

"More diamonds, you said?" Zlatko asked. "Where were the others?"

Soletto looked confused, his thick eyebrows knitted together.

"The killer—the real killer—hid them in the one place he knew was safe. Corrigan's room. He must have gotten in after you had it searched, Commissario. Or did you miss that loose floorboard? A small fortune, maybe more, I'm not a jeweler."

"Those diamonds are evidence!" Soletto bellowed, banging his fist on the table.

"But the case is closed, Commissario. You said so yourself. I will turn them over to the Pontifical Commission, as soon as my investigation is complete. *Buongiorno.*"

I walked out as calmly as I could. There was dead silence until I cleared the door, then more shouting and fist-banging, which told me our little chat had been worthwhile. I'd expected the cold shoulder, for a lot of reasons. A cop protecting his turf and pro-fascist tendencies were at the top of the list.

One thing I could always count on was greed. If there were more diamonds—and outside of a rich dame's ring, they seldom traveled alone—then I'd bet that's what the killer used to pay off Soletto. The phony line about more diamonds unaccounted for might lead Soletto to think the murderer was holding out on him. Or plant the idea he could squeeze him for more. Either way, my hope was that Soletto was now a loose cannon, rolling toward a killer who thought he was home free.

I made it outside without being arrested or shot, which was a relief. Now I had to find Kaz and see if he remembered to check on the keys, or if he'd spent the whole afternoon sightseeing with the princess. Then get a haircut, which might lead to information about Diana, although the connection was definitely lost on me.

I walked back to the scene of the crime to look at it again. I imagined it in the hours before dawn. Severino Rossi asleep, hidden behind one of the colonnades. Corrigan standing by the door, his killer close. They had to know each other, or at least the killer hadn't seemed a threat. It would have been easy enough to yell out, to attract the attention of one of the Swiss Guard, if not a nearby German. Interesting, I thought. This area was close enough to the border line that one of the Krauts on patrol could have seen or heard something.

Too much of a long shot, I decided, so I'd go back over the little I knew for sure.

Corrigan is stabbed, several times, until the knife finds its fatal mark. He collapses, and falls just inside the Gendarmerie jurisdictional line. Or drags himself there. I thought about the blood. There'd been a lot of it, from multiple stab wounds. I could see the killer removing his coat and laying it on the sleeping Rossi, then stealing off into the night, leaving behind a dead monsignor and a sleeping fugitive Jew, covered in a blood-soaked coat.

A scapegoat if there ever was one.

CHAPTER TWENTY

I FINALLY TRACKED Kaz down. Not by finding him, but by asking where Princess Nini Pallavicini hung her hat, beret, or tiara. Being the keen investigator that I am, I cornered Kaz in no time. He and the princess were having tea. My first success at detection in the Vatican.

The princess was housed in the Hospice Santa Marta, not far from the German College. Nuns in steel-blue habits with giant white coifs that looked like sails gathering wind worked in the ground-floor refectory, preparing food for the refugees and families of diplomats who were housed there. Kaz and his princess were in a nearby sitting room, sipping tea from delicate china, while Mary, holding the baby Jesus, looked down on them from an ancient painting.

"Father Boyle, please join us," she said.

"Thank you, Princess, but tea isn't my drink. I need to talk with Kaz, if you don't mind."

"Please, call me Nini. 'Princess' is so tiresome, and Piotr has told me some remarkable stories about you. I feel we are already friends."

"Okay, if you'll call me Billy," I said as I took a seat. "But don't believe everything he says."

"Then you are not General Eisenhower's nephew, and not the great American detective, second only to Dick Tracy?" Nini let a playful smile dance across her lips while Kaz blushed.

"Dick Tracy's only in the funny papers," I said. "And the general and I are distant cousins of some sort, but since he's older, I call him uncle, although not in public. It's not the kind of thing I spread around when I'm in a German-occupied city." I gave Kaz a hard glare, but I wasn't too worried about Nini blabbering to anyone. She looked like a dame who could take care of herself.

"I am sorry, Billy," Kaz said. "It came out in conversation."

"Don't worry about it," I said. "Did you manage to squeeze in any time to look into the matter we discussed, what with sightseeing and teatime?"

"Well, Nini did take a few minutes to show me the excavations in the necropolis under the basilica. Did you know they found what may be the bones of Saint Peter himself?"

"That's great, Kaz, but what about the keys?" Kaz was about the smartest guy I knew. That meant he knew a lot about everything, so sometimes it made it hard for him to focus on just one thing. Especially when a beautiful princess was leading the way.

"Yes, yes, the keys. We found the porter's office in the Medieval Palace. He keeps copies of all the keys hung on the wall behind his desk. He also delivers mail within the building, takes messages, and runs other errands."

"Not to mention he was sound asleep," Nini said. "We could have robbed the poor man blind."

"So anyone could have taken the keys to Corrigan's room, and replaced them?"

"It would be easy," Kaz said. "Within the Vatican, there has been little personal property or theft to worry about."

"Nini," I said, figuring Kaz had filled her in on everything by now, "have you heard anything about diamonds?"

"Other than wonder which Nazi swine stole mine? No. I am sure some of the refugees here have valuable jewels, simply because they are easy to carry and hide."

"Can you think of any reason why Monsignor Corrigan would have one in his room?"

"One makes little sense. If a refugee had diamonds, he might give them to a trusted person to sell for food or identity papers. But one? Let me see it." I gave her the diamond, and she held it up to the light. "Very nice. I can see no flaws. One diamond like this would fetch a good price. A handful of these, a fortune."

"Severino Rossi was a jeweler by trade," Kaz said, apparently having forgotten to share that tidbit.

"Well, he certainly knew his diamonds. It is quite beautiful."

"Had you met him?" I asked. "Helping Monsignor O'Flaherty, perhaps?"

"No, no one by that name. I do not know what he looked like, so I cannot say for certain."

"Where have you been, Billy?" Kaz asked, as Nini studied the glittering diamond.

"Turns out Brackett was actually useful. He got me in to see Soletto. I had to go with an escort from the Pontifical Commission, Bishop Zlatko. A real piece of work."

"Zlatko is pro-Nazi," Nini said. "He is practically an agent of the Croatian puppet state."

"He's also not too fond of Serbs, Jews, Protestants, and the Eastern Orthodox Church. And probably a few others we didn't get around to talking about."

"You must be careful, both of you," Nini said. "There are factions within the commission, and it is obvious that the pro-German side won out. Zlatko will report anything you learned."

"Well, that won't take long. Soletto clammed up, insisting he'd caught the right man. But why did the commission need to send Zlatko along? Soletto is pro-fascist, isn't he? An informer to the secret police?"

"Things are more subtle here, I am afraid," Nini said with a sigh. "Yes, Soletto has connections with the OVRA, the Fascist security force. But they are finished here, since Mussolini fell from power. The factions within the commission operate on another level. They act to steer the Pope one way or the other. To show favor to the Nazis, or the Allies, or to remain steadfastly neutral. All this is beyond a simple informer like Soletto."

"I'm beginning to think we're going to cause more trouble than this investigation is worth," I said. "So far, all I'm certain of is that Rossi didn't do it, unless he's the dumbest killer on record." I told them about my parting shot to Soletto, hoping he'd think his partner in crime was holding out on him.

"If there is a partner in crime," Kaz said. "Commissario Soletto may simply be doing his duty as best he can. Perhaps we are going about this backward, assuming he is in on it."

Backward. Kaz was right. I had something backward. "Kaz, you hit it out of the park with that one." They both looked at me with quizzical expressions. "Baseball. A home run. Anyway, we were puzzled as to why Corrigan dragged himself up the steps to the basilica."

"The blood trail I told you about," Kaz said to Nini, who nodded quickly.

"But we were looking at it backward. He didn't crawl. The killer dragged him up the steps. The struggle took place below Death's Door, but in order for it to come under Soletto's jurisdiction, the killer had to place the body on the steps of the basilica, since Saint Peter's Square itself comes under Italian authority. There was no reason to do that unless he could count on the chief gendarme to close the matter quickly. If the Gestapo or the Fascist police got involved, the whole thing could have spun out of control. This way, the killer was apprehended, declared guilty, and handed over to the Germans. Case closed."

"Piotr, a home run, how wonderful!" Nini said, patting Kaz's hand with hers. He blushed again.

"Oh, it was nothing," Kaz said, waving away the compliment while thoroughly enjoying it. "Your remark about there being more diamonds may work if Soletto is overly greedy, or quick to anger at having been given a paltry payoff."

"He is both," Nini said. "And I would not count on much from Mr. Brackett. That man is depressed much of the time. We don't see him for weeks, then suddenly he appears, full of ideas and schemes. None of them amount to much. Be careful of both men, they can lead only to trouble."

"We are forewarned," Kaz said gallantly. "Billy, Nini has a problem to discuss with us. She needs our help."

"It must be serious," I said, keeping to myself the thought that if Kaz could have handled it, he would have fallen over himself to impress his princess.

"You know we have hundreds of Jews, POWs, antifascists, and even some German deserters hidden within the Vatican," Nini began. "Monsignor O'Flaherty also has placed hundreds of others, mostly escaped British POWs, in hiding places throughout Rome."

"Yes. A huge undertaking," I said.

"Especially feeding all of them. We give money to families in Rome to buy what extra food they can, but here within the Vatican walls, everything has to be carefully hoarded and distributed fairly. The bombings have disrupted food deliveries, and there is little to be had in the markets when we can get to them."

"Billy," Kaz said, "someone is stealing food, here in this building. From a locked room."

"Who keeps the keys here?" Given what Kaz had found in the palace, any number of people could have helped themselves.

"Sister Louise and I have the only keys to the storeroom. In better times, this building is a dormitory for religious visitors. Since so many people pass through, they keep things well guarded."

"How many people know about the storeroom?" I asked.

"It is not a secret, but we don't announce it either. All the sisters and those who help gather the food know of it. It is in the basement, and most residents have no reason to go down there."

"How much is missing?"

"I noticed it three weeks ago," the princess said. "At first only a few things, and I thought perhaps I miscounted. But every few days, more things went missing. A tin of jam or a bit of cheese. I was worried that one of our helpers was taking them, but I couldn't believe it. We all work so hard to bring the food in, and there is never enough." Her hand went up to her mouth, and for a brief moment the stress of danger and responsibility was etched on her face.

"Nini does not think it is one of her people," Kaz said. "The thefts last week were worse, more food taken, the best delicacies. Meat, cheese, tins of fish."

"The meat and fish are carefully doled out, so everyone gets proper nutrition," Nini said. "It could become serious."

"And you find the room locked every time?"

"Yes, there is no trace of forced entry."

"Let me be the judge of that. Show us."

Nini led us downstairs, into a small basement room filled with discarded furniture covered in dust and cobwebs. A workbench ran along one wall, with old tools and wood shavings scattered over it. One bare bulb lit the scene, dimly illuminating a single stout wooden door. Nini reached for her key, but I raised my hand.

"Wait," I said. "Do you have a flashlight, or a match?"

"What?" she said.

"A torch," Kaz supplied. "*Torcia.*"

"No, but I do have a lighter." She flicked it on as I knelt to study the lock. It was an old one, probably from the past century.

"It's a lever tumbler lock," I said, squinting to make out the marks around it in the faint glow. The light went out as it got too hot for Nini to hold, and Kaz took it from her.

"Look," I said, pointing to the scrapes around the lock. "It's been picked."

"Those little scratches?" Kaz said. "They could be from missing the keyhole in the dark. That door has probably been there for hundreds of years."

"Yeah, but this lock wasn't invented until the end of the eighteenth century. In any case, when you miss with a key, it does leave a mark, but a small ding, not a long scratch like these."

"What are they from?" Nini asked, leaning in as Kaz had to let the lighter go out.

"Lock-picking tools."

"Who would have tools like that in the Vatican?" Kaz said.

"Anyone who knows how to use them would know how to make them," I said, walking over to the workbench. I rummaged around until I came up with a length of thick, heavy wire. An awl. A hacksaw, and pieces of scrap metal. "Everything a knowledgeable lock picker would need. Or locksmith, the only difference being in how the knowledge is used."

"The thief made his own tools, here?" Kaz asked.

"Well, I doubt he came with them. All he needed for that lock was a tension wrench and a pick. It's not a simple lock, but for someone who knows what he's doing, it wouldn't take long. Quicker each time."

"So he simply pops down here whenever he's hungry," Kaz said. "Selfish of him."

"So likely not a locksmith," I said. "Most likely a B&E guy who never got caught."

"Breaking and entering," Kaz said, for Nini's benefit.

"Luckily he hasn't taken much, but what he has was the best of it," she said.

"You said the amounts increased recently," I said. "Would that have included a whole salami?"

"Yes," Nini said. "Even Dick Tracy couldn't have figured that out. How did you know?"

"A guess," I said.

"A deduction," Kaz corrected.

Back upstairs, we sat around as the sisters cleared the tea tray. I was getting hungry, and didn't argue when they returned with bread, a bit of cheese, olives, and wine. Deducing is hard work.

"What next?" Kaz asked.

"We wait. And watch."

"Who?"

"The gardener's house," I said in a low voice, putting a finger to my lips.

"That young girl?" Kaz said in disbelief.

"That young girl, who this morning held a bag of salami and other goodies. I didn't think anything of it until Nini mentioned how rationed the meat was."

"Rosana? She has two young children. How could she...?" Nini stopped herself, then said, "Aha."

"Yeah. We may have a love-struck thief. Or one who is trying to impress her."

"There are enough women here among the diplomat families who would give everything for that food. Some enthusiastically. But Rosana has been through a great deal. I don't see her in that light."

"How long has she been here?" I asked.

"Almost two weeks. She came in with the Sunday crowds, and asked a passing priest for help. Luckily he was a friend of Monsignor Corrigan. We were so full up, we had to put her and the children in the gardener's cottage. She has been cooking and cleaning for him, and I think he likes the company."

"Where did she come from?"

"I don't know. Somewhere in the north. She's Jewish, and when her husband was taken she decided to make her way to Rome. She had false papers, but they were not very good. It's a miracle she made it. Should I ask her who gave her the food?"

"No," I said. "She may want to protect him. Kaz, why don't you watch the gardener's place. Nini, do you have any food you could bring in, something to tempt him with?"

"No, but I'm sure John May can raid the ambassador's pantry for a good cause. I will get something tonight and bring it through the refectory when everyone is eating." She picked up a wineglass, her small hand as delicate as the crystal.

"Perfect. Kaz, you find a spot tonight and keep watch. Be careful, and come get me once you spot this guy. Remember, he's a professional criminal, so we don't know what to expect."

"What are you going to do?" he asked.

"According to Monsignor O'Flaherty, I'm going to visit him and get a haircut."

"Oh, you'll like Rino. A charming man," Nini said.

"You know him?" I asked.

"Yes, Rino Messina is one of us. He gives haircuts to the refugees and is a courier for the monsignor. He's also a very good businessman."

"How so?"

"He got the contract to provide barbering services at the Regina Coeli prison. Twice a month he spends a full day there. Rino gives the guards a trim, free of charge. He has the run of the place. You and he should find much to talk about."

"Has he seen . . . ?" I stopped and looked at Kaz.

"Yes, Billy, I told Nina about Sister Justina."

"Has he seen her?" I asked. Hoped. Begged.

"Yes, after she was first taken in a roundup. She was not harmed."

"But that was a while ago."

"Yes. We have had no word since then. Which is not always bad news," she hastened to add. "Relatives are always notified when a prisoner dies in custody. There is hope, Billy." She let her hand rest on my arm, as I tried to find any hope in the fact that Diana was alive but lost in the depths of a Gestapo prison.

CHAPTER TWENTY-ONE

KAZ AND I had dinner in the refectory. Nini served food along-side the nuns and we both took small portions, not wanting to appear greedy after they'd already fed us lunch. It wasn't much. Pasta with a bit of olive oil, garlic, and turnips. It filled the belly, but I found myself getting even angrier at the thief who deprived these people of something extra.

At the long tables, families sat together, parents and children speaking Spanish and Portuguese, languages of the latest nations whose diplomats had sought refuge here. A group of Italian men sat together, looking dejected, eating in silence. Some were dressed in worn suits, others in uniform. After the fall of Mussolini, some Italian troops fought against the Germans when they entered Rome. It was a brave stand, but not well planned. These men were the lucky survivors. The rest of the gathered diners were escaped POWs, their uniforms cleaned and mended, but showing the wear and tear from months or years of captivity. It was easy to spot the newest POWs. Their uniforms were in better shape and they still had muscle on their bones. The others, especially the Eighth Army veterans of North Africa, were thin and gaunt, their light desert khaki shirts barely held together. There were a lot of Brits, with a sprinkling of Americans, mostly airmen who'd been shot down over Italy.

"Do you think the thief is here?" Kaz asked.

"If he's housed here, yes. He couldn't afford to stay away from a meal; it would arouse suspicion."

"Perhaps it's one of those poor fellows captured at Tobruk two years ago," he said. "I could understand that. They look half starved."

"Maybe. But they probably made it through by sticking together, not going each man for himself. Remember, the thefts were small stuff, not enough for a whole squad."

"So we need to look for a loner," Kaz said. "Maybe someone who was recently captured."

"Why do you say that?"

"Because he would have had less time to adapt to privation. Or perhaps he was never captured, but made his way here after he was shot down. He'd owe less to others if he hadn't shared in their suffering."

"Good thinking, Kaz! You're getting to be one helluva detective." He blushed again, and I caught his eye as Nini passed with a tray of dishes. Her smile was dazzling, and it was all for Kaz. "You are one lucky guy, you know that?"

His face went blank, and I knew it hadn't been the right thing to say. A guy with good luck didn't lose his entire family to the Nazis, and then watch the woman he loved die in an automobile explosion.

"I'm sorry, Kaz, I didn't mean . . ."

"No, Billy, it is all right. I know what you meant, and I feel it too. But I feel pulled in two directions. The past contains deep sorrows, and the present offers a chance at joy. I have to convince myself that I am not betraying one for the other."

"Kaz," I said, leaning in and placing my hand on his shoulder. "There is not a single person in your past who would not want you to have joy in your life. You owe it to them to *live*, not simply exist."

"I know," Kaz said in a small, hesitant voice. "But it is so much easier to not feel anything. To not care about living removed all burdens. Now, my heart breaks every time I see her."

"Because she reminds you of loving Daphne."

"Yes."

"Whom you will never forget, until your dying day, no matter what."

Kaz didn't reply. He looked at me from behind steel-rimmed spectacles, his eyes moist. A lift of the eyebrow, a nod, and that was enough. I let my hand slide from his shoulder, and we both fidgeted in our seats, trying to figure out what to say next.

"So, Dick Tracy," Kaz said. "Tell me what to look for."

"Okay," I said, glad of the change in topic. "Look at their hands. Pros will take care of their hands, more than any regular guy. Lock picking takes concentration, patience, and good hand-eye coordination, so watch for somebody comfortable with himself, like a guy who could sit and wait without fidgeting. And if he's a professional criminal, he'll sniff out a cop in no time, so be subtle."

"I am merely a simple priest, Father Boyle. Bless you for your concern."

I slugged him in the arm and left.

At the German College, I knocked on Monsignor O'Flaherty's door. It was opened by a short, wiry man with thick black hair and a finely trimmed mustache. One hand rested on the doorknob and the other held an open straight razor.

"Come, come," he said, waving the razor at me. "I shave the monsignor, come, come."

"Father Boyle," O'Flaherty's voice boomed out. "Meet Rino Messina, the best barber in all of Rome." He was seated in a straight-back chair in the middle of the room, with a towel draped over his shoulders and a half-shaved face.

"Father Billy Boyle," I said, following O'Flaherty's lead to maintain my priestly identity. It was probably a good idea not to share too many secrets with a guy who visited the Regina Coeli as often as he did. "Pleased to meet you, Rino."

"Please, Father, sit and I cut you next." I took that to be a limitation of his English, not a threat. I sat in an easy chair facing O'Flaherty, who gave me a quick nod of approval.

"Rino is one of our close friends," the monsignor said. "He gives haircuts to the wandering souls who show up on our doorstep and makes them presentable. He also smuggles clothes in for the men, right, Rino?"

"Yes, some days I wear three suits in and one out!" Rino had a good laugh over this.

"The POWs I just left were still wearing their uniforms," I said.

"That's a fraction of the boys we've got hidden," O'Flaherty said. "Most are kept in apartments throughout Rome. Rino helps outfit them so they can blend in once they leave here."

"I bring *soldati* anywhere in Rome, safe," Rino said as he finished with the monsignor. "Good shave, yes?"

"Excellent. Father Boyle, a bit of a trim?"

"Sure," I said, getting into the chair and letting Rino adjust the towel around my neck. He worked the scissors the way barbers do before they start in, and then began snipping.

"The monsignor say you ask about Sister Justina, yes?" Rino said as he bent my head forward.

"Yes. Do you know her?"

"Oh, yes. Good nun, she help many people. I go with her, many times, to bring food and lira all over the city."

"To the families who house the escapees," O'Flaherty added.

"Yes. Not much food in Rome, very hard."

"Were you with her when she was arrested?" I asked.

"No. I would not be here if I was. She was taken at checkpoint on Via del Corso. Bad luck, many people arrested."

"For what?"

"All manner of violations," O'Flaherty said, staring out the window like a hunted gangster. "Forged papers, no papers, deserting work details, and so on. The Germans will seal off a block and check everyone's papers at least once a day. They always bag a few that way."

"What was Sister Justina charged with?" I had to stop myself from saying her real name.

"That's what Rino found out on his last visit to the prison," O'Flaherty said, nodding to the barber.

"Black market," Rino said. "She purchase food and have many

lira as well. It is not good, but the Gestapo does not know about the POWs."

"That's great, right? Half of Rome must be dealing in the black market these days." An arrest for dealing in the black market was preferable to a charge of spying.

"True, true," O'Flaherty said. "The punishment for dealing in the black market can be severe, but so many do it that the decrees are seldom enforced. And the fact that they haven't made any connection between Sister Justina and our activities is very promising."

"So how do we get her out?" I asked as Rino finished with the scissors and brushed the back of my neck.

"There is some good news," Rino said, with a shrug and a glance at O'Flaherty that told me the bad news was going to far outweigh the good.

"Give it to me straight," I said.

"Well, me boy," O'Flaherty said, "the good news is that Rino has found someone to bribe. A guard who is thankfully both religious and greedy. He doesn't like seeing nuns arrested, but he wants a stack of lira for his troubles. His regular shift takes him to the gate where food and other deliveries are made. Where Rino goes in and out."

"What about priests? Are they allowed to visit the prisoners?"

"Yes, usually to give the last rites. But it is not uncommon. And to answer your next question, yes, they use the same entrance."

"If two of us go in, he'll let three out, for the right price?" This was sounding like it could actually happen.

"Yes, yes, money is not the problem," O'Flaherty said, somewhat hurriedly.

"What is the problem? What's the bad news?"

"Two things," he said. "First, the jailer in charge of the cells where Sister Justina is kept with other nuns is not bribable."

"He is a fascist pig," Rino said, with feeling.

"Can you get us to her cell?" I asked him.

"Yes. I have cut hair of women. Not nuns, but other women. I go there, and make believe I am good friends with the guard. He is a fool as well as fascist."

"Okay," I said. "What's the other problem?"

"Pietro Koch," O'Flaherty said. At the mention of the name, Rino crossed himself. Not a good sign.

"Who the hell is he?"

"The devil himself," O'Flaherty said. "Italian-Austrian by birth, sadist by temperament, and more fascist than Mussolini, who is said to fear him. He heads up the Fascist political police, and operates with a gang of like-minded Italians and the worst of the Gestapo. He's taken over a small hotel near the Villa Borghese and uses it as a private torture chamber. They call themselves the Koch Gang."

"Banda Koch," Rino said, looking like he wanted to spit.

"Tell me what this has to do with Diana—I mean Sister Justina." I could barely get the words out.

"Koch has requested the transfer of all nuns in the Regina Coeli to his facility at the Pensione Jaccarino."

"Why?"

"Because it amuses him to torture nuns. The man is insane, but connected. He has full powers of arrest, so no one dares speak out. He's also under the protection of the Gestapo chief in Rome, so even the German Army couldn't move against him."

"He doesn't have them yet," I said, praying I'd understood correctly.

"No. The Germans love paperwork, bless their Teutonic hearts. It will take some time. We may have two or three days."

"Rino, when are you scheduled to go back to the prison?"

"In two days. The visits are set by the Gestapo; I cannot go sooner."

"In two days then, I go with you." He nodded his agreement, and began to gather up his things. "Meet me at the monsignor's place on the steps, where he waits for refugees. We will walk to the Regina Coeli. And pray God we return."

"But how in the name of God will you get her out of that cell?" O'Flaherty asked after Rino had gone.

"Monsignor, have faith. I am sure the Lord will provide an answer." Was I? Was I right to put others at risk on the possibility I'd actually get Diana out?

Yes, I decided. I'd gotten this far, and that had to mean something. Maybe it was all due to chance, or perhaps it was the Lord's work. Either way, I had to make the most of it.

CHAPTER TWENTY-TWO

KAZ AND I were hunkered down in the shadows of a grove of conifers, between the Governatorato and the gardener's place. It gave us a clear view of the route between the cottage and Santa Marta. It would have been easier—not to mention warmer—to grab the thief indoors, but there was no place to hide where he wouldn't spot us. We'd donned heavy coats, scarves, and gloves, but there was a cold, damp wind blowing and I would have been tempted to call it a night, except that I wanted this guy for my own reasons.

I'd filled Kaz in on my conversation with O'Flaherty and Rino Messina. He didn't like much of what I had to say, especially the part where I told him I didn't want him tagging along on my little jaunt through the Regina Coeli. He told me he hadn't spotted anyone suspicious, but John May had come up with a carton of canned salmon, which he delivered to Nini in the refectory with enough secrecy to insure that only a practiced eye would catch what was going on. His timing had been perfect: right after dinner, when it was too late to serve the salmon, but when most people were still sitting at the tables. Smart guy.

It was nearing midnight, and I figured we didn't have long to wait. Electricity was rationed, and the power had been off for hours. Vatican City didn't boast much of a nightlife.

"We're doing great on the case of the purloined rations," I

whispered to Kaz. "And I caught a break on getting to Diana. I wonder if we're going to get anywhere with Corrigan's murder."

"For all we know, the murderer could have left the Vatican," Kaz said.

"If that's true, we're dead in the water," I said.

"Look, there!" Kaz whispered as he tugged on my sleeve and pointed to a figure moving from the direction of the Governatorato, but too distant to be heading to the gardener's place. "Perhaps he will loop around, to see if anyone is watching."

"Maybe," I said, but it didn't add up. The Vatican Gardens at night wasn't exactly a high-crime area. In the light of the half-moon, I could make out the dark form, but there was no way to tell who he was or how he was dressed. He cut through a line of shrubs and disappeared. The only thing in that direction was the Vatican radio tower.

"Probably late for work at the station," Kaz said. "I hope he did not scare off our man." Frost plumed from his mouth as he spoke and the cold settled into our bones as we waited, watching the house and the approaches around it. Then we saw him. He kept to the shadows without drawing attention to himself. He didn't dart about but walked confidently, carrying a sack slung over his shoulder, with the jaunty air of someone out for a midnight stroll. A guy used to nighttime getaways. He was headed straight for the cottage. I nodded to Kaz and we made our move.

"Hold it," I said as I ran in front of him. Kaz grabbed the sack and held the guy's arm as I took stock of our catch. He wore a US Army Air Force sheepskin-lined leather flight jacket with sergeant's stripes. "What are you doing out so late, flyboy?"

"What's it to you, *padre?*" He stuck out his jaw defiantly as he spoke in a thick New York accent out of a Dead End Kids movie. "Hey, gimme that back." He made a lunge for Kaz, who was opening the cloth sack.

"Easy, sarge," I said as I grabbed a wrist and twisted it behind his back. "What's in there, Kaz?"

"Youse ain't no priests," he said. "What's your game?"

"Ah, the good sergeant must have been fishing, Billy. He has a nice supply of salmon in here. And a can of condensed milk."

"I got that fair and square, and the milk is for the kids," he said, grabbing at the bag with his free hand.

"Yeah, fair and square with some help from the picks you made for yourself in the basement. What's your name, sarge?"

"Abe. Who the hell are you?"

"That's a long story, Abe. Full name and outfit."

"Abe Seidman, Ninety-eighth Bomb Group. My B-17 got shot down over Viterbo coupla weeks ago. One other guy made it out, but I never hooked up with him. Made my way here and snuck in past them Swiss Guards." His eyes darted about as I let go of his arm, so I grabbed it again to keep him from bolting.

"How'd you manage that?"

"I had a ratty overcoat I picked up to hide the flight jacket, but it wouldn't get me far. So I clocked this Kraut walking alone down the street, with these knuckle-dusters." With his free hand he drew out brass knuckles, fitting them onto his hand. "I took his boots, long coat, and cap and walked in like a tourist. No way I was going to let those Nazi shits nab me. I'm Jewish, says so right on my dog tags. Look, I still got the bastard's boots." I didn't look down to check, but kept my eyes on the lethal brass knuckles.

"Listen, Abe, I'm going to let your wrist go, but after you put those away. Then we talk, okay?" I watched him for some sign of resistance. He had a strong jaw, wide mouth, and dark eyes that darted between Kaz and me, assessing the situation.

"Okay, but I still want to know who you guys are and what the hell you're up to."

"Fair enough," I said, easing up on my grip as Abe stashed his weapon. Bells began to toll the midnight hour from the basilica and all the other nearby churches. They were loud but soothing, the kind of sound that makes you think all is right with the world. But then, a shriek ripped through the night, followed by a louder, terrible scream.

"What the hell," said Abe. "Over there." He pointed to the radio tower.

"Come on," I said. "Abe, stay with us. It's a small place, we'll find you if you hoof it."

"Don't worry about it," he said, taking off ahead of us, leaving the sack with Kaz. We sprinted to catch up, making our way up the hill where the stone tower stood with the tall antennae reaching into the night sky.

We could have saved our breath.

Dark shadows and moonlight played across the body as the wind flogged the branches of the evergreens overhead. Beneath them, yards from the door to the radio tower, Commissario Filberto Soletto lay on his back, mouth open in surprise, or perhaps horror. Soletto's jacket was open, his white shirt stained red. I had the terrible feeling that I had sent him here on a mission of greed, determined to get a larger share of diamonds.

"That's a helluva way for a bull to end up," Abe said. "Took a shiv to the heart."

"How do you know he's a cop?" I asked. "He's not in uniform."

"Pays to case any joint you're going to spend time in, don't it? His name is Soletto, head cop around here. I heard he's on the take with the Fascist police, so I made it a habit to steer clear. Can't be too careful, there's a war on, ya know?"

"What do we do now, Billy?" Kaz asked. Damn good question, too.

Before I could suggest hightailing it, a nearby door opened and several figures emerged. There was no light, even from inside, because of the blackout.

"*La santa madre di Dio,*" a voice said, the speaker almost stumbling on the body as others from behind pushed forward. It was Monsignor Bruzzone, eyeing us uncertainly. "Who did this?"

"No idea," I said. "Didn't you hear the screams?" It seemed they should have made it to the body before us, given the distance we had to cross.

"No, we were in a soundproof room, doing the broadcast." This voice came from Robert Brackett, who stepped closer and knelt beside the body.

"What broadcast?" I asked, wondering about Brackett's mental state after what Nini had told us. He must have been in one of his good moods to be out this late.

"Vatican Radio broadcasts the names of POWs we get from the Red Cross, to let relatives know they are alive," Bruzzone explained. "Tonight it was Americans. We always hand over the list to the ranking diplomat when it is over."

"Monsignor, I suggest you call in the gendarmes. They'll have a lot of questions."

"I can only imagine," he said as he retreated into the building.

Brackett reached out to check Soletto's pulse, but then thought better of it. Dead was dead.

"What is this?" A sharp voice broke through the night air. Bishop Zlatko appeared on the path, carrying a briefcase.

"Commissario Soletto, unfortunately. The gendarmes have been called."

"What happened?" Zlatko asked, glancing around the small group hovering near the body. "Is he dead?"

"Yes. Stabbed."

Zlatko stared at the body, then looked at me, making his opinion obvious. "I said you would cause trouble. I must go inside, I have a broadcast scheduled. I will pray for his soul." He didn't mention my soul or anybody else's. I guess he preferred to pray for the dead rather than the living.

"Not the most charming guy," Brackett said. "Personality or politics."

"Couldn't agree more. You should go inside, too," I said. "The less you're involved, the better."

"Yeah, okay. Hey, Abe, how you getting along?" Brackett gave Abe a small wave.

"Can't complain," Abe replied.

"You two know each other?" I asked, as Kaz told a couple of the radio technicians to move back.

"Sure," Brackett said. "I know all the American POWs who stay here. Part of the job. Abe's not in trouble, is he?"

"Why would he be?"

"For one thing, he's standing over a dead body."

"We were all in the garden and heard a scream. We ran up here and found Soletto like this. Did anyone leave the studio before you?"

"I don't think so," Brackett said as he opened the door. "But I wasn't keeping track of everyone. Who do you think did it?"

"No idea," I said.

"Well, good luck."

I was going to need it. As the door shut behind him, I heard the pounding of boots as gendarmes flooded across the gardens and up the hill.

CHAPTER TWENTY-THREE

DAD ALWAYS SAID to choose the smallest interrogation room there was. Put yourself and your partner between the suspect and the door, and you're halfway home. For all the fancy statues, paintings, and polished marbled floors around here, the Vatican's interrogation room could have been one of my old man's Boston favorites. Small, plain, and cold. One cop across from me, seated behind a stout wooden table. Another in a chair by the door. Me, in the corner, on an old wooden chair that creaked every time I moved. I had to admire the setup. Still, we'd been at it a solid hour, and they showed no signs of believing a damn thing I said.

"We know you are an Allied agent," the guy behind the desk said. For the thirtieth time. He was tall, about my age with short brown hair and a thin slit of a mouth I was thinking about punching. At some other time.

"Everybody knows that," I said.

"You admit this?"

"What? That everybody knows I'm an agent, or that I am?"

"That you are an Allied agent."

"I'm a US Army lieutenant. Sent here to investigate a murder. I was chosen because I was a detective back home before the war," I said, repeating myself with a sigh.

"You were sent to investigate a murder that was already solved? Or were you sent to commit murder?"

"I haven't murdered anyone. And do you really think Commissario Soletto solved Monsignor Corrigan's murder?"

"You were upset with him, yes? About his handling of the investigation? You argued with him in his office, in front of a witness, yes?"

"Yes." It was better to give a short, decisive answer than to argue. It gave him less to work with.

"And then tonight, you arrange to meet him at the radio station and stab him. Why did you do that?"

"I didn't arrange to meet him. Or stab him."

"So you claim," he said, throwing a glance at his partner. His big, silent partner whose eyes bored into me. He was older, thicker at the waist, with a good coat of gray up top.

"What's the Italian word for incompetent?" I snuck in the question as he paused. Interrogators don't like their rhythm being disrupted, and especially don't want to answer questions. A shoe on the other foot thing. But he spoke excellent English, his only accent hinting at a Brit as his language teacher. Maybe he wanted to show off.

"*Incompetente,*" he said. "Now tell me why three of you were needed to kill one man. Or were the other two unwilling dupes?"

"Is the Vatican City Gendarmerie Corps so *incompetente* that none of you can find a murder weapon? Soletto couldn't, and a dozen or so of you couldn't tonight. If I killed Soletto, what did I do with the knife? There were witnesses within seconds of our arrival."

"Ah, within seconds of when you *said* you arrived. You could have been waiting to ambush the *commissario*. You stabbed him, hid the knife, then returned with your accomplices."

"So the knife would be within a hundred yards or so? Not in the radio tower, since it was filled with people. Outside, in the gardens. How long did it take you to find it? Or is everyone who wears that fancy dress outfit *incompetente?*"

His mouth twisted in an angry grimace as he tried to reply. "Why did you kill the *commissario?*"

"What's my motive?" I spread my arms in wonderment. "You're

more pissed off at me than I was at Soletto. Are you ready to murder *me?*"

The big guy interrupted, asking a question in Italian. Thin mouth answered and they laughed. I figured the big guy for his boss, and that he spoke English, but not enough to know what "pissed off" meant.

"*Incazzato,*" big guy said. "Yes, you are making us *incazzato,* yes?"

"I am."

"I think maybe you are police in America, as you say."

"Yes."

"And that you did not kill the *commissario.*"

"Yes." We were on a roll, no reason to interrupt the guy.

"The little priest, Dalakis. He is with you."

"Yes. He's really British Army."

"And the American *sergente?*"

"We ran into him in the gardens. We were all together when we heard the screaming, and ran to the tower." No mention had been made of the salmon and condensed milk, and I thought it best not to bring it up, out of solidarity with cops of any nation. Made me kind of homesick.

"Hmmm," was all big guy said. He nodded to thin lips, who went back to his questioning.

"Who arranged for you to see Commissario Soletto?"

"Robert Brackett, the American deputy chargé d'affaires. Or he asked the Pontifical Commission, in any case. They assigned Bishop Zlatko to be present at the meeting."

"Do you know why?"

"I guess to act as a buffer between us. But Zlatko didn't seem too glad to see me."

"No, the good bishop has made that known," thin lips said, with enough emphasis to tell me Zlatko might not be his best pal.

"What did Bishop Zlatko say at the meeting with the *commissario?*"

"He translated, until Soletto got angry enough to use his English."

"You make him *incazzato* too, eh?" big guy said, laughing.

"It's a gift," I said. "The only thing Zlatko actually said to me was to ask about the diamonds." I watched their eyes for a reaction.

"What diamonds?"

"Listen, I don't want to offend the memory of your boss," I said. I didn't give a rat's ass about the memory of a Fascist informer, but I wanted them to ask me, to demand I tell them my theory. That might open their minds to the possibility.

"Please, speak freely," thin lips said.

"One policeman to the other," big guy said, giving me an encouraging nod.

"Severino Rossi was a jeweler by trade. He left Vichy France when things got too hot for Jews there. He made his way to Genoa, then on to Rome. All we know about him here is that he was found asleep in the columns, near where Corrigan was murdered. He was covered with an overcoat drenched in blood, but he wasn't wearing it. When I searched Corrigan's room, I found a single diamond. My theory is that the killer stole the diamonds from Rossi, who must have converted everything he owned into diamonds, to pay for bribes, papers, food, whatever he needed."

"Why did Monsignor Corrigan leave a diamond in his room?" Thin lips was writing in his notebook as he asked the question. A good sign.

"I don't think he did. I think the killer planted it there, to draw suspicion away from himself and create confusion. I'd bet that the killer paid Soletto in diamonds to finger Rossi as the murderer and get rid of him quickly."

"The blood," big guy said. He was right with me.

"Yes, the blood. After the struggle, the killer dragged Corrigan up the steps, into your jurisdiction. And he learned something too."

"What?" He said it with a lift of the brow that told me he'd already figured that one out.

"He made a mess of things stabbing Corrigan. But he finally found the spot. Up through the rib cage, into the heart. Just like the single thrust that killed Soletto, between the third and fourth ribs."

"Commissario Soletto searched the monsignor's room himself," thin lips said. "But he did so without assistance." He raised an eyebrow in the direction of his boss, who shrugged that most elegant of Italian shrugs, the one that says, *Perhaps, yes, but we will never know, and sadly that is the way of the world.*

"I told Soletto that I had found more diamonds," I said.

They looked stunned. Thin lips looked to big guy, who rubbed his chin. "But that was not true," he said.

"Right. I wanted Soletto to think the killer had held out on him."

Some quick Italian went back and forth between them.

"It appears, then, that you are responsible, at least indirectly, for the *commissario's* murder," thin lips said, writing in his notebook. "You caused him to press the killer for more diamonds, if we are to believe your theory."

"No. Greed caused him to do that. And fear probably caused Corrigan's killer to take another life."

"Fear of being blackmailed?"

"Maybe. Or fear of someone who would always know what he did."

"*Colpa,*" said big guy. "Guilt."

"Yes. Very Catholic, *colpa.*"

"*Andiamo,*" he said to thin lips, who closed his notebook and left the room. "Some things are best said to few people, eh? You think a priest is the killer?"

"I think it is a man with much to lose. There are others here, but refugees have already lost almost everything. My money is on someone who still has position and power. Otherwise, what would be the point?"

"Yes, many have taken sanctuary here. Also diplomats. Brackett. He is a little strange, yes?"

"I've heard that. But not strange enough to kill. I don't think he's the type."

"I agree. He is—*malinconico?*"

"Melancholy. And at times the opposite. I think he has been here too long."

"Like the Germans, yes?" He dug out a pack of cigarettes from inside his uniform jacket and offered me one. I declined, but I was glad we were on friendlier terms now.

"Yeah, like them. You'll be glad to see them go?"

"They and the Fascists with them. Italy is in ruins, all for what? Mussolini and his empire? Bah!"

"I take it you and Soletto didn't agree on politics?"

"You must understand this about the Holy See. There are factions and factions within factions. Yet we all work here, in this same space. For the Church. For His Holiness. We fight among ourselves, but never with him. This is not like the world. Not like your world. You should not have come."

"A murder was committed. A good man was killed."

"Yes, a great loss. But so many people are dead. And now one more. For what? Nothing. The *commissario* did not bring justice, but he also did not threaten the Holy See."

"And I do?"

"Yes, I think so. Before, all sides balance each other. *Capisci?* Now you come, and Soletto is dead. Bishop Zlatko speaks against you to the *Pontificia Commissione.* Maybe the Germans find out about you and come for you. More dead. I do not threaten; I warn. The *commissione* will act. You go."

"How much time do I have?"

"They like to talk. So I give you one day, no longer."

"Then I'd better hurry. May I see the body? Commissario Soletto?"

His narrowed eyes drilled into me as he ground out the cigarette with his heel. Then he stood, and pulled at his blue tunic, straightening it out. "Let us see if he helps you more dead than when he was alive. Come."

We didn't have to go far. The small morgue was down a dank hallway. An attendant wearing a leather apron was pouring a bucket of water over Soletto's naked body, laid out on metal table. His clothes were stacked and folded on a nearby desk.

"Nothing unusual in his pockets," my new friend said after

speaking with the attendant and pawing through the stuff. He leaned over the wound, squinting in the light of the bare bulb above. "Look."

It was pretty much as I thought. Between the third and fourth ribs, left center. He clearly duplicated the thrust that finally brought Corrigan down. No wild slashing this time, but one single wound straight to the heart. I felt the attendant's eyes on me, and realized he was waiting for me to do something holy, but I wasn't in the mood.

"That wasn't a wide blade," I said. The entrance wound was small, a clean cut. "But sharp."

"Of course," he said. "The *misericorde*. How stupid of me."

"The what?"

"Let us collect your friends, quickly. I know where the murder weapon is. If it has been returned."

I followed in his wake as he shouted orders that gendarmes jumped to obey. Doors slammed and men scattered as he moved upstairs. He introduced himself as Inspector Cipriano and still called me Father Boyle, even though he knew differently. Kaz and Abe appeared, and within seconds we were off, trailed by a couple of gendarmes, the first rays of dawn lighting our way. I really didn't need Abe tagging along, but I didn't want to cut him loose either. I had plans for the little crook.

"Where are we going?" I asked, gasping for breath. Cipriano was damn fast for a big guy.

"The barracks of the Swiss Guard. *Arsenale*," he said, searching for the English word.

"Armory," Kaz said, trotting along beside me.

"What's a *misericorde?*" I asked Cipriano.

"A kind of medieval stiletto, designed originally to dispatch badly wounded knights," Kaz said. Of course he would know. "It is from the Latin *misericordia*, meaning mercy. A long, thin, sharp blade, made for going between the gaps of armor plate."

"One was reported missing several weeks ago," the inspector said. "The Swiss Guard keeps every weapon they ever had. One was gone from their collection of *pugnali*."

"Daggers," Kaz explained. Abe gave a little upturned hand gesture that the cops couldn't see. *Don't blame me.*

"Yes," Cipriano said as we passed through the Medieval Palace, guards snapping to attention. "Then one day it was returned. I thought it was harmless at the time; perhaps one of the men misplaced it, or took it to wear."

"Let me guess," I said. "That was right after Corrigan was killed."

"I think so, yes. I am *un idiota!*"

I knew what he was feeling. Sometimes the answer was right in front of you, but you couldn't see it because you'd asked the wrong question. Not where was the knife, but why had someone put it back?

We entered a courtyard and Cipriano made for the far end marked by a castle tower, which I figured was the armory. There were more salutes and we were taken inside, guided by a Swiss Guard in gray battle dress. The vast room was low-ceilinged with several brick archways dividing the chamber. Rows of rifles were arranged alongside suits of armor, long swords, halberds, and crossbows. Machine guns shared space with pikes and medieval helmets. It looked like the guards hadn't thrown anything out in five hundred years.

"There," Cipriano said, pointing to a rack of knives, all long and thin. "Stilettos, rondels, *misericorde.* Yes, this is the one that was missing." He tapped his finger on the pommel and spoke to the guard.

"May I?" I asked, my hand hovering over the knife.

"Yes, but hold it carefully. I doubt there will be fingerprints, but just in case. The guard says the armory is locked but there is no sentry. Anyone with a key and access to the barracks could have gotten in."

I held the knife by the hilt, bringing it up to the light. Cipriano was right; if someone went to the trouble to replace the knife, he certainly would have wiped it down. This one looked spotless, like the others displayed on the rack. I ran my fingers over them, and the faintest trace of dust showed on the upright hilts. Not so with this one, which was clean as a whistle. I licked a fingertip and rubbed it in the groove where the blade met hilt and grip. Tiny reddish flakes stuck to my skin. Soletto's blood.

"This is from the sixteenth century," Cipriano said as he took the knife from me, wrapping it in a handkerchief. I looked at him, wondering what that had to do with anything.

"It has killed enough," he said, sounding sad that this piece of old, cold steel had once again been plunged into flesh. "It has no purpose other than death. Perhaps it feels at home in this century, eh?"

"How many people have a key to the armory?" Kaz asked. Cipriano kept staring at the knife, as if it might speak to him.

"Not many," he finally said. "It should be simple to find who could have gotten in."

"Well, that might not amount to a hill of beans," Abe said, strolling back to our group. I hadn't noticed him wander off. "That door is probably as old as that pig-sticker. It's got a warded lock, looks like original hardware."

"Beans? Pig-sticker?" Cipriano asked. Kaz gave him the basics in Italian, and then nodded for Abe to continue.

"You got a primitive lock there, one of the oldest. There's things inside called wards. They get in the way unless you got a key with notches that match. One of them old-style keys, you know?"

"Well, it's an old place," I said. "What's the problem?"

"The problem is the key. You see, what unlocks the wards is what ain't there. The gaps in the key, ya know? So to make a skeleton key, or passkey, all you need to do is to file away most of the warded center. It'll open any simple warded lock."

"Impossible," huffed Cipriano. "If that were true, half the doors in Rome could be opened with such a passkey."

"Remember, Inspector, this door has its original hardware," Abe said, sounding like he was correcting an overenthusiastic student. "Warded locks did get more complex, with added security. But this one ain't never replaced. It belongs in a museum."

"What makes you so expert?" Cipriano asked, his eyes narrowing in suspicion.

"I was a locksmith before the war," Abe said. "Back in the States, you might find a lock like this on an old cabinet or the like, but not where you want to stash anything really valuable."

"So what are the chances someone could get his hands on a skeleton key around here?" I asked.

"Do you have any idea of how many locked doors there are within Vatican City?" Cipriano said. "How many sets of keys for each, and where they are all stored?"

"No," I admitted.

"Nor do I," he said. "The only thieves we have are pickpockets. We lock our doors to protect areas from the curious and the lost. Not to protect against a murderer stealing weapons. If a resident of the Holy See has access to keys, he is trusted."

Inspector Cipriano shot off a series of instructions to his cops and the Swiss Guard. He handed one of the gendarmes the knife and they scurried off to do his bidding. He told us to follow him, and we did, me at the tail end, watching Abe to make sure he wasn't tempted by any ancient locks.

Cipriano was a cop after my own heart. His next stop was the Swiss Guard mess hall, where the cooks served up what tasted like real coffee.

"I sent my men to look for keys at headquarters," he said. "And told the Guard to find who keeps the keys for the barracks."

"You must have keys for every building," I said.

"Yes, duplicates of all keys are kept at headquarters. But no one checks them routinely. As I said, we have little need for them."

I drank my coffee, and decided to take a chance with Cipriano, who seemed like he might be a decent guy. "Inspector," I said, "what do you know about the Regina Coeli?"

"To stay away from it," he said.

"What's the Regina Coeli?" Abe asked.

"It means Queen of Heaven," Kaz said, which satisfied Abe for the moment. Kaz understood where I was going with this, and wisely didn't want to worry our light-fingered pal.

"I mean who runs it? The Gestapo?"

"No, although they make use of it. It is an Italian state prison, built about a half century ago. Very modern at the time. Why?"

"Do you know anything about the prisoners there, how they're treated?"

"I know it is very crowded. People can be taken in for minor offenses or for treason. If treason, they do not live long. If they violate curfew or are missing identity papers, they may come out soon. The *Organizzazione per la Vigilanza e la Repressione dell'Antifascismo*, OVRA, runs it now. Many OVRA men went north with Mussolini, but some stayed here to work with the Nazis. So it depends on how the prisoners were picked up. If by the Germans in a roundup, there may be a chance. If by OVRA, then less."

"Do you know Pietro Koch?"

"The worst creature in Italy. Do not cross paths with him unless you plan to put a bullet in his head."

"I've heard he wants all the nuns held at Regina Coeli released into his custody."

"Are you certain of this?"

"I have good reason to believe the person who told me."

"I will look into it. If it is true, I will inform Cardinal Maglione."

"The secretary of state," Kaz said. "I hope they will listen to him."

As we debated the usefulness of a Vatican diplomatic protest, both a Swiss Guard and a gendarme showed up and handed keys to Cipriano.

"Look," Cipriano said to Abe, laying them out on the table. They were all the old-fashioned style of key, some tarnished and some polished. "These are the passkeys found here in the barracks and at headquarters. Could any of them open the armory door?"

Abe picked them up one by one. Most of the ends had been cut down to a nub. "These four," he said. "Any of 'em would do the trick."

"Three of them are from the barracks office, one from Gendarmerie headquarters," Cipriano said with a sigh.

"I'd bet there's others," I said. "The porter at the Medieval Palace had a bunch of keys hanging in plain sight."

"Sadly, you are right, Father Boyle," Cipriano said as Abe put the keys back in the pile. "We have a murder weapon, but are no closer to the murderer."

"We know he has access to a passkey and is someone who would not evoke suspicion in the barracks. We know he is smart, to use this knife and hide it in plain sight."

"Yes," Kaz said. "In a peaceful place like the Vatican, it would be unusual to have a knife outside of a kitchen. This is one way to obtain a killing tool and not have to worry about hiding or disposing of it."

"Yes, yes," Cipriano said. "He is a genius. Thank you, gentleman. I will let you know as soon as I hear anything, from the commission or about Koch."

We shook hands, and I chalked it up to the long night that Cipriano didn't notice Abe palm one of the skeleton keys. You gotta love a thief. Especially when he's your thief.

CHAPTER TWENTY-FOUR

"NO I AIN'T," was Abe's response when I informed him he was in deep trouble. We were in our room at the German College, and I'd done my best to set up the interrogation. Kaz in a chair by the door, me in a comfortable armchair, and Abe in the corner. I'd told him to sit on the edge of the bed, thinking that would put me above him. Evidently he'd been in a few interrogation rooms himself, and responded by lying down, plumping the pillow, and crossing his clodhoppers on my clean blanket. "You got nothin' on me. No authority, and them Holy Joes is about to hand the both of youse yer walkin' papers. You got trouble, pal, not me."

"Why were you breaking into the storeroom?"

"I didn't break nothing. I opened the door," Abe said.

"With the picks you made from the metal scraps on the tool bench," I said. "Guy like you, Abe, you could make a set of picks out of most anything. But they gave you tools, everything you needed. It was almost criminal of them, leaving all that stuff around."

"Don't know what you mean. Now you tell me, who the hell are you guys? You ain't no priests."

"We are Allied agents," Kaz said, "sent here to find out who killed Monsignor Corrigan. General Eisenhower wants any illegal activity among Allied forces sheltered in the Vatican dealt with swiftly."

"And we're short on suspects, Abe. Maybe it was you, skulking around at night. Did Corrigan find out you were stealing from the refugees?" We were both laying it on a bit thick, but I wanted Abe to think he was in Dutch.

"You two? Don't make me laugh. If you're here investigatin', how come you ain't come up with anything better?"

"We have suspects," Kaz said, doing a good job of not sounding defensive.

"Yeah, well I hope that bastard Zlatko is one of them."

"You've run into him?"

"If I had, I woulda clocked him, bishop or not. He oughta be wearing a Nazi uniform, him bein' pals with those Croat Ustashi. Bloodthirsty don't begin to describe them. We got briefed on the situation in Yugoslavia, on accounta we flew over the place. How to tell who was on which side, that sorta thing."

"Won't argue with you about the bishop, Abe," I said. "Tell me about Brackett."

"What about him?"

"Anything unusual. He an okay guy?"

"Yeah, sure. Hot and cold, you know? Sometimes real friendly, other times he'll walk right by you, or light into you for nuttin' at all. He and Zlatko didn't get along, not that I'd expect them to be pals." Abe stuffed his hands in his pockets as he eyed the locked door. I could tell it made him nervous, being shut in here with a cop.

"What do you mean?"

"He and the bishop were yellin' at each other, coupla nights ago, in the gardens. I was on my way to see Rosana, so I was kinda hiding in the shrubbery."

"What were they arguing about?" I asked.

"This sounds crazy, but I think they were goin' on about boats. I swear Brackett said 'rudder' a coupla times. I dunno, bein' cooped up here so long probably got to him."

"Yeah," I said, exchanging glances with Kaz. This was top-secret stuff, and there was no reason to let Abe know it meant anything. "Now, tell me about the woman in the gardener's cottage."

"Jeez," Abe said. "You know about Rosana?"

"That's who you swiped the extra food for, right? Beautiful widow, why not? She must have been real glad, huh?"

"You shut your mouth!" Abe was up in a flash and had his hand at my throat. "Shut your damn mouth before I shut it for you. It wasn't nothin' like that."

"Your reaction does you credit," Kaz said, grabbing Abe by the arm. "But now let Billy go." He did, then sat on the edge of the bed, glaring at me.

"Sorry, Abe, I was trying to get a rise out of you. So what's the story?"

"Yeah, well, I forgot you said you'd been a cop. I shouldn'ta fallen for it. I met Rosana the first day she was here. That Irish monsignor, he was bringing her to Nini. You know she's sweet on you, don'tcha?" He directed that last bit to Kaz.

"How do you know? Did she say anything?" Kaz asked, dropping the hardcase Allied agent stance.

"I got eyes. Anyway, I saw Rosana was scared, and I happened to have some extra chocolate on me. So I gave it to her for the kids. She looked at me kinda funny, then started crying. Not sad, ya know, but the kinda tears that come when you can't believe how good you got it. Here she was, on the run from the Nazis, two kids in tow, husband dead, and all of a sudden she's safe on neutral territory, and an American flyboy walks up and gives her chocolate. Still gets me."

"You started calling on her?"

"Yeah, but I couldn't be obvious about it. They don't want too many people wandering around here. Some of the cardinals might get their noses bent outta shape, especially if they have to cross paths with a Jew. I ain't complaining about the Church or nothin', I probably owe my life to them. But it's human nature, know what I mean? You stick with your own kind, like back home."

"Sure," I said. "Now tell me, Abe. You good at what you do?"

"Hell yeah. I'm an armorer-gunner on a B-17. It's a big responsibility. Got two probable kills."

"That's not the job I mean."

"Okay, okay. You caught me with the goods, so I guess I oughta spill. Like I said, I got eyes. I saw all that food going down those steps, so one day I take a look. When I saw that workbench, I knew it'd be a snap. Made a coupla picks, got in, and took a little, to take the edge off, you know?" He raised his eyebrows and tilted his head, as if the theft had been nothing but a prank.

"That's where the chocolate came from," I said.

"Yeah. I wanted to see Rosana again, and I figured with a mug like mine I should come bearin' gifts. So I got a little more, and pretty soon she thinks I'm really something. She don't know nothin' about it, either. You ain't gonna get her in trouble over this, are you?"

"No, we got no beef with her. Or with you, personally, Abe. But you're facing serious charges."

"Billy," Kaz said, with a perplexed look on his face. "Will the American Army charges be worse than the Italian charges?"

"Well, there's looting. The army doesn't like it when enlisted men loot. Doesn't leave as much for the officers. But breaking and entering in Vatican City, that's a new one on me. Either one could mean a lot of time breaking rocks. Be a shame to damage those fingers, Abe."

"Are you guys gonna bust my balls all day or get to the point?" Abe said.

"We need your special skills, Abe," I said. "Tomorrow we're going to go sightseeing, down to the Tiber River. We'll find you a nice suit to wear."

"What you're saying is you want me to break into some joint in Rome, which is swarming with Krauts, while wearing civilian clothes. So if they don't shoot me once for bein' a Jew, they can shoot me twice for bein' a spy."

"We can get into the joint okay," I said. "But we need a door unlocked inside. You do that, we stroll back here, and everything is forgiven and forgotten."

"Well," Abe said, taking a minute to think it over. "I ain't seen Rome except from thirty thousand feet. I guess I could stretch my legs. What kinda place we goin' into?"

"The Regina Coeli prison."

Abe's eyes widened. "No thanks, I'll take my chances busting rocks for twenty years. Are you nuts? That's the one place everyone wants to avoid, and you're thinkin' of waltzing in there? How you gonna manage that?"

"We have an in," I said. "A guy who has the run of the prison. And a guard who's been paid off. We walk in, all official and above board. You open one door, and then we go out with one more person than we came in with. The guard at the exit has been bribed not to notice. Then we hoof it back here in no time."

"You know why I went into pickin' locks? Because I don't have to depend on anyone else. My old man, he was muscle for Monk Eastman on the Lower East Side. The gang always had big plans, too big. Someone talked, or didn't show up, and the whole thing went to hell. When the old man went up to Sing Sing after one of these big scores went south, I decided to go it on my own. This stinks of one of Monk's plans. Too easy and too complicated at the same time."

"Abe," Kaz said, moving over to sit beside him. "Without you, we can get within one door of a lady who needs rescuing."

"Spare the violins," Abe said.

"I am not appealing to your better nature," Kaz said in a hard, even voice. "I am appealing to your sense of survival. Your choice is this. Come with us, and return a hero, in the eyes of the Army and Rosana. Refuse, and for your dereliction of duty, you will be expelled from Vatican City. We will have the gendarmes drag you to the white line and throw you over, into the waiting arms of the Germans."

"You wouldn't," Abe said. I wondered myself.

"Yes, I will, and immediately," Kaz said, rising.

"Goddamn it, okay, okay," Abe said, holding up his hands in surrender. "I go with you. And *if* we get back, you put me in for a medal and a promotion. And keep yer yaps shut about everything else."

"Certainly," Kaz said.

"And when the Army finally gets here, I want a rabbi. An army chaplain."

"Why?" I asked, not taking Abe for the religious type.

"So me and Rosana can get hitched. For an investigator, Billy, you ain't none too bright."

CHAPTER TWENTY-FIVE

ALL I WANTED to do was sleep. We'd been up all night running in circles while the killer probably had a nightcap, congratu-
lated himself on another fine murder, and counted lambs getting
slaughtered until he dozed off. But there was too much to do and
no time for a catnap. It was likely only hours before we got the
boot.

Kaz had gone off to gather civilian clothes for Abe for our jaunt
tomorrow. I'd gone to find Monsignor O'Flaherty and set things up
in case we were thrown out before Rino came in the morning. If I
ended up persona non grata in the Holy See, I wanted to be sure it
didn't keep me from joining Rino on his rounds at the Regina Coeli.
For a minute, when I was dressing it up for Abe, I almost believed
it might be that easy. But Abe had nailed it. There were half a dozen
things that could go wrong and I'd be a fool to believe that at least
one wouldn't.

It didn't matter. I was going to get to Diana tomorrow. Even if
we failed, she'd know I hadn't abandoned her. I didn't want to think
about getting caught, since the Germans would have every right to
shoot me as a spy. But being offered a blindfold and a cigarette didn't
bother me as much as the idea of leaving Diana to whatever fate the
Germans had in store for renegade nuns. Crazy, I know. I did feel
bad about Abe, but if he hadn't been a crook, I wouldn't have had
anything on him, and he'd be just another downed flier biding his

time. That was an excuse, I know, but it made it a little easier to live with myself.

Rudder was a real problem. Neither Kaz nor I could figure why Brackett and Zlatko were tossing that name around. We hadn't had much time to chew it over and I was still shaking my head over it as I knocked on the monsignor's door.

"Ah, Father Boyle, right on time for breakfast," O'Flaherty said as he invited me in. "I was expecting Monsignor Bruzzone, but he must have been delayed. It sounds as if you all had a terrible shock last night at the radio tower."

"Word gets around pretty fast, doesn't it?" I said as I sat at the small table. There were two places set for breakfast, but O'Flaherty had already started in on his.

"It's a small town, and gossip is a cottage industry," he said as he poured me coffee. "You discovered Soletto's body, I understand."

"Kaz—Father Dalakis and I did. Along with an American, Sergeant Abe Siedman. You recall him?"

"Yes. Jewish fellow. We thought it best to keep him here, for his own safety. Most of the escapees are sent out in civilian clothes to live with families, and we think those who have been caught haven't been treated as spies. So many POWs had their clothing worn out by months of constant wear that the Germans tend to not treat them too harshly if they're caught out of uniform, unless it's the Gestapo that picks them up. But Sergeant Siedman was never a prisoner, so they might not look at it the same way. That, plus his religion, made the decision for us."

"Well, he's volunteered to come with us tomorrow. He has a way with locks that may come in handy," I said. "Plus a soft spot for Rosana, in the gardener's cottage."

"Does he now? I'll be sure to be watchful on both counts. Eager to help, you say?"

"Eager to stay out of trouble," I said.

"The man has an odd way of staying out of trouble. You are not very adept at it either, Father Boyle," O'Flaherty said with a knowing grin.

"I think it was a mistake to see Soletto. I didn't get any answers, and I may have caused his death." I told O'Flaherty about the diamonds and my fib to Soletto. A shiv between the ribs made it hard to think of it as a little white lie, but my intentions had been pure.

"Every day, we set things in motion, lad," O'Flaherty said. "What others do weighs on their souls, not yours, as long as you did not act with malice in your heart."

"Malice, no," I said. "But sometimes I don't think through all the consequences. Whichever way you cut it, if I hadn't tantalized Soletto with the thought of more riches to be had, he wouldn't have been dead on the ground."

"It seems to me that a man in your profession could hardly risk even a friendly greeting without it leading somewhere. You consort with criminals and killers, and all the poor souls who live in their orbit. To get the truth out of them, it must be twisted and turned six ways to Sunday. Worry about your soul, my boy, not the earthly consequences of actions taken without intent to harm."

"Body and soul both are what worry me," I said. "I hear Bishop Zlatko is asking the Pontifical Commission to have us thrown out. He thinks we're a threat to the Vatican."

"As am I, as am I," O'Flaherty said. "But if we do not do battle with the forces of Caesar, then what good does it do the world to have all this, the riches of the Church?" He waved his arms around him, taking in his simple room, the building, the basilica, and the treasure of centuries. "Not all cardinals agree with Zlatko. Fewer with the likes of me, but we shall see."

We ate for a while in silence, gazing out the window at the small cemetery below.

"What chances do you think we have tomorrow?" I asked.

"Good. Not a sure thing, but a good chance. I wouldn't risk Rino, nor would he risk himself, if it weren't possible. Now that you've got a man who knows his way around locks, you've solved the hardest part. They are so used to seeing Rino and visiting priests that once you're inside, you should have no trouble. And we've arranged for such a substantial bribe that the guard will desert and go into hiding if he has any sense."

"And you can hold it over his head as well. One word to the authorities and he'd have to explain where the lira came from."

"Why Father Boyle, such a devious mind. I knew we were kindred souls," O'Flaherty said.

We went over the plan, including the meeting place for Abe and Rino in case we found ourselves separated outside the Vatican walls. O'Flaherty gave me the location of a safe house on the Via di Santa Dorotea in Trastevere, not far from the prison, to be used only in an emergency.

"What is next with your investigation?" O'Flaherty asked, after we'd finished the last of the food. "As mournful as Commissario Soletto's death was, it must have narrowed down the list of suspects for you."

"It may be the weapon that narrows it down," I said, and recounted the missing dagger that had mysteriously reappeared in the Swiss Guard's armory.

"Ah, the *misericorde*," O'Flaherty said. "I recall hearing about a missing dagger. The Swiss Guard was terribly embarrassed by that. They are entrusted with all the arms and armor ever held by the Vatican. Their armory is as much a museum as an actual military storehouse."

"Who keeps track of keys around here? It seems pretty loose."

"You have to understand that much of the security here is tradition and custom. The community, beyond the public areas in and outside the basilica, is very small, and obviously religious. There is almost no crime, outside of pickpockets in the square."

"So doors are locked, as they always have been, but with locks that haven't been replaced in centuries."

"Yes, and keys have been lost over the years, copies made, lost, then found again. It wasn't until the influx of refugees that we began to notice what a problem it was."

"What you're saying is that anyone who wanted to could get in to steal that knife," I said.

"True enough. We're a trusting lot, and it would be child's play to lay your hands on anything you put a mind to. Whom do you suspect?"

"I don't know, Monsignor. If I had to name someone, it would probably be the guy trying to get rid of me, if only for that."

"Bishop Zlatko is not someone I'd often agree with. He has one foot firmly in Caesar's world and the other ready to kick anyone who does not agree with him on matters of faith. But he is straightforward, I will give him that."

"Meaning you don't see him as a furtive murderer?"

"No. To be honest, I see him more as a proud mass murderer. Not that he would get his own hands dirty, mind you. But he is one of the more fanatic Croats. Some of the priests in his diocese even work directly with the Ustashi. The chief of the secret police in Sarajevo is a priest, if you can believe it."

"Why doesn't the Pope do something about it?"

"A good question. He has put pressure on the archbishop of Zagreb to restrain the Ustashi regime. The archbishop did recently denounce the murder of Croatian Jews and Serbs, but by the time he did, most were already dead. The Vatican, even before Pope Pius, strongly supported Croatian nationalism, as a bulwark against the Communists to the east. Once the Ustashi took power, they moved faster and more violently than anyone expected," O'Flaherty said, a frown creasing his face. "But the Catholic Church moves slowly, my friend. That leaves room for activities such as mine, but unfortunately Zlatko's as well. But, his time here may be up as well."

"Why?"

"Come, I will explain on the way," O'Flaherty said. "I need to get to my post on the steps of the basilica."

"Are there still escaped POWs coming in?" I asked as he led the way out of the German College.

"Not as many now that the Germans have taken over the Italian camps. But some make it here, along with refugees, downed airmen, and a few German deserters. Some who have been hiding in Rome are afraid that there will be a battle for the city, and gamble that it may be safer on neutral ground." We came to the Piazza del

Sant'Uffizio, where we had to cross that small stretch of Italian territory to get into Saint Peter's Square. O'Flaherty came to a dead stop, then backed up until we stood in the shadow of the basilica. "Trouble," he said.

Trucks rumbled past us, turning at the Bernini colonnades, three proceeding while the last pulled over and halted, the squeal of brakes echoing off the stone buildings lining the narrow street. The German paratroopers on duty along the white border line looked at each other, then at us, with surprise on their faces. The cargo gate dropped with a thud and German soldiers cascaded out, taking up position along the border. Most were regular Wehrmacht troops in their gray-green uniforms, who filled in between the paratroopers. Behind them were the sinister black-leather-coated Gestapo, and a few SS in their gray uniforms and shiny black boots. A regular rogue's gallery.

"Something's happened," O'Flaherty said. "They are sealing off the square completely."

"Are they invading the Vatican?" I asked, suddenly wishing I were packing something with more firepower than rosary beads.

"No, too few of them for that. Come, we'll go around the long way and see what is happening in the square."

"If they closed the border, how will we get out tomorrow?" I asked, not thinking he'd actually have an answer.

"It's more likely they sealed it to prevent anyone from coming in. And that can only mean one thing."

"What's that?" I gasped, struggling to keep up with O'Flaherty's long stride.

"They may have raided some of our buildings. We have people hidden in seminaries, convents, and other properties of the Holy See. They legally have extraterritorial protection, so they are treated as neutral ground. But all that means is a brass plaque by the door."

"Anyone who escaped would make a beeline here," I said.

"Aye. Refugees and clerics alike." He took us through the Sacristy, an ornate building attached to the basilica, which housed the treasures of the Vatican. Swiss Guards opened doors for the monsignor as if he were a general. A marbled corridor took us into

Saint Peter's, but I didn't have a second to play the tourist as O'Flaherty sped to the door amid the worried murmurs of visitors and priests. I followed him down the steps, across the grand piazza, right up to the white line painted in a wide arc at the entrance. A clutch of monks, their brown robes whipped by the wind, stood gaping at the Germans on the other side of the border. Unarmed German soldiers, peaceful tourists a moment ago, filed out of the square between the ranks of their brethren, looking almost sheepish at the display of weaponry.

"Billy." Kaz waved to us. Not surprisingly, he was with Nina.

"What do you know?" O'Flaherty asked of them, his gaze darting across the leather-coated men at the center of things.

"It is the monastery at the *Basilica di San Paolo fuori le Mura*," Nina said.

"Saint Paul's Basilica Outside the Walls," Kaz said, unable to not play the tour guide. "A short distance south, along the Tiber. The burial place of Saint Paul."

"And home to over a hundred hidden Jews," O'Flaherty said grimly. "They should have been safe there; it's Vatican territory. Did any make it out?"

"No. I made what calls I could until the telephone lines went dead," the princess said. "There was no answer at the Istituto Pio."

"Dear God," O'Flaherty said, panic flashing across his face. "That is a Catholic boarding school for boys. When the war began, it was nearly empty. We have dozens of young Jewish boys there, those who escaped the Rome roundup last October."

"How did they know?" Kaz asked.

"Someone could have talked. Torture, or money. Or perhaps they raided a number of locations and got lucky," Nini said.

"There he is," O'Flaherty said, his long arm pointing at a man on the other side of the white line. "Koch."

He walked up to the line, shaking off Nini's hand as she tried to restrain him from the foolhardy gesture. He planted his toes less than an inch from the border, and stood eye to eye with Pietro Koch. Although he had to stare down at him to do so.

Koch was not what I expected. I hadn't had any image of the man in mind, but if I had, it wouldn't have been this. He had an almost gentle look on his face. Serene, even in the middle of all the shouts and clomping boots. His eyes were a bit close together, but they were penetrating, his eyebrows slightly raised as if asking a question. He had a strong jaw, and dark hair slicked back, but there was also something feminine about him. As he flipped through a notebook of photographs, I noticed his hands were delicate, the fingernails manicured. He looked composed, which I thought might be hard to pull off with a giant monsignor, hands on his hips, staring you down.

"*Lè*," he said, pointing to a picture.

"*Sì*," another officer said. "It is he. Monsignor Hugh O'Flaherty. Would you please step this way, Monsignor?"

"Not on your life," O'Flaherty growled. "But tell your boss I will pray for his soul, and likely will be the only one to do so."

Koch flipped the pages again, smiling at Nini as he did so. He stopped, tapped his finger again, and whispered, "*Principessa*," then blew her a kiss. Kaz stepped forward but had the sense to stop. A camera flashed, and Kaz's mug would soon find its way into Koch's book.

"My *capo* says he looks forward to meeting you, in Rome," the other officer said, tugging on the belt of his coat. "You and the princess."

I could feel the tension and anger all around me. I felt like reaching over the line and belting the guy, but instead I drew back, not wanting to draw attention to myself and get my photograph snapped. I figured there was a fair chance these guys might have business at the Regina Coeli, and I didn't want to be fingered as a pal of the monsignor and his gang. That reminded me of old Saint Peter himself, when he was a disciple. At the Last Supper, Jesus predicted that before the dawn, Peter would deny him three times. Of course Peter said he'd lay down his life for his *capo*. Then, when the Romans arrested Jesus, Peter went right ahead and denied he knew him. Three times.

Today, Roman police still inspired fear and silence. Not a lot of progress to show for two thousand years of civilization.

CHAPTER TWENTY-SIX

NINI AND O'FLAHERTY went into a huddle with some of their co-conspirators. Back at the German College, John May was waiting for them, along with a nun and some British escapees in well-worn uniforms. No one had seen Monsignor Bruzzone, and there was a general fear he'd been picked up.

"Odd though," John May had said. "He hasn't been outside these walls for months, not since the trip to Genoa. Said he heard the Gestapo had targeted him, and that it wasn't safe. He must've had an important reason for leaving."

"If he did leave," I said to Kaz as we talked it over, on our way to see Brackett. "Or maybe we have another corpse hidden somewhere. Or he killed Soletto and went on the lam." We passed the Gendarmerie headquarters and made for the Governatorato.

"That does not make sense," Kaz said. "If the Gestapo were after him, why leave the safety of the Vatican? Especially when there is no evidence against him?"

"Yeah, I see what you mean. Maybe he had a good reason to head into Rome, and got picked up by chance. Or he's lying low until the roundup is over." As I thought about it, that seemed the most likely situation. The simplest answers are usually the truest ones, my dad always said.

When we went up the main steps, there were no guards in sight. Everyone must have been called up to counter the German threat at the border. Brackett was in his office, staring out the window, the same view he had been so interested in the first time we met.

"Brackett," I said. He didn't look up. "Did you hear about the Germans?"

"If they come in, do you think they'll send us someplace else? A different view, maybe?" He spoke without moving his gaze from the window.

"Yeah, maybe under six feet of dirt. How's that for a view? I need you to show me the radio tower and where everybody was last night."

"Do you have a cigarette?" Brackett asked. "Lucky Strike, maybe?"

"No, I told you, I don't smoke."

Kaz pulled a half-full pack of Italian Nazionali cigarettes from his pocket and tossed them on the desk.

"The best I could find," Kaz said.

"Filthy things," Brackett said, sighing. He still hadn't moved his head, and I angled myself to get a view of the window. He wasn't staring at the gardens. It was his own reflection, along with enough of the desk to see the pack.

"Enough with the goddamn cigarettes," I said, slamming the palm of my hand on his desk. I waited for surprise to show on his face, or maybe shame. "Wake up and do your job."

"My job?" He picked up the pack of Nazionalis and looked at it as if he'd never seen one before. I wanted to break the window, sweep everything off his desk, and slap him around a bit, all in the name of snapping him out of his daydream, but I knew that would get us nowhere. I stepped around the desk and leaned against the window, blocking his view. I took a deep breath and tried to sound calm.

"Listen," I said. "We need your help. This is the kind of thing that will mean a promotion once Rome is liberated. They'll probably make you an ambassador somewhere. But you've got to pull yourself together. I know it's tough, but we don't have much time."

"Zlatko," he said.

"Yeah, he's trying to get us tossed out, and who knows what will happen with the Krauts lined up outside. Just in case, we need to find out everything we can about what happened inside the radio tower. Can you do that with us?"

"Okay," Brackett said. "I can do that."

It had started to rain. As we crossed the gardens, Brackett hunched up his shoulders and drove his hands deep into his pockets. Kaz and I had decided that we'd wait and ask Brackett about his Rudder conversation with Zlatko after he'd shown us everything we needed. I had the feeling he might go off the deep end soon, and I didn't want to push him to the edge until we'd gotten what we came for. We hustled along the four-story building until we got to the tower, which housed the giant radio masts. Inside, we shook off the rain like mutts and hung our coats. My cassock was soaked where the raincoat hadn't covered it, and the white collar dug into my neck. This was one disguise I couldn't wait to ditch.

Radio Vaticana was a major operation, but this place wasn't all marble and statues like the rest of the Holy See. A long corridor led to a waiting room, with a control room and several studios beyond, all with glass windows and soundproofing. Two were in use. Kaz spoke in a low voice with a sound engineer, who nodded his approval.

"This is the studio we used," Brackett said, pointing to a slightly larger room. Microphones were set up around a table with three chairs. Nothing else.

"You were inside the studio, I think you said, correct?"

"Yes, myself and the announcer. It was an English-language broadcast."

"But Monsignor Bruzzone was there as well?"

"Yes, of course. He brought the list of POWs. It came through the Refugee Commission, which is part of his job. He gave it to the announcer, who turned it over to me after the broadcast."

"Who else was here?"

"The sound engineer. And another announcer waiting for his program."

"Was that Zlatko's broadcast?"

"Sure. He did a Croatian-language hour twice a week. He'd been in earlier to make sure his announcer was there."

"Wait, you mean Zlatko was in the studio, before Soletto was killed?"

"Yes," Brackett said, thinking about it. "Maybe fifteen minutes or so. He talked with his guy, then said he'd forgotten his notes. He had plenty of time, so he went back to his office."

"Did he talk with anyone else?"

"He and Bruzzone chatted for a minute, that's it."

"Was it usual for Bruzzone to hang around, after he'd handed over the list of American POWs?"

"He would stay for the start of the program. Then he'd leave, other times not."

"And he was outside the window the whole time?"

"I guess so. I mean I wasn't keeping my eye on him, no reason to."

"Okay, that's fine. Kaz, ask the engineer if that door to the offices is kept locked at night."

Kaz conversed with him, then reported that it was. Announcers and engineers didn't need access to the offices, so the connecting door was locked after hours. I checked the door. It was fairly new, with a single-cylinder deadbolt lock. Definitely not sixteenth century.

"What's further down the corridor?" I asked Brackett.

"A small kitchen and a bathroom. I think there's a supply closet, but that's it. The radio station is fairly well sealed off from the rest of the building at night."

Kaz and I searched the rooms. I was hoping for a bloodstained coat or gloves, some evidence that the gendarmes might have missed. Nothing. We went outside and searched in the rain, checking tree limbs, shrubs, and any hiding place we could think of. Nothing again.

Back inside, I nodded to Kaz as we approached Brackett, who sat in the waiting room, smoking one of the Nazionali cigarettes Kaz had given him.

"Okay, you've been a big help," I said. "We ruled out a number of options."

"Good for you. You could've gotten any of this from Inspector Cipriano; I gave him the same run-down. I've got to go," he said, as if he had a ton of paperwork waiting.

"I need to ask something else," I said. "Monsignor O'Flaherty mentioned that Bishop Zlatko might be leaving the Vatican soon. Do you know anything about that?" O'Flaherty had been about to explain that when the ruckus in the square started up.

"Sure. Cardinal Boetto is coming to Rome. He's the archbishop of Genoa. Word is he's got information about the deportation of Jews from Croatia."

"And let me guess, Bishop Zlatko is involved," I said.

"That's the scuttlebutt. Boetto is very active in hiding Jews who make it to his door. They come from all over, and probably more than a few from Croatia. Boetto provides them with money and false identity papers all the time."

"So Boetto would be glad to see Zlatko sent back?"

"He and others want the Pope to take a stand against the Croatian clergy participating in the Ustashi killings. Or a stronger one, at any rate. He'd be glad to have the Pontifical Commission act against Zlatko."

"Now I understand why Zlatko is working against us," I said. "It takes some pressure off him."

"Yep, good politics on his part," Brackett said, rising to leave.

"One more question," I said, laying my hand on his arm as he walked by. "How would you describe your relationship with Bishop Zlatko?"

"Relationship? What the hell do you mean? He's a right-wing Catholic Fascist and I'm a Protestant FDR Democrat. We're hardly buddies."

"Do you talk with him? You know, social chitchat."

"I wouldn't be rude, it's not in the diplomat's handbook. But I don't seek him out for conversation, if that's what you mean. And let go of me." He shook off my hand.

"Share any interests? Skiing, any kind of sports?"

"Are you insane?" He looked to Kaz for support, uncertain of where this was going.

"It is just that we have heard of a strange conversation between you and the bishop," Kaz said. "Something to do with boats. A rudder was mentioned. If you and he are not friendly, and share no common interests, why were you talking about rudders?"

"There are some things even wisenheimers like you aren't cleared to know," Brackett said, pushing past us. Cigarette jammed in his mouth, he grabbed his coat, flung it over his head for cover, and slammed the door behind him.

"Haven't seen him that lively in a while," I said.

"Wisenheimer?" Kaz asked.

"You know, I was six years old before I knew my name wasn't wisenheimer, since my dad called me that so often. It's an affectionate way of calling someone a smart aleck."

"Our friend did not seem to have much affection for the question," Kaz said.

"No, but it's interesting that he gave up that information about Zlatko being here earlier. If they're in cahoots, he probably wouldn't have mentioned it."

"We should compare notes with Inspector Cipriano," Kaz said.

"First things first," I said. "Did you get civilian clothing for Abe? I want to get that squared away."

"Not yet. Nini was about to show me where they keep donated clothes for refugees in Santa Marta. She said there would be suits, worn but serviceable."

"Worn is good, it will look more authentic. Let's get that done, and then you check with Cipriano."

"What will you do?" Kaz asked as we stepped outside, where the rain had softened to a mist that floated through the gardens.

"Stay away from the gendarmes." I didn't want to chance getting tossed out of the Vatican or, worse yet, into a jail cell if things went against me. Or us, actually.

"The better part of valor is discretion, as Falstaff said."

I knew Falstaff was from Shakespeare, but since all I recalled was the image of a fat drunk, I didn't comment. That was Kaz's territory, after all. Which encompassed just about anything taught in school.

We made it to Santa Marta a second before the rain let loose

again, pelting down in heavy, thick drops. I laughed at the image of
the Germans guarding the border in their sodden wool uniforms,
but then thought about the Jews who had been taken, and the ones
running scared in Rome, soaked to the bone, unsure of friend or foe,
and the laugh died in my throat.

"Here," Kaz said, opening the door to a long, narrow storeroom.
Shirts were folded neatly on shelves, shoes lined up on the floor, and
coats, suits, and trousers were hung at the far end. They were soft,
well worn, laundered, and patched. Perfect. We found a brown three-
piece that looked right for Abe, and Kaz found a once-white shirt
not too frayed around the collar. I grabbed a tie, a bit loud for my
taste, but it seemed a good fit for Abe. Kaz scrounged around in a
box filled with undergarments, since we didn't want Abe getting
nabbed in case he had to expose his Air Corps BVDs for any reason.

"Billy," Kaz said, his tone far too serious for rooting around in a
box of used skivvies. "Look." He dumped the contents of the box
onto the floor. A crumpled ball of white, stained with the rusty red
of long-dried blood, rolled against my shoe.

"It's a surplice," I said, picking it up and smoothing it out. I
examined it, a white lacey garment worn by priests over the cassock.
The right arm carried a thick stain, with a spray of red at the chest.

"No, actually it is a rochet," Kaz said. "Similar, but the rochet is
usually made of linen, as this is."

"What's the difference?"

"The cotton surplice is worn by the lower orders of clergy. The
rochet is for prelates, bishops, and higher ranks."

"Hmm. Either way, it makes a handy apron to keep blood off
your clothes. You could wear this under a coat, where no one would
notice, and get rid of it afterward."

"Remember the coat hooks by the door at the radio tower?
Anyone could have stepped outside, stabbed Soletto, and removed
the rochet."

"Or," I said, "fold it up real tight and stick it in a coat pocket.
Put it on, slip outside at the right moment, and do the deed."

"It could have been anybody," Kaz said. "We know how easy it is to steal things here. The rochet could have been taken from an unlocked room, the laundry, anywhere." He looked for a garment tag, but there was nothing.

"Or it could belong to a bishop or a monsignor," I said. "These aren't for everyday wear, they're worn at services. It was a cold night, remember, we were buttoned up tight. In the dark, there'd be no way to know if someone was wearing one."

"Perhaps we are jumping to conclusions. It could be a priest with a bloody nose."

"Then why hide it here?"

"Right. It makes no sense."

"Give it to our friend Inspector Cipriano. Let him worry about it. I'll get these clothes to Abe."

The only thing that made sense to me was freeing Diana, and that was a long shot, but I had a better chance at that than at solving this case. Which should have made me happy, but all I did was worry as I carried Abe's brown three-piece draped over my arm.

CHAPTER TWENTY-SEVEN

LUCK WAS WITH me, although running into Bishop Zlatko wasn't the same thing as your horse placing at Suffolk Downs. I had been on my way to look for him when I turned a corner in the Medieval Palace, and there he was, wearing a snow-white rochet over his cassock and hurrying along the corridor, his heels clicking against the shiny marble mosaics. When he saw me, his eyes darted everywhere else but in my direction.

"Bishop," I said, loud enough that he couldn't ignore me, and sharp enough to draw stares from a scurrying monk who had probably never heard a bishop spoken to like that.

"I cannot talk. I am on my way to celebrate midday Mass. Two priests from my diocese have made the arduous journey here, and I promised them a Mass in the basilica."

"I'll walk with you," I said. "Nice rochet, by the way. I learned that word today." His had lace borders. A bit ladylike for my taste.

"I am glad to hear you have discovered something in your time here," Zlatko said, a sneer turning up one lip. He didn't miss a beat. Kept walking at an even pace, hands relaxed at his sides. No widening of the eyes, no flush of red in his cheeks, only quick sarcasm. If it was his bloody rochet, he was doing a damn good job of hiding it.

"Oh, I've learned a lot. About your activities in Croatia, for instance. I wonder what the Pontifical Commission will do when they hear from Cardinal Boetto?"

"Lies! Slander!" He stopped and faced me, fists clenched and the whites of his eyes vivid. "You would do well to not spread unfounded rumors."

"Ah, so that's what your visiting priests are for," I said. "Character witnesses. To refute what Cardinal Boetto will say."

"You are a fool, Father Boyle. But not an unintelligent one."

"Hey, if I were really smart, I'd know why you and Brackett were arguing about boats. Or was it rudders?" I watched for a reaction, and wondered if I'd given too much away.

"Perhaps you are right," Zlatko said, giving away nothing at all. "You are not smart at all."

With that, he was on his way. I still had questions about where he'd been before he'd headed to the radio tower, but they seemed less important now, given his total lack of reaction to my hints about the rochet, and how he threw the rudder mention right back at me. I thought about following him into the basilica and taking in a Mass, but the notion of him at the altar gave me the shivers. I decided on some larceny instead.

Half an hour later, with Abe in tow, we walked down the corridor in the Medieval Palace where earlier Kaz and I had searched Corrigan's room. Checking the nameplates, we stopped at Bruzzone's door and I turned to keep watch as Abe and his picks made short work of the lock. Before I could look both ways up and down the hallway, I heard a click and the door was open. I followed Abe in.

"Piece of cake," Abe said. "You coulda done it, kid. Don't Boston coppers know nothin'?"

"I like to rely on a professional, Abe." The best lock picker we had on the force was Moose Meehan, and he mainly used his right foot. With legs the size of tree trunks, he didn't need picks. Of course, we wore the bluecoats, and it was our turf. This operation required finesse, something the Boston PD at times lacked.

"What're we lookin' for?" Abe asked, looking pleased at the compliment and spiffy in his new brown suit.

"I have no idea," I said. "Sometimes it's better to do something than nothing, so here we are." Bruzzone's rooms were larger than

Corrigan's or O'Flaherty's. Seniority, maybe. He had a small bedroom and a large sitting room, with a pair of chairs by a window gracing a view of courtyards below.

"He skip town?" Abe asked.

"He didn't show up for breakfast with Monsignor O'Flaherty this morning," I said. I checked the bedroom. His bed was made, and an armoire held several pairs of black trousers, a cassock, and shirts. One surplice, no rochet. A hairbrush sat on a washstand, set below a small mirror. A book lay on his nightstand. Next to it was a bottle of pills.

"Abe, you know what *sonniferi* means?"

"No, but I think *sonno* means sleep. Maybe he needed some help with his shut-eye."

"Not the kind of thing to leave behind if you're going on a trip, is it?" I shook the bottle. It sounded half full.

"What are you doing?" a loud voice from the other room demanded. It was Bruzzone, looking none too pleased to find us in his bedroom. He looked scruffy, too. Unshaven, wrinkled clothes, his hair in need of that brush. "How dare you enter my apartment!"

"I'm sorry, Monsignor," I said, placing the bottle of pills back on the nightstand. "It appeared you had gone missing, and we were concerned."

"Who gave you a key?" Bruzzone asked, studying Abe for a second. "And who is this person?"

"He's a locksmith in civilian life," I said. "He's the key."

"You broke in?" Bruzzone looked rattled, as if he couldn't absorb what we were telling him.

"Let's sit down, Monsignor." I led him to the chairs in the study and we sat down. Abe edged toward the door, trying to look invisible, ready to bolt. "We were just looking for some clue as to where you had gone, or been taken. After the killing last night, we were worried."

"Thank you for your concern," Bruzzone said. "It was simply a shock to find anyone in my room. I assure you, I am fine." He brushed grime from his pants and pushed back his hair, pulling himself together.

"Where were you, Monsignor?"

"In Rome. It is not a crime, is it?"

"Not at all," I said, playing the helpful but confused pal. "Monsignor O'Flaherty was worried when you didn't show up this morning. He was expecting you for breakfast."

"I completely forgot. I will apologize to Hugh. And I must apologize to you as well, for being so rude. I thank you for your concern, but I simply could not sleep and went out. I often wake before dawn." He sighed and slapped his hands on his thighs. All done, time to move on, or so he hoped.

"It must have been something quite important," I said, "to cause you to leave the Holy See. I'm told you haven't crossed the border into Rome in quite some time."

"That is true, not since my last trip to Genoa, working with Cardinal Boetto. We had some close calls, and I thought the Gestapo was following me. I felt it prudent to not take any chances here. What is the American expression? To lie low?"

"Yes," I said. "What was so important that you left after the murder of Soletto?"

"Why do you say that?" Bruzzone asked. I wasn't entirely sure, except that he had the look of a guy who'd slept in his clothes, if he'd slept at all.

"Because you look like you've had a rough time of it. My guess would be that you were out after curfew and had to hide out somewhere."

"That would have been difficult. The Germans enforce a curfew, and are guarding the perimeter. They would have picked up anyone crossing over."

"But you got in okay?" I asked.

"Certainly. As a citizen of the Vatican State, I have no problem during the day."

"So where were you? Whenever it was you were there?"

"I am sorry, Father Boyle. That must remain confidential. Even you are not privy to everything here. Or in Rome."

He sounded remarkably like Brackett had, when I'd hinted to

him about Rudder. Or Zlatko, for that matter. There was a certainty in his voice, as if he were backed up by some higher power. Not *that* higher power, but one backed up with hardware.

"Abe, wait outside for me, okay?" I wanted to try something, and it would be better if Abe didn't hear. He didn't need coaxing to leave the scene of a crime, and I heard the door shut behind him. I let the silence settle around us, and watched Bruzzone's eyes. He was nervous. But anyone would be, lying to a cop as he was.

"What is it now? I have matters to attend to," he said, shifting in his seat. He couldn't wait to get rid of me.

"Tell me this, Monsignor. Are you Rudder?" He stopped fidgeting. His eyes widened for a split second, showing a flash of white that faded as he sat back, sighing as if I'd knocked the air out of him.

"We all have our burdens in this war, my son. That is the last thing I will say about it."

It was all I needed to hear. I collected Abe and we headed back to the German College.

"You need to break in anywhere else?" Abe asked as we walked behind Saint Peter's. "I hear they got a ton of jewels and stuff stored over there in the Sacristy. That church they got hangin' off the basilica."

"Yeah, you and me could clean up, Abe." I knew Abe wasn't serious, at least not too serious. But it was his line of work, and I understood that he couldn't help but case out the joint, even if the joint was the Vatican. "But how would we ever get it out of here?"

"Cut in a Kraut or two, and we're all set. Gotta be a coupla those bastards who'd take a bribe, know what I mean?"

"Yeah, I do," I said. Abe had triggered something buried deep within my mind, but not so deep that it didn't wake up to the notion of a German as a way out of here. I was already busy juggling what I knew about Brackett, Corrigan, Zlatko, and Bruzzone, so I hadn't had time to think it through, but it had taken root anyway.

"Abe, we all set for the morning?" I asked as we entered the German College.

"Yeah. I get you at O'Flaherty's room at 0830. If you ain't there, I go with Rino the barber. We meet at the safe house in Trastevere."

I told him to get some chow and a good night's sleep. There weren't a lot of alternatives, but for a guy who had a way with locks and a new civilian suit, there might be temptations.

Kaz had left a note in our room saying he was over at Santa Marta, and to meet him for dinner there. Not surprising, since that's where Nini hung her hat. I strolled over, enjoying the fresh, cool air. The rain had passed and everything felt clean and new. Be nice if only it cleansed people, too. But perhaps there would never be enough rain to wash away the sins of this war.

"Where's Nini?" I asked when I found Kaz in the refectory, sitting alone.

"Helping to prepare dinner," he said. "We had time for tea. It was quite civilized. I do wish I weren't wearing this priestly clothing though. It inhibits me."

"Maybe we'll get you a new suit like Abe's. How did it go with Cipriano?"

"The inspector will canvass all clerics above the rank of bishop to see if anyone is missing a rochet. I assume that does not include Pope Pius himself. There is a store that sells clerical clothing, near the printing office, and he will check to see if anyone recalls one being sold recently. He thought there was a fair chance of finding out if one had been stolen, since they are expensive, with all that lace handwork."

"All that will tell us is more about the lousy Vatican locks."

"Well then, I hope you found something more useful in Bruzzone's room," Kaz said, a bit offended.

"I did. Bruzzone."

"Alive?" Kaz asked. A reasonable question.

"Yes, and looking like he'd spent the night somewhere else. He walked in on us, but I sold him on the story that we were worried about where he'd gone."

"Which was where?"

"He wouldn't say. He was nervous until we got to that question, then he grew a backbone. Sound familiar?"

Kaz took a moment to think it through. "Brackett," he said. "At the radio tower. When you asked him about Rudder."

"Right. And I asked Bruzzone point-blank if he was Rudder. He stonewalled me. As did Zlatko when I put it to him, although he'd stonewall me for the hell of it."

"Are all three involved with Rudder?" Kaz said, furrowing his brow. "No, wait. O'Flaherty said Corrigan was Rudder. What's going on here?"

"Correction. O'Flaherty said that Corrigan was Rudder. Big difference."

"I don't understand," Kaz said.

Now Kaz is the smartest guy I know, when it comes to stuff they teach in college. But sometimes the simplest things elude him. Like this. "If everyone is Rudder, then no one is."

Kaz went silent, and I could see the wheels turning. He put all that brainpower into high gear, and it took him about thirty seconds. "You mean, no one is the *real* Rudder," he said. "The Germans have captured or killed him, whoever he was, and are feeding us false reports."

"You got it," I said, imagining how it might have gone. "The OSS team sets up in Rome, where the Germans nab them and their radio. They turn them, or replace them after they wring out all their secrets. Then they recruit agents and begin harvesting information. That way, they know what's going on behind the Vatican walls, and control what gets communicated back to headquarters. So we get the real dope on Soletto, for instance. That was in the OSS report we read."

"So Brackett and Bruzzone think they are helping out the OSS, and their contact tells them under no circumstances to reveal their role to us."

"Yes," I said, suddenly taking in the implication. "Which means the false Rudder knew about us."

"Both Brackett and Bruzzone knew we were coming, so it is not surprising," Kaz said. "But what about Zlatko? He hardly seems the type to spy for the Allies."

"I don't know. Maybe he stumbled onto it somehow and was threatening Brackett."

"Or," Kaz said, "he was a plant. To watch the other two. Or three, I should say, counting Corrigan."

"Could be," I said. "It would be a good story. He tells them he's really pro-Allies, but has to hide the fact in Croatia because it would be too dangerous. He could say he's feeding the OSS dope about the Ustashi. It would sell."

"Billy," Kaz said, "perhaps it is too dangerous to enter the Regina Coeli tomorrow. You might not leave."

"I can't stay away, Kaz. I don't think I could live with myself if I did."

"You may not live if you do."

"It's a helluva spot to be in, isn't it?" I took in a deep breath, as if a little extra oxygen might help things make sense. "I could stay safe tomorrow and regret it for the rest of my life. Or take the risk and live with the consequences."

"Perhaps you need some spiritual guidance," Kaz said. "There is no shortage of that here."

Kaz was right, but the problem was the guidance went in twenty different directions. Seeing the Vatican up close wasn't what I'd thought it would be. Instead of a spiritual sanctuary, it seemed more like city hall at election time. Politics and deception, all in the name of the greater good. Monsignor O'Flaherty was a brave and decent guy, but I wondered why there weren't more like him, and no Bishop Zlatkos at all.

Nini came to sit with us, but I made my excuses and left them to themselves. Or to be alone myself, I guess. I wandered through the gardens, trying to think through everything that might happen tomorrow. That drove me crazy, so I gave it up pretty quickly. I found myself in Saint Peter's Square, and decided to go into the basilica, uncertain if there'd be another chance.

As before, I was overwhelmed by the sheer size of it. I felt small and insignificant under the grand, high ceilings, and immediately wished I hadn't entered. I needed to be bucked up, not humbled. I turned to leave, not finding what I wanted in the holiest of holies. To my left, I saw a sculpture. I recognized it from pictures I'd seen in *Life* magazine. The *Pietà*. Its title meant pity in Italian.

I was drawn to it, even as I tried to make for the door. The white marble gleamed even in the faint interior light. The dead body of Jesus draped across his mother Mary's lap, her hand raised as if questioning, *Why?*

There were no answers here, only sadness and sorrow.

CHAPTER TWENTY-EIGHT

RINO MESSINA WAS right on time, Abe looked good in his new suit, and the gendarmes had not taken me away during the night. I figured we were off to a good start.

"Carry this, me boy," O'Flaherty said as he placed a Bible in my hands. "You'll look more the part. And don't worry about looking a wee bit nervous. No man in his right mind would whistle while he works in that hellhole."

"Yes," Rino said. "I am there so often it is easy. But even for the guards, their first time is hard. Strange, yes?"

"Yes, strange," said Monsignor O'Flaherty, leading Rino out the door before he could tell us more about how the place gives even the guards the willies.

"You sure about this?" Abe asked.

"Sure enough," I said, trying for a jaunty tone. "We'll be fine."

"Good luck, Billy," Kaz said, shaking my hand. We'd agreed that there was no reason for Kaz to come along, and some danger if he did. Koch had his photograph, and there was no sense in risking his neck on the streets of Rome. "If all goes well, we will dine here with Diana tonight."

"That sounds grand," I said, trying for a confidence that didn't come as easily as I'd wished. Kaz clasped his other hand over mine, and then let go, turning away to stand at the window.

"Now, Billy," O'Flaherty said as we stood outside in the small piazza by the German College. "You should prepare yourself. Sister Justina has been held for quite a while. She may have been interrogated. Harshly. There's simply no way to know what her condition is."

"I know," I said. It was all I could say. I knew about Gestapo kitchens. I knew about degradation.

"That's not what I mean, son," he said in a whisper. "She may not be able to move under her own power. You will have to judge if it's safe for all of you to go out if you have to carry her. It may attract too much attention."

"Judge?" I said. "I can't judge anything. All I can do is try my damnedest to get her out. I'll send Rino and Abe out ahead of me if I have to. If there's any risk."

"Life is a risk, Billy. God be with you. I will pray to Saint Michael the Archangel for you."

"Send one up to Saint Jude as well, Monsignor." Saint Michael, the patron saint of police officers, was the defender of heaven, having chased Satan and the fallen angels into Hell. He was a righteous holy warrior, but I felt closer to Saint Jude, the patron saint of hopeless causes. Michael had strength, but Jude had faith, and there was so much strength deployed against me that faith was all I could count on.

"I will pray to them both," O'Flaherty said. "I'll not walk you to the border line. It will be better if you're not seen with me. Farewell, Billy."

With that, he was gone. Abe, Rino, and I walked out of the piazza, crossing the white line, not giving the German guards a second look. I clutched the Bible to my chest as we took a hard right onto the Via delle Mura Aurelie, putting distance between us and the cordon of guards. Abe carried Rino's leather satchel, holding the tools of the barber's trade.

"It is longer this way," Rino whispered, glancing around at the few people out on the street. "But fewer *Tedeschi*. Now, no more talk. You pray."

Fewer Germans and a prayer or two sounded like a fine idea.

Abe walked with his gaze riveted to the sidewalk, as he'd been instructed. We meandered through side streets, the mustard-colored walls leaning toward each other above our heads. Laundry hung damp and motionless from windows, the occasional sound of a baby crying or a child laughing breaking the silence. It was as if the city was holding its breath—for me, for Diana, for all the hidden souls. For liberation. I prayed, but not coherently. It was a begging, the big *all in*, the wager of my soul if only this worked and Diana came out safely.

A narrow passageway led us out onto the Via della Lungara, the main road alongside the Tiber. I was jolted out of my dreams by the sight of the river and the city arrayed on the other side. Low buildings along the river, their orange-tiled roofs lit by the rising sun, and the rest of Rome beyond them.

Rino touched my arm. To our right was a blood-red flag, the black swastika hidden in its folds. One block away stood the *Carcere Giudiziaro Regina Coeli*, the Queen of Heaven herself. I tried to take a deep breath, but my heart was pounding too fast for my lungs to catch up. My legs shook and it was all I could do to move ahead. An icy stab of fear choked back all my prayers and bargains with God, leaving only terror and shame at the intense desire to turn and run radiating out from my gut, cleansing my body and mind of all thoughts but that of self-preservation. But before I knew it, I was following Rino as he approached the two stone-faced guards at the door, my Bible clutched in sweaty palms and Abe in lockstep.

One guard was German, the other Italian, in the black-and-gray uniform of the *Guardia Nazionale Repubblicana*, Mussolini's Fascist security police. Rino nodded as we passed, the sentries bored and apathetic. No one got out, and no one wanted in. They had a lonely job. We turned a corner and followed a narrow passage between two wings of the prison. Broken crates and squashed produce told me we were at the entrance where Rino's pal was on guard duty. It smelled like the back alley of a restaurant. Grease, piss, and rotting vegetables.

Inside was different. We walked down a wide, tiled hallway, our heels sending echoes eerily off the stone walls. At the end of the corridor, a guard stood at a lectern, a notebook open in front of him. Opposite stood another GNR soldier, Beretta submachine gun slung over his shoulder and pointed in our general direction.

"*Il padre ed il mio apprendista sono con me,*" Rino said to the guard with the book, ignoring the one with the submachine gun. I held the Bible to my chest and gave a little bow to the guy with the gun, figuring it was a standard priestly move. He surprised me with a brief nod, his eyes darting to the passageway beyond. I glanced in that direction, but there was no one there. Maybe he was waiting for coffee, or nervous about his sergeant showing up.

I listened to Rino and the other guard speaking in quick bursts of Italian. He signed the book, they laughed, and Rino left a package of cigarettes to show they were all friends. The guard waved us through, into a large square room lit by high windows, the morning sun creating a mosaic pattern on the floor. It was spacious and bright, not like any prison I'd ever seen.

Rino leaned in close and whispered, "We have twenty minutes only. Marcello's shift changes early." Abe's eyes widened for a split second, then reverted to the bored indifference of an apprentice barber toting his master's gear. That was the advantage to working with an experienced thief. I could count on him to keep a poker face and not draw attention. Me, I wasn't so sure of.

Certain that the pounding of my heart could be heard by the sentries out on the street, I followed Rino as he waved casually to the guards and policemen in the hallway. I willed him to hurry, but he kept to a slow, rolling gait as I pressed the Bible close to my chest. Finally, we entered a circular room with four corridors leading off like spokes on a wheel. The windows were three stories tall, topped with graceful arches. The room was painted bright white and the four directions of the compass were set in the floor, a colorful mosaic that cruelly showed the inmates every direction they had no chance of taking.

Rino took the hallway to the right, which led into a wing of cells, three tiers tall. Circular stairs at each end gave access to catwalks, where guards patrolled, looking down as we entered. Each catwalk extended to the far wall where they curved around out of sight, connecting to more cells. Moans echoed from the far end, as a sharp, loud cry of pain came from the cell opposite us. I jumped at the sound, but Rino hauled himself up the stairs, as if it were just another day at work.

There was a ruckus on the second tier, raised voices in Italian and German. Three men in black leather overcoats were yelling at a jailer, who was fumbling with his keys at the door of a cell. He finally got it open and two of them hauled out a prisoner. Barely able to stand, his clothes filthy and in tatters, his face a palette of bruises, he was propped up against the railing as the next door was opened, and another prisoner was pulled out. This guy had no marks, and his appearance told me he'd been in the cell for a couple of days, tops. Unshaven, grimy, and disheveled, but standing on his own.

The third man turned to face the second prisoner and spoke to him in Italian. It was a gentle voice, soothing and calm. But I knew it masked something else. The speaker was Pietro Koch. He wore the same wisp of a smile I'd seen on his face at Saint Peter's as he nodded to his two leather-coated accomplices. They tipped the bloodied prisoner over the railing, and watched him fall to the hard floor below.

It wasn't that far to fall, but he fell flat, the sharp sound of cracking bone followed by silence. Deep-red blood seeped out from under the body. His legs gave a final thrash, and then the body was inert, the inescapable pose of death—all gravity and finality as the physical body became nothing more than a leaking bag of bones and blood.

Koch gave an appreciative laugh, and patted his prisoner on the shoulder, as if complimenting him on watching the spectacle. Handcuffs were produced and Koch's henchmen led the prisoner toward us as the jailer protested. One of them replied in German, the other in Italian. I didn't understand the words, but the meaning was clear. *Go to hell.*

They brushed past us, the prisoner wearing a stunned, vacant look on his face. Koch came last, stopping smack in front of me, his languid eyes looking deep into mine, as if they could see my thoughts, hook into my brain, and pull the truth out into the open.

"*Prega per lui,*" he said, then patted my shoulder as he had the prisoner's. He chuckled, a gentle, amused laughter, as he waited for me to respond. Behind him, Rino lifted his hands, palms together in prayer. *Pray for him,* he was telling me.

"*Sì,*" I said in a whisper as I kissed the Bible and took the stairs, praying indeed, but for Koch not to say another word, to not hear the sound of steel on leather, a pistol being drawn, a shouted command to halt. All I wanted to hear was the sound of my own shoes on the metal stairs.

"*Ma non per me!*" Koch shouted out, and laughter followed from the other two thugs. That I understood. But not for me. No worries there. We went up, they went down, as the guards on the ground floor directed two prisoners to drag the body away.

The third tier had a guard posted at the top, seated at a small desk off the landing. This must be the unbribable Fascist that Rino had told us about. Along the catwalk, a woman guard stood gazing at the scene below. Prisoners were bringing in mops and pails to clean up, and it looked like this was the high point of her day. Rino signed a sheet on the guard's desk. He'd explained that since this tier was the women's section, there was this last checkpoint, mainly to keep idle guards away from the female prisoners. Rino and the guard laughed over something, and another package of cigarettes appeared. The jailer thanked Rino and opened the pack, leaned his chair back against the wall, and lit up. This put him out of sight of the catwalk, maybe so he wouldn't have to share his smokes. Whatever the reason, it gave us a break.

We walked toward the female guard, who waved at Rino while making eyes at Abe. He winked at her, being either a great actor or a consummate ladies' man.

"*Buongiorno, Fabrizia,*" Rino said. Fabrizia smiled as she opened one of the cell doors. Abe played his part well, admiring the curves beneath the uniform. Fabrizia moved to another door and opened it, playing with her hair and chatting with Rino, maybe asking if he could give her a trim. Her hair was black and curly, popping out from under her cap in all directions.

I passed each door as she opened them. Inside the first were two women, huddled in fear on their small, narrow cots. One was bruised and bloodied, another had a dirty bandage covering one eye. Haircuts were probably the last thing on their minds.

Now there were three doors open. I caught a glance of Rino nodding toward where the catwalk curved around the wall. We wanted cell number 321, and we were in front of 313. With Rino consulting Fabrizia about her hair, and the open cell doors blocking her view, Abe and I rounded the corner. He stopped at a barred door that connected to a circular staircase at the opposite end of the wing from where we had entered. This door was out of sight of the guard and would be our exit route. Abe got out his picks and made quick work of it, leaving it unlocked behind us. We had to move fast, and I trusted Rino to disengage from Fabrizia and join us. She'd have to stay by the prisoners or lock up, and either way it gave us some time. Not much, but enough.

A red sign greeted us as we came to the last of the cells. Limitato. Restricted.

Each cell had a Judas hole that was latched shut. Beneath that was a thick iron bar that was set into a lock welded onto the door. Cell 320 was unlocked, probably empty. But number 321 was closed up tight.

"Kee-rist," Abe whispered. I shielded him with my body as best I could as he knelt to work his picks into the lock. He cursed under his breath as he went. This lock seemed tougher than any of the locks in the Vatican. I pressed my hand against the cold steel door, the only thing that stood between Diana and freedom. Or me, at least. Freedom was a few more doors away, and we had only minutes before the shift changed and our bought-and-paid-for guard went home for the day. Voices rose from the main hall, but it was only the prisoners cleaning up. The clatter of pails echoed against the walls, but I still heard the *click* as Abe picked the lock. With a grin on his face, he pulled the iron bolt back and opened the door.

I expected the worst. I knew she'd be in rough shape, even if the worst hadn't happened. But the last thing I expected was to see Diana seated at a table, dressed in a clean gray skirt and white silk blouse. Two empty chairs faced her. Her light-brown hair was pulled back from her face, which looked pale but otherwise undamaged. Her expression was full of apology, or sorrow, I couldn't tell, but either way it wasn't good.

Her eyes were rimmed with tears as she gave a quick glance to my right, where a German officer lounged against the wall.

"Lieutenant Boyle," a familiar voice said. "I believe you are acquainted with Miss Diana Seaton, also known as Sister Justina?"

CHAPTER TWENTY-NINE

"DIANA! WHAT'S GOING on?" I barely got the words out before shouts echoed from the catwalk outside.

"Do not worry, Lieutenant Boyle," Erich Remke said. "Your comrades will not be hurt. Now, sit down. We must talk."

I'd encountered Remke twice before. Once when I was on the wrong side of the bars in a Vichy French jail cell, and another time in Sicily, when we were vying for the allegiance of a Mafia boss. I hoped he wasn't sore about how that had worked out.

"I prefer to stand, Major Remke," I said, trying not to look concerned about the scuffle outside the door, and to overcome the shock running through my brain. What was happening here?

"It is Colonel Remke now, Lieutenant," Remke said as he sat down. "And you are still a lieutenant? Does the American Army not recognize officers with initiative?"

"What's going on here?" I asked. Still standing. It was about the only thing I had control over.

"Go ahead, Billy, sit down," Diana said. She tried for a smile, and it almost worked. So I sat, and our eyes locked on to each other's.

"There, now we can talk, the three of us," Remke said. He spoke excellent English, with more of an Oxford accent than a German one. He was tall, with a chiseled face, all angles and soldierly intent. He wore his uniform well, the green-gray fabric well tailored. On

one sleeve was a cuff with *Brandenburg* in Gothic script. I knew that
was a special commando outfit attached to the Abwehr, the German
intelligence service. Remke noticed my glance. "Yes, as you can see,
Miss Seaton and I are engaged in the same work. Intelligence, or
what passes for it."

"What do you want?" I asked. I'd been thinking of doing what
we'd been told to do if captured, which was to give name, rank, and
serial number, then clam up. But this was all too elaborate, too complex. We were way beyond the protocols of the Geneva Convention.

"Are you not glad to see Miss Seaton well?" Remke demanded.
"You must know the reputation of this place. This is a pleasant surprise, is it not?"

"Diana, did you tell him your name?"

Remke leaned back and nodded to Diana, giving her the floor.
They were a bit too much at ease with each other. Something was
up, something that I needed to figure out, fast.

"No, Billy. He knew it. And, I know this sounds odd, but it's so
good to see you," she said, her lip quivering. I reached out with one
hand to take hers, but Remke held me back.

"I am sorry, Lieutenant Boyle. For now, we have important matters to discuss. Later, you and Miss Seaton may embrace. But not
yet."

"You're Rudder," I said. It was chancy, but if I were right, it might
throw him off. It did.

"Very good," Remke said, surprise flashing across his face. "How
did you come to that conclusion?"

"You're here, for starters. You know Diana's name. A few clues
from the Vatican. Too many people claiming to be Rudder, or being
in contact with him."

"Yes, I am Rudder. We captured an American OSS team four
months ago, radio and all. We had been watching them for some
time, and monitoring their transmissions. Once we took them, we
kept transmitting and recruited new agents."

"So the people in the Vatican thought they were helping the
Allies? Brackett, Corrigan, Bruzzone?"

"The first two, yes. Monsignor Bruzzone was not recruited. He has kept a low profile since Genoa, where I hear he was almost trapped by the Gestapo." Score one for Bruzzone; he hadn't lied to me about Rudder.

"Even Bishop Zlatko?"

"No, not the good bishop. He is working with us, trying to curry favor with the high command. He reported on activities within the Vatican while he tried to ferret out information about Tito and his Partisans, but he is of little use to me. He has peddled the same information to the Gestapo, who have him on their payroll. That has become inconvenient for him, of course. The last I heard, he was trying to convince an American diplomat that he was a double agent, and on the side of the Allies. I think he is planning for the future."

"I doubt the Allies will take him seriously."

"Or the Wehrmacht. The violence of the Ustashi left even the SS stunned, which is a remarkable achievement." His eyes avoided mine, and I wondered at the atrocities he'd seen to make that judgment.

"I'm sure that kept you up nights. Now what is this all about? You could have picked us up on the way here. Why bring me all the way to Diana's cell?" As I spoke, I remembered the situation in Algiers, when Remke found Colonel Harding and me in that Vichy jail cell. He let us live for his own purposes, to help free one of his agents also being held by the Vichy police.

"Because I have a task for you, Lieutenant Boyle. One that is especially suited to the nephew of General Eisenhower."

"How did you know . . . ?" I'd never let that slip, and I didn't believe Diana would have told him. I also knew the OSS hadn't included that tidbit in any of their transmissions.

"After our encounter in Sicily, I began to build a file on you, Lieutenant William Boyle, late of the Boston Police Department. A distant but trusted relative and confidant of General Eisenhower."

"Very distant, and as you point out, still a lowly lieutenant, so don't count on me being worth much in a trade." I figured Remke wanted to swap me for one of his agents, and if Diana wasn't enough of a bargaining chip, maybe he thought I was.

"No, Lieutenant Boyle. I do not want to exchange you. I want you to help me end the war."

That was the last thing I'd expected to hear. Looking at Diana, I could tell she wasn't surprised. Remke had filled her in, and from the way she held herself, I knew she believed it. There was no fear, no hesitation in her eyes, more of an eagerness to draw me in. I wanted to trust her instincts, but this was happening too quickly.

"Perhaps you should have thought of that sooner," I said. It's always easier to fall back on a wisecrack when you don't know what else to do.

"We did," Remke said, leaning back in his chair. "Allow me a brief history lesson. In 1939, Admiral Canaris of the Abwehr began to recruit intelligence agents with links to the Vatican. Canaris sent Josef Müeller to Rome to meet with the Pope. The message was that an anti-Nazi circle existed and that plans for the assassination of Hitler and a coup d'état were in place."

"You're telling me that the top ranks of the German Intelligence service are all anti-Nazi? That's hard to believe."

"I am telling you nothing that is not known to the highest ranks of your own intelligence services. Now, in late 1939, Müeller met with the Pope's private secretary, Father Leiber. He laid out the plans for him and asked that the Pope contact the British and help determine if they would support the coup and not attack Germany while the anti-Nazi forces were struggling for control."

"The SS probably wouldn't give up easily," I said. "Even with Hitler dead."

"Exactly. We needed to be assured that England would not strike in the midst of a German civil war. That would only turn the nation against us."

"So what did the Pope do?"

"He agreed to help. He met with the British ambassador, Sir D'Arcy Osborne."

"I know him," I said, trying to take in the enormity of what I was hearing.

"Yes, I know," Remke said. "You dined with him the day you arrived."

"How do you know that?"

"Through an Italian boy who works in his kitchen. Sir D'Arcy is well aware he is an informant. The trick in Rome is to know who is informing on whom, and to tailor your comments accordingly. In any case, Pius told D'Arcy of the plot, and the ambassador forwarded the information to the British Foreign Office. Cables were exchanged, and for a while it seemed as if the English took us seriously."

"But they didn't?"

"Not in the end. In February 1940, they were given the plans for the invasion of France and the Low Countries. They reacted by demanding a list of all the conspirators, their ranks, roles in the new government, and so on."

"Wait a minute. You're saying that the British had the plans for your invasion of France in 1940?"

"Yes. They were passed through the Pope's offices to Sir D'Arcy, and then on to the Foreign Office. They are probably buried deep in a locked room somewhere in London, if they have not been destroyed. Quite embarrassing, if the truth came out. Admiral Canaris also informed the Dutch directly about the invasion plans, but they thought it a trick and ignored him."

"There was no coup in 1940," I said, trying to get back on track.

"No. As you can imagine, no one thought it wise to hand a list of the top opponents of the regime to the British. They could easily have used it in an attempt to destabilize Germany, which would have only cost the lives of many good men."

"And then Hitler defeats France and the British hightail it out of Dunkirk, and he's in the catbird seat."

"The British depart in a great hurry, and Hitler is left in an enviable position," Diana translated, noticing Remke's confused expression.

"Ah, American idioms. Wonderful use of language, I must admit," Remke said. "Yes, without a guarantee of cooperation, and given Hitler's victories, nothing could happen in 1940. His success in France was our greatest undoing. With the non-aggression pact with the Russians, our eastern border was secure. In the West, France was ours and England stood alone. Some thought it would end with a negotiated peace, and others believed Hitler was the genius he insisted he was. Instead, that little Austrian fool decided to attack Russia when he became bored with sacrificing his Luftwaffe over England. Since then, there have been several attempts on his life, but nothing even close to success."

"You've got something in the works," I said. I was beginning to see a glimmer of hope. Remke was naming names, and that meant either he was gambling for big odds or he didn't plan on either of us ever repeating any of them.

"I am only a courier. Admiral Canaris put this plan together. I reported to him when I uncovered your relationship to Eisenhower. Then, when we heard you were coming to Rome, things began to fall into place."

"Is that why you grabbed Diana? Sister Justina?"

"No, Billy," Diana said. "I was picked up in a routine identity check. I was carrying food for some of our guests, and the police arrested me for trading on the black market."

"But you knew who she was," I said to Remke. "And you used her as bait to get your hands on me."

"Yes. What better place to meet than the Regina Coeli? The Gestapo would never guess we were using the prison for our rendezvous. And I wanted a certain leverage, to guarantee you play your part. This place is quite suitable for that purpose."

"To blackmail me, you mean."

"If you should prove recalcitrant, this visit should serve to remind you of what could happen to both of you. Many are left to their fate in the Regina Coeli every day. Two more would not be noticed."

"I haven't been mistreated, Billy," Diana said. I knew what she meant. Diana had been tortured and raped in Algeria by a psychotic Vichy officer, and it had been a long road back for her. And us. Since the war began, Diana had seen more action than many men. Serving with the British Expeditionary Force in 1940, as a switchboard operator in Lord Gort's headquarters, she was one of the lucky ones who made it out of Dunkirk, just ahead of the Germans, only to have her destroyer blown out of the water courtesy of the Luftwaffe. She'd watched wounded soldiers on stretchers slide off the decks into the cold Channel waters as the ship went down, and barely survived herself. Since then, Diana had constantly flirted with death, perhaps to test herself to see if she deserved to live while so many around her had died. I looked into her eyes, and nodded. It was very good to know.

"If you should fail me, I can promise Miss Seaton will never leave this prison alive," Remke said. "Nor your comrades."

"That doesn't leave me with much of a choice," I said.

"Good," Remke said, his attitude softening. "I was quite glad to hear that you had rescued Miss Seaton in Algeria."

"And your agent as well," I said. In the group that had been taken hostage by the renegade Vichy, at least one had been a German agent. We never knew which one, and I hadn't really cared, since I got Diana back.

"Yes. I was also pleased that the situation was resolved. I would have done so myself, but we were 'hightailing' it for Tunisia at the time." Remke smiled as he used his new Americanism. I had resolved the situation with a knife, and while it helped, there was too much hurt for revenge alone to heal.

We sat in silence for a minute, the small cell thick with the past. Maybe Remke knew the details, or maybe he felt them in the air.

"So basically, you're going to hold Diana and the men who came with me as hostages, to insure I take some crazy message to the Pope, which you hope will end the war. The same message that the British disregarded four years ago, before Germany burned, looted, and murdered all across the map of Europe."

Remke glowered at me. He wasn't the sort of officer who liked being talked back to by a lieutenant, even one related to Ike. A lot like another colonel I knew. "It is all the more important now," Remke said, slamming his fist on the table. "How many more will die as you crawl your way up the Italian mountains? How many more when you invade France? How many civilians will die in the terror bombings? How many more tens of thousands of soldiers will die on the Eastern Front? How many Jews, Gypsies, political prisoners, and others will die in the camps in the east? And how far will the Soviets go when all is said and done?"

"How do I know you care about all those lives?" I said, moving closer to Remke to match his anger. "Maybe all you want is to protect Germany from the Russians. There's going to be one helluva butcher's bill to pay when they cross your border." Maybe this was why they wanted to approach the Vatican. With their well-known desire to keep the godless Soviets away from Eastern Europe, Pius and his advisors would probably see eyeball to eyeball with the Germans on this one.

"I must admit, personally, to some truth in what you say. My family is from East Prussia. They will be the first to encounter the Russians if they get that far."

"When they get that far," I said. "Not if. Otherwise you wouldn't be here."

"None of us would be here if the English had dealt with us seriously in 1940," Remke said. "Remember that. Ask your own Colonel Samuel Harding. If he doesn't have access to that information, he can certainly obtain it."

"Stop it," Diana said. "Both of you. If there's a chance, Billy, you should take it. And Colonel Remke, tell Billy what you have to offer." We both stared at her. "Now."

"What are you offering? Besides our freedom?"

"Your freedom will come, for all of you, once you deliver the message and I have confirmation. There is nothing to this that is injurious to the Allied armies. Quite the opposite, I hope."

"So what's the offer?"

"This," Remke said, withdrawing a folded stack of papers from his jacket pocket and tossing them on the table. "The Auschwitz Protocol."

"It's the proof we've been looking for, Billy. Of what is happening in the camps," Diana said, casting a glance at Remke, who had leaned back in his chair as if to put distance between himself and the document. "I've read it, and it is damning."

"Two Slovakian Jews, Alfred Wetzler and Rudolph Vrba, were transported to Auschwitz in 1942," Remke said, as if reciting from a report he'd read many times. "They witnessed everything that went on in Auschwitz and the nearby work camp, Birkenau. Selections for gassing. Random murders, starvation, brutality. They escaped quite recently and made their way to Slovakia, where an underground Jewish organization interviewed them and wrote up this report. The first version was in Slovak, and has been translated into German."

I picked up the typewritten sheets. I couldn't make heads or tails of the German, but there were hand-drawn diagrams showing the layout of a giant camp complex. "What is this?" I asked, pointing to an oddly shaped building.

"Gas chambers and a crematorium for disposing of the bodies," Diana said. "On a massive scale."

"Can you read any of this?" I asked her.

"A little. This passage, for instance, from February 1943. It speaks of two large transports coming into the camp." She traced her finger along the text, translating slowly. "'Polish, French, and Dutch Jews, who in the main, were sent to the gas chambers. The number gassed during this month is estimated at ninety thousand. Two thousand Aryan Poles, mostly intellectuals.' It goes on and on."

"Now, Lieutenant Boyle, are you satisfied?" Remke asked, his eyes glancing away from the document, away from me and Diana. He seemed to find no place to rest his gaze. "The shame of my nation is laid before you. The fruits of our inaction. We have tried to stop this madness and failed. We have warned our own enemies of invasion and betrayed our oaths, only to see Hitler and his Nazis win at every turn. All I ask is for you to simply deliver a document to the Vatican."

I was overwhelmed. Finding Diana, listening to the unbelievable numbers in the report, trying to figure out Remke's real motives—it was all too much. I was just a dime-a-dozen lieutenant, an ex-cop who happened to be on a general's family tree.

"Do you know Milton, Colonel Remke?" Diana asked, giving me time to think.

"Fairly well," he said. "My English professor at Heidelberg had us read it in the original. Why?"

"Deluded with a shew of the forbidden Tree springing up before them, they greedily reaching to take of the Fruit, chew dust and bitter ashes. The proceedings of Sin and Death," she recited.

"Paradise lost, indeed," Remke said. They both looked at me.

I knew Milton was some sort of poet, but I didn't understand what they were getting at. I only knew I didn't want to regret what I did next and remember nothing but dust and bitter ashes in *my* mouth.

"Yes, I'll do it," I said. "But I want something else."

"What?" Remke asked, sounding weary, impatient, and angry at the same time.

"Severino Rossi."

CHAPTER THIRTY

REMKE DIDN'T HAVE time to ask who Severino Rossi was or why I wanted him. One of his men stepped into the cell and hurriedly whispered in his ear, glancing nervously in my direction. Remke nodded, then stood and gathered up the Auschwitz Protocol. "Follow me," he said. "We must leave immediately. The Gestapo knows about Miss Seaton."

He barked orders to his men and within seconds we were descending the stairs to the main floor. Rino and Abe, their hands bound, cast startled glances at us as Remke hurried Diana and me past them, our hands noticeably free. "Don't worry," I said as I went by, but I doubted that gave them much comfort or answered the questions forming on their lips.

"*Ruhe*," said one of the Germans, which I knew meant quiet. Rino and Abe took the hint.

We were out the door in under a minute and Remke hustled us into the rear of an idling staff car. He took the front seat and the driver sped off before his door was closed. Behind us I saw Abe and Rino getting the same treatment. Their handlers were pros, laying hands on the crowns of their heads, pushing them into the automobile as cops back home did. It made me wonder what the hell an honest cop would do under the Nazis, and glad that I didn't have to make that kind of choice.

"Where are we going?" I asked.

"Your friends are going to an Abwehr safe house," Remke said. "They will stay there until you have completed your assignment. Then we will return them to Vatican territory."

"And where are you taking us?" Diana asked, clasping my hand in hers.

"To dinner, of course," Remke said, as the church bells of Rome began to ring in the midday hour. "At the Excelsior Hotel." He had to be joking, playing with us while he figured out how to sidestep the Gestapo. I held onto Diana's hand, her touch my only truth. Even here, in uncertain captivity, it was enough.

We crossed the Tiber and wound through narrow side streets, empty of traffic. On the main thoroughfare, the only vehicles were German. Trucks, staff cars, and motorcycles, most heading south to the front at Anzio. We turned off onto the Via Veneto, and I had a feeling we were entering one of the ritzier sections of town. Like Beacon Hill back home, the Via Veneto was on the high ground, and the buildings had a well-kept look, matched by the few pedestrians out for a stroll. A couple of cafés were open, and even with a chill in the air, these elegant Romans were enjoying their espressos outdoors.

The car pulled up to a hotel entrance, the six-story gleaming white building topped by a dome at one corner, the name Excelsior wrapped around it in big green letters, in case you didn't get the point that it was a really fancy joint.

"Welcome to the German military headquarters in Rome," Remke said. "Do not speak, and follow me."

He opened the door for us and I offered Diana my hand, but she had the sense to remember I was dressed as a priest and walked up the steps liked she owned the place. Remke led me by the arm, maybe thinking I was going to sprint off, holding up my cassock the whole way. Inside, the palatial lobby was lit by chandeliers, the black-and-white marble floor dazzling. Shiny black boots clicked up a wide staircase as officers with red-striped trousers—signifying generals— went about their duties. A younger German officer, also wearing the Brandenburg cuff, rose from the couch and gave Remke a discreet nod. He opened a waiting elevator and accompanied us to the third floor. Without speaking, he opened the door to a suite and checked the rooms as we waited.

"Forgive the cloak-and-dagger dramatics," Remke said, leading us into a spacious room where a table was set for three. Heavy gold curtains were draped over ceiling-level windows, and tapestries hung between ornate Roman columns. This place was gaudier than the finest suite at the Copley Square Hotel. "Banda Koch has raided convents and monasteries in Rome and found hidden Jews and Italian antifascists. Someone undoubtedly talked and identified Sister Justina as part of the O'Flaherty organization. It didn't take long for the Gestapo to realize she was in custody for black-market violations."

"Those buildings all have extraterritorial status as part of the Holy See," Diana said. "How can that be allowed?"

"Pietro Koch is a monster, in a world of monsters," Remke said. "I have heard even Mussolini fears him. The Gestapo lets him operate because he is effective, and his status as a Fascist police commander allows them to disavow his actions when he goes too far. There has already been a diplomatic complaint lodged by the Vatican, and apologies are being made by the German ambassador."

"But Koch was able to torture enough refugees to get the information he wanted," Diana said.

"Yes. But now, we shall sit and eat. We must not let Koch ruin your appetite, Miss Seaton," Remke said, pulling out the chair for her.

"After the food at the Regina Coeli, it will take more than one psychotic Italian to do that," she said, and Remke looked almost embarrassed. I studied Diana as she sat, pulling her light-brown hair back, adjusting the starched white napkin on her lap. Strange, how normal even the most absurd moments can seem. That morning I hadn't known if I'd find her half dead or if I'd be put against a wall and shot. Now here we were, with bone china and cut crystal set out before us. A table prepared in the presence of mine enemy.

"What is this document you want me to take to the Vatican?" I asked, trying to shake the confusion and cobwebs loose. "Something other than the Auschwitz Protocol, if I understand you."

"First, we will eat. I must leave Rome soon, and the way the war is going, I may not have another chance to enjoy the delights of the Excelsior's kitchens."

So we ate. I was actually hungry, despite dining under the noses of the German high command, with an Abwehr agent who'd probably saved Diana from torture and death at the hands of the Gestapo, and who wanted me to be his personal messenger boy to the Pope. We started with artichokes, along with plates of olives and mozzarella, then salmon and asparagus with pasta. Washed down with a couple of bottles of wine. I needed to be taken prisoner more often.

Remke inquired after Colonel Harding, and I told him he was fine. I asked about his aide, whom I'd last seen in Algiers. Dead, Remke said. On leave to visit his family in Hamburg, he was killed in a nighttime bombing raid. Except he called it terror bombing. I didn't debate the point and we moved on to more pleasant conversation. He and Diana chatted about Bernini and Caravaggio and other artists I'd never heard of. Finally, when the dishes were cleared away and coffee was brought in, we got down to business.

"First, the conditions," Remke said. "I will give you a document. You must deliver it to Monsignor Giovanni Montini, in the Vatican State Department. We understand he is involved in smuggling funds to refugee organizations in the north. He is most likely to be sympathetic and pass this on to Pope Pius."

"Monsignor O'Flaherty mentioned the refugee work," I said. "He should be able to get me to see Montini."

"I do not care how you do it. But when you speak to O'Flaherty, warn him to keep within the Vatican walls. The Gestapo wants him dead. There was even talk of a sniper picking him off from outside, but fortunately that operation was canceled."

"I doubt he'd ever give up his post on the steps of the basilica, sniper or not. But I'll give him your message. Now, what's so important about this document?"

Remke leaned in, his voice almost a whisper, even with no one else in the room. "There will be another assassination attempt in the near future. We almost succeeded last month, when one of our men was selected to demonstrate new winter uniforms for Hitler. He had dynamite in a briefcase, which he was ready to set off as the Führer approached."

"What happened?" Diana asked.

"Herr Hitler canceled at the last minute. That man has the devil's own luck. Now another officer, who is often called upon to brief Hitler on the Russia front, has volunteered to shoot him at the next opportunity. He is scheduled to go to the Berghof, Hitler's mountain retreat, next week."

"The document lays this all out?" I asked.

"Yes. This time, there is more information about the conspirators. My name, among others. I am handing you a noose with which you could hang us all," Remke said. "Give it to Montini, and ask him to forward it to the English. There are two copies. I will count on you to send one to General Eisenhower, likely through your Colonel Harding."

"You know Churchill and Roosevelt agreed to nothing less than the unconditional surrender of Germany," I said.

"I have to believe that is nothing but propaganda, to mollify the Soviets. It is the greatest gift they could possibly have given the Nazis. Now they can state that no mercy will be given, that Germany will be lost unless the war goes on. It is ridiculous," he said. "Once the coup has succeeded, we will disarm the SS, arrest the surviving leadership, and retreat from Italy up to the Alps. We will request a cease-fire with the Soviets, and pull back to our borders as they were at the start of the war. All this will take time, and we need to know the Western Allies will not act against us as we do so."

"Just like 1940," I said.

"Yes, but in 1940 the Soviets were our allies. Now the Russians march west, and will not stop until they have swallowed all of Europe."

"And in 1940 the world didn't know about the extermination camps," Diana said. "If there's a chance to stop the war and save tens of thousands of lives, it's worth taking, Billy."

"What happens to Diana?" I asked, not quite as eager as she was.

"She will remain here, as my guest. In somewhat better accommodations than the Regina Coeli. But under lock and key, guarded by a female agent. Until you complete your mission."

"I guess it is worth a try," I said, meaning that it was worth keeping Diana out of jail. I doubted Remke's plan would work, even if they did manage to knock off Hitler. I wasn't as sure as Remke that the unconditional surrender demand was window dressing, and I knew the Russians, after losing millions of lives, would not let the German Army slip away intact. From what I knew of them, it wasn't their way of doing business. "How will you know if I've done my part?"

"I will require an acknowledgment. From Monsignor Montini. A receipt, if you will. Written confirmation that he has the documents in hand."

"And then Diana is free? My two friends also?"

"Yes. You have my word."

Remke seemed like the sort who'd take offense if I questioned his word, so I let that slide. "You don't want an acknowledgment that I passed it onto Colonel Harding?"

"How could you not?" Remke said. "That document and the Auschwitz Protocol are probably two of the most valuable intelligence finds of the war. Your colonel would be quite displeased if you did not deliver them immediately."

"Okay," I said, knowing he was right. Harding would kill for this stuff, and Diana had made it her mission to reveal the truth about the camps. It had haunted her when she began to hear bits and pieces after first coming to Rome. We'd been able to grab a few hours together between assignments not long ago, and she'd told me about the trains, the transports to the east, and thousands disappearing. Industrial killing, on a scale so inconceivable that it was hard to accept, and even harder to convince her superiors that the reports were not exaggerations or deliberate propaganda.

"Now tell me about this person you want," Remke said, rising from the table and walking to one of the windows. "A prisoner, I assume?"

"Severino Rossi, and I hope he still is," I said, watching Remke as he pulled a drape back, looking like a gangster checking to see if John Law was on his tail. "He's a French Jew who made it to the Vatican and got fingered for the murder of Monsignor Corrigan. Commissario Soletto turned him over to the police in Rome, without much of an investigation."

"If it has been more than a week, I doubt Monsieur Rossi is still in Rome. Or alive, I regret. This is the crime you were sent to investigate, yes?"

"It is. I haven't had much success yet. I need to talk to Rossi and find out what he knows, before the killer strikes a third time."

"Who else has been killed?" Diana asked.

"Soletto. Last night," I said.

"Really? I did not know that," Remke said. He didn't sound as if he was used to secondhand news. "Who do you think is responsible?"

"Hard to say. There were a lot of people around the radio tower, where it happened. Might have been Bishop Zlatko, but he's on the top of my list mainly because I don't care for the man. Monsignor Bruzzone was there, along with Robert Brackett, the American diplomat. Radio technicians, Swiss Guard, gendarmes, various refugees, the list goes on."

"There is a slight chance Rossi was not sent for transport if he was involved in a criminal case. I will look and see what I can find out. If Rossi is alive, and you keep your end of the bargain, I will give him to you." Remke let the drape go, apparently satisfied with the street scene.

"How will we make contact?" I asked.

"I will give you a military pass, which allows you to go about the city unmolested. Be at Piazza Navona tomorrow at noon, precisely. Stand by the *Fontana dei Quattro Fiumi* and I will meet you there. At that time, I will tell you what I have found out. You must have the acknowledgment from Montini by the next day."

"Two days? What if he won't see me?"

"Make it your business to see that he does. If not, I will be forced to take Miss Seaton with me to Germany as my prisoner, and your two comrades will be back in the Regina Coeli."

"But—"

"Two days. Excuses are irrelevant. I will leave you both alone now, for twenty minutes. Do not attempt anything foolish. My men are in the corridor and on the street."

With that, he left the room. Diana and I were alone, two pawns in a game of giants. The only thing a pawn can do is to move ahead, slowly, hoping to reach that final rank where it can be anything it wants.

I figured I was halfway there. Maybe even a little further, I thought, as I looked into Diana's eyes, inhaled her scent, felt the coolness of her skin, and fell into her embrace.

CHAPTER THIRTY-ONE

ANOTHER TRIP THROUGH narrow Roman streets, only this time I was alone in the backseat of Remke's staff car. The little swastika banners on the fender snapped as the BMW sped down the Via Nazionale, the driver leaning on the horn as he encountered traffic and slow-footed pedestrians. Soon it would be Chryslers barreling through these streets, but for now a black BMW with blood-red pennants still had the right of way.

"Here," Remke pointed out from the front seat as we passed the Piazza Navona. "It is only a short walk from the Vatican. The Fountain of the Four Rivers is at the center. We are on the Corso Vittorio Emanuele, named for the Italian king."

"I met him," I said. "Wasn't impressed."

"I agree. A small man, in many respects. Too often, nations do not have the leaders they deserve. Instead, they are burdened with the weak, the stubborn, or the blind."

"That's the good thing about living in a democracy. We can get rid of them every few years."

"Perhaps. But your President Roosevelt seems to be under the spell of Stalin, and I doubt he will be thrown out of office for that offense, even though it should be a crime. Churchill, now there is a man who knows how to govern as well as fight."

"You're hoping he will talk Roosevelt into accepting a negotiated peace?"

"He must. Otherwise Europe will be a wasteland."

I bit my tongue. The Germans had gotten a good start on the wasteland business all by themselves, but there was no percentage in antagonizing Remke when he was about to let me go. I needed him to free Diana, as well as Rino and Abe. Ending the war, that was a chance in a thousand; but getting those three on neutral territory, I figured the odds were more like four to one in my favor, so I kept my trap shut.

Remke beat a rhythm with his fingers on the door, his arm out the open window. His head swiveled to the left, then the right, taking in everything happening around him. He was obviously a professional, a soldier and spy who knew what he was doing. But something had clouded his judgment. Something had him in its grip, causing him to miss the big picture. No matter how logical the plotters' plans were, even if they got Hitler this time, the die was cast. Soviet tanks and armies of men were moving west, surging toward Germany. Not like the painful crawl of our few divisions up the boot of Italy. Not even like the invasion of France, whenever that would be. No, there were hundreds of divisions, all out for blood and revenge. And a single emotion blinded Remke to that inescapable fact. Hope.

This plan gave him hope, not only for his nation, but for himself and his family as well. He didn't strike me as a man who believed all the Nazi propaganda about the pure Nordic race. Instead he seemed an honorable man for an enemy. I had to admire him, but all I believed in right now was getting Diana out, and freeing Abe and Rino. I knew I didn't want their deaths on my conscience. Well, maybe that was blind hope too. I'd have to watch out for that.

We had to wait to cross the Tiber. A column of half-tracks and trucks about a mile long snaked its way along the road ahead, blocking the intersection. I lay back, closed my eyes, and savored the memory of twenty minutes alone with Diana.

We'd sat on the couch, wordlessly holding each other, grasping at the minutes as they slipped by. I hadn't known what to say, what sentence I could possibly form that would make sense in this upside-down

world of elegant prisons, disguises, and German rescuers. Our desire
to touch, to caress lips, cheeks, and hands, to feel the physical sensation of being together was overpowering, our bodies having survived
so much danger, abuse, and separation. We kissed, but ultimately our
passion was trumped by relief, fear, sadness, and the ticking clock,
and we simply held onto each other like drowning swimmers. When
it came time to depart, we gripped each other so tightly that I must
have left a bruise on Diana's arm as I struggled to draw her in, to
bring her close, to remember the feel of her, the smell of her hair,
the contours of her shoulders, arms, waist, and hips. Everything was
sharp and clear, my mind on high alert to drink in every detail, even
as Remke took me by the arm and closed the door, leaving Diana
standing alone, tears glistening on her face.

We hadn't spoken a single word.

The driver floored it as soon as the column had passed, wakening
me from my daydream, back into the nightmare of Remke's fantasy.
The bronze statues of Winged Victory on pillars flanking the bridge
would have laughed at our pathetic plotting if they hadn't seen so
many thwarted plans and dashed hopes before. Mussolini must have
tipped his hat to them once or twice, and look where that got him.
We skirted the massive Castel Sant'Angelo, where popes used to
hide out back when the Huns came calling. Not our modern motor-
ized Huns, but their ancestors on horseback. The castle was useless
now, pretty to look at, but nothing that would stand up to a few
well-placed howitzer rounds.

We zipped up the Via della Conciliazione, the wide stretch of
road Mussolini put in to connect the city with Saint Peter's Square.
It was supposed to be about conciliation between Rome and the
Vatican, but it seemed to me tailor-made for armored vehicles.

We pulled up close to the white border line, a stone's throw from
the great granite obelisk at the center of the piazza. I got out, taking
note of a thin figure in a black cassock walking nervously back and
forth a few yards from the line. It was Kaz, but he hadn't spotted me
yet, probably not taking into account that I'd hitch a ride with a
German colonel.

"Remember, Lieutenant Boyle," Remke said, stepping out onto the curb. "Two days, no more."

"And you remember, Colonel Remke, I want Severino Rossi. I hope we can both walk away winners."

"As do I. I will find Rossi, if he is alive to be found," Remke said, then pointed to the piazza. "Is that not your friend Lieutenant Kazimierz, dressed as a cleric as well? Baron Piotr Augustus Kazimierz?"

"Yes," I said, figuring Remke knew for certain anyway. "Your people wiped out his family, so he probably wouldn't be offended if I didn't introduce you."

"You Americans can be quite hypocritical, but I do not believe you have the self-awareness to realize it," Remke said, his lips pressed into a thin, angry line. He moved to get into the car but halted, his face red with fury. "Does it come from the superiority you imagine you possess, secure on your continent, surrounded by oceans instead of rivals, competitors, and enemies in every direction? You Americans and your English allies, who have shown nothing but disdain for all our efforts to dispose of a madman, you do not hesitate to lump me and other honorable men in with Gestapo and SS thugs. With the Nazis. 'Your people,' you say. Was it not *your people* who wiped out the Indians and enslaved the Africans? Is that not how you built your sanctuary from the wars and cruelties of old Europe?"

Remke turned away and the car sped off, leaving anger and suspicion in the air. I tried to think of what I would've said if he'd given me half a chance, but I had nothing, so I stepped across the white line in case he changed his mind and came back.

"Billy!" Kaz ran to me, a look of confusion on his face. "What happened? What were you doing with that Nazi? Where are Rino and Abe? Did you see Diana?"

"It's a long story," I said, deciding not to correct Kaz on Remke's party membership. "Let's find O'Flaherty and I'll explain everything."

"Is it good news or bad?" Kaz asked as we walked to the German College.

"Diana is alive and well, that's the good news. As for the rest, we've been had."

"Tell me now," he insisted.

"They knew our every move. They meaning the Abwehr. Diana and I spent the afternoon having lunch with a German colonel at the Excelsior. He wants us to help him end the war, but he's keeping Diana, Abe, and Rino hostage in case I don't go along with it."

"If you don't want to tell me, Billy, just say so."

"Holy Mother of God," O'Flaherty said minutes later. "Slow down and start over. I don't think I've ever heard such an incredible story." We were in O'Flaherty's room, seated around the table where I'd laid out the documents Remke had given me.

"There is no Rudder," I said. "The Abwehr nabbed the OSS team a while ago, and have been recruiting agents under that name and radioing in phony reports, probably salted with enough real information to make them credible. Brackett thinks he's reporting to an Allied agent, but he's been feeding dope to the Jerries. Corrigan too, I'm sure."

"It would be a kindness not to tell Brackett," O'Flaherty said. "It probably gave some meaning to his life here. But this means Rudder, or rather Colonel Remke, knew all about your arrival."

"Yes. When he came across my name, he started putting the plan together. He'd found Diana in prison, where she was being held under her alias as Sister Justina. He may have known about Rino and his connection with you, Monsignor. He's aware of your work, and that warning about the Gestapo was certainly in good faith. In any case, he was waiting for us."

"This document is unbelievable," Kaz said, reading through the Auschwitz Protocol. "It details the inner workings of an extermination camp. We've had word of atrocities, terrible mass murders, but this is—inconceivable."

"I think he may have given us that to help change attitudes among the high command," I said. "Perhaps Remke thinks Roosevelt and Churchill will deal with the anti-Nazi conspirators if it will help put a stop to these mass murders. It's the other document we have to deal with first."

"I should be able to see Monsignor Montini easily enough," O'Flaherty said. "Giovanni and I have worked well together before. He's channeled money and resources to many refugee organizations. But a written acknowledgment." He paused to consider that requirement. "That will be more difficult."

"Why?" I asked. "It's only a receipt."

"Yes, but a receipt that could be used against the Holy See. Plotting with traitors to the Third Reich, working as a conduit to the British secret service. It would be enough to send a regiment of SS troops into the Vatican. Oh no, me boy. This is a dangerous piece of paper. Very dangerous."

"If I don't deliver in two days, he takes Diana with him to Germany. And Rino and Abe rot in the Regina Coeli."

"Do you trust the man?" O'Flaherty said. "To do what he says, whichever way it goes?"

"I do," I said. Remke didn't impress me as a liar. Too spit and polish for that, even if he worked for the Abwehr. "But he's walking a tightrope. This plan, the plot against Hitler, it means everything to him. If we don't get what he wants from Montini, he'll take Diana."

"You've got his number, I think," O'Flaherty said. "There's no going back for a man like Remke, if you're right about him."

"Then we must find a way," Kaz said. "We must get that letter."

"There's one other thing," I said. "I asked him to find Severino Rossi, if he's still alive."

"Admirable, Billy," O'Flaherty said, a tinge of exasperation in his voice. "Here we are discussing the deaths of millions, the killing of a dictator, and a possible end to the war, and you're still itching to find the murderer of a single man."

"Two men," I reminded him. "Two men the war wouldn't have gotten, at least not yet."

"Fair enough," O'Flaherty said. "A soul is a soul. What do you think Severino Rossi will tell you?"

"Something I may already know," I said. It had to do with hope. Rossi and Remke were from different worlds, but I was beginning to see a similarity. Both had come to Rome out of hope. Hope for themselves, for the world that they used to inhabit, now upside-down with violence and death. Rossi had come to Rome for something specific, I was sure of it. He'd made it out of France and to Genoa. Why not stay there? What drove him to journey to Rome, without identity papers, and hide in Saint Peter's?

"He wanted to see Corrigan?" Kaz guessed.

"No," I said, and then something else clicked. Another favor I should have asked Remke. Now I'd have to wait until noon tomorrow. "Kaz, we need to see Zlatko now. Monsignor, I'd like to leave these documents with you, for safekeeping. We'll check with you soon about Montini."

"I'll take them, boy, but it's a heavy burden we must share. I thought it was hard enough to care for dozens, then hundreds of poor souls. But this, how many thousands of lives stand in the balance?" He stared out the window, as if trying to keep his eyes from the papers on the table. There was no need to answer.

CHAPTER THIRTY-TWO

"YOU ARE CERTAIN Diana is in good health?" Kaz said for the tenth time.

"Kaz, she's at the Excelsior. Even in a locked and guarded room, how bad can it be? Remke had her on ice at the Regina Coeli, but she was well-treated. All we have to worry about is getting that letter from Montini."

"Is that why we are looking for Bishop Zlatko?"

"No. I figure we have a little time before things heat up over Remke's documents. So I want to try something with Zlatko."

We were headed through the Vatican Gardens, and as we passed the gardener's house, I saw Rosana peering out from a window. I felt a twinge of guilt as I put my head down and hustled up the hill to the radio station. Maybe I should tell her Abe was on a mission. Maybe I should apologize for getting him captured. Or mind my own business, but it was kind of late for that, so I focused on Zlatko. He was due for a radio broadcast in Croatian, and we had to hustle to catch him.

"Bishop," I said, waving as he drew near on a path leading to the tower. He carried a briefcase and appeared to be in a hurry. Or maybe he'd spotted us already.

"Gentlemen, I have no time to chat. I have a radio address in five minutes." He walked faster, and we matched his pace.

"Colonel Remke sends his greetings," I said. Zlatko kept his head down, but the tip of his shoe caught on the gravel and he almost lost his balance.

"I do not know of anyone by that name," he said. He seemed short of breath. Lying is hard work.

"I'm sorry, I meant to say Rudder. You know, the German agent you've been feeding information to. In violation of the Holy See's neutral status."

"How dare you!" Zlatko stopped and faced us.

"Interesting that you want to get rid of me as an Allied agent, when all along you're working for the Nazis. Gives neutrality a bad name."

"Where did you come up with this fairy tale?" Zlatko said, his chin held high. He must've been practicing the Mussolini look.

"Colonel Erich Remke. Today, while we were lunching at the Excelsior Hotel. You should try it. Or maybe you have? It's the German military headquarters; you'd feel right at home."

That got to him. His eyes widened and he didn't deny it. I could see him calculating the value of the truth versus a lie. "Yes, I have been in contact with the colonel," he said, giving up the charade. "I will do whatever it takes to protect the church against the godless Bolsheviks."

"But the struggle against Communism didn't preclude you from hedging your bets with Brackett, did it? You tried to tell him you were a double agent, to be on the winning side when the Fifth Army rolls into Rome. Did you threaten him? Tell him you'd reveal his connection to Rudder, and have him expelled from the Holy See?"

"What could that weakling do for me?"

"He could put in writing that you were working for the Allies," Kaz said, his eyes latched onto Zlatko's. "Then you could murder him, perhaps as you murdered the others."

Zlatko flinched. "I am not a murderer," he said. It came out slowly, as if he wished he'd thought of killing Brackett and was kicking himself for it.

"But you did get a letter from him," I said.

"I do possess evidence that I provided information to the Allies," Zlatko said, working the Mussolini chin move again.

"I'm sure that will come in handy when the Pope sends you back to Croatia. You can show it to the Soviets. You'll need to at your trial for war crimes."

"Where did you hear that?" Zlatko asked, apparently not in a hurry to get closer to the Russian front.

"I have connections," I said. "Tell you what, you do me a favor and I'll do one for you. Get me a list of informers within the Vatican. Anyone feeding the Germans or the Italian secret police information. By first thing tomorrow. Then I'll put in a good word for you."

"That is impossible," Zlatko said. "There are informers every-where. How am I expected to know them all? This is Rome, for God's sake!"

"Then it should be easy. Start with the Germans. That may be enough. Come up with the goods and I'll fix it so you stay in Rome."

"But how can I—"

"Aren't you late for your broadcast, Bishop?" Kaz said. We walked away, leaving him to return to his calculations. This time it was the value of cooperation versus confrontation. The way I had Zlatko figured, if cooperation would save his hide, I'd have names by sunset.

"Good play," I said to Kaz. "How'd you come up with that bit about the letter?"

"It occurred to me that such a document would be very useful, especially if the person who wrote it could not retract it at a later date. I had been thinking how your Colonel Remke was quite smart to only request a letter acknowledging receipt of his peace offering. It requires little commitment while at the same time attaching importance to the document."

"Let's talk to Brackett and see what he has to say."

"That should make Zlatko call off the proceedings to have us removed from the Holy See," Kaz said as we crossed the gardens and descended to the Governatorato. "Was that why you wanted to question him?"

"Partly. If word gets around he's naming names, we may stir things up a bit."

"So Zlatko is the scapegoat, staked out for the killer?"

"Wouldn't sacrificial lamb be a better description, since he's a man of the cloth?"

"Either way," Kaz said, "he is an excellent choice."

We found Brackett in his office. His desk was a mass of papers and he had a drink in his hand, getting a head start on the cocktail hour. He offered us a drink but we declined. I wouldn't have minded a belt, but I didn't like drinking with a guy who did it to pass the time. That sort of thing ended in a fistfight, blubbery tears, or worse yet, both. I wasn't in the mood.

"We came to warn you," I said. I remembered what Monsignor O'Flaherty had said about letting Brackett down easy, so I decided a white lie would do. "The Rudder network has been turned."

"Why tell me?" Brackett said, pouring himself another brandy.

"Because we know you're one of Rudder's agents. It's something we stumbled onto during the course of the investigation. I thought you'd want to know."

Brackett went for his pipe, fiddled with it for a moment, then tossed it down on the desk. "All right," he said. "How long has it been compromised?"

"It happened two days ago. When's the last time you made contact?"

"Four days ago. Whenever I have something to report, I walk along the border at nine o'clock in the morning, circling the Bernini colonnades. Enrico—that's my contact's code name—comes into the piazza."

"Enrico may not know," I said. "Stay away from him, all right?"

"Sure," Brackett said. "You certain about this?"

"It has been confirmed," Kaz said. "You have been of great service. You are to be commended."

"It saved my life, I'll tell you that," Brackett said, a regretful sigh escaping his lips. "This place is a prison at best, a lunatic asylum at worst. It has broken some people, you know. The Peruvian minister disappeared one day, vanished. The Honduran drank himself to death—in my opinion, mainly from being cooped up with his wife."

"What was the last thing you reported to Enrico?" I asked.

"The status of your investigation. He said Rudder wanted to be informed. I figured we're all on the same side, so it wouldn't matter. Right?"

"Well, it's hardly top-secret stuff. What else?"

"Oh, Soletto and Bishop Zlatko, that sort of thing."

"What do you mean?" Kaz asked.

"Listen, I didn't mean to do anything wrong," Brackett said, finishing off his drink and topping off the glass from a brandy bottle.

"The letter," Kaz prompted him.

"Right, the letter. How did you find out? Oh, never mind. Anyway, I didn't want to chance it that Zlatko would really blow my cover. So I gave him the letter. I said he was a valued Allied agent, that sort of thing. Only, Soletto found out."

"What?" Kaz and I both said at the same time. This was news.

"Yeah," Brackett said, slurping his brandy and smacking his lips. "He sent for me, and waved the carbon copy under my nose."

"You kept a copy on file?"

"That's what we do here. Type things in triplicate. I never thought—well, let's just leave it at that."

"What did Soletto want?"

"Information. The usual. He also hinted that by not turning me in for violating Vatican neutrality, he was helping the Allied cause. Sort of like Zlatko, who thought it was amusing when I told him. Blackmail and patriotism all rolled up in a nice, neat package. But the joke was on Soletto. Can't say I was sorry to see him go." Brackett raised his glass, drank, and then studied the remaining amber swirl. It required all his attention.

"Well, you're certainly a brave man," I said.

"Oh, it wasn't so dangerous," Brackett said. "Wait a minute, what do you mean?"

"Now that Soletto is dead, you're the only one who knows the letter is a fake. Sure, you had to write it to protect your cover, but it puts you in a tough spot. Zlatko could get in a lot of trouble if you rescinded it."

"You don't mean Bishop Zlatko would harm me?"

"Not harm," Kaz said. "Murder."

"No, he wouldn't," Brackett said, swallowing a slug of brandy and slamming down the glass. "He's not a bad guy, really." He poured another, determined to talk himself into believing that one.

We left the Governatorato, feeling a lot less sympathetic toward Brackett than when we arrived. Now we knew Zlatko had a motive for shutting up Soletto. Maybe Brackett did too, but he'd probably been halfway through a brandy bottle when Soletto took a knife to his heart.

"An odd man," Kaz said. "Tragic, the way he took to being sealed in here. Even in a POW camp, you at least have your comrades. He is the only American here."

"And not a Catholic, either," I said. "FDR was sensitive about the anti-Catholic vote, so he made sure the diplomats posted here were Protestant. He was alone in many ways. Not surprising he leapt at the chance for excitement and a break from the bottle."

"Are you sure he didn't take up other hobbies, such as murder?"

"I don't know. He doesn't seem the type."

"You told me once that there was no type when it came to murder, that anyone could be a killer," Kaz said. We stopped in front of a small church tucked under the shadow of Saint Peter's grand dome. The façade was plain, a muted rusty color that needed attention. It looked like it could barely accommodate a small-scale South Boston wedding.

"Yeah, but it depends on the state they're in. I'm sure Brackett could be pushed to murder, but it would have to be over something he cares about. The only thing that's going to get him excited is a break from monotony or an unopened case of brandy. So right now, he's not the type, he's too morose and self-involved. Just like this little church could never be a basilica, Brackett may dance around the edges of spying and a bit of danger, but it's not his world. He's simply not a dangerous man."

"Still," Kaz said, "it is a pretty church. Ninth century, if I recall. Back when a man would kill at the slightest provocation."

"Yeah, well maybe Corrigan insulted his alma mater. Let's pay Inspector Cipriano a visit."

The Gendarmerie Office was only a few steps away, and we found Cipriano in his office, holding a telephone and nodding. He occasionally opened his mouth as if to speak, but that was as far as it went. He gestured vaguely at chairs in front of his desk, then held the telephone away from his mouth as he struck a match and lit a cigarette. Fortunately, I'd never risen high enough in the ranks at the Boston PD to endure a call like that, but I'd seen plenty. Someone high up was shoveling a mountain of trouble down Cipriano's way.

"Please, do not ask if I have found the missing rochet," Cipriano said, hanging up the telephone with more emphasis than was necessary. "I have done nothing but listen to clergymen complain about being questioned."

"No luck at all?" I asked.

"*Sfortuna*. But I did find this," he said, tossing a sheet of paper across his desk. The carbon copy of Brackett's letter to Zlatko.

"We know about it," Kaz said. "Brackett felt pressured by Bishop Zlatko."

"The good bishop is practiced at pressure," Cipriano said. "It was he who complained the loudest about my search. Keep the letter. Better yet, burn it. Signore Brackett does not deserve to get in trouble with his government because of a man like Zlatko."

"That's decent of you, Inspector."

"Any chance to act decently these days should be grasped with *vigore*," Cipriano said. "I was a Rome policeman before I joined the Vatican force. I left behind the hard choices that my colleagues had to make during the past years: serve the Fascists or suffer the consequences. I sat out the war, much like Signore Brackett, within these walls, tending to small matters. So I am glad to do one decent thing for him."

"Nothing new on the knife?"

"All I have are more questions and a headache," Cipriano said, rubbing his temples with his fingers. "For instance, I found something odd in the *commissario*'s report about Severino Rossi, the refugee charged with Monsignor Corrigan's murder."

"What?"

"Correspondence with Regina Coeli, requesting that the prisoner not be turned over to the *Tedeschi* for transport. You know what transport means for Jews, yes?"

"Death camps," Kaz said. "But why is that surprising? It is a case of murder. Wouldn't Soletto and the Rome police want the suspect kept here?"

"The only police left serving in Rome are the worst of the Fascists," Cipriano said. "Commissario Soletto himself said they would do us a favor by putting a bullet in Rossi's head. They would be glad to oblige, too. Especially Pietro Koch and his gang. But the odd thing is that this request was made the day after the murder."

"As if Soletto had thought things over and changed his mind," I said.

"Yes, *esattamente*," Cipriano said. "Why would he do that? He was not sympathetic to Jews. Or anyone."

"Because Rossi had some value to him," I said.

"Rossi knew who the real killer was?" Kaz suggested.

"He did not name anyone," Cipriano said.

"You saw him yourself, that night?"

"Yes. It was early morning by the time I arrived. They were just taking him away. He seemed disoriented, perhaps in shock. One often sees this after a violent crime."

"Did he say anything to the Swiss Guard who found him? He must have shaken Rossi awake, right?"

"He was not coherent. And it was not a Swiss Guard who found him," Cipriano said.

"That's what was in the report," I said.

"Ah, the official report, from this office," Cipriano said. "The one kept under lock and key." He was enjoying himself.

"Well, we know how much good keys do around here," I said. "Who found him, then?"

"Your American friend, Robert Brackett. His name was kept out of the written report."

"Why?"

"Because Signore Brackett was returning from the bedroom of a lady. A married lady, at that. Her husband, one of the South American diplomats housed here, was elsewhere, likely sharing a different bedroom with another man's wife. These diplomats, they have nothing to do all day, so they find much to do in darkness."

"Have you interviewed her?"

"As delicately as possible, yes. They are quartered on the Via del Pellegrino, in the same building as *L'Osservatore Romano*, the Vatican newspaper. The times match, and Brackett found a Swiss Guard on duty and brought him to the scene. So the report—the one you could not have read—was correct in everything but Brackett's presence."

"Correct in all regards, except for the man who found the body."

"*Sì*," Cipriano said, with only the slightest of shrugs to show his professional embarrassment. "I thought Soletto would have told you. What do you think Rossi might know?"

"If not the identity of the killer, then something worth keeping him alive," I said. I decided not to mention that Remke was looking for Rossi. If he'd survived the last week or so, it made it more likely Remke could find him. But there was no reason to advertise the fact.

"Perhaps," Cipriano said. "What have you been doing?"

"You wouldn't believe me, Inspector, and telling you would only make your headache worse."

"Thank you for not burdening me with the truth," he said. "I prefer a knowing silence."

He picked up his lighter and handed it to Kaz, who took Brackett's letter and lit it over the ashtray on the inspector's desk. It flamed quickly, the words disintegrating into ash.

CHAPTER THIRTY-THREE

I HADN'T GOTTEN much sleep during the past thirty-six hours. None was more like it, and it had caught up to me. O'Flaherty informed us we could see Montini at nine o'clock in the morning. Kaz said he was going to walk in the gardens with Nini, to discuss the case, of course, and ask her about what she knew of Severino Rossi and the Genoa connection, since he'd come through there while Corrigan and others had been in that city as well. I thought that was a fine story, and wished him well. I grabbed some quick chow in the refectory and then hit the sack. I was bone tired, but my mind wouldn't stop working the details. What did we know about Rossi? Or Brackett and his late-night bedroom visits? And what about Corrigan, Zlatko, even stand-up guys like John May and Hugh O'Flaherty? Why did Monsignor Bruzzone disappear for one night? For that matter, why had he not left the Vatican for months prior to that?

May and O'Flaherty were involved in the black market. Had they unknowingly brought in a deadly partner?

But the biggest puzzler was still Corrigan himself. Why had he been murdered? By all accounts he was one of the good guys. Even with his college connections to Wild Bill Donovan of the OSS and his unwitting intelligence work for Remke, he was a straight arrow who'd done good works. It made sense that, as an American at the Vatican, he'd responded to the phony Rudder the way he had, passing along tidbits of information. So why was he killed?

Money. Corrigan, Bruzzone, and O'Flaherty had all carried money to Genoa, along with forged identity papers, worth a small fortune. Worth a life. Money and papers equaled hope. There it was again. Those three carried hope with them, bearing it as a gift to Jews and other refugees in Genoa. Had they crossed paths with Severino Rossi in Genoa? Had hope passed him by, and was he seeking revenge?

My eyelids felt heavy, and I thought I was still going over the case, but suddenly I was watching Rossi walking the streets of Boston, down in the Dorchester Hill neighborhood. In threadbare clothes he shuffled along the street—it looked like Blue Hill Avenue, with its tailor shops, meat markets, and dry goods stores— his neck craning at the signs in English and Yiddish. I couldn't quite make them out, the words evaporating as I tried to focus on each one.

The Hill was a Jewish neighborhood. Mostly Polish Jews, those who had escaped the pogroms in Russia and Poland and settled in Boston and Chelsea. I followed Rossi, turning down a side street lined with two-family houses and three-deckers. I wanted to ask him what he was looking for, but I never could quite catch up to him. He disappeared, and I turned around to find myself in South Boston, miles away.

I was with Dad, at M Street Park. We were in uniform, me in my bluecoat and Dad wearing his brown suit, hitching up his pants the way he did when his badge, cuffs, and revolver began to weigh him down. It was a cold day, the wind flapping his jacket and stinging our faces. The old brownstones behind us hid the sun, and in front of us a dead man was slumped against a tree.

I awoke with a start. I'd been dreaming, confused images of home and Rossi roiling my unconscious. I'd liked the memory of home, and I recalled the case at M Street Park. I remembered Dad didn't speak when we first arrived. It was always that way when he brought me along to a crime scene. I was there for crowd control and to get coffee when the detectives wanted it. Plus the overtime, sure. But his real reason was to teach me.

I circled the body. His legs were stretched out on the ground. His head lolled to the left. A gunshot to the right temple had blasted bone, brains, and blood against the tree trunk. A .38 revolver lay on the ground near his right hand. The question was, suicide or murder? Dad never assumed suicide, preferring not to rule out foul play even in the most obvious situations. To me, it looked obvious at first glance. But Dad always said a detective doesn't glance.

I didn't touch anything but knelt near the body and looked for clues. Dad had pounded that one into my thick head. Anything is a clue. The clothes on a corpse can tell you what the guy planned to do that day. The wear on the soles of his shoes could tell you if he drove for a living or walked with a peculiar gait. I looked at his hands. No ring on the left hand. Powder burns on the right. I leaned in closer. There was a yellow nicotine stain between his first two fingers. I sniffed, hunting for the aroma of smoke. It was there, despite the wind and the smell of blood and gunpowder. I stood, studied the ground. I looked at the horizon.

"He was murdered," I said.

"Tell me more, sonny boy," Dad said.

"He's a heavy smoker. But there are no matches on the ground, no last cigarette. Maybe he had his last smoke elsewhere and came here to kill himself, but that doesn't feel right."

"Why?"

"This is a nice park. Nice buildings on three sides. But the way he's facing, toward East First Street, there's a power plant and water-front buildings. The way I figure it, a suicide would sit facing the other direction, have a cigarette, take in a view of the trees and the park, then do the deed."

"So what happened here?"

"The killer grabbed him, brought him here. I can't tell for sure, but I don't see a pack of cigarettes in his shirt pocket, which he probably was never without. Plunked him down here, facing away from the houses so no one would notice right away."

"And then told him to shoot himself?"

"No. The killer shot him, then put his hand around the weapon and fired a second round into the ground to get those powder burns on it."

"Good thinking, Billy. Now bring that boy over here. The lad who found the body."

The kid was maybe twelve or thirteen. He was gangly, shivering in the cold wind.

"You touch the body?" Dad asked him.

"Wouldn't touch a dead guy," he said, staring at the ground.

"Don't blame you," Dad said. "You're a good lad, I can tell. Some folks would have rolled him over and taken his wallet. You did the right thing." Dad clapped him on his bony shoulder, but didn't let go. He pulled him closer and patted him down, producing a pack of Raleighs from his jacket pocket, Sir Walter himself staring at us. "The lighter, boy."

"It was on the ground, honest," he stammered as he dug a Zippo out of his pants pocket. "The smokes too. I figured nobody'd want 'em anyway."

"Were there butts on the ground?"

"Yeah, two. I cleaned 'em up so no one would take notice of the missing pack."

"You're too young to smoke, kid. I ought to tell your folks," Dad said. He let the kid beg and promise never to take anything again before telling him to shove off.

"You had a good theory, Billy," Dad said as we both looked out toward the harbor. "But Walt Hogan here, he worked across the way. Owned one of them warehouses. So he did have his last smoke here, looking out at something that was important to him."

"Why'd he kill himself?" I asked, as we walked out of the park, past rows of narrow houses.

"Oh, I don't know. Maybe money problems, maybe trouble with the law we don't know about yet. We'll find out. What's important to remember, aside from not trusting whoever finds the body, is that there are more reasons for killing than you can shake a stick at. Makes little difference if it's your own death or another's."

"Is hope a reason?" I asked.

Before Dad could answer, the front door of a house opened and Severino Rossi stepped out. He opened his mouth to speak, and then I awoke with a sharp gasp, only to see Kaz shutting the door in our darkened room. Somewhere along the line I'd fallen asleep again, and Rossi had found his way back into my dream.

"What time is it?"

"Almost midnight," Kaz said. He pulled the blackout curtains tight and lit a lamp. "Did I wake you?"

"Yeah," I said, planting my feet on the floor and untying my shoelaces. "I was dreaming about a case my dad took me on. Turned out to be a suicide. But Severino Rossi was there too. It was all mixed up. Rossi was about to say something when you came in."

"About the suicide?"

"I don't know. I'd just asked my father if hope was a reason for killing. Loss of hope, I meant."

"Was it an actual case?" Kaz asked, kicking off his shoes.

"It was. Guy was a warehouse owner named Walter Hogan. Dad found out later that he'd gambled away the company payroll. Then he borrowed from a shyster, and lost all that on the horses. He was going to get the broken-leg treatment, lose his business, and betray the people who worked for him."

"It sounds like hope had passed Mr. Hogan by long before he pulled the trigger," Kaz said.

"I don't think so. He probably had hope up until the last race, which could have won him everything back. That's the thing about hope. The thought of it bucks you up for one more try."

"Like Colonel Remke," Kaz said.

"And maybe our killer. If only you'd stayed out later, Rossi might have told me. How was your walk with Nini?"

"It was raining, Billy. We went to her room after supper."

"Kaz, are you blushing?"

"No, not at all. It is warm in here."

"These rooms haven't been warm since August. Imagine, a baron and a princess. They could make a movie about you two."

"Who would play me, do you think?" Kaz asked, kicking off his shoes.

"Jimmy Cagney," I said, knowing that would please Kaz. He was really more of a Leslie Howard type, but he'd been shot down last year over the Bay of Biscay, so I didn't mention him. "Did Nini know anything about Genoa? Or were you too preoccupied to ask?"

"Duty comes first," Kaz said, hanging up his cassock. "She did say that Monsignor Montini channeled a good deal of money to Cardinal Boetto in Genoa. Boetto works with a Jewish relief agency, the *Delegazione Assistenza Emigranti Ebrei.* The cardinal, along with a group of priests, nuns, and lay people, help them with funds, forged documents, and smuggling routes into Switzerland."

"And Corrigan, Bruzzone, and O'Flaherty were the go-betweens?"

"Yes, until a few months ago. The Gestapo raided the cardinal's offices but found nothing. They left him alone, but are hunting several of his aides, who have gone into hiding. Nini said our three monsignors had all left Genoa moments ahead of a roundup."

"Which is basically what Bruzzone told us," I said. "That's why he didn't leave the Vatican for so long."

"Nini thought that he was overcautious," Kaz said. "Corrigan went into Rome often and was not picked up. O'Flaherty only stopped recently, since his activities here have attracted so much attention. Even so, he continues to go over the wall at night, in disguise."

"Maybe Bruzzone simply lost his nerve. Hard to blame the guy."

"We should ask him more about that," Kaz said, turning off the light. "But now I have to sleep. I am exhausted."

"I'll bet," I said.

Kaz threw a shoe at me, missing by a mile.

CHAPTER THIRTY-FOUR

WE HAD AN escort of six Swiss Guards the next morning, surrounding Monsignor O'Flaherty, who had a firm grip on the briefcase that held the documents from Remke. Monsignor Bruzzone was along as well. O'Flaherty had told us over an early breakfast that he'd shown the documents to Montini the night before, and that we were sure to get a favorable hearing.

We crossed Saint Peter's Square, the sky a dense gray that matched both the damp paving stones and the uniforms of our escort. Passing between a pair of guards at the Bernini colonnades, we entered the Cortile di San Damaso, a small courtyard within the Apostolic Palace, where Swiss Guard stood at attention at the entrance to the Pope's personal quarters. We went the other way, entering the Medieval Palace under an archway just as heavy raindrops began to splatter the ground.

O'Flaherty led us into a room that was a riot of color compared to the dreary day outside. It was huge, probably forty by sixty feet. The floor was white marble with the papal crest inlaid in gold. The walls were papered in yellow and white, topped off by ornate moldings with angels tucked into the corners. Couches and chairs were arranged around three sides, all done up with some florid chintz of yellow flowers and vines. It looked like a vision of what a classy whorehouse back home might aspire to, except for Bishop Zlatko, who stood sour-faced, looking everywhere but in our direction.

We sat, facing an empty table. The door opened and a thin man in his forties strode in and sat alone at the center. His hair was thinning, and his eyes were hooded by heavy brows, his forehead wrinkled in worry.

"I think it will be easiest if we all confer in English," he said, speaking slowly but precisely. "I am Monsignor Giovanni Montini, Minister of Ordinary Affairs for the Secretariat of State. I have asked the good Bishop Krunoslav Zlatko to attend to us. Bishop, I understand you had lodged a complaint about our visitors, but it is now withdrawn. Is that correct?" Montini nodded in our direction, but his eyes were on Zlatko.

"Yes, Monsignor," Zlatko said, rising from his chair. It must have irritated him to have to defer to a mere monsignor. But among the Roman Curia, a monsignor could have the Pope's ear while a dozen bishops cooled their heels in the palace hallway. "I was concerned for the safety of His Holiness and our neutral status. But I have conversed with these two young men on several occasions, and I believe their intentions are honorable. I would only counsel discretion on their part." In other words, we'd worked a deal and he had something that would insure my silence.

"Very well, Bishop Zlatko. Thank you. Do not let me keep you from your duties." Zlatko looked stunned at the dismissal, but recovered quickly. As he passed me, he made eye contact and gave a slight nod toward the door. We'd meet outside.

"Gentlemen, I have unfortunate news," Montini said after the door had shut behind Zlatko. "I have just spoken with His Holiness. He is much disturbed by the activity of Banda Koch. They invaded the extraterritorial properties at Saint Paul's Outside the Walls. They took over sixty refugees, Jews, antifascists—anyone without papers."

"It is terrible," O'Flaherty said, a touch of belligerence in his voice. He took a deep breath and tried to calm himself. "What is the Holy Father going to do about it?"

"He feels this may be the first step in a German takeover of the Vatican," Montini said. He had a pained expression that said he thought this was wrong, even foolish. "We have heard rumors of a plan by the SS to invade the Vatican and place the Pope under Nazi protection. In Germany, of course. His Holiness believes that the actions against our properties may be the first step in implementing this plan." Montini sighed, not making eye contact.

"What are you not telling us?" Bruzzone asked.

Montini folded his hands on the table as if in prayer. Then he spoke, so quietly that I had to strain to hear him. "In order to avoid giving the Germans a pretext for invasion, His Holiness has directed that all guests be expelled from Vatican properties outside these walls. It is to be done immediately."

"That is outrageous!" O'Flaherty barked as he stood. "I don't believe it." Bruzzone pulled him back down onto the flowered couch, where he sat, teeth gritted against the anger straining to burst out of him. He struck me as the kind of priest who had to really work at obedience.

"What will you do?" Bruzzone asked.

"I have managed to dissuade the Pontifical Commission from making this their work. If I had not, this would be an official meeting with the cardinals present, instead of a gathering of steadfast friends. And their welcome guests."

I could feel O'Flaherty exhale. "You are going to throw a monkey wrench into the works, then," he said.

Montini waved his hand and shrugged, granting the point even if he didn't understand what a monkey had to do with a wrench. "Do you recall when the commission ordered the Swiss Guard to turn away Allied prisoners entering the piazza?"

"Yes," O'Flaherty said. "The order was never enforced."

"And once His Holiness has ignored an order—his or the commission's—it remains ignored. So leave it to me. No one will be expelled. But it means this is a difficult time to ask the Pope to engage in espionage."

"Again, Giovanni," O'Flaherty said. "He did so in 1940. We know much more now about what is happening in these camps. It makes it even more important."

"Yes, I agree. But in 1940 there were no German divisions in Rome. The SS did not run Italy."

"Sir, may I speak?" I half rose from the chair. I wasn't sure of my status here, but I figured I had little to lose.

"Yes," Montini said, smiling. "Mr. Boyle, is it?"

"Yes sir. I understand how this is a delicate matter, and that timing is important." I took a deep breath, willing myself to slow down and make sense. "But remember, what Colonel Remke is asking for is simply an acknowledgment that you've received the document about the planned coup. He mentioned you by name, Monsignor. Not the Pope."

"True," Montini said. "But as an officer of the Secretariat, I speak for the Pope. It would have been different if this colonel had asked Monsignor O'Flaherty to sign such a letter. He could do so, without repercussion. Would that satisfy the colonel?"

"No. He was quite clear about you, given your position here."

"Monsignor?" Kaz rose and walked toward Montini.

"Please, feel free to speak, Baron Kazimierz."

"You have seen the Auschwitz Protocol as well?"

"I have. We have heard many reports, but this is the first detailed documentation. It is beyond belief. Shocking."

"Yes, Monsignor. It would not be espionage, would it, to accept receipt of this report?"

"No. We often receive reports from other parts of occupied Europe. Why?"

"He is onto something, Giovanni," O'Flaherty said, slapping Kaz on the back, almost sending him reeling. "Listen to the lad, it could save three people from the Germans with no risk at all."

"Go on," Montini said.

"You could give us a letter acknowledging receipt of the Auschwitz Protocol. An experienced diplomat such as you could also insert language which the knowledgeable reader would understand referred to another, separate document."

"Will that work?" Montini asked. "Would it free Sister Justina and the others?"

"It's better than nothing, Monsignor," I said. "If you absolutely can't acknowledge the information about the plot, at least do that. It will give us a chance."

"I agree," Bruzzone said. "It may work, and you can sign such a letter without fear of incident. You have drafted letters for His Holiness on this very subject, responding to reports from bishops in Poland."

"Perhaps," Montini said. He rose from his seat and approached O'Flaherty and Bruzzone. All pretense of an official meeting was gone. The three men huddled together, conversing in Italian. They had an easy familiarity, their places in the Vatican hierarchy less important now than their common bond as friends and conspirators.

"Do you really think it can work?" Kaz whispered to me.

"It has to," I said. "That was sharp thinking. It's a good-faith effort on our part, which has to count for something. I wonder if we should have pressed Montini more, though."

"If the Pope is nervous about the Germans taking the Vatican, I doubt he would associate himself with any document that would put him in league with the Allies and the anti-Nazi plotters."

"Gentlemen," Monsignor Montini said. "I believe I can craft the letter as you suggest. I will work on it today. Meanwhile, Monsignor Bruzzone will deliver both documents to Sir D'Arcy. He can get them to Switzerland, I imagine."

"I made copies last night," O'Flaherty said. "We will keep those for when the time is right. I have a priest working on a translation of the Auschwitz Protocol into English. I'll give you a copy, Billy, when that's done."

"This must be kept secret, for the moment," Montini said to Kaz and me. "I trust the monsignors implicitly. We have worked together many times during this war, to help the unfortunate among us. They are both good men, as you are, I am sure. Can I trust your silence?"

"Yes," I said. "But I will have to report this to my superiors, once this mission is complete."

"Of course," Montini said. "Have you made progress in your investigation?"

"We have," I said. "As soon as we return with Diana—Sister Justina—I expect we will be very close to finding the killer."

"Excellent," Montini said. "We were greatly saddened at the loss of Monsignor Corrigan. The work we do is not without danger."

"How soon can you have the letter ready?" I hoped he'd say within the hour. All I could think of was Diana crossing that white line.

"Not until later today. I have other pressing duties to attend to. Have Monsignor Bruzzone bring you to my office in the Papal Palace at three o'clock." So much for my high hopes. One more day, then.

"Grand work, boys," O'Flaherty said after Montini left us. "That ought to do the trick. Monsignor Bruzzone will get you the letter this afternoon. I must leave you now. We have a bit of a crisis in one of our houses."

"In Rome?" I asked. "Remke warned you about the Gestapo, remember?"

"And I'm glad he did, boy. That's why I'll be disguised so my own mother wouldn't recognize me."

"Be careful, Hugh," Bruzzone said as we filed out of the room. "There's no disguising your height."

"Don't worry about me. I'll see you all tonight. Good luck."

"I shall bring the documents to Sir D'Arcy immediately," Bruzzone said as we stepped outside. "I will meet you at the German College before three o'clock, to take you to the Palace."

We stood under an archway in the courtyard, watching the two monsignors dash off in different directions, the collars of their coats turned up against the cold rain. Something that had been said in the fancy yellow room was not sitting right. Maybe I was thinking too much about Diana and was distracted. Or maybe there was something important that had been said. Or not said. I glanced around for Zlatko, but didn't see him. The covered archway kept out the rain but not the biting cold. Maybe he got cold feet, either kind, and went indoors.

"Billy, is there a reason you didn't mention your meeting at noon with Remke?"

"No reason to," I said. "O'Flaherty knows about it. Montini didn't have enough time to prepare the letter anyway."

"Is something bothering you? Things went fairly well in there. You should be glad."

"I should. How come I'm not?"

"Worry," Kaz said.

"Isn't that what makes cowards of us all?"

"No. That's conscience, as Hamlet says."

I looked around for Zlatko, and thought I caught a glimpse of him as we made for the Hospice Santa Marta. But bishops in black and purple were a dime a dozen around here, and I figured he'd come around with his list of informers sooner rather than later.

CHAPTER THIRTY-FIVE

REMKE HAD SHOWN me the south entrance to the Piazza Navona. So I'd studied my map and found the route to the north entrance. I donned extra layers of clothing—scarf, hat, gloves—courtesy of Nini. Mistrust I had enough of already. The rain had turned to a damp mist that felt even colder than the earlier downpours, and I clenched my hands in my pockets as I trudged along the Tiber, checking to make sure I had the safe-conduct pass from Remke close by, along with my Vatican identity papers.

I passed under the looming Castel Sant'Angelo and the huge Hall of Justice, built out of so much heavy white stone that it had created a sinkhole and almost toppled into the Tiber River, according to Nini. She and Kaz worked so hard at being nonchalant around each other that I was certain they were both head over heels. Good for Kaz. He'd suffered more than most, lost more than most, and had cared less for life than most. The princess and the baron. It sounded like a happy ending, but those were in damn short supply these days, and I worried about my own chances for one.

Kaz didn't have a get-out-of-jail pass, and Koch had his photograph, so he stayed behind to look for Zlatko. If things went smoothly, I'd be back in an hour, and we'd have some pieces of the puzzle in place. Of course, if smooth had been in the cards, I wouldn't be out in this weather. Head bowed into the wind, I crossed the bridge and took the Via Agonale, which led into the north end of the square. Neptune stood in a fountain with his trident like a sentry, his gaze fixed on the obelisk where I was headed.

I skirted the left side of the square, mixing in with pedestrians who were walking between the few open restaurants and shops; mainly German officers going in for an early lunch, with a few leather-coated civilians thrown in for good measure. Any of them could have been on the lookout for me. Or just hungry. I did a full circuit of the square and didn't spot Remke. I arrived back at the Fountain of the Four Rivers, with its Egyptian obelisk, a trophy from another war.

Kaz had told me the four rivers marked the extent of papal authority, back in the days when God's kingdom was as much of earth as of heaven. Each river was represented by a statute. The Danube, the Rio de la Plata, the Ganges, and the Nile. Kaz had explained that the figure representing the Nile had his robe pulled over his face to symbolize that the source of that river was unknown. The guy was as much in the dark as I was, so it seemed like a good spot to wait.

"Follow me, Lieutenant Boyle," a voice whispered to me. It wasn't Remke, but I didn't get a chance to protest. He headed south out of the piazza, taking a narrow side street, which led to a hole-in-the-wall restaurant, the Piccola Cuccagna. The walls were the familiar rusty red, and the smell of rotting garbage wafted up from the alley. Not one of Rome's finer attractions, but out of the way and dry. A good choice.

My escort opened the door, and the aroma of warm food from the kitchen made it an even better choice. Remke sat at a corner table, alone, a single glass of red wine at hand.

"What news do you have? Don't worry about speaking English, we have the restaurant to ourselves." As he spoke, his men closed the curtains and doused most of the lights. "These officers are all loyal to me and our cause, so you may speak freely."

"I will get the letter from Montini this afternoon. I met with him this morning, and he agreed to write it." When you need to lie convincingly, the truth can be convenient. I glanced at Remke's men, who gave me approving nods. Nice to have a vote of confidence from the enemy.

"You are certain? You will have it tomorrow?"

"I can have it for you later today. Why don't we do a switch this afternoon?"

"Impossible. I have generals to brief later, and they all like to talk, and drink. A waste of time, but necessary. Tomorrow will be soon enough. I will have your friends nearby. If you deliver, they will be freed."

I didn't inquire as to the alternative. "I will. Have you found Severino Rossi?"

"Yes." Remke signaled for a glass of wine for me. I took that to be a bad sign.

"I don't need a drink, Colonel. I need Rossi. Is he alive?"

Remke looked uncomfortable, and I wondered if he were the type who felt he had to deliver on a promise, no matter how hard. He was reminding me more and more of my own Colonel Harding.

"Yes, he is alive. But getting him out will be difficult." Remke had said he would give me Rossi if I held up my end of the deal. For him, that meant all in. If Rossi had been dead, he wouldn't lose a moment's sleep. But not delivering on a promise, that would keep him up at night. "When the jailers at Regina Coeli did not receive any further instructions from Soletto, they didn't know what to do. Yesterday, when you encountered Koch at the prison, he was there for prisoners. They gave him Rossi."

"Prisoners to torture."

"Yes. He does it both to extract information and for the pleasure it gives him."

I took a large gulp of wine. "Would he release him to the Vatican Gendarmerie?"

"Koch would laugh at them. Their jurisdiction means nothing to him. He is clearly insane, although I am told he is devoted to his wife and children, as well as his mistress."

"Would he release him to the Abwehr?" I locked onto Remke's eyes, daring him to take the step I was suggesting. We had a bond now, a bond made of new loyalties in a changing world, where enemies were friends and friends were not to be trusted.

"Perhaps the question is, could the Abwehr take him from Koch? Giving is not in his nature."

"Colonel, I respect what you're doing against Hitler. But my story to Colonel Harding will sound a lot better if you take an active role in rescuing a Jew from the clutches of this crazy Fascist cop. It would help me sell the whole package, especially if I were an eyewitness."

"Sell the package? You sound like a UFA producer. This is not a film script, Lieutenant. If we go after Rossi, and take you, it could mean your life."

"I have to go. I know what he looks like."

"All right, my American friend. We will go. But you must dress the part. So we can sell this package to Koch." Then he laughed, and I couldn't decide if he had a healthy sense of humor or a death wish. He rattled off some German and his men gathered around.

The next thing I knew, I was changing clothes with a Wehrmacht captain who was about my size. There was a lot of nervous laughter and kidding among Remke and his band of four men. Five, counting me. It was the kind of banter you'd hear in any unit before an operation, especially if one of the guys were down to his skivvies and switching clothes with a phony priest. It was a barrel of laughs.

"You are familiar with the Walther?" Remke asked me as I pulled on the leather belt and holster. The boots were a tight fit and the sleeves a bit long, but other than that I looked like any well-dressed Kraut.

"The Walther P38?" I said. "Sure. You point the barrel at the bad guy, right?"

"Do not forget to pull the trigger," the newly frocked priest said. Even Remke laughed.

"All right," Remke said, once we were ready. "Dieter will drive, and Carl will stay in the car with him, in case anyone wonders why a priest is driving a German staff car. Hans, you stand guard at the door and cover our exit. Lieutenant Boyle and I will go in with Bernard. Boyle is with us to identify Severino Rossi. We go in very

serious, very angry, but not at Koch and his men. They are our colleagues, and it is the incompetent fools at Regina Coeli who deserve
our wrath. Understood?"

Heads nodded. It was a good approach. Smart.

"Lieutenant Boyle," Remke said. "Koch is set up in a small hotel,
Pensione Jaccarino, not far from the Excelsior Hotel. Remember, we
are there for one man. You will likely see others in great need. You
must ignore them."

"Okay, but call me Billy, Colonel. Everyone does."

"Well then, so I must, Billy. The hotel is small, narrow corridors
and many rooms. Do not become separated from us, and obviously,
do not speak. The men of Banda Koch are the worst of the worst.
The Gestapo calls them a Special Police team, but all that means is
that they are the cruelest of the Fascist Police, the Gestapo, and the
SS combined."

"So if there's trouble?"

"Shoot to kill, Billy," Dieter said. "The world will be a better
place."

We crammed into the staff car, Remke explaining that his men
would walk back to the Excelsior if we got Severino out. Meaning
he probably wouldn't be in shape to sit up straight. We drove up the
Via Veneto again, this time turning right after the Excelsior and
coming to a stop on the Via Romagna, outside a modest three-story
hotel. The rain had stopped, but the air was colder and slick patches
of ice coated the pavement. Bernard, Remke, and I went up the steps
and the colonel tried the door. Locked. He pounded on it, shouting
in Italian. Hans walked up and down the sidewalk, checking the
alleyway, giving the all-clear signal.

Finally the door opened. A stocky guy, short but solid, stood in
the doorway. His shirtsleeves were rolled up, his suspenders hanging
off his waist. Sweat beaded his brow. He looked Remke over and
fired a volley of Italian at him. Remke held up his hands, shaking
his head, probably telling the guy he had it all wrong, it was the *idioti*
down at the prison who were responsible for this mix-up.

It was enough to get us inside. The stocky guy beckoned us into a room that had probably once been a parlor for guests. Newspapers littered the floor, an empty schnapps bottle lay on its side. In the next room, down a dingy hallway, a phonograph was playing loudly, an opera of some sort. He cupped his hands to yell over the music, obviously calling for his superior, or at least another German to deal with this officer.

"*Un momento,*" he said. So far so good. Heavy footsteps sounded as the scratch of a needle across vinyl signaled the end of the music. But the soaring operatic voice seemed to go on, terribly out of tune and without accompaniment. It was a scream. A piercing shriek at the edge of madness, a rising cry that stopped only for desperate breath before starting up again, climbing the scales of disbelieving pain.

"*Basta!*" the stocky guy yelled, gesturing at someone in the room, telling him to stop. A tall, thin man with sunken, dark eyes and a two-day growth of beard sauntered out of the room, a pair of bloody pliers in one hand. He wore a leather apron, stained with both fresh and dried blood. The screams lessened to cries and whimpers, the opera in intermission.

"*Siamo qui per il prigioniero che si chiama Severino Rossi,*" Remke said. "*Koch è qui?*"

The two Italians shook their heads. No, Koch wasn't there. They argued a bit with each other, and then the short guy seemed to win. He pointed upstairs, and beckoned us to follow. We passed the room where the tall guy had returned to his work. In it, a figure was tied to a chair, his face unrecognizable. Four fingers on his left hand were ruined, the pliers having done their work. You save the thumb for last. If it was Rossi, I wouldn't have had a chance at recognizing him. The opera of pain began again, louder and more insistent. I could feel my heart pounding as I fought to control myself and act as if this were just another day on the job.

Upstairs, a room had been converted into an office. A man sat at a desk. He was dressed in civilian clothes, nicely tailored at that. White shirt with silver cuff links, blue silk tie, charcoal-gray wool suit. Large photographs covered one side of the desk, mostly mug shots, some of crowds on the street. He was working his way through a stack of files, a fountain pen poised above a notepad. There were no traces of blood to be seen, but ink had leaked from his pen, a trail of blue spots seeping into the blotter.

"*Was wollen Sie?*" he asked, without looking up. His dark hair was slicked back and the odor of a perfumed pomade wafted toward us. I glanced at the photographs and saw Kaz, his face upside down but clear as day. And my own mug in the background.

"*Was ist ihr Name?*" Remke demanded sharply.

"*Hauptsturmführer Becher. Und Sie?*"

"*Oberst Remke von dem Abwehr.*" Remke's tone made it clear that as a colonel, he outranked the plainclothes SS man Becher.

"*Der Gefangene Severino Rossi,*" Remke said. "*Schnell.*"

They started to argue, so I feigned boredom and eased out of the room, hands clasped behind my back and boot heels clicking against the floor, like an arrogant Aryan. I glanced into the rooms leading off the main hallway. In one, a woman lay on a bare mattress, her hands manacled to the iron frame. She had one black eye and a look of hopelessness in both. The next room didn't even have a bed, only a crumpled blanket with a monk curled up on it, his hands clasped in prayer. Maybe he'd been picked up in Koch's recent raid on Vatican properties. Neither met my eyes, which was fine with me.

In the third room, two men were slumped in opposite corners, like fighters between rounds. Their faces were bloodied and both had their eyes swollen shut from a fresh beating. The walls were sprayed with blood and a bucket half filled with water was by the door. I wondered whose job it was to clean the place up.

From the corridor I heard raised voices, but they didn't have that edge of danger to them. They were aggrieved, but not violent. It sounded like a dustup over paperwork down at the precinct.

I stepped into the room, and nudged one of the men with my boot. He didn't move. I squatted down to get a closer look, but I couldn't make anything of his face. His hair was wrong, though. Short and dark brown, not black and curly. I stood, and as I did he fell to the side, his head hitting the floor with a disquieting sound. He was dead.

I grabbed the pail and doused the other guy with water. He moved, grimacing as he did. Although his hair was matted with dried blood, I could tell that it matched Rossi's. The face I wasn't so sure of, but he was thin and gaunt, as Rossi had looked in the picture. Footsteps and mutterings were headed my way, so I stepped back as Remke and the other German entered the room. The civilian, or cop, or whoever he was, consulted a clipboard. He was unconcerned with the dead body, so I figured he'd gotten what he wanted from him.

"Rossi," he said, pointing to the heap in the corner, which had begun to moan at the mention of the name.

"*Danke*," said Remke, with a quick click of the heels, very Prussian. He snapped his fingers and pointed to Rossi. Bernard and I grabbed him under the arms and made for the stairs, not in too much of a hurry, but not taking in the sights either. As we came downstairs, the volume of the opera lowered. The Italian stood in the doorway of the torture chamber, wiping his hands on a towel.

"*È morto*," he said, shrugging his shoulders. No reason not to enjoy the music, I guess.

Remke went ahead and opened the door. We dragged Rossi along, his feet bouncing on each step. He cried out, and that in turn caused him pain. He gasped, and I realized he was able to see through those black eyes, since there was Pietro Koch, black leather trench coat and all, staring at us from the sidewalk. Two similarly garbed men stood behind him, hands deep in their pockets and eyes on us.

"*Ho bisogno di questo prigioniero per l'inchiesta*," Remke said, as Carl opened the rear door of the BMW. Carl stood with one hand on the open door and the other resting on his holster. The snap had already been undone, in case Koch didn't buy the explanation, which was something about needing the prisoner for questioning. Becher appeared on the doorstep, looking down at us, a pistol in his hand hanging loosely at his side.

"*Colonnello Remke, sì?*" Koch said, his eyes darting to the doorway of the pensione, then back to the group around the car. His words came out on frosted breath, his cheeks as rosy as a schoolchild's.

"*Sì,*" Remke said, with that click of the heels again.

Koch walked around the car, his eyes settling on Dieter, who wore my coat buttoned up tight to cover the white collar. Remke and I got in, me in the backseat with Rossi, trying to hold him upright. Carl and Bernard crossed the street, taking up stations behind a parked car. Koch looked in the window, his gaze on me, and I nodded, as if to say thanks for the loan of the half-dead prisoner. Koch's dark, beady eyes stayed locked on mine until he broke into a smile and nodded back. He stood, thumped the hood of the car, and headed into the building.

Dieter put the car in gear and waited for a truck to pass. The vehicle slowed, and I cursed silently as Rossi slumped against me. His breath was ragged and wheezy as he mumbled in French. I glanced up at Koch and Becher, who were watching us from the doorway to the pensione, and saw their eyes dart to the sidewalk.

It was Zlatko. He wore an open coat, his purple bishop's sash bright against his black cassock. He was yelling to Koch, his hand thrust accusingly in our direction. I could only make out one word, but it was enough.

"*Americano!*"

Becher raised his pistol, and my hand went to my Walther, but Dieter peeled out into the road, speeding around the lumbering truck, sending a motorcycle skidding onto the sidewalk. Pistol shots echoed in the street, and I saw Koch and Becher diving for cover as Carl and Bernard fired in their direction before disappearing down a narrow street.

"It appears Bishop Zlatko has found a new sponsor," Remke said.

"We should have shot him and Koch," I said.

"That would not have been wise," Remke said, watching me from the front seat. "Killing Koch would result in the Gestapo and the Fascist police turning the city upside down. It would make things difficult for both of us."

"Yes," I said, holding onto Rossi. "Although I don't think you are a man who goes through life choosing the wisest course."

"Oh, I am," Remke said, with a sharp laugh. "But perhaps wisdom has come too late for me."

"I sure could have used some," I said. "I had a deal with Zlatko, but it looks like he double-crossed me."

"He must have followed you," Remke said. "Or at least he saw you leave the Vatican and came to inform Koch."

"That means trouble for you," I said.

"It will be more than trouble for you, Billy, if we are stopped before we reach the Vatican border. As for Koch and his gang, they are often embroiled in conflicts with the Wehrmacht and even the regular Italian police," Remke said, as Dieter drove calmly through the military traffic, his eyes checking the rearview mirror every few seconds. "Bernard and Carl fired high, simply to force them to cover so we could get away. If a complaint is made, it will be deemed a matter of mistaken identity. But Koch is not one for official channels. An ambush is more his style, so we must take care."

"We should change the meeting spot," Dieter said. "In case Zlatko did observe it today."

"Yes," Remke agreed. "We will meet at the Trinità dei Monti, the church at the head of the Spanish Steps. Do you know the Piazza di Spagna?"

"I saw it on a map. I'll be there."

"What was your arrangement with Zlatko?" Remke asked as Dieter barreled down one narrow, twisting street after another, staying away from the main thoroughfares.

"Information in exchange for doing my best to keep him in Rome. I don't think he's a big fan of the Russians, and he has a lot to answer for in Croatia."

"As do we all," Remke said, turning away and staring straight ahead.

CHAPTER THIRTY-SIX

"ONE MORE THING, Colonel Remke," I said as the staff car drove along the south side of the Bernini colonnades, making for the entrance nearest the German College. "I need to know—"

"*Halten Sie das Auto hier auf,*" Remke said to his driver, pointing to the end of the colonnade. "You, my American friend, are in no position to ask for further favors. I have done this because I said I would, as a gesture of good faith. But nothing else until you make good on your part of the bargain."

"I will," I said, with more fervor than I felt. "And when I do, if you happen to know the name of anyone in the Vatican who was an informer for the Gestapo in Genoa, I wouldn't mind hearing the name."

"Genoa?" Remke said. "Why Genoa?"

I knew I had him hooked. I never met an intelligence officer who could resist asking questions. "Because something very bad happened to Severino Rossi there," I said. "Something that caused him to make the journey to Rome without identity papers, and left him on the steps of the basilica with Monsignor Corrigan murdered at his feet."

"Genoa, you say? There is a lot of refugee traffic there. Coming from France or Yugoslavia, or trying for Switzerland. We may be able to find something, but you will only learn of it when you have fully completed your task. Now, leave the belt and the pistol on the seat and take Monsieur Rossi with you, if he is still alive. Hurry."

"I would appreciate the return of my uniform," Dieter said as we carried the unconscious body of Severino Rossi over the line. Remke had intercepted the curious German guards and turned them away. Two Swiss Guard in their gray uniforms advanced with rifles at the ready, suspicious of a bloodied body being manhandled by Germans. "When it is convenient, of course."

"Sure," I said, feeling his boots pinch my toes. I looked around for a familiar face, and quickly spotted Kaz and Nini peering out at us from the shadows of the colonnade. I saw Kaz's eyes widen as first he recognized me, and then saw the wreck of a man Dieter and I were holding up. He and Nini ran to us, speaking to the guards as they passed them. Officially, refugees were to be turned away. But, like most of the Swiss Guard, these two were sympathetic to Monsignor O'Flaherty, and stepped back, keeping a wary eye on Remke as he leaned against the hood of the car, one long step from the white border.

"Is this Rossi?" Kaz asked, taking one arm and hoisting it over his shoulder. He took in my clothes on Dieter and the uniform I wore, and gave Dieter a curt nod.

"Yeah," I said. "We had to get him back from Banda Koch."

"We?" Kaz asked as Nini felt Rossi for a pulse.

"It is a long story, Baron," Remke said, raising his voice from the other side of the line. "Your friend is not without nerve. I trust tomorrow will not require it in a similar quantity."

"Noon," I said. "All three of them, and the names, Colonel."

"In my army, lieutenants do not give orders to colonels," Remke said.

"Yet you take them from an Austrian corporal," Kaz said. After what the Germans had done to his family following the invasion of Poland, he had little love for any German, even one with a gun pointed at Hitler's head.

"Yes, Baron. But perhaps not for long. Any demands from the lieutenant will only be considered once his obligation is met," Remke

said, his eyes hard and narrow. "Nerve will count for little if I am
disappointed in this. Until tomorrow then." He bowed in Nini's
direction and ignored me, which was good, since I was sure I wasn't
hiding my worry well.

"We must take him to Santa Marta," Nini said. "The nuns have
a small clinic there. He needs help, his pulse is very weak."

"Okay, but not the clinic, it's too public. We need a safe place to
hide him," I said.

"Hiding people is what we do," Nini said. "I will ask Hugh—"

"No," I said, as we clumsily carried Rossi through the Gate of
the Bells. "Not even Monsignor O'Flaherty should know where he
is. Where can we bring him?"

"My God, do you not trust even him?" Nini asked.

"It is to protect this poor soul," Kaz said soothingly. "The fewer
people who know where he is, the safer he'll be."

"All right then. We will take him around to the side entrance
and he can have my room. The sisters know how to keep a secret."

We skirted the German College and kept to the shadows as we
crossed a small piazza to the Santa Marta. Nini produced a key ring
and unlocked a side door. Rossi began to moan as we carried him
up the narrow stairway as gently as we could.

"Who could do such a thing?" Nini said once we'd gotten Rossi
laid out on her bed. She had a small sitting room and a separate
bedroom. Spartan, but luxurious by Vatican standards. She began to
clean the dried blood from Rossi's face with a wet cloth, and
instructed Kaz to fetch Sister Cecilia and her medical kit.

"Don't worry, Billy," Nini said after Kaz left. "Sister Cecilia is a
trained nurse and quite discreet. I only hope this boy can be healed.
He is the one they say killed Monsignor Corrigan, isn't he?"

"That's what Soletto said, but I wouldn't put much faith in that."

"Because he was murdered also?"

"Yes. I think Soletto was paid off by the killer to cover things
up, and then got too greedy."

"How much would you have to pay a policeman to cover up a
murder?" Nini asked.

"Apparently more than Soletto did," I said.

Rossi winced as Nini dabbed around his swollen eyes, which was a good sign. You had to be alive and conscious to feel pain.

"I'm pretty sure there were diamonds involved, but I don't know in what quantity. Good quality, though." Kaz and I had kept things quiet about the diamond we'd found in Corrigan's room so far, but it seemed safe to tell Nini.

"That's odd," Nini said, pressing a damp cloth to Rossi's lips.

"Why?"

"What you said about good quality. About a month ago, an envelope was left for the Mother Superior. In it were three diamonds."

"Of excellent quality?" This was quite a surprise; perhaps Kaz and I should have told Nini about the diamond sooner. It would have helped to know this.

"Yes, and that was what was remarkable. As you know, diamonds are useful currency for refugees. We've seen some, but usually small and flawed. A jeweler told me these were excellent specimens."

"You have no idea where they came from?"

"None at all. We were simply glad to be able to buy food with what we got for them. Quite a lot of food, and some bribes as well."

"It's sort of an open secret that Santa Marta houses hidden Jews and refugees, isn't it?"

"That's a good way to put it," Nini said. "I always thought the diamonds came from a man who had money and identity papers, but was perhaps Jewish himself, and wanted to help without revealing who he was."

"The diamonds were his," I said, pointing at Rossi.

"Oh no," Nini said. "Is that what this is all about? Simple greed?"

"I don't know," I said, and I didn't. People killed for greed all the time. But if the motive had been greed here, why give away a small fortune in diamonds? A greedy man wouldn't part with beautiful gems to help refugees. No, not a greedy man, or at least not a man greedy for lucre.

Sister Cecilia swept into the room, steel-blue habit swirling, medical kit in hand. She took charge, sending Nini for more water and shooing Kaz and me out of the room.

"You seem to have changed tailors," Kaz said as he poured us both a glass of wine from a side table in Nini's parlor.

I sat in an easy chair facing a wide window with a magnificent view of the dome of Saint Peter's. It was odd how this place revolved around the basilica—physically, spiritually, and aesthetically. Even so, its aura of majesty and serenity did little to alter the human drama all around it. Was it mocking us, with our conflicts and struggles? Would it be here in another thousand years, when this war was forgotten? I didn't know. All I knew was that my feet hurt.

"It belongs to Dieter. One of Remke's men," I said, pulling off the boots with some effort. "He has small feet."

"I assume he didn't simply take a fancy to your priestly attire," Kaz said, sitting on the couch opposite.

"No." I took a healthy slug of vino and unbuttoned the collar of my—Dieter's—tunic. "Remke found out that Pietro Koch and his gang had taken Severino Rossi from Regina Coeli, for no other reason than to torture him."

"Nini has told me stories," Kaz said. "Koch was forced to move to his current location from his previous hotel after the neighbors complained about the cacophony of screams day and night."

"Yeah. They had an opera going full blast on the phonograph to cover the sounds of torture. Anyway, Remke agreed to take Rossi from them, since he'd told me he would get him if he were still alive."

"Interesting," Kaz said. "A man of his word, it seems."

"That might work against us, if he doesn't like the letter we give him. We might not get Diana and the others back."

"Perhaps," Kaz said. "But why the uniform?"

"I'd seen a photograph of Rossi, so I was the only one who could recognize him. We had no idea what we'd walk into, so it seemed best that I go along."

"They gave Rossi up?"

"Yeah, Remke fed them a line about needing him for questioning, and there being a mix-up at the prison. Typical bureaucracy and they bought it. But that's not the big news. I know where Zlatko disappeared to."

"Tell me where, and I'll tell you why," Kaz said, raising a wine glass to his lips.

"Okay. He showed up at the Pensione Jaccarino, just as we were driving away. It wasn't a coincidence, either. He pointed me out as an American to Koch, and there were a few wild shots fired to cover our escape. Now, why was he there?"

"Because Cardinal Boetto from Genoa arrived with a report on Bishop Zlatko's activities in Croatia. A number of witnesses place him at a concentration camp run by a Franciscan monk. Also, his superior, Archbishop Ivan Šarić, has taken a number of Jewish properties for church and personal use, including one estate he signed over to Zlatko. Boetto wants Zlatko stripped of his bishopric, which would be an embarrassment for many in the Vatican who overlooked the clergy's support of the Ustashi in Croatia."

"It sounds like everyone was lining up against Zlatko," I said.

"Yes. Since he is here, he is a convenient lightning rod for righteous indignation. The news got to Zlatko and he was seen crossing the border by one of the Swiss Guard."

"Remke said that German intelligence hasn't valued what Zlatko has been feeding them, but that Koch might take him on. It could be the only place Zlatko has left to go, if he doesn't want to face the music here or back in Croatia when the Soviets roll in."

"I pity the man if Banda Koch is his last resort. But he's proved his worth to them already, by alerting them to your presence today. Leaving the Vatican tomorrow may be too dangerous, Billy."

"We've changed the meeting spot to the church at the top of the Spanish Steps. I'll dress in civilian clothes. There's no sense in going out as a priest again."

"Or a German," Kaz said.

"Hard to believe we've thrown in with a German intelligence officer, against an Italian Fascist and a Croatian bishop."

"The Vatican is not quite what I thought it would be," Kaz said. "I am not a religious man, and what happened to my cousin colored my view of the church hierarchy. But there is much good here, as well as evil. In Poland, the priests were executed by the Nazis, along with all the others they butchered. In Croatia, it is the priests who lead the butchery, and the church does little to stop it. Yet many here risk their lives to save others. It leaves one confused, doesn't it?"

"Only if you expect revelation," I said, gazing out at the basilica. "I find it easier to set my sights lower. Just because people wear fancy robes, they don't necessarily act decently. It's who they were before they put on the robes that matters."

"I think the robes do matter, Billy. Once they are donned, this becomes a place of absolutes. No shades of gray, only the glittering dome of heaven or the descent into hell. From O'Flaherty to Zlatko, they all act in the name of God, don't they? I don't know why I am surprised; perhaps I had more faith than I thought."

"And now you're disappointed?"

"It does leave me wishing for simpler times."

"To simpler times to come," I said, raising my glass and draining the last of the wine, wondering when those times might be. Kaz finished his drink and we sat quietly, the rays of the setting sun gathering around the dome, bathing the basilica in pure light.

"Do you think Remke can succeed with the plot against Hitler?" Even here, in private, Kaz lowered his voice to a whisper.

"If it can be done, it would take a man like Remke to do it. He won't be the one pulling the trigger, but he does seem the type to set things in motion."

"Speaking of him, we should get the letter from Montini. After I find you some new clothes."

I went to the window as Kaz left to find a new set of duds for me. The sky had turned a deep red, the dome now dark against the fading light. Rossi cried out from the next room. I hoped my prayers about tomorrow actually meant something, and that I wasn't committing a sin for thinking they didn't.

CHAPTER THIRTY-SEVEN

I WAS DECKED out in a nice blue suit, a little shiny on the knees and elbows, but it fit. I didn't mind swapping the clerical collar for a dark-blue polka-dot tie either. Kaz ditched his cassock as well, since everyone within Vatican City seemed to know who we really were.

Monsignor Bruzzone was at his desk, and didn't seem unhappy to leave the paperwork behind. "I suppose you have heard about Bishop Zlatko," he said as he led us out of the Medieval Palace. "He has left the Holy See."

"Just a step ahead of Cardinal Boetto," I said.

"It appears so. His archbishop and Archbishop Boetto are bitter enemies. Since Bishop Zlatko is close at hand, he knew he would incur the wrath meant for Archbishop Šarić."

"Not without reason," Kaz said as we neared the entrance to the Apostolic Palace.

"No, of course not," Bruzzone said, halting in the middle of the courtyard. It was cold, and not a single light showed anywhere. "I simply meant that the bishop saw the handwriting on the wall and acted to save himself. Or, perhaps he is the killer you seek, and thought you were close to apprehending him. Have you made any progress that might have frightened him?"

"No, nothing," I said. "Once the business with this letter is settled, we might have something to investigate."

"Ah yes, that is more important, isn't it? Come, I will take you up." Bruzzone pointed to the top floor of the darkened palace. Above us, the last remnants of light cast an inky glow across the sky. I shivered, and followed.

"Alois, come stanno sua moglie ed i bambini? Franco, come stai?"

Bruzzone chatted with Alois and Franco, who wore capes over their gray field uniforms. I heard our names and Montini's mentioned, then the doors were opened and the guards gave us friendly nods.

"You and Monsignor O'Flaherty both seem to know all the Swiss Guard well," I said.

"Of course we do. In our business; it pays to befriend those who stand guard at the gates, yes? I got to know them even more closely when their chaplain fell ill and I took over his duties for a brief time. They are good men, many of them willing to turn a blind eye when POWs or refugees show up in the piazza. Others even give their assistance willingly."

"It seems orders from the top are not always carried out to the letter," I said, remembering what Montini had said this morning about ignoring the Pope's directive for refugees to be turned out of papal properties.

"But is it not the spirit we should be concerned with here?" Bruzzone gave a wink, and we followed him up the marble staircase to the third floor. He had a point, and I recalled what Kaz had said about this being a place of absolutes. True, there wasn't a lot of middle ground between heaven and hell, but some of these guys managed to find room in the shadows to rationalize their own actions. As long as it was to my benefit, I had no problem with that. After all, a Boston cop learns rationalization at the knee of his daddy.

"Monsignor," Bruzzone said as he knocked at the open door. Montini did double duty, working afternoons as the papal secretary. His office was at the edge of the Pope's private living quarters, which stretched around one corner of the top floor. The single window was covered in blackout drapes, and heavy wood paneling deadened the sound, making Bruzzone's voice sound meek and fearful.

"Yes, come in," Montini said, rising from his chair. "You are here for the letter, I assume?"

"Yes, Monsignor," I said.

"You have given up the priesthood, both of you?" Montini said with a sly grin. "I despair of losing two such resourceful candidates for the clergy."

"By now most people within these walls know we're not for real," I said.

"Correct. If prayer flew as quickly as gossip, all the saints in heaven could not keep up with it. But take care when you cross the border line to deliver this." Montini handed Kaz a thick white envelope. "There is a copy in English as well as in German. I thought the former might imply delivery to the English or Americans."

"That's smart, Monsignor," I said. "But what does the letter actually say?"

"It is addressed to Colonel Erich Remke, Excelsior Hotel, Rome," Kaz said. Then he read.

> As Minister of Ordinary Affairs for the Vatican State Secretariat, I acknowledge receipt of the document referred to as the Auschwitz Protocol, along with other documents related to the conflict which now engulfs the world.
>
> The Holy See has received many reports of vast atrocities involving noncombatants, tormented as they are, for reasons of nationality or descent, destined to exterminatory measures. When soldiers turn their weapons against noncombatants to exercise these measures, whether from the air or on the ground, such acts are no longer part of jus ad bellum, the criteria for a just war, but must be called murder. Such reports beg the question, How should the honorable man act?
>
> Should he not, over the ruins of a social order which has given such tragic proof of its ineptitude, gather together the hearts of all those who are magnanimous and upright, in the

solemn vow not to rest until a vast legion shall be formed of those handfuls of men who, bent on bringing back society to its center of gravity, which is the very law of God, will take just action?

Mankind owes that vow to the countless dead who lie buried on the field of battle: The sacrifice of their lives is a holocaust offered for a new and better social order. Mankind owes that vow to the hundreds of thousands of persons who, without any fault on their part, sometimes only because of their nationality or race, have been consigned to death. Mankind owes that vow to the flood of tears and bitterness, to the accumulation of sorrow and suffering, emanating from the murderous ruin of this dreadful conflict and crying to Heaven to liberate the world from violence and terror.

"It is signed by Monsignor Montini," Kaz said, offering me the letter. I shook my head, and he placed it in the envelope.

"The Christmas message?" Bruzzone asked.

"Yes," Montini said. "I took the words His Holiness used in his Christmas message to the world in 1942. Since he had already uttered these sentiments, I saw no reason why they could not be stated once again."

"It's a lot of words," I said. It seemed to me that they were so convoluted and dense that it would take a dozen philosophers to decode it. Maybe that was the idea.

"It is the style of writing which the Holy See calls for," Bruzzone said apologetically. "Ornate, one might say."

Inscrutable and obscure, I might have added, but I didn't want to sound ungrateful. It was all we had, and I knew it was all Montini could give. "Thank you, Monsignor Montini. I am sure it will appeal to Remke, especially the part about weapons from the air. He called it terror bombing."

"Please remember that while we work to assist those who are persecuted by the Nazi regime, we also pray for all those civilians whose lives have been taken in this war, however their deaths were delivered. We are indeed neutral, no matter how sympathetic we may be to decent men such as you."

"Thank you," I said, although I wasn't certain what exactly I was thanking him for. The slightest of compliments, following the condemnation of our air war?

"You expected more, I know," Montini said. "But there are limits to what can be done without involving His Holiness. Or with his involvement, as you know we cannot risk the neutrality of the Holy See."

"Men and women risk their lives for others all the time," I said. "Even carpenters."

"God's blessing on you," Montini said, ignoring my remark and dismissing us as he returned to his paperwork.

Bruzzone invited us back to his office for a drink, which sounded like the best idea of the day. We settled into chairs, our coats still on against the chill of the room, as he poured out three brandies.

"*Salute*," Bruzzone said. The brandy felt hot in my gut, and I declined a second. I needed my head screwed on straight to figure out how best to play the letter.

"What do you think your Colonel Remke will make of Montini's letter?" Bruzzone asked.

"I don't know. He might buy it, even without a direct reference to the coup."

"I am not so sure," Kaz said. "From what you've told me, Remke sounds like a man who also deals in absolutes."

"*Assoluto?*" Bruzzone asked.

"Billy and I were talking about how religion, particularly here at the Vatican, causes people to see the world in absolute terms. Heaven and hell, with little in between. No offense, Monsignor, but it does seem to come naturally to those who believe strongly."

"Yes, I understand. Anyone who believes strongly—in overthrowing a tyrant or in his own religion—such a person must believe absolutely. How could it be otherwise? Where else would your strength come from?"

"The problem is that tyrants are the ultimate absolutists. It's fine to believe in religion and the church, but if all it gets you is a watered-down letter using last year's Christmas greeting, then I can't say I'm impressed with the mighty power of the Vatican."

"You must understand how things work here, my friend." Bruzzone leaned across his desk, as if proximity might improve his logic. "The Holy See is not of the temporal world. The church exists outside time, outside of the normal limits of human understanding. His Holiness—and yes, his advisors such as Monsignor Montini—they do not consider a problem in terms of months or years, but centuries. The rise of fascism in Europe is merely one incident in history. Tyrants come and go. They rise, they murder thousands, burn monasteries, shut down churches, propagate evil of all kinds. But they do not last. They never have. Words do nothing against them in the short term, so we bow to the storm winds and wait. We wait, and we have faith. The leaders of the Church are planning for eternity. What is the 'Thousand-Year Reich' in comparison to that? It will not last out the decade, and will soon be gone from Europe."

"But what of all who have died, while you bow into the wind?" Kaz asked. "All of the innocent noncombatants Monsignor Montini wrote of so eloquently?"

"You ask us to solve that problem, a temporal problem, which we had no part in creating," Bruzzone said with a heavy sigh. "You wish us to take a side in this struggle, and risk His Holiness, the Holy See, the treasures of the Church here in Rome. But we are not an army. We are not the Red Cross or the League of Nations. You wish for a stronger letter, to save your friends. This I understand. But such a letter, in the wrong hands, would bring the Gestapo down upon us. Here, where Saint Peter built his church. What good would that do, to deliver His Holiness into the hands of Hitler?"

"Your words make sense, Monsignor, but they are words spoken in a safe place, with good brandy at hand," Kaz said. "Out in the world, beyond the white border line, things are not so clear."

"Do not forget, I too have been out in the world. I know what it is like to be hunted. Do not judge us too harshly, my friends. Our job is to care for souls, and do the best we can while we are here on earth. Perhaps we are weak and fearful, perhaps we make mistakes, but that is because we are human."

Bruzzone folded his hands in front of him. With his words hanging in the air, I slid my glass toward the bottle and he filled it. For that small gesture I was glad.

CHAPTER THIRTY-EIGHT

I STOOD AT the foot of the bed, willing Severino Rossi to wake up. He was the key to solving the murder, I was certain. He looked much better, but I knew that was because he'd been cleaned up, laid out on clean sheets, and his filthy clothes replaced with white pajamas. His eyes were still swollen shut and wine-colored bruises decorated his cheeks. He had a splint on one arm and a bandage wound tightly across his thin chest. Each breath was labored, each gasp ragged. He looked like he'd been in a fight with Joe Louis and then stepped in front of a milk truck.

"What do you think?" Kaz asked in a whisper. Sister Cecilia was asleep in an armchair near the bed and she blinked an eye open as we spoke.

"I think we aren't the only ones waiting to see if he wakes up," I said, guiding Kaz out of the room.

In the sitting room, Nini had laid out plates of pasta and glasses of wine. "*Aglio e olio,*" she said. Garlic in olive oil. It was pungent enough that I thought Severino might rise up and ask for a bowl.

"Has he spoken at all?" I asked.

"He whispered something in French," Nini said. "I couldn't make it out."

"In case anybody asks, say he's in a coma. Probable brain injury."

"It may well be true," Nini said. "Sister Cecilia says he was severely beaten, and certainly sustained a concussion. He should be in a hospital."

"We couldn't protect him there," Kaz said.

"You must," Nini said, her hand clenched into a fist. "That boy has suffered too much already."

"Kaz should stay here," I said. "If that's all right with you, Nini."

"Certainly. What do you think could happen?"

"That's just it—we don't know. The killer could be anyone, even someone we all trust. Nini, you'll have to be on guard against everyone," I said.

"Perhaps now is a good time to show you this," Kaz said, pulling a Beretta automatic pistol from his coat. "I took this from that Fascist officer at the train yard. I didn't tell you because I didn't want you to worry."

"We were under orders not to bring any firearms in neutral territory," I explained to Nini. "But I'm damn glad you did," I said to Kaz. "And that you didn't tell me at the time. You may need it if the killer makes a move against Severino." I reached for my wineglass, and when I rested my hand on the table, I saw it tremble. I hadn't thought about the train yard in days. About killing the Italian. Necessary, we had told each other at the time. It was, but my hand still shook at the memory of it.

"Then perhaps you should tempt him," Nini said, with a glance at my hands that told me she'd noticed. "If we tell two people that he was awake and speaking, two hundred will hear that message within the hour."

"Not yet," I said. "I have to deliver the letter to Remke tomorrow. I don't know how long I'll be gone. But as soon as I get back, we'll let it slip that Rossi made a miraculous recovery."

When I get back tomorrow. With Diana, Abe, and Rino in tow. There was no other option, nothing else I could think about but their safety. Abe and Rino were my responsibility. Diana was everything else. I struggled to focus on Rossi and work out the best way to use him to our advantage. When all that was behind us, I could focus on finding Corrigan's killer. It was easy to forget the orders that had brought me here, being so far removed from the brass. One of the advantages of dangerous work: you don't have senior officers watching over your shoulder.

"You should take this," Kaz said, sliding the Beretta across the table.

"I will," I said, pushing it back to him. "But you keep it tonight and stay here. Block the door and shoot anyone who tries to force their way in."

As Kaz reached to take the pistol, the door to Nini's room opened and a stooped figure in a threadbare coat stared down at us. He was covered in dust from boots to beard, and he wore a blue workman's coverall over his clothes. Kaz snatched the Beretta up and leveled it at the stranger's belly. "*Chi è?*" he demanded, asking the man's identity.

"Would you shoot a harmless priest, Baron?" The Irish accent was unmistakable.

"Hugh!" Nini exclaimed. "You know better than to sneak up and frighten people with your disguises. One day you *will* get yourself shot."

"Excuse me, *Principessa*. I thought I'd receive a warm welcome, but I never dreamed it would involve a small cannon. I'll go wash up and return a changed man while the Baron puts away that *pistola*." As he spoke he straightened himself, gaining six inches in height. Nini shook her head, as if exasperated at the antics of a young boy, and I thought that for all the danger to himself and others, Hugh O'Flaherty did manage to squeeze a sense of enjoyment out the situation. Ten minutes later he was at the table with us, the fake whiskers gone and the rest of him fairly well dusted off. I gave him a quick summary of the day's events.

"Can you keep things quiet about Rossi? His presence here puts Nini in danger, you know," he said, taking a sip of wine.

"Kaz will stay here tonight to guard them both," I said. "We got in without too many people seeing us, so I hope that will buy some time."

"Are you satisfied with the letter from Montini?"

"No, but it's the best he could do. We'll keep our fingers crossed."

"Do you know," O'Flaherty said, pausing to take in a mouthful of pasta, "that crossed fingers were a sign the early Christians used to secretly identify each other? Making the cross, you see? It's a good sign to make, but I'll add a prayer or two tonight for your success."

"What were you doing today, Monsignor, to need such a disguise?" Kaz asked.

"Trouble in some of the houses where we have people hidden. I had to travel across the city. Workmen are part of the background scenery in Rome. It helps me blend in, and the stoop does away with some of my height."

"What kind of trouble this time?" Nini asked.

"All personal problems, nothing worse. It's hard for a man to be hidden away in a home and not able to speak the same language. There was a British officer who was sure the family he was with hated him, since they dined separately. Served him his meals in a hidden attic room. He became afraid that they were going to betray him. It turned out that they were giving him the lion's share of their food. If they got one egg, it went to him, to keep his strength up."

"And they didn't want him to see what little they were left with," Nini said.

"Aye. I explained it to him and then there were tears and the shaking of hands all around. I promised to get more food sent to them. Then onto another family, where a young South African sergeant was paying too much attention to the wife of the house. I have to say, I'll be glad when the Allies get here and take these fellows off our hands."

"How do you get around? You must wear out a lot of shoe leather," I said.

"With the help of the unsung heroes of the occupation of Rome," he said. "The trolley conductors. Good fellows, each one. See, I used to conduct the early Mass in Saint Peter's. Before dawn it was, and I'd finish up just before the first shift started for the trolleys. So I got to know them, and they me. Now I can go anywhere on a Rome trolley car. I give the driver a wink and he sees through my disguise, lets me ride for free. Plus they know where all the roadblocks and identity checks are."

"I bet they can spot a tail as well," I said.

"They have a nose for policemen, sure. Do you want to take the trolley to Piazza Navona tomorrow?"

"The rendezvous has been changed to the Spanish Steps. It would be good to know if anyone's following me from here. Zlatko must have told Koch all about us by now. It would be a feather in his cap to pick me up, and he's sure to have a blood feud going with Remke."

"Still at noon?" O'Flaherty asked in a low voice.

"Yes. But I'd like to get there early and scout around. Koch could be following Remke as well as me."

"Smart. Let's hope Colonel Remke is as wary and takes precautions himself. You can wait in the Trinità dei Monti church at the top of the steps, which will give you a good view all around. I'll fetch you at seven o'clock for breakfast."

"In disguise, of course," Nini said.

"To be sure. Only, which one shall it be? I don't make a very handsome nun, but it's been done."

"You're kidding, right?" I asked.

"I don't make a habit of it," O'Flaherty said with a wink, finishing off his wine in one gulp.

CHAPTER THIRTY-NINE

KAZ HAD A gun and a girl. I had neither.

Instead I was alone in a darkened room, wishing for sleep, hoping that tomorrow I'd be here to say the same. I'd left Kaz and Nini with Severino, who still hadn't moved as much as a finger. I'd waited until I heard them drag a bureau against door, then prowled around inside the building, watching for intruders and drawing irritated glances from the nuns who were still up and about. From there, I went outside, turning up my collar against the cold night air. I crossed to the Sacristy and kept to the shadows, eyeing the entrance to Santa Marta. Nobody else was out; no killer was casing the joint.

I gave up on the stakeout and went back to the German College. The bells tolled midnight as I lay alone, thinking of what might happen tomorrow on the Spanish Steps. Or not happen. What if I came back empty-handed? What if, what if, what if? I heard the bells again, once, then twice.

A sharp rap at the door jolted me awake. It was daylight, and Hugh O'Flaherty greeted me in an unlikely getup. If he hadn't spoken, I might not have known it was him.

"Get dressed, Billy," he said, barely keeping down a grin. "I've letters to deliver." He was dressed in a postman's blue uniform and cap, complete with a leather bag bulging with mail. A thick mustache completed the disguise. He tossed me a hat, a gray snap-brim fedora. It was a good fit, and helped shadow my face.

I followed him to the refectory. His bag seemed to curve his body into a slouch, hiding a few inches of his height. We were served coffee and bread fresh from the oven by nuns unsurprised by the outfit.

"One advantage to rising early," O'Flaherty said, stuffing a piece of warm bread into his mouth. "I've been to Mass as well. It feels good to get a head start on the day, don't you think?"

"It's better than the day getting a head start on me," I agreed, as we left for the Santa Marta. "You must have raised a few eyebrows at Mass in that outfit."

"No one begrudges a letter carrier his worship," he said. "And folks here have grown used to seeing me in all manner of garb, as you could tell. Monsignor Bruzzone himself joked with me about the nun's outfit just this morning. That was no tall tale, Billy, but I'll tell you all about it tonight when I trust we'll be having a celebration."

"A celebration. Yes," I said, trying not to think about it, since that meant thinking about the alternative. When I first heard that Diana had been taken, hundreds of miles and an enemy army had separated us. I never imagined I'd get this close to her, and be able to free her. I couldn't bear the thought of failure now. What would Diana think of me, I thought, if I left her in chains to be brought to Nazi Germany? What would I think of myself, I wondered, as we made our way to Nini's room. We announced ourselves, and Kaz pulled the furniture away for us to enter.

"A regular fortress you have here," O'Flaherty said. "Any change in your guest?"

"I was able to give him some sips of broth earlier," Nini said. "Sister Cecilia went to the kitchen and said I wasn't feeling well, and brought the food up. No one suspects Severino is here, I am sure."

"That's right," Kaz said. "It was quiet all night."

"Good, good," O'Flaherty said. "Well, collect your armament, Billy, and let's be off. I've sent up my prayer to Saint Gabriel this morning, so I've done all I can."

"Why Saint Gabriel?"

"He's the patron saint of letter carriers, he is! Come on, have a cheer, my boy. Things will go well, you'll see. But if things go awry, I'll be nearby. The offices of Propaganda Fide are in the Piazza di Spagna, which is the square at the bottom of the steps. It's Vatican territory, so if you need refuge, go there. Follow me when I get off the trolley and I'll point it out."

"Thanks for your help, Monsignor. And your prayers," I said.

"We Irish have to stick together, don't we? Now let's be off. The sooner the better."

"I wish I were going with you," Kaz said, handing me the Beretta.

"Me too," I said, pocketing the weapon. "Hold tight, okay?"

"We will be waiting," Kaz said. "For all of you."

We left through the Porta Angelica, near the barracks of the Swiss Guard, avoiding most of the German guards. O'Flaherty went first, bent over his bag, sorting his mail. I trailed him by a few steps, hands stuffed into my pockets, shoulders bunched against the cold, trying to look like another Italian out on business or coming from Mass. The key was not to look around, not to betray any of the nervousness I felt with one glance too many at the bored Wehrmacht guards or the plainclothes secret police hovering a few yards behind them.

O'Flaherty was a good actor. He was a convincing mailman, with a delivery around every corner. After twisting through a few side streets and confirming we weren't being followed, we entered a main thoroughfare, the Via Cola di Rienzo. Traffic was light, mostly military. A trolley car rumbled down the road, and I joined a line at the stop, O'Flaherty right behind me. A hand on my shoulder, a wink to the conductor, and we were aboard.

We changed trolleys twice. From what I knew of Rome from the map I had studied, we were taking the long way around, across the Tiber and then up to the Quirinal Palace, where Mussolini and the king of Italy used to run things. Now *Il Duce* was up north, under the German thumb, and the king was down south, under Allied thumbs. Both were relics of history, pitiful jokes that history played on this poor, beautiful nation.

The trolley barreled downhill on the Via Sistina, picking up speed. The bell rang for a stop and O'Flaherty motioned for me to follow. On the street, a few shops were open, but only halfheartedly. No customers, not much food to sell. There was a line outside a bakery, and one jewelry store had so many watches in the window, I figured hungry shoppers must have sold them for bread. I kept O'Flaherty in view, which, considering the length of his stride, took some doing. As the street opened into a small piazza, he stopped at the base of an obelisk in the center of the square, adjusting the strap on his mailbag. I stopped and craned my neck, admiring the Virgin Mary standing at the top of the column.

"The building to your right," he said in a low voice. "See the yellow-and-white flag? That's Propaganda Fide. Where we plan our missionary work, although there is precious little of that these days."

"Got it," I whispered.

"Follow the piazza in the other direction. You'll be at the base of the Spanish Steps. The church is at the top, to your right. *Go gcuire Dia an t-ádh ort.*"

"I'll wish you the same, Monsignor, but I'd say God's already put his luck on you."

He left me looking up to the Virgin Mary, trying to remember a prayer or two. I got my bearings: Propaganda Fide faced the square at the south end, guarded by Mary on her column. Three stories tall, beige stucco. I knew where I was.

Many of the windows along the way were shuttered tight. This winter of German occupation didn't make for much of a tourist trade. I strolled along the piazza, which widened as I approached a fountain. The Spanish Steps ascended to my right, but I tried not to gawk. I had more than two hours before the meet, and I was here to watch for signs of a setup, not to sightsee.

A gaggle of German soldiers, apparently on leave, given their soft cloth caps and cameras hung around their necks, chatted and smoked cigarettes, tossing their butts into the empty fountain. From the northern end of the square I heard the distant sound of marching boots. The few civilians in the piazza all began to walk in a different direction, and I took the hint. I cut down the Via della Croce, and made a long loop around to arrive back at the square, in time to see the tail end of a formation of ten German soldiers leaving the piazza. I guessed that sergeants were alike in every army, and some Kraut felt the need for useless early-morning exercise.

I was heading in the direction of the Spanish Steps, so I ascended them, stopping midway as if I needed to catch my breath. It wasn't hard to pretend. There were a helluva lot of steps. Below me I saw a mailman, but it wasn't O'Flaherty. Above, a couple of workmen in blue coveralls were cleaning the steps, dragging their trashcans and emptying their sweepings into them as they went.

I took a few more slow steps and turned. It was hard not to admire the view. Saint Peter's rose above the rooftops, the crosses and spires of lesser churches dotting the landscape. The morning clouds were breaking up, and shafts of sunlight fell on the city, reflecting off windows and giving the buildings a soft, golden glow. The wind was strong, so I turned my collar up and pulled down the fedora, glad to have a good reason to hide my features. It's hard to spot a guy if you only have a photograph or have only seen him once, doubly hard if you can't see his whole face.

I passed the church without a second glance, trying to look like a Roman late for a morning appointment. Next to the church was the Hotel Hassler, and the German-sounding name drew me on. What better place for Remke to stash his men, and perhaps prisoners, than in a nearby hotel. Of course the same thing went for the Gestapo. The place could be crawling with them.

I pushed open the polished brass door and felt the welcome warmth of the lobby. Marble floors and columns extended the length of the building. On either side, plush red velvet armchairs and couches were situated for those who wanted to see and be seen. I chose a chair in the corner, which gave me a view of the street and the lobby. I picked up a newspaper and leafed through it. The Italian was bewildering, but the pictures of Mussolini and Hitler were plentiful. I pretended to read, sweeping my gaze across the lobby and out the window, looking for anything out of the ordinary.

A line of monks shuffled down the street, probably heading for the church. A German Wehrmacht general made for the elevator with a beautiful dark-haired woman on his arm. Two aides grabbed chairs on the other side of the lobby and lit cigarettes. It didn't take a detective to figure that one out. Street sweepers worked their way past my window, their brooms pushing litter from the gutters. They looked straight down, not side to side, which meant they were intent on their work. That alone made me suspicious. Sweeping the streets sounded like boring work. Why were these guys so focused? Overacting?

I was about to get up and check out the sweepers more closely when two heavyset thugs in trademark Gestapo black leather trench coats walked in from the street. I brought my newspaper back up to read, not wanting them to think I was leaving because of them. They heaved themselves into two nearby chairs, their Nazi Party badges prominently displayed on their lapels. They didn't speak, but stared disdainfully at anyone who met their gaze. I studied pictures of Italian troops fighting with the Germans at Anzio, and words such as *vittoria* gave the impression that the brave Fascists where about to drive the Allies into the sea. Victory at last.

Maybe they were. I'd been out of touch for a while, and the situation in the Anzio beachhead had never been good. It was only thirty or so miles away, and as I snuck a look at the Gestapo men and the other officers idling in the lobby, I wondered if they ever heard the guns when the wind carried toward Rome, and feared for what was in store for them. They were the lords of Rome, but there had been plenty of those over the centuries. The thought gave me courage, so I put the newspaper aside and rose, adjusting my fedora at a jaunty angle, and made for the door.

One of the Gestapo men rose and pointed a finger at me. "*Darf ich Ihre Zeitung lesen?*"

I stopped, feeling a cold sweat at the small of my back. I didn't understand him and had no clue what to do. I struggled not to say a word, since anything I said would betray me.

"*Giornale,*" the other one said, pointing at my newspaper.

"*Sì*," I said, happy that I could get away with a one-word response. I smiled and nodded my head. "*Sì*," I said again, figuring one more time couldn't hurt. I got a polite "*Danke*" in return.

As I departed, I could sense them following me with their eyes. I put my head down and walked away from the church, in case they were onto me. I took a left to get off the street and found myself not far from the Excelsior Hotel. German headquarters was not a good destination, so I reversed course and watched the road from a corner. No Gestapo. That was either a good sign, or they'd cordoned off the area.

I took my time, gazing in shop windows and watching for the reflection of a tail. There was nothing out of the ordinary beyond what passed for city hustle-bustle in wartime Rome. Lots of uniforms and skinny civilians pretending life was perfect. I followed suit and made my way down to the piazza, ready for another run at the Spanish Steps.

The day had warmed, so I unbuttoned my coat and pushed back my hat. I took the steps more quickly this time, passing the same sweepers I'd seen before, even though the steps didn't seem to need another cleaning. No one paid me much mind, as far as I could tell. In front of the church, the two sweepers I'd seen from the hotel were returning in the opposite direction, working their brooms and dustpans like there was no tomorrow. Poor choice of words, I thought grimly.

I climbed the steps to the church entrance. That bit of extra height gave me an extraordinary view of the city. Maybe when we took Rome, I thought, Diana and I could come here and enjoy the sights. Have a drink at the Hassler. Be the lords and ladies of Rome.

Inside, the church was long and narrow, with small chapels along either side. Sunlight filtered in through the high stained-glass windows, and the footsteps of worshippers and curious soldiers echoed off the marble floor. Germans took photographs. Old women, hunched over in black dresses, knelt and prayed. Half a dozen monks, probably the same group I'd seen earlier, sat in the front pew, their heads bowed. No Remke, no Gestapo, as far as I could see.

I left and made another circuit, walking down the Via Condotti, looking at the sites, then going back up, giving me a direct view of the steps. I could make out the same blue coveralls among the field-gray and dark overcoats. I hadn't seen much of the city, but I don't think I'd seen that many municipal workers that hard at work in my life. Not much like Boston.

If it were a setup, they would have made me already. So why hadn't I been taken? Because they wanted Remke? Maybe they had no idea about me, but knew Remke would be here, out in the open. Maybe. Maybe I was nervous in the service.

The hell with it, I told myself. I crossed the piazza, stopping to browse the wares of a few sidewalk vendors who had set up tables at the foot of the steps. Secondhand clothes, books, china knick-knacks. A few paintings. No food in sight. These were probably families who were selling off their possessions, hoping to trade for bread. But the Germans were the only ones who had money and food, and what did they care for an Italian's castoffs? They could snatch whatever they wanted.

I retook the steps, ignoring the sweepers, not caring why they were wearing down the steps with their brooms. I checked my inside pocket, the feel of the folded papers reassuring. At least I had a chance. Probably more than the poor souls in the piazza selling off Grandma's crockery had. Entering the church, I let my vision get used to the dim light and walked the perimeter, admiring the artwork in each chapel and eyeing the other gawkers and worshippers.

The monks were gone; no, two of them were standing near the confessional. Maybe one of their pals was inside confessing his sins. How much trouble could a monk get into, anyway? A couple of nuns walked past, their rosaries clicking as they moved. I took a seat in a rear pew, drawing my coat around me. It was cold in the church, and I shuddered. I had about a half hour to go. I checked the letters for the hundredth time. I checked the Beretta, feeling the grip, remembering the Fascist I'd killed in the rail yard. I glanced at the confessional, and decided against it.

The harsh click of boot heels sounded to my rear. The footsteps were determined, not the casual stroll of a sightseer. I stood, ready for the worst.

"Billy," came a whisper at my back. "You forgot my uniform. Not to mention the handmade Italian leather boots. Now follow me."

I stood, waiting for Dieter to get a few steps ahead, marveling at how cool and collected he seemed. Which was probably the point of being cool and collected. The church remained quiet, a few nuns still at prayer, the monks at the confessional. One of the camera-toting soldiers strode ahead of Dieter and opened a door adjacent to the main entrance. He held it for both of us, and I wondered how many of the sightseers were actually Remke's men.

The light outside was blinding after the dim interior, and I blinked my eyes to adjust. We were on a staircase leading to the side door of the church, with a high balustrade that gave some cover. Remke stood with his back to me, surveying the piazza below.

"What do you have for me?" His tone was sharp, demanding.

"The letter from Montini," I said, reaching into my coat. Dieter flinched, his hand going to his holster. Force of habit, I figured. I withdrew the envelope slowly, letting him see it. I thought he might give a smile and an apology, but his hand stayed where it was. Only his eyes moved. Remke snatched the envelope and opened it. He read, the breeze fluttering the edge of the pages. It seemed to take forever. I scanned the crowds, wondering where Diana might be.

"I didn't like the looks of the street sweepers," I said. "Too many of them."

"They are ours," Dieter said. "We've been watching you."

"What about the two Gestapo men in the hotel lobby?"

"They are watching a general who is having an affair with the wife of a Turkish diplomat. Decidedly un-Aryan of him."

"This," Remke said, his voice grim and his hand shaking. "This is all you have?"

"It's diplomatic language," I said, trying to calm him. "You have to read between the lines."

"Idiots!" Remke shouted. "What do they expect to come of this watered-down drivel? I give you a valuable document about the crimes of the Nazi regime and your friends at the Vatican cannot even acknowledge that we are risking all to topple them? This is dishwater. Nothing. I could have given that report to a newspaper in Switzerland and gotten more out of it."

"It was the best Montini could do. Koch's raids on Vatican properties in Rome have gotten the Pope nervous about an invasion of the Holy See, so he didn't want to risk bringing it to his attention. He thought half a statement was better than none."

"Did he now?" Remke stuffed the papers into his pocket. "Well, you shall have the same choice. You delivered half of what I wanted, so you decide on which half of your payment you will take. Miss Seaton, or the Italian and the American? One woman or two men? Read between the lines of that bargain and see how you like it."

Remke went down the steps, leaving me rooted to the spot. It never occurred to me he'd split the difference, but it made a perverse sense. It was no more than what we'd done. Diana, I told myself. Take Diana. But I couldn't get the words out. Rino and Abe were my responsibility; I couldn't leave them behind. And knowing Diana, she'd not want their fate on her conscience. It had taken her long enough to get over the guilt of surviving Dunkirk. I didn't need to bring up that burden all over again.

So it was on my head. I had to leave her behind or on a train to Germany, wherever Remke had in mind to keep her under wraps. I had to count on him not to turn her over to the Gestapo. I didn't think he would, but I wasn't taking any chances. I had nothing but a bluff.

"Give them all to me," I said, following Remke to the sidewalk. "Or I burn your documents. They'll never get to London."

"Then I give you nothing but a bullet," he said. "You are an American officer out of uniform. I could shoot you now as a spy and be done with it. Make your choice."

"How do you know I won't get word to the Gestapo about your plans?" It was weak, I knew, but I needed time to think of something else. Anything that might give me an edge. Remke only laughed.

"If you were English, I would worry about it. But you Americans are too naïve to play that game. You have thirty seconds to decide," he said. "Then we leave."

The wind picked up, swirling paper and dust in spite of the phony street sweepers' hard work. I shielded my eyes and took a look around. He must have had them all close by. My hand closed around the Beretta in my pocket as I wondered what my chances were against Remke with Dieter at my back.

There was none. "The two men," I said, my words condemning Diana. I couldn't look Remke in the eye. As I spoke, two monks approached from behind him and the door above us flew open. The monks hurried forward, the rush of air blowing back the first monk's cowl.

Becher. I recognized him from the Pensione Jaccarino. Koch's pal.

I pulled my pistol and pushed Remke aside with my left arm. I shot Becher twice, dead center. I waited for a bullet in the back, either from Dieter, if he hadn't picked up on what was happening, or from Koch's men bursting through the door. The other monk hesitated as Becher hit the ground, then backed up, raising his pistol to fire. I knelt and shot twice again, sending him to the pavement.

Above me more shots echoed against the stone church. Remke stood with his arm outstretched, squeezing off shots from his Walther. Two monks rolled down the stairs, their pistols clattering uselessly against the stone steps. Dieter struggled to his feet, his arm drenched in blood, likely from one of Remke's stray rounds.

Pairs of street sweepers in their blue coveralls ran to the scene, brooms exchanged for MP-40 submachine guns they must have had hidden in their trashcans. Civilians ran in every direction and off-duty soldiers dove for the nearest cover. We were knee-deep in dead monks.

"Look," I said, pointing to a figure in a black trench coat, peering around the side of a statue fifty yards away. There was no mistaking the dark, slicked-back hair and the close-set dark eyes. Pietro Koch, who probably thought he had a ringside seat for the capture of the German who had kidnapped one of his victims. Or me, an American agent.

"Koch," Remke said, pointing him out to his men. But he was already gone, vanishing into the panicked crowd. "*Sind Sie schlecht verletzt?*" he said, turning his attention to Dieter, who held a hand over his right arm, blood dripping between his fingers.

"*Nicht schlecht,*" Dieter said. I think he was saying he was all right, but his face was white and he was losing blood. "I saw Becher, but his men knocked me over when they burst out of the church."

"It seems I owe you my freedom, if not my life," Remke said to me, supporting Dieter. "But know this; someone betrayed you and it was not my people. Only three of us knew of the change to this location. Someone *you* told must have informed Koch."

"Bishop Zlatko?" Dieter suggested.

"No, he hasn't been seen at the Vatican," I said. "Are you certain it couldn't have been someone at your end?"

Sirens began to echo in the distance, and the more curious of the onlookers were gathering to stare at the blood-drenched corpses in monks' robes.

"I stake my life on it," Remke said. "And now we must leave before too many questions are asked."

"What about—?"

"Yes, yes," he said. "Your actions have relieved me of the need to detain anyone. Consider all debts paid."

He snapped his fingers, and two sedans left the curb and stopped in front of us. The driver's door opened and Bernard stepped out, pistol at the ready. Remke gave a curt nod, and he held the door for me. Diana sat up front, Abe and Rino in the back, their eyes wide, confusion etched in their faces.

"Back to being enemies, then?" I said, my hand on the door. I should have hated Remke. If things hadn't worked out, he would have left Diana to rot in prison, I was certain of it. But in that moment I hated *myself* more, because I understood. Remke did exactly what had needed to be done. He was gambling with the lives of thousands, and one life more or less wasn't going to stop him. I should have hated him, but all I felt was awe at his focused intent, and pity for what it must have done to his soul.

"Yes. Until we set things right in Berlin," Remke said.

"Now I must insist on the return of my uniform," Dieter said, trying for nonchalance but coming up short as he wavered unsteadily, blood seeping through his fingers.

"And the handmade boots," I said. "If you can get to the Vatican tomorrow, head for the Arch of the Bells at noon."

"Until then," Dieter said, as Bernard helped him into the other vehicle. I extended my hand to Remke. He hesitated, then shook it.

"Good luck," I said, then jumped into the car and floored it, putting as much distance between us and the damned Spanish Steps as I could.

CHAPTER FORTY

"WHAT'S HAPPENING?" DIANA demanded, her hand pulling my sleeve. "What was the shooting about?"

"We were betrayed. Those were Koch's men disguised as monks. They had set a trap," I said, heading away from the church. "Rino, where's the nearest bridge?"

"Take this right, the Via del Corso," he said. We passed ambulances heading in the other direction, and a squad of Germans double-timing it on foot. In the rearview mirror I saw the Germans stop traffic and seal off the road. Diana noticed it too.

"They'll set up identity checks at the bridges," she said. "It will be a while before they realize it wasn't a partisan attack."

"So step on it," Abe said from the backseat. "I ain't plannin' on a stretch in a POW camp. Or worse. We're in civvies, for Chrissakes."

I looked at Diana. She nodded, and gripped the seat with both hands. "Okay," I said. I leaned on the horn and watched pedestrians and a few bicyclists scatter. I dug into my pocket and gave Diana the Beretta. "Three or four rounds, that's it."

"This left!" Rino shouted, and I took it hard, tires squealing. Diana rolled down her window and held on, the Beretta at the ready. A block ahead of us, the Ponte Cavour spanned the Tiber River. A lone German military policeman stood at the intersection, a red-and-white sign in his hand. Halt. Behind him, on the bridge, we could see other Germans moving a barbed-wire barricade on a wood frame into place.

They were *Kettenhunde*, or "chain dogs," as the common German soldier called them, for the metal gorgets they wore around their necks. They were cops, of a sort, but hardly brothers in blue.

"Go!" Diana said, and leaned out the window, firing a shot at the German. I swear she hit the sign, which spun out of his hand as he dove out of the way of the speeding car. Soldiers were stopping traffic on the road that ran along the Tiber, allowing us to pass right through the intersection. Nice of them.

The road dipped as it met the bridge, and the car shuddered with the impact as it lurched forward at high speed. It swerved, and I fought to keep control as we sped toward the line of Germans. If we crashed we were dead, one way or the other. One officer drew his pistol and held up his hand. Diana fired two, three more times, and the soldiers dropped the barricade and threw themselves on the pavement, rolling to the side of the bridge. We flew through the opening, sending shattered wood flying as the car struck the ends of the frames. Barbed wire stuck to the front bumper and headlights, and one of the barricades trailed us, still hanging by a strand, spinning out of control, cartwheeling on the roadway and insuring no one tried to be a hero.

All that was left was one officer, standing at the far end of the bridge. No barricade, no backup, just one Kraut in his peaked cap, wearing the chain dog gorget. And holding a submachine gun.

"Get down!" I screamed, and pressed the accelerator hard, hoping that a few thousand pounds of metal at high speed might give him something to think about.

It didn't. He raised the MP-40 and fired a burst at the windshield. It hit high, probably from the recoil, shredding the roof. I was closer now. Rino was swearing or praying, I couldn't tell. Bullets stitched the hood, leaving jagged holes that spewed steam from the radiator. The German didn't move; he kept firing, the spent shell casings arcing brightly in the sunlight. The last few yards seemed to take forever, as if I could count the casings as they flew from his weapon and bounced on the pavement. Abe cursed, Diana screamed, and I prayed the bumper could take it.

A heavy thud. His body slammed against the windshield, cracking the already pockmarked glass. His face, the dullness of death already upon it, was pressed against the glass for a second before his body slid off the hood, his arm trailing in a dead-handed farewell. Dumb bastard. He'd be alive if he had simply stepped aside and let us go.

Smoke poured from under the hood as the windshield finally gave in and fell like ice off the eaves right into our laps. I glanced at Diana, who looked wild-eyed but unhurt, her mouth still open in the scream I had heard before impact. There was a helluva racket behind us, part of the barbed-wire barricade still along for the ride. I took a quick turn, and the wire finally snapped, leaving the barricade blocking the street behind us.

"You ain't a half-bad getaway man," Abe said, twisting around in his seat to check our six. "Now let's ditch the car before she lights up."

"Good idea," I said. We *were* a bit conspicuous. I pulled into a piazza behind the Palace of Justice, which seemed like the perfect spot to leave a shot-up sedan. Diana tossed the empty Beretta on the seat and we walked in the direction of the Castel Sant'Angelo, trying to look casual as we turned a corner, putting the smoldering car behind us. My heart was pounding and sweat dripped down my temples as a muted *whump* signaled the combination of leaking gasoline and creeping flames.

"Follow me," Rino said. "I know the back ways." He and Abe went ahead a few paces and disappeared into a palazzo. We followed through the large oak doors, pulling them shut behind us. Rino led us through the building and onto the next street. We'd walk a block, then duck into another building, wait until the coast was clear, and repeat the process.

"We are close," Rino said as we huddled in a passageway. "This is the Via di Porta Angelica. See, the Gate of Sant'Anna, there." He pointed down the street. "I am friends with many of the Swiss Guard, we will have no difficulty."

"All we need is a distraction to get past the German sentries,"

Diana said. German paratroopers, in their distinctive helmets and smocks, strolled along the white line, rifles slung idly over their shoulders.

"It looks quiet," Abe said. "Maybe they ain't sounded the alarm on this side of the river yet."

We pulled back, out of sight of the street.

"Rino, do you have your identity papers?"

"*No, sono spiacente*, they took everything. I know some of the Germans by sight; they are used to seeing me and may let me pass. But that would do you no good, my friends."

We withdrew into the shadows, waiting for an edge to get us the last fifty yards to the safety of neutral ground.

"Billy," Diana whispered as we leaned against the wall. "You did it. You got us out." She clasped her hands over mine and drew them close. I leaned into her and we kissed. It was hungry, a kiss born of life and death and the precious seconds in between. We could have been in front of a firing squad or in bed alone; it wouldn't have made one bit of difference. Our cheeks brushed and I felt warm tears as we leaned against a cold stone wall. I should have told her right then, but I couldn't find the words to speak the truth. How could I tell her I'd been about to leave her behind? She buried her face against my shoulder, and we held onto each other, not quite believing we were together, afraid we might not make the last few yards.

"Was it hard to get Montini to write the letter?" she finally said.

I was happy to talk about that instead of my near abandonment. "Yes. It wasn't everything Remke wanted, but I guess it was enough. Montini mentioned the Auschwitz Protocol specifically, but the reference to the coup was vague."

"Well, you must have convinced Remke. He'd been apologetic to us, but said he intended to keep his word if you didn't come through. He was going to take me to an Abwehr prison in Germany. I've had enough of jails. Enough for a lifetime, thank you very much."

"Well, we're not home free yet. If Koch figures we're headed this way and moves fast, he could seal off the Vatican."

Several vehicles passed by and we pressed ourselves more tightly against the wall. Rino stuck his nose around the corner and came back shaking his head. "Perhaps we should try walking into Saint Peter's Square," he said. "They may not be checking papers."

"If they aren't now, they could start any minute," I said. "We don't know if Koch was after Remke or me. Or you."

"What's so special about you anyways?" Abe asked.

"I'm the guy who's going to finger the killer, and I think he knows it," I said. "Other than that, I'm just your average Joe."

"So this bastard drops a nickel on you? Gets Koch to do his dirty work?"

"Either that, or Koch had it in for Remke. Probably Koch was happy to pitch a doubleheader. Regardless, we're stuck here until we can figure out how to get by those sentries."

"Doubleheader?" Rino asked.

"Baseball, pal," Abe said. "Remember I was telling you about the Brooklyn Dodgers?"

"Dem Bums," Rino said, delivering the Brooklyn accent perfectly.

"Go Roma," Abe said in return. "Italian football. Roma won the *scudetto* back in '42. We didn't have much else to talk about the last coupla days."

We settled into the shadows, listening to the sounds of the street, wondering about our chances. Maybe we could simply walk in. Maybe we'd be nabbed and end up guests at Pensione Jaccarino.

"Listen," Abe said.

"What?" Diana said, tilting her head to catch the sound.

Abe closed his eyes and lifted one finger, signaling us to wait. "B-24s," he said. "Not as pretty a sound as B-17s, but they're coming."

I caught the heavy drone a second later. A noise like no other, four-engine bombers headed in our direction. Once you've heard it, you don't soon forget it.

"Come on," I said, edging closer to the street. "How soon will they be overhead, Abe?"

"Any minute," he said. "They're a little to the south." He edged around the corner and checked the street and the sky. "The Krauts are all looking up."

We walked out into the street. Everyone was looking up, Germans, Swiss Guard, nuns, priests, passersby. The droning grew louder as we watched the planes passing far above the city rooftops—scores, maybe hundreds of them—flying across Rome, heading toward some target to the west. A few puffs of antiaircraft fire added to the show, but the bombers flew on unscathed. Abe nodded and we stepped out into the street, our heads craned skyward like everyone else, hands shielding eyes from the sun. We walked slowly, moving through the crowd like ghosts, unseen. Every soul around us was united in curiosity and relief that such a devastating force was going elsewhere, passing over with their bomb bay doors closed, the gods of war having decreed one more day of life and sunshine.

Such was the joy that no one noticed us as we stepped over the line, into the safety of the Holy See.

CHAPTER FORTY-ONE

"COME, QUICKLY, YOU must not be seen," O'Flaherty said, beckoning us with an impatient wave of the hand, as if we were dawdling schoolchildren. Rino had asked one of the Swiss Guard to telephone the monsignor, who'd left a message for us to stay put. He arrived in two minutes, out of breath and with a worried look on his face. We were well within the Vatican walls, so I didn't understand whom we were hiding from. "Here, inside."

He held open the door of the Church of San Pellegrino and ushered us into a small chapel not far from the Swiss Guard barracks. Set between two larger buildings, it looked like an afterthought of the Vatican bureaucracy.

"You are all in one piece," he said. "Thank the Lord. We heard reports of gunfire; you're none of you hurt, are you?"

"No, Monsignor," Diana said, laying her hand on his arm. "It was close, but we got away. Koch was waiting for us. Or for Colonel Remke."

"The only good thing about Koch is that he provides proof of the very devil in our midst. And you, my dear, I'd almost not recognize you. Quite a change, quite a change," O'Flaherty said, letting a smile creep over the concern on his face. I hadn't had the time to notice, but Diana *was* nicely turned out. She wore a dark-blue dress and a fitted jacket under a stylish tan raincoat. She looked like she'd been shopping, not kept under house arrest.

"What's the problem, Monsignor?" I asked, saving my questions about Roman fashions for later. "We're safe now, aren't we?"

"For the moment, yes. I take it you have not heard?"

"Heard what?"

"The Americans have bombed Monte Cassino. This morning, over two hundred bombers attacked the abbey. It is completely destroyed and many civilian refugees have been killed. Trouble is brewing over this, and the Germans are making the most of it."

"What's special about this abbey?" Abe asked. "We've bombed whole cities, so what makes this one joint so important?"

"The Abbey of Monte Cassino sits on the highest ground above the town of Cassino and overlooks the Liri and Rapidio valleys," O'Flaherty said. "The hill is part of the German defensive line. They hadn't occupied the abbey, but having control of the area around it gave them an extraordinary position for observation. Allied soldiers have been hit hard trying to take it."

"You know for sure the Krauts weren't inside?" Abe asked.

"Yes, we have had regular reports from the abbot, and the Holy See received official assurances from Field Marshal Albert Kesselring that no German troops would set foot inside. The occupants were monks, refugees, and priceless works of art. It was founded in the year 524 by the Benedictines, and took centuries to complete. Today it was destroyed by American bombs in one morning. Some cardinals want His Holiness to protest directly, but he has not yet made up his mind."

"Surely we're not in any danger?" Diana said.

"Many in the College of Cardinals are very angry over the bombing. Some because they still harbor fascist sympathies; others are genuinely appalled at the senseless destruction. There has been talk of expelling all Allied escapees within the Vatican. Not to mention you and the baron, along with Miss Seaton. Depending on what action His Holiness takes, you may indeed be in danger of expulsion."

"What about his order to expell refugees in the other Vatican properties?" I asked.

"Monsignor Montini has managed to derail that idea,"

O'Flaherty said. "But there is so much anger against the Allies now that he may not be able to do the same if the cardinals demand action. To make matters worse, the Allies have also announced they may bomb Castel Gandolfo, the Pope's summer palace in the mountains above Anzio, claiming it is occupied by German troops, which is ridiculous! There are over fifteen thousand refugees there. Can you imagine the carnage if they bomb it? I must say, your generals wield their bombers with an indiscriminate hand. Now I've got myself worked up telling you this, but understand, you may need to leave soon, and quickly at that."

"We need to get Abe to a safe place," I said. "Bomber crew may not be the most popular guys around here. Best for him to lie low."

"Rino," said O'Flaherty, "will you take Abraham to my room? And perhaps you should stay as well, in case you were recognized by Koch. It might not be safe for you on the streets of Rome."

"Yes, a good precaution," Rino agreed. "We shall go through the gardens, less chance of us being seen."

O'Flaherty checked the street, and motioned for them to leave. We decided to go out separately, in case anyone was looking for a group of four.

"You are safe with most of the Swiss Guard," O'Flaherty said. "After helping me smuggle escapees in, they will have little heart for tossing them out. There may be a few with pro-German leanings, but not many."

"What about the Vatican police?" Diana asked.

"With Soletto gone, someone may take over the role of chief informant for the Fascists. You are safe with Cipriano, I am sure of that. But I wouldn't announce myself at headquarters. Any over-zealous gendarme could arrest you for violating Vatican neutrality at the drop of a hat."

"How is Rossi? Any improvement?"

"Bad news, I'm afraid. He died a few hours ago."

"Damn! Who knows about it?"

"No one but myself, the baron, Nini, and Sister Cecilia. You wanted his presence kept quiet, so I decided that meant in both life and death. Sister Cecilia and I moved his body to the mortuary. He is listed as unidentified, and no one's the wiser."

"You're sure no one got to him?"

"Positive, lad. The room was fortified and the story put out that Nini had come down with influenza. Everyone steered clear. Only Sister Cecilia went in and out."

"Who exactly is Rossi?" Diana asked.

"Severino Rossi was the one man who could have identified the murderer of Monsignor Corrigan. And he still might," I said.

"This is the Holy See," O'Flaherty said. "But do not expect we can raise the dead, me boy."

"What I had in mind was that celebration you mentioned, remember? Think we could throw a little party tonight, to toast the return of Diana and the others?"

"Of course. But why, and who is invited?"

"About a dozen people. Here's what we'll need—"

"*Ciao?*" a voice asked from the open door, spilling light into the darkened room. "Hello?"

"Who's there?" I asked, blinded momentarily by the brightness.

"It is Monsignor Bruzzone, Billy. You are safely returned?"

"Yes," I said. "We had a bit of trouble, but we're fine. I don't know if you've met Diana Seaton? Formerly Sister Justina."

"No, I have met neither. Pleased to meet you, Miss Seaton," Bruzzone said, extending his hand.

"*È un piacere di conoscerla,*" she said.

"Did Monsignor O'Flaherty call you here?" I asked, wondering at Bruzzone's sudden presence.

"No, no, I am here purely by accident. I am preparing for midafternoon prayers. This is the chapel of the Vatican Gendarmerie Corps. As I mentioned, I sometimes fill in for their chaplain, as I must do today. There is a shift change at the Hour of None, and many come to the service."

"Well, we must be going," I said, not wishing to fight through a crowd of cops to get out.

"You will not stay for the prayers?" Bruzzone said, looking at O'Flaherty as well as Diana and me.

"No, unfortunately we have a sick friend to visit," I said. "But I hope you'll join us tonight, to celebrate our safe return."

"Certainly," Bruzzone said, then went to prepare for the service.

We left, stepping into the street, the cold outside not as biting as in the old church. The sun was already low in the sky, with dark-gray clouds creeping in.

"What is the Hour of None anyway?" I asked as we made our way through the Vatican Museum. I wondered about the coincidence of Bruzzone showing up.

"The ninth hour after dawn, observed at three o'clock," O'Flaherty said. "Part of the Divine Hours, the schedule of daily prayer. I would wager you didn't pay much attention in confirmation class, Billy."

"I must have missed that one," I said.

"The death of Christ is commemorated at None," Diana said. "And legend says that was also the hour of the day when Adam and Eve were driven from the Garden of Eden."

"Ah, a lass who knows religious lore. 'Tis a pleasure to converse with you, Diana," O'Flaherty said as we descended a marble staircase, colorful frescoes on either side. "Are you aware that nine is considered an incomplete and unlucky number?"

"Yes, as opposed to the perfection of ten," she said. "Isn't the novena for the dead derived from the nine days of mourning?"

"From the ninth day, to be exact, my dear," O'Flaherty said. "The funerary day."

They chatted back and forth like that, but I didn't pay much attention. I'd lost count of how many days we'd been here, but for sure I wanted to leave before that ninth day came around.

CHAPTER FORTY-TWO

"SO WHAT'S WITH the new threads?" I asked.

"Do you like my new look?" Diana asked as we climbed the steps to Nini's apartment.

"I thought you were locked up, waiting for me to rescue you," I said, maybe with a touch of pique. It was one thing to snatch the woman you loved from her captors, but it was another thing to find her decked out in high fashion when you did.

"Colonel Remke sent out for new clothes for me. An Italian lady friend of his went out to a nearby shop. Thank goodness the Germans set up headquarters in the richest part of town. I certainly like it better than my nun's habit, unless you'd like to see me back in the clothes of chastity and prudence?"

"That didn't stop us in Switzerland, remember?" We'd had a brief encounter on that neutral ground when Diana came across the border to report to her spymaster. I put my arm around her and we stopped short of Nini's door. "I can't even put words to it, Diana. I'm so glad you're free. And we're together."

"Me too, Billy," Diana said. We kissed, long and languorously, until a door opened and we both jumped.

"Diana!" It was Kaz. They embraced amid laughter and tears.

"It has been so long, Kaz," Diana said. "How are you?"

"Aside from the war, I am wonderful," he said. "Have you met Nini?" At the mention of her name, she came out of the room and stood next to Kaz, linking her arm with his. I noticed Diana glance at the intimate touch.

"I know of Princess Pallavicini, but we haven't met. Diana Seaton," she said, extending her hand.

"Please, call me Nini. Kaz has told me so much about you. And Daphne as well. I'm glad to meet you."

For a moment there was silence, and I was afraid the mention of Daphne's name had put a damper on things. Nothing like reminding a girl of her dead sister the first time you meet. Especially when you've been sleeping with the dead sister's lover. Glancing at Diana, I saw a tear in the corner of her eye.

Suddenly the two of them embraced. I heard a brief, muffled sob, and then they headed into Nini's apartment, arms intertwined, leaving Kaz and me in the hallway.

"Kaz, do you understand women?"

"A bit more than you do, Billy, but not much," he said, as we followed them in.

Inside, Nini poured wine and we toasted. "To a safe return," she said.

"For all of us," Diana added. Hard to argue with that sentiment, but I noticed Kaz grasp Nini's hand. A safe return for him meant parting with Nini, and I could see that idea held little appeal.

"We're so sorry to have lost Severino," Nini said. "Sister Cecilia said he must have had severe internal injuries."

"Did he regain consciousness? Say anything?" I asked.

"Nothing," Kaz said. "Nini fed him broth, and he reacted to that, but no words. His head was so bruised he may have had an injury to the brain. And I know what you are going to ask next, Billy. No one got in. He died of his injuries."

"Okay then, here's the plan. We're having a gathering tonight at the German College. Monsignor O'Flaherty is setting it up now. He's providing food and wine to celebrate Rino, Abe, and Diana making it back safely. We figure with food rationed, no one will turn down an invite."

"Who is on the guest list?" Nini asked.

"Robert Brackett, the American deputy chargé d'affaires. Monsignors Montini, O'Flaherty, and Bruzzone. John May, butler to Sir D'Arcy. Inspector Cipriano. And Bishop Zlatko, if he's turned up back in the Vatican. Plus our three guests of honor."

"To what end?" Diana asked. "Although a good party is reason enough after the Regina Coeli."

"To smoke out a murderer. We may be sent packing any time, and I want to get to the bottom of things. Severino Rossi is the latest victim, even if he didn't die at the killer's hand."

"Catch me up, Billy," Diana said, taking a healthy sip of wine.

"Rossi was blamed for Corrigan's killing. He was set up by the killer and Soletto, who turned him over the Fascist police. They in turn held him until Koch came looking for more victims. It was his handiwork that killed Rossi, but he was a dead man anyway. He would have been on a train to a death camp by now if Koch hadn't taken him."

"What will happen at the party?" Kaz asked.

"That's the part of the plan O'Flaherty is working on. We're going to announce that Rossi is back, and recovering. We expect him to be able to speak by the morning."

"You think the murderer will try to kill him?" Nini asked.

"That's the great part of this plan," I said. "You can't kill a dead man."

The destruction of Monte Cassino was on everyone's lips. O'Flaherty had commandeered a small dining room at the German College for the party, and provided ample wine and food. Breads, cheese, olives, sardines, bruschetta, plates of antipasti, bowls of pasta with garlic and olive oil—it all smelled like heaven, but the topic was still hell on earth. The bombing.

"I had to stand and listen to Cardinal Maglione tell me it was a colossal blunder, a stroke of gross stupidity," Brackett was complaining. "When I told him the American government would help to rebuild it, he said that even if they built it with diamonds, it would never be the same abbey."

"He's got a point," I said as Brackett tossed back a gulp of red wine. "And we can't rebuild the lives of the civilians who were killed either."

"We'll pay compensation. But Cardinal Maglione is none too happy about your continued presence. He called it an insult for you to remain after the wanton destruction of the abbey. So take a hint, and wrap up your investigation toots sweet." Brackett moved in close. His breath smelled of garlic and alcohol. "How's it going?"

"We should have it wrapped up by morning," I said, steering him away from the others. "I was going to report to you tomorrow, but I might as well now. We got Severino Rossi back from the police. He's here."

"Rossi? The guy who Soletto arrested?"

"Yeah. Turns out he witnessed the murder of Corrigan and was set up for it. He took a few beatings while he was in custody, but he's starting to come around. He should be awake and talking by morning. We've got him stashed upstairs, in a room right across from Monsignor O'Flaherty. He's keeping an eye on him."

"Then what's he doing here?" Brackett said, pointing to the monsignor across the room.

"I'm sure somebody's watching him. But I'm not worried. No one knows he's here. Keep it under your hat, okay?"

"Sure," Brackett said, cutting a hunk of cheese for himself. The session with the cardinal hadn't affected his appetite one bit. "Let me know what happens."

"You'll be the first to know," I said.

I crossed the room to the table where the food was laid out, buffet style. Abe had brought Rosana along, and was introducing her to Nini and Diana. Rosana was quiet, her dark eyes flitting about the room, assessing each person, wary even in the midst of friends and abundant food. She was a survivor, a tough cookie who'd kept herself and her children alive, no small feat in occupied Italy. I wondered how she'd adjust to peace and comfort. How we all might struggle with letting our guard down.

Diana was sparkling. Nini had given her makeup and the loan of a string of pearls, which set off the rich fabric of her dress. They both took Rosana under their wings and soon had her smiling. Abe beamed, and gave me a wink.

Everyone had shown up, except for Zlatko. A message was left at his room and his office, but no one claimed to have seen him. Monsignor Montini and Inspector Cipriano were seated together, finishing up their plates of pasta.

"Mind if I join you?" I asked.

"Please," Montini said. "I am so glad you all came back to us safely. The letter worked, I take it?"

"I can't say. We were interrupted by Banda Koch. I don't know if they were after me or Colonel Remke, but after we fought them off, Remke took the letter and let everyone go." An honest enough answer.

"My sources in the city say you saved the colonel," Cipriano said. "Were you armed?"

"If your real question is am I armed, the answer is no. We have no weapons here."

"That is good," Montini said. "I am sure you have heard that feelings against the Allies are running high since Monte Cassino. The Allied High Command has compounded this tragedy by threatening to bomb Castel Gandolfo. The abbey was not Vatican territory, so while we mourn the loss of life and such a grand monastery, it is not considered an attack on the Holy See directly. But to bomb the Pope's residence, where thousands have taken refuge, that would strike against all notions of neutrality and safe haven."

"I understand, Monsignor. As soon as I return, I will make every effort to pass that message on."

"That is good to know. Your return may need to be sooner than you like. Cardinals are pressuring the Secretariat for some action in response to the bombing. Your expulsion may satisfy them. I am sorry if this interferes with your investigation."

"Not at all," I said. "We were successful in getting Severino Rossi released."

"Where is he?" Cipriano demanded.

"He can't be moved," I said. "And you can't turn him over to the

Rome police again. They beat him to within an inch of his life. He's here, in the German College. I give you my word he won't be going anywhere."

"Has he told you anything?" Cipriano asked.

"A little, just a few hours ago. He said he didn't do it, and that he saw a figure approach Corrigan. He couldn't speak further. Sister Cecilia says he needs a good night's rest, and tomorrow he should be well enough to tell us more."

"I should see him immediately," Cipriano said. "He is a murder suspect, after all."

"Please, let him rest. Until tomorrow morning, at least."

"I think we can honor your request," Montini said. "After all, this poor soul was already turned over to the Fascists once. We do not need to persecute him further. We will come together tomorrow and decide what is to be done."

"Very well, Monsignor," Cipriano said. He drained his wine and then looked to me. "Where?"

"Upstairs," I said. "The room directly above Monsignor O'Flaherty's. It was empty, so we set him up in there. Please, keep this confidential."

They both nodded agreement, Cipriano nervously drumming his fingers on the table. I could tell he didn't like it, and I couldn't blame him. No cop likes being overruled by a civilian.

"Gentlemen, thank you so much for coming tonight," Diana said, gliding up to the table. Montini and Cipriano both rose, the inspector giving a little bow and kissing her hand, all very suave and continental.

"I am happy you are returned to us, my dear," Montini said. "Even if we have lost a sister." We all laughed dutifully.

"I wanted to ask about the documents," Diana said. "Have they been passed on?"

"They should be in Switzerland by now," Montini said, keeping his voice low. "Our ambassador there has been instructed to turn them over to the Allies. I hope something good may come of all this."

"Will His Holiness speak out?" Diana asked. "This is so important, so many lives are at risk."

"The situation is quite difficult," Montini said. "As you know, Pius does not want to grant the Germans any pretext for invading Vatican City. He feels this may give them the excuse they hope for. Then all the people in our care, here and in the other properties, will be forfeit."

"But he's the Pope," I said. "Shouldn't he say something?"

"To what end, that is the question," Montini said. "Words cannot stop transports to the east. Every time we have protested, the Nazis have increased their brutality. We have had reports from our own priests in the concentration camps asking us to not speak out, since the reprisals visited upon them are so harsh. Believe me, if words could free these poor souls, I would beg the Pontiff to speak them." He paused to sip from his wineglass, and shook his head as if losing an argument with himself. "But I think words fail us. Only actions seem to have any effect. Actions such as giving sanctuary."

"I'm glad I'm not in your shoes, Monsignor."

"Nothing is easy in this wicked world," he said.

I left them to brood as Diana went to fetch a fresh bottle of wine. I picked up some food and stood by Bruzzone and O'Flaherty, who were in a corner speaking in hushed tones.

"Billy, I'm afraid I spilled the beans to Monsignor Bruzzone," O'Flaherty said. "I told him about poor Severino, in the room across from mine."

"Just keep it quiet, okay?" I asked Bruzzone. "We don't want word getting around."

"Of course, you have my word. Has he told you anything yet?"

"A little, but we wanted him to build up his strength. By morning we should know everything."

"Good, good," Bruzzone said. "You know that might be all the time you have. The College of Cardinals is meeting tomorrow. You could be expelled before nightfall. I was telling Hugh he may want to prepare a safe house in Rome for you."

"Thanks for the warning," I said, wondering just how safe any house in occupied Rome might be.

"Let me know if I can help," he said to O'Flaherty, and then returned to the table for more food.

"Billy, I don't like deceiving a friend," O'Flaherty whispered.

"It has to be done this way. Think of it as excluding a friend as a suspect."

"Still, it's a lie."

"Cops lie all the time. It's often the best way to get at the truth."

"Now there's one for the philosophers," he said.

I cornered John May and confirmed that Sir D'Arcy had received a copy of the Auschwitz Protocol and Remke's letter. May knew about the documents going to Switzerland. May knew most everything that went on, but not the Severino Rossi story. His version had Rossi in O'Flaherty's room. I asked him to pass on the news that we might have the investigation wrapped up by tomorrow, and that we needed passage out of here. He had his own communications network in place, and I didn't want to know details, except for when Kaz, Diana, and I could get out.

And maybe Nini, I thought, as I watched her and Kaz together. As I did, the door opened, and Bishop Zlatko strode into the room. Everyone stopped talking and stared.

"Now you all see that I was right when I said these spies should be cast out," he said. "The Allies have desecrated Monte Cassino, and will destroy the Vatican itself!"

"Bishop Zlatko, this is not the place for accusations," Monsignor Montini said, rising from his seat.

"You are right. Tomorrow will be the time. I only hope Monsignor O'Flaherty will also be dealt with. He is obviously an Allied agent consorting with these provocateurs."

"Bishop, I know we don't agree, but come break bread with us," O'Flaherty said, clearly doing his best to keep his temper at bay.

"Bishop, please, for the peace of this house," Montini said, gesturing toward the table.

"Yes, of course," he said, visibly calming himself. "Forgive my rudeness. The news of Monte Cassino has been quite upsetting." He came to the table and I poured him a glass of wine.

"So, what happened to our deal?" I asked.

"I did act to stop proceedings against you, as I said I would."

"But you didn't get me the list of informers I asked for. Instead, you headed straight for Koch's headquarters."

"Of course, that is where I was going to get the information. What better place? I was simply surprised when I saw you there, in that German uniform."

"So then I guess you know we have Severino Rossi?"

"What of it?"

"He's about healed up enough to tell us who killed Monsignor Corrigan."

"You would believe a Jew? He'd say anything to save his own skin," Zlatko said, his lips twisted in disgust.

"That describes a lot of people. What about the informer?"

"Oh, I know exactly who it is. But I have no reason to tell you now. You have no standing here and there is nothing you can do against me. You will be tossed out into Rome proper soon enough. Thank you for the wine, it was mediocre." He barked out a harsh laugh, turned on his heel, and left, not even slightly curious as to where Rossi was.

CHAPTER FORTY-THREE

"NOW WE WAIT," I said. I'd gone outside with the last of the guests, to make sure everyone had left the building. John May was the last to go, and I watched him walk through the cemetery in the courtyard of the German College.

"Do you think it will work?" O'Flaherty asked.

"It already has," Nini said. She stood at the table where she'd been cleaning up. "The cheese knife is missing."

"Are you sure?"

"Absolutely. It had a white bone handle and a long, thin blade. Sharp enough to slice through that pecorino."

"Okay, we need to move. Rino, take Nini and Diana back to Nini's place. Abe, take Rosana home, okay?"

"Good luck, Billy," Diana said, giving me a kiss. I squeezed her hand and then she was gone, no protest, no argument about staying to help. It wasn't like her. Whatever the reason, I was glad to have her out of harm's way.

"Kaz and I will be in your room, Monsignor," I said as the three of us took the stairs up. "With the door cracked open we'll have a view of the hallway. I doubt Montini is our man, but he and Cipriano think Rossi is in the room above yours. In case it's either of them, I want you upstairs in the room opposite that one."

"I cannot believe either the monsignor or the inspector is guilty."

"That's because you see the best in people, Monsignor.

Occupational hazard for a cop is to see the worst." We stopped on his floor. "We've got three possibilities. John May was given your room, and Brackett and Bruzzone were told it's the room across."

"Too bad Zlatko did not take the bait," Kaz said.

"He still could have heard a rumor. Or maybe he's certain of getting his information from someone else. We have to watch for him as well."

"Are you sure the best place for me is upstairs?" O'Flaherty asked.

"Yes," I said. "We could miss a light tread on the staircase. Sound the alarm if you hear anything, and we'll come running."

"All right, me boy," he said, opening the door to his room. "Let's catch a killer before the night is over. I took a lot of abuse moving people out for the night. I hope it was worth it. Arm yourselves." He took a golf club from a bag by the door and hefted it. "I haven't played since the Germans took over. It will feel good to swing a nine iron."

Kaz and I settled in after O'Flaherty went upstairs. I figured we had time, as the killer would wait for at least an hour to be sure everyone was asleep. It wasn't quite ten o'clock, but for the Vatican that was the middle of the night. I decided to make one quick circuit of the building. I grabbed a three iron and left Kaz staring through the slim crack of the open door.

Downstairs I checked the kitchen, making sure no one was hiding there. I went out the back door and circled the grounds, watching for anyone approaching. Nothing moved but the frost on my breath. I came in through the cemetery, where the tall stone markers and the evergreens cast shadows in the faint moonlight. Part of the cemetery wall was being repaired, and I stepped carefully around a pile of bricks and scaffolding. A series of arches ran along one wall, creating a covered walkway that led from the cemetery. The main door was off this walkway, and I checked to be sure it had been left unlocked. On the side of the courtyard, an exterior staircase went up to the second floor. That door was locked fast. Good. Only one way in. I retraced my steps, checking the courtyard as I did. There were no lights showing, no sign of activity anywhere. A balcony ran along the second floor, where doors led to the rooms opposite

O'Flaherty's, but there was no access from the outside. The staircase was a separate structure, and with that door locked, passage was blocked.

I thought I caught movement out of the corner of my eye. I entered the cemetery garden, watching the breeze rustle the pines. Maybe that was all I saw. I waited, letting the night settle in around me. No sounds other than the wind came to me, so I left the cemetery behind. That was time enough with the dead.

Back in the room, Kaz shrugged, indicating nothing out of the ordinary. We waited some more. The bells tolled eleven. We took turns watching through the crack in the door. Anybody coming up the staircase from the main entrance would be in our line of sight, whether or not they were headed to our floor or the floor above. I hadn't wanted to insult the monsignor, but I preferred him out of the way. First, he was too important to all the POWs and refugees hidden in Rome, and second, he seemed too kindhearted for the work that might need to be done tonight.

More time passed, and the bells chimed midnight. I began to have doubts. Corrigan, Soletto, and Rossi might not have the justice they deserved. Maybe I'd overthought things. Maybe I was dead wrong.

I heard a noise. So did Kaz from his post at the door. He moved it open, wincing as it squeaked. No one was in the hall. Another sound, this time from the room across the hall. We both tiptoed, golf clubs in hand, and I had a fleeting thought of how ridiculous we must look. I put my hand on the door handle, and slowly opened it.

Another noise, but the room was empty. The bed, where we had made up pillows and blankets to look like a sleeping man, was pulled apart, feathers from the pillow strewn about.

The door to the balcony was open, and I sprinted outside in time to see a form drop from the balcony onto the staircase. Bruzzone, Zlatko, or Brackett, I couldn't tell.

"Kaz, go out the main door," I whispered.

I went out on the balcony and saw in an instant. He'd come up from the staircase, using a drainpipe for leverage, and pulled himself up over the balcony. I leapt onto the stairs, losing my balance, tumbling down, the golf club slipping away. There was a sharp pain in my knee, and I rolled over, trying to get up, but my knee buckled.

"Is there no end to this?" It was the voice of Monsignor Bruzzone, a white-handled knife grasped in his hand, feathers still clinging to his black shirt. He towered over me, his arm pulled back, ready to plunge the knife into my chest.

There was a thud, and Bruzzone sank to his knees, the knife dropping from his hand. His eyes rolled up as he wavered for a moment, then fell over.

"*There's* an end for you," Diana said from behind him, wielding a length of stout lumber from the scaffolding in the cemetery. O'Flaherty, with Kaz one step behind, came on the run and skidded to a halt in front of Bruzzone, a look of stunned admiration on their faces.

Kaz and O'Flaherty dragged Bruzzone's unconscious hulk inside and up the stairs to the monsignor's room. We needed some privacy. I limped behind them, Diana helping me along.

"Thanks," I said. "You saved my life. Was that you I spotted earlier?"

"Yes. And I'm happy to return the favor," she said, her arm tucked under mine. "I knew you would argue with me about waiting outside, so I decided not to mention it. It worked out well, wouldn't you say?"

"Can't argue," I said. "Let's call it quits though, okay? No more needing to be saved for either of us."

"Deal," she said, even though we both knew it might be a promise broken.

Kaz got Bruzzone trussed up in a chair while O'Flaherty cleaned the blood from his head. Bruzzone moaned, half conscious at best after Diana's whack with a two-by-four.

"I cannot believe it of him," O'Flaherty said. "Did you suspect him more than the others?"

"I was suspicious about his leaving the Vatican. Abe had made a crack about a heist and cutting in some German guards right after Bruzzone returned. It made me think about the reasons he might have for sneaking out overnight. One possibility was to enlist the aid of the Krauts, to help him get away. It was the only thing that made sense, for a guy who had been afraid to step over that line for so long."

"Aye, he refused to explain himself to me as well," O'Flaherty said with bitterness as he threw a glass of water into Bruzzone's face. "Wake up and explain yourself!"

"Let me go," Bruzzone said thickly, blinking his eyes and wincing from the pain. "I have done nothing."

"No," I said. "You only happened to steal a knife, scale a balcony, and then shred a pillow in the room where we told you Severino Rossi was sleeping."

"No, I was out going to prayers. Matins."

"I saw you come out of the room," Diana said. "I didn't see you go in, but it was you plain as day coming out."

"Hugh, are you going to take the word of these spies?" Bruzzone's eyes were wide with fear, beseeching his comrade.

"Listen to yourself, Renato, my friend. You sound like Bishop Zlatko. What have you done, man? This isn't the fellow I knew when we worked up north," O'Flaherty said, moving in on Bruzzone as anger overcame him and his voice rose in a shuddering rage. "What happened to you? Who have you become?"

Bruzzone had started to put up a good front. Sometimes, in the face of overwhelming evidence, the best thing to do is deny everything, blame everyone else. I'd seen high-priced lawyers make that work in court. But this wasn't a Beantown courtroom. This was a guy tied up in a chair in the dark hours of the night, blood trickling down over his white clerical collar.

I picked a feather from Bruzzone's sleeve and let it drop in his lap. Then I held the knife in front of him, not threatening, just letting him see it.

"You were going to murder Severino Rossi, God rest his soul, with that very knife!" O'Flaherty yelled. "You, a priest, who has saved lives. How could you possibly take one?"

"I have done nothing," Bruzzone said. He shook his head and

gazed down at the floor. I had the feeling he was speaking truthfully, but not about the murder.

"You betrayed Severino Rossi, didn't you?" I asked, as gently as I could, trying to pry the truth out of that statement.

"Leave me alone, please," Bruzzone said, his eyes avoiding mine.

"Renato, we all trusted you," O'Flaherty said. "Tell him it cannot be true, for the love of God!"

Bruzzone faltered in the face of his friend's anguish. His lip quivered, and I watched him begin to slowly disintegrate as his façade of respectability and innocence crumbled. The small quiver turned to a grimace as he tried to hold back the reservoir of emotion that had been dammed up for so long. I saw it shatter, the guilt and shame overflowing, wiping away his desire for survival, his ability to lie and scheme, to believe his own protestations. He burst into tears, like a child reprimanded by an angry but loving parent. I'd seen it before, in interrogation rooms and back alleys. The desire to be freed from a great and terrible burden overwhelming the instinct for self-preservation.

"Why did you do it, Monsignor?" I whispered. Bruzzone held his head in his hands, tears dripping through them. I pulled his hands away, holding them in mine, knelt in front of him, and asked again, eyeball to eyeball. "Why did you do it?"

"Because I was afraid," he wailed. "I did not want to die. I did not want to suffer the pains they promised me. Do you understand? I am a coward, and I did not want to die!"

"Tell us how that led you here tonight," I said, as soothingly as I could, coaxing him along like a recalcitrant child.

"Once I began, once I gave in, I was too ashamed to be found out for what I had become. I lusted for my own life, and sacrificed others. Forgive me, *scusami*."

Tears without end seeped from his eyes, a constant flow that soaked into his black shirt.

"It began in Genoa, didn't it? Where you first met Severino Rossi?" I asked.

"He is dead, truly?"

"Yes. After you had him turned over to the Fascist police, Koch took him and tortured him for sport. We got him out, but it was too late."

"*Il mio Dio,*" he said. "Yes, in Genoa."

"How did you know that?" O'Flaherty asked me.

"The diamonds," I said. "Rossi was a jeweler by trade, and he came through Genoa, where Monsignor Bruzzone had been doing his good works. Soletto was paid off in diamonds for the cover-up, which he engineered for the killer. We found a single diamond in Corrigan's room, when Bruzzone brought us there to search it. It's my guess Bruzzone planted it there. Soletto wanted more for his part in the cover-up, and put the pressure on for more. But my guess is that there weren't any more, that the killer had felt guilty about possessing them. Isn't that right, Renato?"

"Yes, yes, I gave them quietly to the princess, to help with the food, never in a way that she could discover where the money came from. The one I left for you to find was the last of the accursed things. I did not want them, I didn't want any of this."

"How did this happen?" O'Flaherty roared. "Explain yourself, will you?"

"It began in Genoa, of course," Bruzzone said. He took a deep breath, and seemed to relax. I'd seen it before, with even more brutal murderers. Once they began to tell their story, it was like a great weight had been lifted from their souls, and they became eager for an audience, to explain themselves, to rationalize their behavior, even to demonstrate their skills at evading discovery for so long. "Severino was there with his family, his father, mother, and sister. God help me, we had become friendly. They were kind people. His father was a jeweler and had taught Severino the trade. They gave me their diamonds for safekeeping. The elder Rossi said I should use them as a bribe to free his children if they were taken."

"But you stole them," I said.

"No, no, it was not like that at all," Bruzzone said, eager to prove himself only a murderer, not a thief. "I had obtained identity papers for them, genuine Vatican passports, Hugh, like we gave to so many. I was on my way to the house where they were hidden when the

Gestapo took me. They had been watching Cardinal Boetto, and had seen me go in and out many times. They found the passports, and the diamonds."

"They let you keep the diamonds?"

"First, they showed me the cells at Gestapo headquarters. It was horrible, the tortures they made me watch. Fingernails pulled out. Bones broken—my God, I can still hear the crack of a shinbone," Bruzzone wailed. He looked at each of us, as if we might grant absolution. "They wanted to terrify me, and they did. Hugh, if I could have died quickly, I would have been glad to do so. But they are experts at deferring death and prolonging pain, greater pain than even our Lord endured upon the cross. They gave me a choice. They said they didn't care about diamonds or priests, they wanted Jews. If I gave them Jews, I could go free, and take the diamonds."

"Dear Mother of God," O'Flaherty muttered.

"You have not seen what they do to the human flesh, Hugh." Tears streamed from Bruzzone's eyes, and O'Flaherty wept with him as we all felt the horror of what Bruzzone had carried within him. "I am not a saint, I found that out quickly. I have never felt such terror as I did then. And to give me a choice! It was diabolical. I begged, I prayed, but in the end I told them where to find the Rossi family. The next day, they let me go. They said the Gestapo in Rome would be in touch. I found myself on the street in Genoa, diamonds in my pocket and a stain upon my soul. I prayed that no one would ever find out what a coward I'd been. I felt sick with myself, and returned here as quickly as possible. I didn't want the Gestapo in Rome picking me up. I knew I would do whatever they demanded, God help me."

"Which is why you never set foot outside the Holy See again," O'Flaherty said.

"Until the other day," I said. I wanted to keep Bruzzone talking, telling us any detail that came to mind, so when we got to Corrigan's murder the truth would be the only logical choice. "Where did you go?"

"Why, to the Gestapo, of course. I thought if you were to find out I was responsible, I would need protection. I asked to have safe passage north, and offered to give them whatever information they needed. But they beat me and threw me out into the street. They laughed. They had no record of what happened in Genoa, and called me a fool. It is almost comical, yes, all this time to have been worried?" No one answered him.

"Yesterday, you tried another approach. You called Koch at his headquarters and told him about my rendezvous," I said.

"I did. I thought if you were removed from the investigation, I would be safe. Since the Gestapo did not believe me or value my services, I thought Koch would."

"Renato, I told you about that meeting in confidence," O'Flaherty said, the hurt evident in his voice. "At Mass this morning, it was!"

"I am sorry, Hugh. We are not all paragons like yourself. A giant among men, the holy warrior, happy in his work. Sometimes I think you are the greatest fool of them all."

"Tell us what happened with Monsignor Corrigan," I said, feeling almost sorry for this pitiful creature.

"He came to me one day, and said Severino Rossi had been in Saint Peter's Square, accusing me of betraying his family. Corrigan had met him in Genoa when they first went to Cardinal Boetto for help. I had no idea Severino had escaped. I was so ashamed of what I had done, I wanted only to forget. But Severino alive would not let me."

"Corrigan believed him, didn't he?" I asked.

"Yes, so I told him that I had evidence that would clear me of those charges, and that I would produce it that night. I said Rossi was crazed with loss and fear, and didn't know what he was saying. I waited until I saw Severino in the square and told him to meet me at the Door of Death that night, to give him his diamonds as well as proof it had not been I who betrayed his family." Bruzzone hung his head, shamed at his own admission.

"The sleeping pills," I said. "You had sleeping pills in your room. You gave them to Severino." I'd wondered why Rossi had stayed near the body, and now, remembering the sleeping pills in Bruzzone's room, it all made sense.

"Yes, I gave him food with the ground-up sleeping pills mixed in. He ate it all, and I sat with him until he fell asleep. Then Monsignor Corrigan appeared at the hour we had agreed upon. It was more difficult than I thought it would be. There was so much blood, and he would not stop struggling."

"The dying cling to life," O'Flaherty said. "As do sinners."

"Do you know was the irony is?" Bruzzone said. "The tortures I brought upon myself were far worse than the physical pain I would have felt at the hands of the Gestapo. There were times I yearned for the torture chamber." He looked wistful at the thought of it.

"You had a deal with Soletto, right?" Kaz asked, getting us back on track.

"Yes. I knew he was a greedy man, that he would take care of things for a few of my diamonds. He agreed to arrest Severino and to insure Monsignor Corrigan's body was found outside of Vatican jurisdiction."

"But the monsignor managed to drag himself back to the steps under the Door of Death," I said.

"I had never killed a man before," Bruzzone said. "I could not believe he had any strength left. I stabbed him once, and thought that was all it would take. He fell, but asked me why, why was I doing this? I pulled the knife out and thrust it in again and again until he was quiet. I had no idea he had any life left within him, there was so much blood. Soletto came as soon as a guard found the body, and acted promptly. Severino was taken away and I thought it was over. But Soletto was insatiable. He wanted more, and he would not believe me when I told him all the diamonds were gone. I used my last one when I placed it for you to find in Corrigan's room. I had hoped to implicate Rossi as the murderer."

"So Soletto had to go, right?"

"If you understand logic, you know that once you set upon a course, you must keep to it. Otherwise, what is the point?" Bruzzone said. "As you pointed out, this is a place of absolutes."

"You used the *misericorde* because you had access to the Swiss Guard armory," O'Flaherty stated.

"It was the perfect weapon. It is what it was made for," Bruzzone said, a note of defiance creeping into his voice. "And there are few weapons to be had."

"Logical," Kaz said.

"Yes, and it is logical that you must let me go," Bruzzone said, taking a deep breath. The tears were gone now, he'd gotten everything off his chest and he felt better. Time to go home and put this all behind him. Strange, how the mind of a killer can rationalize every action, every thought, twisting everything to fit in with his own needs and desires.

"Why?"

"What crime have I committed on Vatican ground? The mutilation of a pillow?" He smiled, wiping away the dampness on his cheeks.

"You have just confessed to murdering Monsignor Corrigan," Kaz said.

"I was present, yes. But the crime occurred outside the boundary, as determined by the Lateran Treaty. And the Vatican Gendarmerie has already turned the murderer over to the authorities in Rome."

"Soletto," O'Flaherty said. "He was murdered well inside the walls."

"I never said I harmed him. Simply that once a course is set, it must be followed." He straightened his shoulders and held his head high, a newfound confidence replacing the display of weeping sorrow. "Please, call Inspector Cipriano, and ask him what charge can be brought against me. Actually, it was I who was assaulted tonight. Only *my* blood was shed."

Kaz, Diana, and I retreated to the hallway, leaving O'Flaherty standing guard over Bruzzone.

"I don't like it," Diana said. "He is probably a little crazy, but smart. He went right back to his original story."

"He's gotta be a little nuts. We should have had Cipriano here to see all this," I said. "But he was a possible suspect too."

"Bruzzone was obviously under a lot of pressure," Kaz said, "keeping everything bottled up. Now that he has confessed his sins, he has retreated into self-preservation. After months of deceit, it is likely second nature to him. What should we do? He is right that our standing here is precarious as best."

"I'm going to try something," I said. We went back into the room.

"Are you going to let me go?" Bruzzone asked.

"I think we can put together a case against you with Inspector Cipriano," I said.

"Of course, I forget. I stole a cheese knife as well. Good luck, my friend."

"Okay," I said, shaking my head as if we'd been outfoxed. "Let me congratulate you. You're doing everything right. Stick to your story, I'm sure that you'll be able to hang on here until the Allies arrive."

"Yes," Kaz chimed in, already with me. "Then there will be a different police force in Rome. They will certainly take up the case of the murder of an American monsignor."

"So sit tight," I said. "You know that Corrigan was friends with Wild Bill Donovan, head of the OSS? I'm sure he'll send in a team with the first Allied troops to enter Rome. It may be a month or so, but your day will come. Enjoy the time you have left."

"I will go to the Germans. I cannot be kept here against my will."

"Don't you be so sure, Renato," O'Flaherty said. "Inspector Cipriano may put you in protective custody. Monsignor Corrigan has a lot of friends here who may wish you harm, regardless of the legal issues. It would be for your own good." O'Flaherty was quick on the uptake himself.

I watched Bruzzone's eyes go from calm and confident to wary and worried. We had him. "There is another way," I said.

"What?" he asked.

"I need to close out this case. Write out what you told us here—"

"Never!"

"Just as you told us. Nothing about crimes committed in the Vatican. But Genoa, Rossi coming here, contacting the Gestapo, Koch, all that. Nothing that Cipriano could arrest you for."

"And what will you do for me?"

"I will get you out of here by noon today. I'm in contact with a German intelligence officer who can take you north. He'll want to hear about you contacts with the Gestapo and Koch. Maybe they'll set you up with Mussolini in Salò, on Lake Garda. Ought to be nice there in the spring. The Fascists could use a tame priest, don't you think?"

We went back and forth for a while before Bruzzone caved. I had him convinced it would be either a short wait for the Allies and a possible OSS assassination team or a chance to leave the Vatican behind and head north with a German escort, putting miles and a lot of munitions between his own precious self and the advancing Allies. By the time he'd written out his statement, he was chuckling over what a great deal he'd made.

CHAPTER FORTY-FOUR

A FEW HOURS of sleep later, Diana and I stood by the white border in Saint Peter's Square, her face turned up to the warming sun. Kaz and Abe stood a few yards back with Bruzzone, each of them grasping an arm. It was a pleasant day.

"What's the purpose of the statement, Billy? You can't use it for anything. Nothing legal, anyway," she said.

"Right, but I needed Bruzzone to believe it was worth something to me. And he thinks it will put him in the good graces of the Germans, having warned them of an Allied agent at the Spanish Steps."

"But he doesn't know that you are turning him over to one of Colonel Remke's men."

"Exactly. I mentioned an intelligence officer, but he didn't put two and two together. He was so desperate to find a willing sponsor to take him north, away from the Allied armies, he didn't consider that possibility."

"So the confession is really for Remke," she said, her eyes still closed and lifted toward the sky. "Funny."

"What?"

"That if Bruzzone were not so desperate for his own life, he might have taken the time to think it all through. Now, his lust for life will be the death of him." I didn't agree that it was funny, but I didn't quibble about it either.

A few minutes later, a staff car rolled up and stopped by the white line. Bernard rolled down the driver's window and gave a wave. Dieter got out on the passenger's side, his arm in sling, but with a smile on his face. Nice to have pals among your enemies.

"It seems you owe us an automobile as well as a uniform," Dieter said, clicking his heels and executing a slight bow in Diana's direction. I decided the friendliness was especially directed toward her. But I was used to that.

"I didn't think you'd want the car back full of holes. But I do have your uniform, cleaned and pressed. Boots shined as well," I said, as I handed him a small valise.

"Thank you, Billy. I do not think I will see Italy again for a long time. I am glad at least to leave with my hand-tailored uniform and good Italian boots."

"I have something else for you," I said, handing him the paper and gesturing with my thumb toward Bruzzone. "A murdering monsignor. He's the guy who tipped off Koch about our meeting."

"And the man who killed Monsignor Corrigan and Commissario Soletto?" Dieter asked.

"Word gets around," I said. "Your informers are quick off the mark. Yeah, that's him."

"Why give him to us?" Dieter asked. "Not that I mind getting my hands on the man who was the cause of my wound." He rubbed his arm as he eyed Bruzzone.

"Certain legal questions have been raised. The Lateran Treaty, jurisdiction, that sort of thing. There's a chance he could get away with it, given the current situation."

"He doesn't look worried," Dieter said, glancing at Bruzzone.

"Well, he doesn't know who you are. He was trying to get in good with the Gestapo, so they would protect him from any charges. He thinks you're the next best thing. I promised him you'd take him north."

"He is the murderer, you are certain?"

"We are," Diana said.

That seemed to settle that. "He will be taken north, you have my word." Dieter nodded to Bernard, who bundled Bruzzone into the back of the car. I thought I saw a look flash across his face, concern perhaps, or maybe the ache in his head had worn off and he was thinking more clearly. But it didn't last. I could see the killer's wheels spinning, the process of rationalization kicking back in. He was telling himself a story and willing it to be true. He was going north, yes.

We waved good-bye.

"Let's walk through Saint Peter's," Diana said after we'd watched the car drive off. Rino and Abe had disappeared, and we were as alone as we'd been in a while, the huge square behind us.

"I don't know," I said as we neared the entrance. "I don't know if I want to go inside."

"Billy, it's beautiful. Awe-inspiring. And I'm not even Catholic."

"That's just it. I am. But the people I've seen here are no different from people anywhere. Some decent, some bad, and a lot in between. I thought it would be different at the Vatican, like a shining city on a hill. But it's just another town on high ground, with good and evil pretty well evened out. For every Zlatko there's an O'Flaherty, and too many Bruzzones—weak and willing to trade their souls."

"I saw a lot of good here, Billy," Diana said. "But then it did not have to live up to my youthful ideals. That's a lot to ask for."

"Not here. It shouldn't be." I'd sent a man north, knowing what that meant. Even though he'd murdered and betrayed people who trusted him, it weighed on my mind. The Vatican didn't seem worthy of my childhood vision of it, and at the same time I felt the stain of death upon me and wished I could have found more solace here.

"All right then," she said. "Let us stroll in the gardens. I can't tell you how many times I walked through them and thought of you by my side."

We agreed on the gardens, and I didn't look back as we left the basilica. We passed the gardener's cottage, and saw Abe and Rosana sitting on the front step. Abe nodded a brief greeting, and then turned his eyes upon Rosana with her two children at her side. A happy ending, for them at least.

We walked along the old Leonine Wall, the ancient fortified wall of the city. We skirted the radio tower with its association with sudden death. It felt like springtime, green grass and early flowers blooming in the bright sun. A starling chattered in a treetop, and we grinned like idiots at such a simple pleasure.

"Billy!" It was Kaz, trotting up the walkway. In a hurry. Good-bye to simple pleasures. Diana sighed and looked away.

"What?" I said, trying not to take it out on Kaz.

"John May wants to see us. We need to leave. The three of us," he added, seeing the look on my face. Kaz turned abruptly and we followed as I wondered what his face looked like.

"This has nothing to do with the situation here," May said as he served tea in Sir D'Arcy's sitting room. "Monte Cassino, I mean. It is simply that everything is in place to get you out. Tides and the moon, that sort of thing. We have an excellent forgery on a travel pass. It will get a truck to the coast without a search."

"How good a forgery?" Diana asked.

"Practically the original," May said. "We have three lieutenants in one house who were going stir-crazy. They convinced their host to take them to the opera. So they dressed up in the finest clothes they could find, and she took them to her box. Wealthy woman. Right in the next box was none other than General Rainer Stahel, the military commander of Rome! So the lady begins flirting with him outrageously. She evidently thought it the best way to distract his attention from the very quiet young men sitting with her. At intermission, she asked him for his autograph, if you can believe it, and he scrawled it on her program. We have copied it and used it several times. Always works like a charm."

"The best defense is a good offense," I said. "When do we leave?"

"Within the hour. We need to get you down to Fiumicino before nightfall. It's a little fishing village on the coast."

"Can you take four of us?" Kaz asked.

"The princess?" May asked. Kaz nodded. "Yes, one more should be no problem." That put a smile on Kaz's face. We all dashed to

Santa Marta to give Nini the good news. We found her in the refectory, but her response was not what Kaz expected.

"I cannot leave with you," she said, wringing her hands. "There is so much work with the refugees. And Hugh needs me. You know what it is like, Piotr. I have a duty, even though I am not in uniform. I am Italian, and so many of these are my people, Christian and Jew alike. I cannot leave them."

"You do not want to?" Kaz asked.

"I wish to, with all my heart," she said. "But I cannot." She kissed me on the cheek, hugged Diana tearfully, then took Kaz by the hand and led him upstairs.

We waited. It wasn't like we had a lot of bags to pack. Diana was still wearing her expensive duds, and I had my coat on, so we were as ready as we needed to be. A half hour later, Kaz came downstairs alone. He didn't say a word.

John May didn't ask about Nini. Maybe he'd known what her answer would be. He packed us in the back of a very old truck of indeterminate vintage, and threw blankets over empty crates shoved in front of us. He slapped the side of the vehicle, and a silent driver took us through the Sant'Anna Gate and out of the Vatican City State, into the unknown. I didn't mind one bit.

CHAPTER FORTY-FIVE

"*Uscire qui*," THE driver said after two hours of slow roads and one checkpoint. May had been right. We had been waved right through.

"This is our stop," Kaz translated. It was the first thing he had said since we'd left.

We jumped from the back of the truck and stretched our stiff limbs. We were on a wharf, a scattering of fishing boats bobbing on the tide. The setting sun sparkled on the water. If we weren't being smuggled out of enemy territory, it would have been downright pretty. The driver pointed to the most dilapidated craft in the harbor, at the far end of the wharf.

Walking toward the fishing boat, I felt exposed. Anyone along the shore could spot us, and there was no cover, nowhere to run. Our footsteps echoed on the weathered planks, the only other sound coming from the gulls squabbling for fish guts.

Our boat was thoroughly rusted, with what paint there was peeling off in great chunks. I saw movement in the cabin and wished I still had that Beretta.

"That you, Billy?" A large shadow emerged from the boat.

"Big Mike!" Diana said, running to give him a hug.

"Quiet down out there!" a rumbling baritone echoed from below deck.

"Come on," Big Mike said, grinning as he helped Diana aboard. "We're ready to shove off."

We cleared the harbor as the sun vanished below the horizon, the only light coming from the distant stars. At the wheel, Lieutenant John Hamilton checked his compass with a flashlight, its red filter protecting his night vision.

"Will you tell this big lummox to stay out of the way?" Hamilton said. "I'm about ready to throw him overboard." Hamilton had two crewmen along, Yugoslavian pirates by the look of them. They laughed, and I could tell it had become a running joke.

"What are you doing here, Big Mike?" Diana asked after we settled into the small cabin.

"I brought Billy his orders to go to Rome," he said. "Then I figured I oughta hang around and make sure the OSS got him out okay."

"It's the only reason we're here," Hamilton said, keeping his eyes on the horizon. "Because then Big Mike will go back to London and leave us alone."

"You look familiar," Diana said to Hamilton. "Have we met before?" That got more laughs.

"You're looking at a real movie star," Big Mike said. "Sterling Hayden himself."

"Never heard of him," Diana said. Hamilton laughed loudest at that one.

He explained we were only going about twenty miles out, to rendezvous with a British submarine. They'd taken the boat up from Anzio last night, mingling with the fishing vessels that the Germans allowed out along the coast. We had about two hours, and he wanted all hands on deck to watch for German patrol boats. This was a quiet sector, most of the action was down around Anzio, but that was no reason to take chances.

Diana and I went out on the bow and squinted into the blackness, watching for any shapes moving against the stars. Time passed, the sound of the motor blending into the night, the blackness encompassing us until it seemed as if we weren't even moving, but floating in a watery dream.

"How is Kaz taking it, do you think?" I asked in a whisper.

"It is another loss. But not terrible, and perhaps temporary. They seem quite in love, don't you think?"

"Yes," I said. "That was a tough choice she had to make."

"Every choice in war is a loss, one way or the other," Diana said. She shivered, and I took off my coat and draped it around her shoulders. I wanted to tell her about the choice I had made and almost had to live with. I don't know why, but it felt like a secret I shouldn't keep from her. Guilt, maybe, as I thought of Bruzzone, his story spilling out of him like water over a dam.

The sound of gunfire echoed across the water. It was distant, the dark sky to the south lit with faint red flashes. Destroyers or PT boats, maybe, too far away to cause us any trouble.

"Sometimes it's hard to know which loss is worse than the other," I said. "Diana—"

"Look!" She pointed off the port bow. White foam churned and a black shape blotted out the stars in front of us. I thought it was a whale, about to crush our flimsy craft.

"Submarine!" Hamilton shouted. He slowed the boat and turned toward the sub. "Prepare to disembark."

Figures spilled from the conning tower, and launched a rubber raft in our direction.

"We're going home, Billy!" Diana shouted, her face wild with excitement as she hugged me. "What were you about to say?"

"Nothing," I said. Instead of talking, I kissed her. There, in hostile waters, bobbing on the bow of a fishing boat in the Mediterranean, with one of His Majesty's submarines waiting for us as exploding shells created fireworks on the horizon, and with a pair of Yugoslavs shouting their encouragement, we kissed—a kiss of pleasure, joy, and forgetfulness.

Some things are better left unsaid.

Author's Note

Although Colonel Erich Remke of the German Abwehr (military intelligence) is a fictional character, the plots against Hitler and the Nazis orchestrated by that agency and its head, Admiral Wilhelm Canaris, are factual. This includes the use of the Vatican and Pope Pius XII as a conduit for passing information to the English and French about the German plans to invade France in 1940. The Pope did indeed help the anti-Nazi circle to contact the English and provide warnings of the invasion, but these efforts bore no fruit, perhaps because the English were too suspicious or shortsighted.

The assassination attempt described by Remke is based on an actual plan that was to take place on March 11, 1944. Cavalry Captain Eberhard von Breitenbuch, an anti-Nazi conspirator, had offered to smuggle a pistol into a planned meeting with Hitler and shoot him in the head. Convinced that the war would only bring about the complete destruction of Germany and that Hitler had to be stopped, he was willing to sacrifice his own life in the attempt. Breitenbuch, an aide to Field Marshal Ernst Busch, made it to the door of the conference room, only to be stopped by a duty sergeant, who explained that Hitler had suddenly ordered that no adjutants be admitted. As Remke said, Hitler did have the devil's own luck when it came to avoiding assassinations.

The Auschwitz Protocol is real, a document written in hand by two Slovakian Jews, Rudolf Vrba and Alfred Wetzler, who escaped Auschwitz in early 1944. Initially referred to as the Vrba-Wetzler report, the papers were combined with earlier documentation smuggled out of Auschwitz by Witold Pilecki, a member of the Polish underground (as described in *Rag and Bone*), and as such were referred to as the Auschwitz Protocols. The documents did make their way to the Vatican and other governments. The wide publicity given to these reports caused a halt to the deportation of Hungarian Jews to Auschwitz for a time. The deportations began again after a fascist coup in Hungary, but heavy diplomatic involvement of neutral embassies in Budapest as well as that of the Vatican's papal representative, Angelo Rotta, saved tens of thousands of Jews from being transported to death camps. The Swedish Embassy alone, under the leadership of Raoul Wallenberg, saved an estimated 70,000 Jews in Budapest.

Monsignor Hugh O'Flaherty is one of those true-life characters that a novelist could never invent. O'Flaherty and his organization hid an estimated 4,000 escaped prisoners of war and Jews, along with Italian antifascists and other refugees. In addition to his network, it is estimated that the Church hid about 5,000 Roman Jews in the Vatican and the surrounding areas, including thousands within the Pope's summer residence, Castel Gandolfo. John May, butler to the English ambassador, also played his part as a master scrounger.

Sterling Hayden, or John Hamilton, as he insisted on being called while serving in the military, is another larger-than-life character who nearly threatened to take over the story. Hayden was a sea captain and adventurer who happened to work in the movie business. He smuggled arms to Tito and the Partisan Army in Yugoslavia as described in these pages. He parachuted into the Balkans and received the Silver Star for gallantry and a commendation from Marshal Tito for his support of the Yugoslavian resistance.

Monsignor Montini was a Vatican priest working to aid, feed, and hide refugees in Vatican extraterritorial properties. At the request of Pope Pius, he organized the *Pontificia Commissione di Assistenza* to provide assistance to escaped POWs, Jews, antifascists and others on the run in German-occupied Italy. In 1963, he began his pontificate as Pope Paul VI.

Finally, much has been written about Pope Pius XII and his role in regards to the Holocaust. Many share the assumption that I held before I began my research: that Pius was vaguely complicit with the Nazis, or at least could have saved lives by speaking out. This view was supported by the text of *Hitler's Pope* by John Cornwell, published in 1999. Cornwell charged that Pius was anti-Semitic and that he did not speak out enough about the Holocaust during the war. However, Cornwell's views changed upon further research. In 2004, he stated, "I would now argue, in light of the debates and evidence . . . that Pius XII had so little scope of action that it is impossible to judge the motives for his silence during the war, while Rome was under the heel of Mussolini and later occupied by Germany."

The fragile neutrality of the Vatican City State during the Second World War must be understood in order to see the past through the eyes of those who lived it. The small state was only ten years old as a political entity at the start of the war, the Lateran Treaty of 1929 having guaranteed the independence and sovereignty of the Holy See. The threat of military invasion by the Germans to take Pius XII into protective custody was a real and present danger. The Pope felt he did need to maintain strict neutrality. Unfortunately, he was often neutral by omission, not publicly condemning the killing of 1.8 million Catholic Poles by the Nazis or one million by the Soviets either. When Pius XII did speak out, his diplomatic phraseology was so circuitous and convoluted, in the manner of the time, that his message was often robbed of any impact.

There is also the real question of what would have come of any vociferous denunciation of Nazi genocide. The Pope did have moral authority and the threat of excommunication for Catholics, but it seems unlikely that those engaged in the killing machine of Nazi extermination would have cared much about what the Pope had to say.

There is no way to know if Pius's course was the right one. Pinchas Lapide, a Jewish theologian and Israeli diplomat and historian, has written the best summation I have found:

When armed force ruled well-nigh omnipotent, and morality was at its lowest ebb, Pius XII commanded none of the former and could only appeal to the latter, in confronting, with bare hands, the full might of evil. A sounding protest, which might turn out to be self-thwarting—or quiet, piecemeal rescue? Loud words—or prudent deeds? The dilemma must have been sheer agony, for which ever course he chose, horrible consequences were inevitable.

Acknowledgments

Once again, I acknowledge the deep debt I owe to my wife Debbie Mandel for her unswerving support and assistance in the conception and writing of these stories in the form they appear here.

Edie Lasner continues to provide invaluable help in the usage of the Italian language. Any errors should be chalked up to my lack of linguistic skills and any well-turned phrases are solely due to her expertise.

I am grateful to Tom Mandel and Cathy D'Ignazio for their gracious hospitality in providing the use of their Block Island house as a writer's retreat, where significant portions of this and other novels have been written during quiet winter weeks.

The manuscript was also improved through the assiduous reading and editing of Michael Gordon, who has saved me from any number of mistakes in this and other books.